S0-ELL-881

REALMS UNREEL

AUDREY AUDEN

REALMS UNREEL
Version 1.3.0
Copyright © 2011 by Audrey Auden
All rights reserved

Published by Temen Books, an imprint of Studio Shah LLC

http://temenbooks.studioshah.com/
temenbooks@studioshah.com

Cover design by Sumul Shah

∞

This is a work of fiction. Names, characters, places, and events described herein are the product of the author's imagination or used fictitiously. Any resemblance to actual persons, businesses, or events is purely coincidental.

∞

No part of this book may be reproduced, stored, or transmitted by any means without the written permission of Studio Shah LLC. To request permission, email temenbooks@studioshah.com.

∞

ePub ebook ISBN: 978-1-937262-00-6
Kindle ebook ISBN: 978-1-937262-01-3
PDF ebook ISBN: 978-1-937262-02-0
paperback ISBN: 978-1-937262-03-7

REALMS UNREEL

For Sumul, who never gave up on me

Reality is an activity of the most august imagination.
— *Wallace Stevens*

CHAPTER 1
The Underground River

On the first chill day of autumn, Dom looked up and saw Ava watching him from a distance. He set down his chisel and raised his hand in a hesitant greeting. He did not quite trust his eyes. Ava had been absent for weeks, and whenever she left, whether for a season or a century, he started to find her shape in every shadow.

But this was no shadow. Ava waved to him in answer and began to approach. A breeze off the snow-capped mountains rolled down into the valley, blowing her saffron robes and scarlet mantle before her, carrying her across a plain of tall grasses. She alighted in the clearing where Dom stood and made her way to his side.

Her eyes swept over the twelve carved panels of pale red stone that Dom had arranged in a circle around him. Each panel rendered the graceful form of a single tree designed by Ava's own hand. Almond, walnut, apple, cherry, persimmon, pomegranate, apricot, pear, plum, fig, chestnut, olive. She reached out and traced her fingers along the lines of each carving in turn.

She settled a warm hand on his dusty arm and smiled up

at him. She was a diminutive woman with wide brown eyes framed by a wild tangle of dark curls. Her skin was smooth and golden as a hazelnut shell, untouched by time. She might have been the same girl Dom first met long ago in the cool cedar forest by the sea. But when he looked into her eyes, he saw the accumulated sorrow of ages. He knew that light-hearted child had drifted from the world long ago, lost in visions.

"It is beautifully done," she said.

Her words would once have thrilled him, but Dom knew that beauty had long since ceased to be Ava's concern. She had designed these carvings to adorn a shrine to the underground river flowing beneath the valley. Their purpose was to placate the Oracle, nothing more.

A troubled look came over Ava, and her eyes shone with tears.

"What is it?" Dom asked in surprise. In all the years they had spent together, he had never known Ava to cry.

"Serapen," she said, letting out a shaky breath, "Serapen came to me and delivered my answer from the Oracle."

A chill of foreboding washed over him. She should have been overjoyed by this long-awaited visit from Serapen, the foremost Mohira among the priestesses of the Mohirai. Ava had toiled for centuries in the hope of receiving this answer.

"What did Serapen say to you?" Dom asked warily.

Ava pushed back the curls from her forehead and recited slowly,

"'Your answer lies in the tree at the heart of the temple.'"

Her eyes drifted past Dom out toward the lone hill that marked the center of the valley, the heart of the living temple.

"How can that be?" he scoffed, following her gaze, "We

must have stood there a thousand times before."

Ava's hand trembled on his arm.

"There was something else," she said softly.

Her tone stopped the breath in him, and a stillness came over the valley as Ava closed her eyes and said,

"Serapen told me the way I seek leads through Death."

∞

Dom's faith in Ava's vision had never wavered since the day she first told him of the land that lay beyond Dulai. Her visions had always proved true. He had believed her that their labors would be rewarded a thousandfold when at last they found their way to that distant country. But surely no place, however wonderful, could merit the risk of passage through Death.

Dom took Ava by the shoulders.

"We cannot go that way," he said, his voice hoarse with fear.

A tear slipped down her cheek, and she took his hands in her own, tracing the rough callouses formed by his long years of devoted service to her.

"I never imagined … I never thought to ask such a sacrifice of you. But," she looked up, her eyes searching his, "We were never meant for this world, Dom. There is nothing left for us here."

"How can you say that?" he cried, sweeping his arm out across the valley. The gesture encompassed a living temple, the work of both their hands, the likes of which had never before been seen on the face of Dulai. Somehow Ava saw it not, so lost was she in longing for another land that lay hidden from her.

Dom now wished Ava had never seen that land. Serapen had warned her — she had warned all the children receiving their calling from the Oracle — not to gaze into the sacred pool. There was no telling what might appear to one who looked upon it unprepared, Serapen had said. But Ava had looked. It was an accident, Ava had said.

Serapen had been delivering the Oracle's words, calling Ava to join the Mohirai. Ava had looked back unthinkingly to grin at Dom, who stood waiting with the other children to receive his own calling. Her face had shone with delight at the prospect of initiation into the priesteshood. Then her gaze had fallen, just for an instant, upon the reflection of the sacred pool.

In that instant, a vision had unfolded before her. Ava had described it for Dom many times. There was a land, she said, where wise men read the mysteries of the universe in the stars, their gaze pushing ever outward. Great cities spread across the globe, she said, their towers rising into the heavens. Countless voices rose in song, she said, creating a common tongue for the heartbreaking beauty of life. Ava's words had carried Dom with her into that land, and they had spent many an evening together imagining life in such a place.

Reverie had seemed at first enough to satisfy Ava. Her mind was otherwise occupied with study of the Mohiran mysteries, just as Dom was devoted to learning the craft of the Artifikes, the order of builders to which the Oracle had called him. But as the ages had passed and the novelty of her service to the Mohirai had faded, Ava's desire to visit that unknown land had consumed her, pushing out all else from her waking thoughts and sleeping dreams. In the end, despite Dom's efforts to dissuade her, Ava had returned to the Oracle. She said she would have no peace until she knew what road might lead her to the land she had glimpsed in the waters of the sacred pool.

Ava had known as well as Dom the danger of questioning the Oracle. The price of an answer was a task of the Oracle's choosing. Such a task, once accepted, could not be set aside.

It was Serapen who had again delivered the Oracle's words. If Ava would have her answer, said Serapen, she must first build a temple to the sacred mystery of fertility.

Ava had been relieved, even pleased. In her years as a Mohira, she had overseen the construction of many a temple. She had believed this would be a simple task. Even so, Dom had had his doubts. The Oracle had never been known to grant a simple task.

But Dom had never doubted he would follow Ava, even though her task was not his to complete. He too desired to see the land of her vision, and ever since they built their first city of acorns and river-stones together as children, they had relied upon each other in their work. Dom relied on Ava's expansive imagination, and Ava relied on the meticulous work of Dom's hands. Together, they could build anything.

And so Dom had journeyed with Ava through the lands of Dulai as she searched for a place to build her temple. He had stood by her side when they first looked down upon this broad valley. He had spent centuries with her here, building monuments, terracing slopes, laying beds of herbs and flowers, cultivating trees and vines. The work might have given them both great pleasure as children, but it had become for Ava a source of sorrow as the years passed by. The Oracle had remained silent.

And now all their toil had led only to this: the Oracle's emissary bearing words of madness. Dom's jaw clenched in anger at the injustice of it. Ava pressed her hand to his chest, and he could feel his heart pounding there.

"I too am afraid," said Ava, her eyes locked on his, "But I know what I saw. I know what awaits us. Will you trust me, Dom? Will you follow me once more?"

Dom drew a shuddery breath. He had followed her so far, in hope of seeing the land of her vision, yes, but also because he could imagine no life without her. He could find no words, so at last he only nodded. That was enough. Ava beamed at him. He felt her small hand slip inside his own, and then they were running.

Ava's bare feet flew along an unseen path through the gardens, vineyards, and orchards. Dom struggled in his heavy boots to keep up. Startled songbirds darted from bushes, and grazing herds of goats bleated in surprise. When Ava reached the foot of the hill at the center of the valley, she let go of his hand to hike her saffron robes up to her knees. Her scarlet mantle flapped around her shoulders as she scrambled up the grassy slope.

"Ava!" called Dom, now out of breath, "Wait!"

She paused, looking back at him, tossing a curtain of dark hair behind her shoulder and smiling a little as she said,

"Have we not waited long enough?"

And yet she stepped back to take his hand once more. They reached the top of the hill together.

Dom followed as Ava slowly wandered the ancient grove shading the top of the hill. She moved silently from tree to tree, looking up into the branches of each before moving on to the next.

At last, when the sun began to sink beneath the peaks of the western mountains, Dom sat down wearily beneath a gnarled pomegranate tree. Before him, the fountainhead of the spring that fed the underground river bubbled up from a deep pool. Ava came to sit beside him.

"The Oracle said I would find it here," she said mournfully, pressing her hand to the twisted bark of the pomegranate tree, "Here, in the heart of the valley."

"Perhaps the Oracle torments us," he said, his voice hardening as he tried to suppress a surge of fury toward the Oracle, "Perhaps you asked an impossible question."

Ava hugged her arms to her chest. Dom felt the sting of her disappointment as if it were his own. He reached out to comfort her, but she pulled away, standing so quickly she nearly slipped on the wet stones surrounding the pool. She fell back hard against the trunk of the pomegranate tree.

"Careful," said Dom, climbing to his feet and lending his arm to steady her.

The branches overhead rustled, and a bright red pomegranate dropped into the pool with a plunk. Dom and Ava turned to watch it bobbing and drifting on the slow-moving surface that concealed a powerful undercurrent. The spring drained into a great crack in the foundation of the hill, and as they watched, the bobbing pomegranate vanished, swallowed up by the underground river that watered the valley.

Ava stepped forward.

"Look," she breathed, pointing.

The rippling surface of the pool had grown smooth, mirroring the molten sunset. In the reflection, the pomegranate tree seemed to sway in a high wind, its leaves rippling in an unseen current, the flowering tips of its branches writhing and stretching into the reflected heavens. Dom looked up into the branches above him. Not a leaf stirred. He felt an icy chill creep down his spine.

Beside him, Ava was looking up into the branches as well.

She stretched up on her toes and plucked a ripe pomegranate from the tree. She regarded it thoughtfully, then broke it open, crushing a few of the seeds in the process. A blood-red trickle ran down her wrist, and the clusters of ruby seeds glittered in her hands.

She looked up at him, her lips parted in amazement.

"The fountainhead, Dom," she said wonderingly, "This is the way beyond Dulai."

Dom looked down at the dripping fruit, his stomach churning, his head spinning.

"I do not understand."

Ava extended her hand to him, one half of the pomegranate cradled in her palm.

"I see the way on from here, Dom. The river passes through Death. Come with me. I will show you."

There was a slight rumbling in the ground below them, and then all was still. Dom looked at Ava in alarm.

"What was that?"

"The time has come," she said, looking out at the sun slipping below the western horizon, "We must hurry."

Dom felt numb as Ava took his hand and led him to the edge of the pool. They stepped in, and the water rose around them, ankle-deep, knee-deep, chest-deep. Ava's scarlet mantle floated on the surface like a pomegranate blossom. Dom's boots sank as if made of lead. He took one last breath and closed his eyes as the water closed over his head.

In the stillness beneath the surface, Dom gripped Ava's hand. The icy undercurrent wrapped around his ankles, pulling him down, down, down. Terrified, he opened his eyes in the clear water, and with blurred vision he saw beneath his feet the dark maw of the underground river, open wide, sucking hungrily.

Fear took over him, and Dom kicked with all his strength against the powerful undercurrent. In his struggle, Ava's hand slipped from his fingers, and Dom thrashed frantically through the water, searching for her. Seeing her scarlet mantle swirling before him, he grasped the fabric tightly and began to pull her back to him. But the mantle tore from her shoulders.

A silent scream rose in Dom's throat as he watched Ava disappearing into the darkness below.

A sudden surge carried him upward, spitting him out onto the edge of the pool. He thought his body was convulsing until he realized that the ground was shaking violently beneath him. He heard a great explosion, and to the west he saw a column of smoke rising into the darkening sky.

The stones at the edge of the pool slid around him, and he hauled himself away from the water, scrambling on hands and knees as small pebbles and then great boulders scraped down into the spring. Clenching Ava's muddied mantle in his hands, he watched in horror as the fountainhead disappeared. He fell prostrate upon the shaking earth.

"Dom."

A voice cut through the terrible noise of the earthquake. Dom looked up from the ground and saw the edge of a white robe gleaming softly in the twilight. Above him stood Serapen, serene as the moon, unmoved by the tumult.

"Please," Dom cried, eyes wild, "Please. Help me!"

Serapen looked down at him impassively. Enraged by her indifference, Dom staggered to his feet and cast Ava's mantle aside, splashing into the shallow basin that was now all that remained of the fountainhead. He seized a small boulder and grappled with it, the callouses on his hands shredding, the muscles beneath his sodden tunic tearing, until at last he cast the stone away. He reached down and took another between his hands.

"The way is shut," said Serapen, her voice ringing out over the groans of the earthquake.

"No!" he grunted, straining with all his might to lift the rock, "I must follow her."

Serapen watched his futile struggle for a moment before saying,

"Then you must go by another way."

Dom slowly released the stone from his hands and straightened up unsteadily, struggling to keep his balance as the ground tipped beneath him.

"Show me," Dom cried, desperation driving all caution from him.

Serapen's eyes flashed.

"Consider your words carefully," she said, "Are you certain you wish to ask this of one who speaks with the voice of the Oracle?"

The memory of the darkness that had swallowed Ava coalesced into an icy knot of fear in Dom's chest.

"Yes," he growled at last, his voice merging with the rumble of the earth, "This I ask of the Oracle: What must I do to follow her?"

The ground fell still, and in that moment of calm, Serapen's eyes locked on his, luminous in the darkness, twin pools of green and gold flecked with red and black.

"You will have your answer, Dom Artifex. But first," her voice rose, filling the warm night air, surrounding him, "you must build a temple to the mystery of enduring beauty. A fitting dwelling place for the Oracle."

Dom closed his eyes, his mind swimming with the heady mix of his rising frenzy and the seductive voice of the Oracle.

"Do you accept your task?" said Serapen.

Dom looked down at the water seeping up through the immovable rock now concealing the path Ava had taken. Ava had given him the chance to follow her, but in his fear he had let that chance slip away. A pact with the Oracle offered him a second chance to stand at the entryway to darkness. He had never before fully understood what desperation had driven Ava to accept a task from the Oracle. Now his own extremity forced his mouth to shape the words,

"I do accept this task."

Serapen nodded, sending a ripple down the curtain of shining white hair that fell almost to her knees.

"Very well," she said.

Serapen knelt to lift Ava's sodden mantle from the place where Dom had dropped it. Dom lunged forward, hand extended to grab the mantle from her, but Serapen stopped him with a warning gesture. From her belt, she withdrew a small flask of oil, which she emptied into the folds of fabric. She laid the mantle in a loose circle around the base of the pomegranate tree, lifted two flat stones from the ground, and struck them together with a great crack, showering the fabric with sparks. Dom gave a shout of horror as a small flame rose from the mantle and crept slowly up the trunk of the tree, gradually engulfing the twisted bark, the spreading branches.

"This is the sign of our covenant, Dom Artifex," Serapen intoned, eyes dancing with flame, "Now you must leave this place. Do not look back."

The ground trembled, and a great river of fire began to run down the slopes of the smoke-spewing mountain in the west. The blazing tree and the burning horizon momentarily blinded Dom. When his vision returned, Serapen was gone.

He was about to turn and run when he caught a glimpse of the scarlet mantle, still twisting in the flames at the base of the tree. Heedless of the searing heat, he rushed forward and seized the burning cloth.

He plunged the mantle into the shallow water pooling above the buried fountainhead, extinguishing the flames and cooling the burns that even now were healing on his hands. Falling to his knees, he pressed the charred fabric to his heart. Every fiber of his being cried out,

Lost. Lost. She is lost to me.

And so she was, for a time.

CHAPTER 2
Emerald Bridges

Dom raised his arm and delivered another stroke of his hammer. The ring of metal on stone faded into the rustle of the white pavilion shading his makeshift studio. He stepped back to survey his work.

An unfinished marble statue of a woman stood before him atop a pedestal. Her robes flowed in elegant folds down to bare feet planted in a bed of herbs and flowers. In her left hand she held a ripe pomegranate, split open to reveal clusters of plump seeds. A cascade of loose curls fell over her shoulders. Her head tipped slightly to one side, lips parted in the delight of understanding. In his mind's eye, Ava always took this form, the embodiment of his ancient regret.

A sharp sting ran down his arm, and he winced. He rolled back his sleeve, turning his palm up to scan the web of fine pink lines just visible beneath the skin of his forearm, a tidy grid overlaid on the irregular paths of blue and violet veins. Near his wrist, one line stood out brighter than the rest, a scarlet thread having just been pushed to the surface by the straining of his muscles.

He stepped toward the bench and found a small leather

pouch, from which he withdrew a fine needle. Tracing its sharp point lightly over his wrist, he freed the end of the emerging thread and drew it out. The long, damp filament swung slowly from his fingers as he threaded it through the needle. He gripped the needle tightly as he touched the sharp point to the mark at his wrist that had already healed over. He bore down into the sun-browned flesh and worked the needle from wrist to elbow, burying the remnant of Ava's mantle in the only hiding place he had found from the prying eyes of Serapen and her handmaids.

The mantle of a Mohira was one of the greater mysteries, woven from living thread and bound to the one who wore it. By defying the Oracle's command and saving Ava's mantle from the flames, Dom had preserved not merely a memento, but an enduring connection to her.

Just as the last inch of scarlet thread disappeared beneath his skin, the world tilted, and Dom fell to his hands and knees, dropping the needle into the grass beside him. He gasped as the threads woven into his skin constricted from his neck all the way down to his ankles. Despite the pain, his heart leapt.

He scrambled on hands and knees to close the heavy flaps of the entryway. Enclosed by the relative privacy of four canvas walls, Dom crawled back toward the center of the pavilion. With his back pressed to the cool marble base of the statue, he let go of his grip on Dulai.

∞

Ages had passed since Dom watched Ava disappear into the underground river, and nineteen years since he last felt the pull of her awareness along the living threads of her mantle. Now she had returned once more.

Dom closed his eyes as gravity vanished. He felt his disembodied consciousness slipping into the void between the worlds. He forced down a rising panic, focusing on the pull of Ava's awareness. At last, light and sound flooded around him. The tension that had guided him slackened, and he felt himself drifting weightless in an enclosure that slowly resolved into a small pink room. With some effort, he gathered his diffuse sensations into a single position, reorienting himself.

He found himself standing beside a narrow bed looking down at a dark-haired woman in a loose white robe. In her arms rested a newborn wrapped in a soft yellow blanket. Here was the new life that Ava had chosen.

A fair-haired man leaned over the mother, his fingers tracing the rounded lines of the baby's face. A middle-aged woman dressed in blue bustled about the room gathering loose linens. She paused at the foot of the bed to smile at the baby's parents, until a beeping sound outside the door caught her attention.

"Everything all right in here for now?" she asked briskly.

The parents nodded, and the woman slipped out the door.

Father and mother adored their child in hushed tones, awestruck, until the mother looked up and said,

"Should we let them in, Travis?"

Dom saw the woman's face for the first time, and his eyes widened in surprise. Anatolia. She had grown up, but there was no mistaking her.

"Are you sure you're ready?" the father, Travis, asked with a grin.

Anatolia smiled ruefully.

"Do your worst."

Travis left the room, and Dom resumed watching the baby. Anatolia was whispering to her, kissing the dark down on the top of her head, touching her tiny hands and lips. Dom wondered whether Anatolia might recognize in this infant form the essence of the sister she had lost nineteen years ago.

Travis returned a few minutes later to usher in three eager visitors. Dom looked up at their approach, scanning the faces that would form the backdrop of Ava's new life.

An older woman with bleach-blonde hair entered speaking loudly into a headset ("We're going in now! I'll call you back!"). Behind her followed a tall scarecrow of a man with a high, lined forehead and thinning hair through which his sunburned scalp could be seen. He carried a sleepy-eyed, tow-headed little girl.

"Ah! She's beautiful," the woman exclaimed, eyes sparkling as she leaned in over her grandchild and said to her headset, "Yes, yes. Yes. Okay. Bye." Anatolia winced almost imperceptibly. Dom recalled the comparatively calming presence of Anatolia's own mother.

"Grandpa," the little girl said solemnly, "Would you please put me down?"

"Of course, my dear," the grandfather said with equal dignity.

Once on the floor, however, the little girl lost her composure entirely. She rushed to the bedside and squealed,

"Mama! She's so tiny! Can I hold her?"

"Can you be very, very careful?"

"Ple-e-e-ease?"

The little girl reached up, arms wide, and Travis knelt to show her how to cradle the baby. He eased the yellow bundle into her arms, and the little girl rocked the baby gently, prattling to her quietly.

The door burst open, and Dom looked up to see a lively young man with spiky blue and green hair enter, waving a pair of eyeglasses before him.

"Travis!" he cried, "I think I figured it —"

The young man shut his mouth at the glare from the grandfather and folded the glasses, chastened. He hooked the glasses carefully to the collar of his form-fitting, glistening black shirt, which did not quite cover an elaborate tattoo that stretched from his shoulder to his elbow. A row of green LEDs blinked on the shiny metallic belt holding up his skinny jeans.

"Do you know what you're going to call her?" the grandmother asked Travis.

"We were thinking of naming her after Ana's mother. Isidora."

"Isidora. That's a pretty name. Is it Turkish?"

"Greek, Ma. Ana's mother is —"

"Right, right, right. Well, it's a nice name."

A wail of protest interrupted them, and all eyes turned to the little girl holding the baby. Her grip had slipped a bit, and the baby was squirming in her arms.

"Careful, Ollie!" Anatolia said sharply to the little girl.

"She's fine, Ana," Travis soothed, reaching down to adjust Ollie's hands.

"Oh, look!" Ollie squealed, "Look, Mama!"

The baby had turned an unfocused gaze up at her sister, revealing vivid green eyes. Anatolia stopped mid-scold and pressed her lips together, her eyes welling up. Travis took her hand.

"What is it, love?" he asked gently.

Anatolia shook her head, pulling back her hand to brush away her tears. She sniffed and gave him a watery smile.

"Nothing, just ... Those eyes. Just like my sister's." She reached out and touched the baby's head. "What about Emerald? Emerald Isidora Bridges."

"Emerald," said Travis, drumming his fingers against his lips, "Hmmm. Emerald. Emmie. I can see that."

"Emmie," Ollie said, wiggling her forefinger, which Emmie was now grasping tightly in a tiny pink fist, "It's so nice to meet you."

The young man with the shiny belt surreptitiously slipped on his eyeglasses and began narrating softly into his collar, the fingers of his right hand sliding along the front of his belt while his left hand pressed the side of his glasses.

"We're recording!" he said. Dom realized with amazement that the eyeglasses must contain some sort of camera. The speed of technological change on Earth continued to accelerate since Ava's last appearance here. "Okay, it's April — what day is it, now? — April sixth, 2012, and we're welcoming little Miss Emerald Isidora into the Bridges clan. There she is!" he said, swooping down over Ollie until his eyes were three feet away from the baby, then backing up to say, "What do you think about your new little sister, Ollie?"

"Jesus Christ, Frank! Will you cut it out with that video scanner?" the grandfather exploded. Dom drew back, alarmed by the outburst.

"Patrick!" the grandmother scolded, "Language!"

The room fell silent. Patrick, the grandfather, took in the anxious looks and slowly exhaled.

"I thought he had finally managed to break those damn glasses," he grumbled.

Travis and Anatolia exchanged an amused glance. Frank

cleared his throat, then edged over to Travis.

"So," said Frank in an undertone, switching off the patch mic on his collar, "Did you ask her?"

Travis considered Anatolia, who was carefully overseeing the transfer of the baby from Ollie's arms into her grandfather's. Travis cleared his throat.

"Sweetheart ..." he began, "So, Frank and I were wondering ..."

Anatolia looked up, waiting for him to finish before seeming to realize what he meant. She rolled her eyes, saying,

"Oh, all right. But —" Frank hauled Travis from the room by the arm before Anatolia could change her mind or even finish saying, "— I still don't see why we can't just video conference."

"What are they doing, Nanna?" Ollie asked her grandmother.

"I'm ... well, it's something your daddy and Uncle Frank have been working on over at the Lab. Sensory augmentation —" she flapped her hands, unable to find the right word, "Sensory projection? Something. There are some fancy clothes involved. I guess we'll see in just a minute."

"Just a minute is probably a bit ambitious, Marie," Anatolia laughed.

Nearly an hour later ("We're almost there! Just give us five more minutes ..."), Travis stood in the middle of the room wearing a form-fitting black shirt and glasses like his brother's, as well as a pair of dark gloves enmeshed in golden seams. He was speaking patiently through a headset to his mother-in-law, as he had been for the last forty-five minutes. At last, he turned to Frank.

"Okay, she's got it on. You can switch to projection."

The background hubbub that the rest of the group had

kept up for the last hour subsided somewhat.

"Thank God," said Frank, heaving a sigh of relief. He tapped out something on his shiny belt, and a three-dimensional, translucent projection of an older woman with chin-length silver curls and stylish square-rimmed glasses appeared facing Travis.

Dom's mouth fell open in astonishment, and he drew nearer to the projection, circling it slowly. Here stood Anatolia's mother, Isidora, or so at least it seemed. She had perhaps grown a bit plumper, and the smile lines around her eyes and mouth had perhaps deepened, but she exuded the same warmth he remembered from nineteen years ago.

"Hi, Yaya!" cried Ollie, bouncing up from the seat beside her mother to wave at the projection.

"Hello, my darling," said Isidora, waving back. A light source in the unseen room where Isidora stood glimmered on the golden seams of her gloves and the black threads of her form-fitting shirt.

"Isidora," said Travis, "I just need you to press this patch on the belt near the — yes, that's the one."

"Oooh," Isidora straightened up, "That felt strange."

"Good. That means it's on. Now, just mirror my movements," said Travis, "Frank?"

Frank snapped to attention and transferred baby Emmie expertly from her mother's arms to her father's. When Frank stepped away, Isidora mimicked Travis uncertainly, cradling empty space in her arms. Then she gasped. In her projection, a baby had appeared.

"I can feel her in my arms!" Isidora exclaimed.

Dom shook his head in wonder. This world Ava had so longed to inhabit was truly miraculous.

"Touch her cheek, Travis," Frank urged.

"Isidora," said Travis, "Watch me."

Travis stroked the baby's cheek with the fingertips of his gloved hand. Isidora repeated the movement, shaking her head as she murmured,

"Amazing. Amazing."

After admiring her granddaughter's tiny face, hands, and feet with the help of Travis and their linked sensory augmentation gear, Isidora turned, still cradling the projection of the baby, and said to Anatolia,

"I wish I could be there, my love. Papou does, too. We will come to visit soon, just as soon as the semester ends."

"I wish you could see her, Mama," Anatolia said softly. Dom saw her eyes glistening as she looked from the real baby in Travis' arms to the simulated one in Isidora's, "I mean, really see her. It's just not the same as having you here."

"Pretty damn close, though!" Frank muttered to Travis.

∞

The Bridges brought Emmie home in a streamlined silver car that ensconced its passengers in preternatural silence as they glided over the uneven surfaces of a tangled freeway system. Dom sat unseen in the back, wedged between Emmie, who was sleeping in her car seat, and Ollie, who was fidgeting in hers. Ollie kept up a stream-of-conscious dialog with her parents, who patiently predicted when the baby might crawl and walk and talk, denied Ollie's request to sleep in the baby's room, and suggested that Ollie's teacher might not like her to take the baby to school for show-and-tell.

As they slowed to a crawl at a particularly ill-conceived juncture, Dom considered that, while the quality of vehicles had changed since his last sojourn on Earth, the quality of city traffic had not.

"Travis," Anatolia murmured. Dom turned to face the front seat. Anatolia was gripping her husband's knee and pointing. They were approaching a disturbance in the road.

Ahead of them, a sign-waving crowd, hundreds strong, was marching up an exit ramp toward the oncoming freeway traffic. Four police officers in navy blue uniforms were climbing out of a pair of police cars parked at the top of the ramp. Sirens wailed in the distance, and seconds later another half-dozen police vehicles swept past.

"It'll be fine, Ana," Travis said calmly, squeezing Anatolia's hand, "They're just making a spectacle."

"It was just a spectacle at city hall, until it wasn't. Is there another way around them?"

"Mama?" said Ollie, picking up on her mother's worried tone, "Why are those people walking on the freeway? Aren't you not allowed to do that?"

"They're protesters, Ollie," said Anatolia, forcing the anxious note out of her voice, "They want people to know that they're very angry, so they're breaking the law."

"What are they angry about?" said Ollie, pressing her hands to the window and staring out wide-eyed as they inched by the gathering crowd on the exit ramp. Dom read the signs — some scrawled by hand on dirty canvas, some printed neatly on shiny banners — waving above the crowd. *Heal America. Take Back Oakland. This Is My Occupation.* Though the car muffled the sound impressively, Dom could just hear the dull roar of the protestors' chants.

"Well, they're angry about a lot of things," said Anatolia, watching the front line of the crowd edging toward the police cordon, now twenty officers strong, "But the biggest thing is that they can't find any work right now. So they don't have anything better to do than —"

"Ana," Travis shook his head, sounding mildly exasperated. He looked at Ollie in the rearview mirror, "Mama's right that it's hard for people to find jobs, but people are angry because they think the government is doing a bad job, and that big companies are to blame."

"Are they mad at you and Uncle Frank?" Ollie asked in alarm. Travis laughed.

"No, sweetheart. Our company isn't nearly big enough to catch their attention."

They came through the traffic in the end without incident, and a few miles later they turned onto a road that ascended a forested incline and wound its way along a ridge cut into a steep hillside. Stands of tall redwoods and silver eucalyptus gave way at intervals to sweeping views of the flatlands below.

A few miles later, Travis turned onto a short driveway that led to a tiled deck projecting out over a cliff. A second car containing Travis' parents and younger brother pulled up behind them.

As Travis and Frank hauled bags out of the car, Ollie skipped off to a low pedestal at the edge of the deck. She pressed her palm to the pedestal, and a section of the deck slid away before her feet. She descended from view.

Dom followed Anatolia curiously as she carried baby Emmie from the car to the opening into which Ollie had just disappeared. He found himself looking down a broad staircase that descended into a spacious but minimally-furnished living room adjacent to a large kitchen and dining room. At the far wall, floor-to-ceiling windows looked out over the lowland flats of Oakland and Berkeley toward the well-trafficked waters, bridges, and islands of the San

Francisco Bay. Dom followed Anatolia down the stairs, admiring the improbable cliffside construction with the eye of a craftsman.

Anatolia sank into the deep cushions of the sofa facing the grand windows, rocking the baby in her arms. The rest of the family descended the stairs noisily behind her.

"Who wants Nanna to make breakfast?" called grandmother Marie.

Several hearty shouts of approval met this offer, and everyone but Anatolia passed through to the kitchen.

"Do you want anything, love?" Travis shouted back to Anatolia.

"Just some quiet time, for now."

In the relative peace of the living room, Dom stood looking down at Anatolia and the child. As he leaned over her, Anatolia shivered. She pressed the baby to her breast, looking up apprehensively at the place where Dom stood unseen.

Dom drew back. Perhaps he could spare the child this lifetime, let go of their connection, set her free. She must desire that, in some ways. Even so, he felt Ava's pull, strong as ever. Perhaps she could not let him go, either.

For now, though, he could let her enjoy the fleeting obscurity of childhood. He loosened his hold on her and reached for the body that anchored him to Dulai.

∞

Night had fallen, and Dom's awareness returned to a body cold and stiff, still propped against the base of the statue. He rose unsteadily, reaching out in the darkness for the flask at the end of his tool bench. Finding it, he threw back a long draft of water to moisten his dry throat, then rubbed his arms and legs, which tingled with the taut awareness of his renewed connection to Ava.

He made his way slowly toward the closed entryway, guided by the dim glow suffusing the canvas walls of his pavilion. He pushed through the flap and stepped out into the light of the full moon. To the east, across the dark, still waters of a vast lagoon, loomed a massive wall of volcanic rock scaled by the delicate marble tiers of the Temple City, the work of his hands and his offering to the Oracle. The city gleamed in the moonlight.

The sight of the child had kindled in him such fierce longing to be free of this place that for a moment he thought he must scream with the frustration of it and rouse the sleeping city. Yet he knew well that whether he raised his voice in defiance or bowed his head in obedience, he was bound as surely to his task now as he had been the day he accepted it. He turned away from the city, facing westward and listening to the long inhalations and exhalations of the sea as it washed the unseen foot of the cliff far below him. Feeling his desperation ebbing somewhat, he returned to his pavilion.

He tossed and turned on his sleeping mat all through the night. In his mind, the face of the newborn child merged into the faces of a thousand other children. From each he had hoped to learn the secret of crossing into Death, but each had slipped away from him too soon.

He was awoken from his restless sleep hours later by the sound of someone entering his pavilion. He jumped to his feet and faced the entryway. There stood a skinny girl in blue novice robes, silhouetted against the rosy light of dawn. A length of fine red ribbon fluttered from her fingers.

"Dom Artifex?" she said timidly.

He gazed at her expressionless for a long moment before answering,

"Mohira?"

"I —" she swallowed, "I bring you word from Serapen."

Dom's nostrils flared, but he beckoned her to approach. However much he despised Serapen, this girl was not to blame.

"Speak, then," he said.

The girl stretched the ribbon between her hands, reading aloud from the pattern worked into the threads,

"Come to Musaion at dawn. The Oracle summons you."

Dom ground his teeth. In the ages that had passed since Ava departed, these occasional summonses from the Oracle had lost their power to inspire hope and now served only to taunt him. His question remained unanswered.

He dismissed the girl with a gesture and waited impatiently for her to leave, but she shifted nervously from side to side, her eyes darting from his face to the unfinished statue behind him.

"Would you like to take a closer look?" Dom asked brusquely. The girl nodded. "Well, go on."

She edged around Dom, stopping an arm's length from the statue. She reached up and traced one finger over the perfectly sculpted pomegranate seeds, an echo of the statue's thoughtful expression in the line of her chin, the curve of her lips. She glanced back at Dom and said,

"She is very beautiful. Is she one of the Mohirai?"

Dom looked away.

"Not any more. She ..." he searched for words a novice might understand, "She left Dulai to cross over into Death."

"Death?" said the girl, mouthing the strange word,

"Where is that?"

Dom's jaw worked for a long moment until he managed to growl through clenched teeth,

"That is one of the secrets you Mohirai keep from me, in your great wisdom."

The girl shrank away from the harsh words, eyes wide in her pale face. She bowed and departed hastily. Dom remained rooted to the spot, fists shaking, burning with anger.

∞

Dom did not hurry to answer his summons from the Oracle. Whatever else the Oracle might be, she was not impatient. Only when his anger had cooled did he depart.

A steep, narrow trail through the sunburnt grass led from the ridgetop where his pavilion stood down to the shoreline. There stood a lone dock, fashioned by Dom from some of the scrubby trees that grew atop the ridge. The dock projected over the jagged rocks of the shoreline and out to the water. He stood at the end of the dock and looked out across the vast lagoon.

The pilgrims' ferry crossing from one end of the great volcanic caldera to the other came into view, and Dom hailed it. The ferry took a long time coming, and when it pulled up alongside the dock, he jumped aboard wordlessly. He ignored the half-dozen other passengers as the ferry made its way slowly across the still waters toward the Temple City.

At the Temple City harbor, broad, shallow stairs emerged from the dark blue depths of the lagoon. The stairs climbed up to meet the lowest tier of the city before continuing on a steeper and narrower path that scaled nearly one thousand vertical feet to join the domed temple crowning the city. The marble tiers connected by this central staircase formed the shape of a stylized tree, white branches spreading across dark stone.

Two barefoot girls in bright blue robes hiked up to their knees stood on a low stair, ankle-deep in the water, ready to secure the ferry to the heavy metal rings bored into the stairs. The pair of novices offered their hands to help him ashore, but Dom stepped off without looking at them, leaving his fellow pilgrims behind.

He ascended the stairs swiftly, cutting through the slow current of foot traffic on the boulevards and promenades that interrupted the staircase at intervals, pulling the hood of his traveling cloak over his face to avoid the curious eyes of the young priestesses in their colorful robes and mantles.

The long climb concluded at a white marble plaza. Dom stepped out upon it, facing the massive domed form of Musaion, the jewel of the city, his greatest offering to the Oracle. Even this had not been enough to satisfy her.

The great doors of Musaion stood open, and Dom passed through the archway, pausing for a moment at the threshold to let his eyes adjust to the dim light of the vestibule, the first stage of the elaborate ritual of enlightenment.

At the far wall, between two narrow archways, stood a woman arrayed in the saffron and scarlet that signified an initiate of the mysteries.

"Greetings, Mohira," he began, inclining his head just enough to indicate respect.

"Greetings, Artifex," she replied, "What business brings you to Musaion?"

"I come seeking audience with the Oracle."

"You are most welcome," she said, involuntarily spoiling

her attempt at solemnity with a bright-eyed smile. She was a new initiate, then, still delighting in her role as Musaion's gatekeeper.

She turned to a small recess carved into the wall between the two archways. Water spilled from a silver spout at the back of the recess into a shallow stone basin, spiraling down an open drain. She lifted a chalice from its place beside the basin, sprinkling a handful of herbs into it from a pouch suspended from her belt, filling it from the fountain and raising it to Dom's lips. He drank, knowing no amount of sweet herbs could take away the bitterness of that cup.

Smiling again, she ushered him through the rightmost archway, the entry to the inner chamber.

The hall beyond the archway turned almost immediately to the right, and then again to the left, a light trap that plunged Dom into complete darkness, the second stage of the ritual. He pressed his hand to the wall to steady himself, his fingers tracing unseen symbols carved in relief upon the stone. He walked slowly along the winding path through darkness until at last he saw the light up ahead.

He emerged blinking into the inner chamber, which drew his eyes irresistibly upward.

Soaring above the immense space, a massive central dome of translucent white stone seemed to float atop four golden half-domes that vaulted the great semicircular wings flanking the central chamber. Filtered sunlight illuminated wall frescoes of staggering scale and fell soft upon the free-standing sculptures arranged on the white tile floor. Echoes of women's voices and footsteps drifted through the open archways leading out from each of the four wings, but the only other person in sight stood upon a dais at the center of the temple. He crossed the great space between them, stopping at the foot of the dais.

Before him stood Serapen, pacing back and forth before the great loom that ordered Dulai and the lives of all within it, her bare feet padding over smooth white stone, brown fingers guiding the shuttle through the warp, snowy robes and long white hair flowing in waves behind her. The finished lengths of fabric that lay in folds upon the dais were threaded missives in which the Mohirai would read small pieces of the Oracle's will. To Dom, the indecipherable rags were simply a reminder that the knowledge he so desperately sought was hiding in plain sight all around him.

"Greetings, Dom Artifex," she said, running her fingers along the gathering threads one last time before turning to face him. She looked down upon him, eyes glowing with living colors. He held her gaze, trembling but unable to look away.

"Greetings, Serapen Mohira."

Serapen tipped her head to one side, considering him for a long moment before saying,

"You sought the counsel of the Oracle once, Dom, did you not?"

Dom closed his eyes, remembering the desperation that had led to this foolishness. After a long silence, he said,

"I did."

Serapen's voice grew lower and fuller as she intoned,

"And so you must respect the Oracle's words. Complete your task. If you would follow Ava, first you must let her go."

Dom felt the Oracle's command closing in around him, one more link in the chain that bound him to this place. He bowed his head and forced his voice to say,

"I submit to the word of the Oracle. Let it be so."

But in his heart, he rebelled. Whatever the consequences,

to him or to the newborn child, he knew now that he would stop at nothing to escape the life that had, in Ava's absence, become a source of unending sorrow.

CHAPTER 3
The Alternet Generation

Dom made a show of diligent obedience to the Oracle, but he used his labors on the Temple City to mask sojourns to Emmie's side. The construction of a new library wing gave him weeks of solitude between rising stone walls. Sculpting a fountain for the plaza before Musaion allowed him afternoons of reverie within the canvas pavilion of his movable studio. And, when all other attempts to find privacy failed, his nights overlapped Emmie's days, giving him many uninterrupted hours in which to withdraw from Dulai and immerse himself in Earth. This was how Dom watched Emmie's early years unfold against the backdrop of her father and uncle's Emerging Media Lab.

Uncle Frank's omnipresent video scanner captured Emmie's first steps across the bare cement floor of the Lab's makeshift lounge and into her father's arms before a cheering audience of engineers.

"Oh, no, Travis," Anatolia groaned through her three-dimensional projection, watching the replay from her law office a few blocks away, "How are we going to child-proof that place? You know she'll head straight into that death trap if you give her half a chance."

"The spliner's not a death trap, Anatolia," Frank blustered, his face turning almost as red as his freshly-dyed hair.

"We're working on putting walls around it," said Travis, walking over to an unprepossessing square of spongy grey material covering a large section of floor. The programmable extrusion mechanics of this expensive new device could replicate three-dimensional environments with great accuracy, enabling the Lab to use interactive, life-sized terrain models as they tested out their sensory augmentation prototypes. Travis pointing out to Anatolia the chalk lines where the walls and door would go. He met his wife's eyes through the projection and said solemnly, "We'll keep an eye on her. Don't worry."

"You could just put her in daycare, you know," grumbled Frank.

Anatolia bit her lip. Until now, Frank and Travis had accepted without criticism the neurotic overprotectiveness that rendered her unable to leave Emmie in the care of anyone outside the extended family of Lab team members. Dom felt a pang of sympathy for her, seeing in her anxiety the legacy of her sister's death.

"Let's talk about this later, Ana," said Travis, shooting a warning look at his brother, "We just wanted to give Emmie her moment in the spotlight."

Anatolia directed a strained smile at Frank.

"Thanks for helping me be a part of it," she said, "You boys are the best."

Regardless of the origin of Anatolia's fears, her concerns about safety at the Lab were more than a little justified, as Dom learned firsthand over many months at Emmie's side.

The Lab, housed in a sprawling warehouse near the West Oakland waterfront, was a trove of experimental electronics of all shapes, sizes, and degrees of quality assurance. A litter of sharp metallic thread snippets, button-sized batteries, and tiny microelectronics covered the floor. Travis more than once caught Emmie on the verge of swallowing a shiny, blinking, mouth-watering prototype, before the engineers learned to keep their work out of little arms' reach.

Though that would have been enough to worry any mother, the warehouse was also an active construction site. Dom watched with interest as the Lab team methodically repurposed the building as a hardware prototyping facility. Emmie's father invested heavily in workstations and lab benches but maintained a guise of dereliction about the building exterior to blend in with its immediate surroundings. West Oakland was a battleground between community reclamation efforts and socioeconomic deterioration, and baby Emmie became accustomed to an occasional gunshot from beyond the slapdash security fence.

Despite the apparent hazards of the neighborhood, the Lab's interior showed every sign of a healthy, growing enterprise. Spread out across makeshift lab benches of reclaimed plywood and cinderblocks, beneath the glare of bare light bulbs, the team assembled retinal projection glasses and sensory feedback garments, motion simulation headsets and olfactory augmentation patches. In the fenced-in lot beside the warehouse, the team ran daily gauntlets of simulation and feedback tests with their product prototypes, dictating and typing copious notes, initially with the aid of run-of-the-mill tablet computers, but increasingly, as time went on and their prototypes improved, with a few taps of fingers on a wrist or a few jabs in the air with a stylus. Notes in hand, they trooped back into the warehouse, ripping and replacing, reworking and tweaking, and returning to the testing lot once more. The bright lights of the Lab burned round the clock.

Though the curious goings-on at the Lab might have provided a welcome diversion from his unending labors in the Temple City, Dom observed everything with a pragmatic eye, knowing Ava had not chosen this place and time lightly.

∞

"You've got to see this!" Frank called up to Travis, who was crossing the newly-constructed catwalk connecting two upstairs office wings, hurrying back to his office after an important conference call with the Lab's investors.

Dom looked up from the corner of the Lab where Emmie was giggling at a life-sized three-dimensional projection of her Papou, sitting behind his desk in Massachusetts. Grandfather and granddaughter were engrossed in a game of peek-a-boo, Papou having offered to watch Emmie for a few hours that afternoon when the usual Lab babysitter had needed to cancel at the last minute. Dom found Frank watching another three-dimensional projection across the room, beckoning to Travis.

"What is it?" said Travis, descending the stairs. He stood next to his brother, and together they watched as Frank replayed a recording of a recent product test. The recording began with seven men and five women — product testers — standing in a row on the fenced-in lot outside the warehouse. Each wore a headset and form-fitting sensory augmentation clothing.

Travis leaned in closer as the recording flickered. The

product testers now appeared dressed in formal evening wear, standing on a crowded dance floor beneath a star-studded night sky. Twelve glowing green spheres pulsed slowly above the avatars of the product testers.

The three-dimensional projection now split into two separate projections. The first showed the recording of the physical lot: twelve product testers in headsets and sensory augmentation clothing. The second showed the recording of the ballroom simulation: twelve product tester avatars surrounded by a simulated crowd.

"Please wait for your dance instructor, who will take you through the steps of the waltz," a woman's voice instructed.

In the ballroom, twelve new avatars stepped out from the simulated crowd and onto the dance floor. Six of these avatars had glowing red spheres pulsing above their heads. The other six were marked with glowing blue spheres.

"The live instructors," murmured Frank, pointing out the six red markers, "and the simulated instructors," he said, pointing out the six blue markers. Travis nodded, his eyes never leaving the projection.

The soft strains of a waltz began to play. In the recording of simulated reality, the six live and six simulated instructors demonstrated the steps of the dance, eventually taking hands with their partners and beginning to swirl around the dance floor, coattails and ballgowns fanning out behind them. In the recording of physical reality, Dom watched with interest as six live couples danced across the asphalt alongside six solo product testers dancing with unseen partners.

When the music stopped, the six live and six simulated instructors bowed, said farewell to their partners, and departed the dance floor. In physical reality, six live instructors slipped out of the test lot through a back door and into the Lab.

The woman behind the camera prompted the product testers to remove their headsets. Several of the testers, emerging from the simulation, nodded at one another, evidently impressed. A pair of Lab engineers set up a circle of metal folding chairs in the center of the lot, where the twelve testers sat for a follow-up interview.

"Here we go," said Frank, rubbing his hands together in anticipation.

A Lab intern scribbled notes while one of the hardware engineers asked questions about the fit and comfort of the sensory augmentation gear. One of the designers asked questions about the quality of the simulation content, trying to identify what aspects were particularly realistic versus particularly unconvincing. After discussing the product testers' thoughts on these points, the designer said,

"Before you go, we'd like you to fill out a brief survey to rate the quality of your dance instructor on several metrics. Six of you had our live instructors, while the other six danced with projected instructors from a studio in San Francisco. Just note which type of instructor you had using the checkboxes at the top of the survey. And, thanks, everyone!"

The intern handed out a dozen paper surveys with clipboards and pencils, and Dom watched as the product testers scribbled down their answers and turned them in before thanking the woman behind the camera. The recording stopped.

Travis turned to Frank, looking excited.

"Well?" Travis said impatiently.

Frank rustled the stack of surveys in his hand, grinning as he said,

"Twelve for twelve."

"You're kidding me."

Frank grinned from ear to ear in answer, and Travis smacked his forehead in amazement.

"We rocked it!" Travis hollered across the hall toward a group of engineers in the midst of a heated debate over the merits of a new heat-dissipating conductive fabric. Baby Emmie turned around, startled by the noise, a wire-seamed glove with blinking fingertips dangling from her hands.

Travis called the rest of the team down to the first floor. Dom stood beside a young woman with square-rimmed glasses, pink hair, and a form-fitting sensory augmentation tunic over black leather pants. Frank sat on the edge of the bench just behind Travis.

"Listen up, guys," Travis said, pacing the concrete floor before the group of men and women looking up at him expectantly from the lab benches, "Today's a big day for the Lab. A big day for the whole sensory augmentation community. These users —" he pointed to Frank, who waved the product tester surveys at the team, grinning, "These users just experienced a simulated human interaction so convincing that it was for them indistinguishable from physical reality."

This pronouncement was met with shouts and cheers and a great deal of applause. When the ruckus died down a bit, Travis continued,

"This is a huge step forward. The holy grail is within our reach. High-fidelity simulated reality is coming. We're going to erase the boundary between the real and the unreal.

"I know there have been a lot of long days. And nights. And weekends. I thank you for that. Because of you, I'm finally going to be able to tell my dad that those long hours playing video games in the basement weren't wholly wasted."

"Will you tell my dad, too?" someone called out amidst

the general laughter. Travis smiled and said,

"Tonight, we celebrate. Drinks on me. Then I want you to go home and get some rest, because we've still got a long way to go."

∞

Three-year-old Emmie sat under the bridge table that Daddy had set out on the deck. Daddy took out the table once a week when Nanna and Grandpa came over to play bridge. Emmie emptied a box of crayons onto the tile floor. She picked the red, blue, green, and purple. Next to the crayons, she placed the Jack of Spades and the Queen of Diamonds. These cards had fallen onto the floor when Daddy and Grandpa got up from the table to go to the kitchen. Emmie considered the crayons, thinking very hard about which color she should use first.

She looked up expectantly and saw the dark-haired man in the funny dress and big leather belt, hiding under the table next to her. He always came when Emmie was trying to make hard choices like this. He reached out his hand and tapped the red crayon. She considered the red, then nodded in approval and began coloring over the long white hair of the Queen of Diamonds.

Above her, Mama was talking while Nanna shuffled cards.

"I wish I could get him to leave all these sensory augmentation devices back at the Lab," Mama said to Nanna.

"Good luck," Nanna laughed, "We could never keep those boys apart from their toys."

"We don't even know how any of this technology affects the adult brain, much less the brain of a developing child," said Mama. She sounded angry.

"We said the same thing about video games," said Nanna, "But the boys turned out —" her phone rang, and she said, "Just a second. I need to take this."

Nanna's office assistant called her all day long. Grandpa didn't like that. Nanna said a few things to her phone, then said to Mama,

"Sorry, Ana. What were you saying?"

"I just worry that, with all this simulated reality, Emmie won't get to have any *real* experiences," said Mama.

Emmie perked up at the mention of her name, but Mama didn't say anything else about her. Emmie kept coloring the Jack and Queen, now using the green crayon. They would live in the dollhouse hovering before her, projected from the smartcom. Daddy had given Emmie her very own smartcom. It could make a hundred different dollhouses, and dolls, too, but Emmie liked drawing dolls for herself.

"There's nothing less *real* about simulated reality, Ana," said Daddy. Emmie saw his feet and Grandpa's coming back up from the stairs that went down to the kitchen. Emmie heard the tinkle of some bottles and glasses above her on the table, then the beeping of Daddy doing something on his smartcom. "Look," he said.

"Hi, Dad," said Ollie. Emmie looked up at Ollie's voice and came out from under the table. Beside Daddy, she saw a projection of her sister, who was sitting behind a big table. Emmie waved happily at her sister. Ollie had been gone for almost two weeks, and Emmie missed her.

"Ollie! Hi, Ollie!" she said.

"Hi, Emmie!" her sister waved back.

"How's math camp, sweetheart?" asked Daddy.

Ollie rolled her eyes and tugged the end of her long, blonde braid.

"Are you going to make me do this *every* summer? I get A's in math. Is it really that important for me to *like* it, too?"

Daddy reached out toward the projection and put his hand under Ollie's chin so that she looked up at him. Ollie wrinkled her nose and rubbed her chin. Daddy's special headsets made your skin feel funny sometimes.

"Someday," Daddy said to Ollie, "when you learn about groups, rings, and fields, you'll thank me."

Ollie sighed.

"I've got to go. I've got loads of homework. Loads." She sounded very grown-up and serious, but Emmie knew Ollie loved homework.

"All right, babygirl. Give me a call if you need any help."

"Cheers, Dad."

Daddy switched off the projection and turned to Mama.

"See?" he laughed, "It's as good as having her right here."

Mama opened her mouth, but before she could say anything she looked down and saw the cards Emmie was coloring under the table.

"Oh, Emmie!" she scolded. Emmie felt hot tears filling her eyes. Mama was upset with her again. Then Mama smiled and said, "It's okay, sweetheart. Here, let's get you some real paper."

She picked up Emmie and started carrying her toward the stairs that led down into the house. Emmie looked back and saw the man who had been sitting with her under the table disappear, and she giggled. That funny man could hide better than anyone else. Mama called back to Daddy,

"You hear that, Travis? She needs *real* paper!"

∞

41

Five-year-old Emmie lay on her belly atop an empty server rack in her father's office, swinging her sensory augmentation headset over the edge like a metronome.

"Are you almost done?" she whined. She had been waiting practically forever for Daddy to stop writing email and come play with her in the spliner. With his authorization code and a few pieces of sensory augmentation equipment, the spliner could become almost anything. The forest simulation was what she had in mind: the perfect place for a game of chase.

"Just one more minute, sweetheart," Daddy said distantly. Emmie grumbled and made a face, but he never looked up from his laptop.

The office door swung open, and Uncle Frank burst in.

"You've got to read this," he said, waving a stapled printout in his hand.

"Busy," said Daddy, "Email it to me."

Uncle Frank dropped the printout on Daddy's keyboard. Daddy pushed back angrily from his desk and threw up his hands.

"I'm the goddamn CEO! What do I have to do to get a minute of peace around here?"

Emmie stopped swinging her headset and stared at her father wide-eyed. He sounded like Grandpa. Uncle Frank looked like he wanted to step back out of the office.

"Sorry, Travis," he said, "You're still sorting out those malfunction complaints?"

Daddy nodded, closing his eyes for a moment, his mouth set in a straight line. He let out a deep breath and looked down at the paper on his keyboard.

"It's okay. Sorry for yelling at you. So, what's so important?" He slipped on his reading glasses. "The Death of the Internet …" he read aloud, trailing off as his eyes traveled down the page.

"So, what?" Daddy said, looking up at Uncle Frank, "She's not the first grad student to complain about government surveillance of the internet. She also sounds pretty paranoid and misinformed."

"I think she made some good points. But anyway, it's the response that's interesting."

Daddy turned to the next page.

"Alternet Protocol Specification, by The Anonymous Collective …" He read on silently, flipped to the next page, then the next. Emmie could see black and white drawings on the pages as he turned them. When he came to the last page, he took off his reading glasses and said,

"I don't know that much about complex adaptive systems, but — Yeah, I guess you could work around communication monitoring with a network like that. But who would bother? Most people don't care about government snooping that much."

"It's not just about government surveillance. The internet is becoming so heavily regulated now that, pretty soon, only the big guys will be able to play on the network. The startup economy is tanking already, and it's only going to get worse."

"Da-a-ad," Emmie whined softly, apprehensive that a long and boring conversation was about to take place.

Uncle Frank looked down at her.

"Ah. Waiting for spliner time?"

Emmie nodded.

"I've got a new African safari simulation that could use an expert opinion. Want to check it out?"

Emmie grinned up at him. Uncle Frank was fun to play with. He even let her wear some of the prototype sensory augmentation gear, if she promised not to tell her mother. Uncle Frank glanced at her father, who said,

"That'd be great. Chase another time, okay, Emmie?"

She nodded and ran happily after Uncle Frank to go on safari.

∞

Just a few weeks later, Emmie heard Uncle Frank talking excitedly about the Alternet Protocol Specification again. He said the people who made it, the Anonymous Collective, had written a manifesto. They said that the Alternet Age had arrived, and that they had set up eight places for people to connect to the alternet. Uncle Frank said that pretty soon there would be places to connect to the alternet everywhere in the entire world.

One of the eight places turned out to be in the community garden toolshed just a few blocks away from the Lab. Uncle Frank took Emmie with him to see it.

"You'll be able to tell your grandkids that you were here the day the alternet was born," he said, looking down at her as they walked along the uneven sidewalk toward the community garden.

"But what *is* the alternet?" said Emmie.

"It's just a protocol now," said Uncle Frank, "That means it's a way for a lot of computers to talk to each other. A protocol is a language that a bunch of computers all understand. The internet started as a protocol, too. The internet is just millions and millions of computers, all talking to each other using the same protocol. Big computers, like the servers at the Lab, and little computers, like the ones you see on mobile phones and smartcoms, they can all talk to each other with the internet protocol."

"Why does there need to be another protocol, if the computers can all talk to each other already?"

"That's a very good question. It's because, on the internet, there are these highways. Computers that want to talk to each other have to send their messages to other computers over the highways. Like how we use the freeway to travel from home to the Lab. And different people own the internet highways. The problem is that sometimes the people who own the highways don't let everyone use them. Sometimes they even read messages that don't belong to them."

"Why do they do that?"

Uncle Frank smiled grimly.

"Some people like to control information. But information wants to be free."

Emmie didn't understand that, but she didn't have a chance to ask any more questions because just then they came to the chain link fence of the community garden. Uncle Frank opened the gate, and they followed the path between twelve well-tended raised beds that led to the toolshed. Uncle Frank pointed at the roof, where a black box topped by a palm-sized solar panel glinted in the sun.

"That's it?" said Emmie, disappointed.

"Yep. That's it," said Uncle Frank, grinning.

Uncle Frank was right. Pretty soon, Emmie saw little black boxes, and all sorts of other kinds of alternet connection points, everywhere.

"That's because the information routing application runs on pretty much every consumer electronic device," Uncle Frank had explained. He seemed very excited about this. "It's very well designed. Peer-to-peer, anonymous, and lightweight. It's spreading like wildfire."

That sounded pretty worrisome to Emmie. A group of teenagers had started a wildfire last summer by one of the biggest houses in the Berkeley hills. Daddy said it was sad because it gave all the protestors a bad name. Mama said it was sad because they were so ignorant. Emmie thought it was sad because a lot of people had died. She had even been able to smell the smoke from her house.

Later, though, Emmie decided the alternet wasn't scary at all. In fact, the alternet turned out to be one of her very favorite things. People starting putting the most wonderful things on the alternet, and, with all the immergers Uncle Frank and Daddy let her use at the Lab, she suddenly became able to visit worlds she could never have imagined.

∞

Over the next several months, Dom observed an escalation of activity at the Lab as retinal projection devices, sensory feedback garments, audiovisual motion simulators, and environment modeling tools poured from the shelves of the warehouse. The rapid growth of the alternet and the proliferation of the multi-sensory content that the new protocol supported drove sales of Lab sensory augmentation equipment through the roof. In the year that followed the appearance of the public alternet access point in the community garden toolshed, Dom noticed several new words enter the Lab lexicon.

The first was *alternet domain*. A domain was a collection of alternet content, often contained in a three-dimensional representation of some kind of physical environment.

Fast upon the heels of *alternet domain* was *immersion*. Immersion was accessing alternet content that provided a convincing multi-sensory experience.

To the delight of the Lab, their own team coined the word *immerger*, which gained traction in the tech community. An immerger was anything that aided immersion, including most of the products the Lab designed.

And finally there was *Tomo*. Tomo Yoshimoto was the Japanese alternet domain designer whose alternet domain *Kaisei* epitomized immersion. *Kaisei* and its creator had become an international sensation.

Comparison to Tomo became the highest praise Travis could bestow upon his own designers. Frank's engineers engaged in an ongoing battle of one-upmanship to improve the experience of Tomo's *Kaisei* through ever more subtle refinements to their sensory augmentation gear. The Lab's entire mission might have been understood as the enablement of Tomo-quality immersion experiences.

Dom followed Emmie for days after the launch of *Kaisei* as she explored the domain in full head-to-toe immergers. He was as awestruck as she by the acres of Japanese gardens through which users entered the domain. The expansive content beyond grew only more ethereal and wonderful. Dom might have wandered the subdomains of *Kaisei* at Emmie's side indefinitely had not the first day of kindergarten arrived.

∞

"Everybody hates me," six-year-old Emmie wailed, bursting into her sister's bedroom one day after school. Twelve-year-old Ollie stood staring into space, probably immersed in alternet research for school.

Ollie blinked, refocusing her eyes from the visual overlay

rendered by her retinal-projection glasses. She quickly took in Emmie's running nose, red with rubbing, and puffy eyes, wet with tears. She pushed back her glasses, peeled off her immerger gloves, and hauled Emmie up onto her bed. They flopped back onto the squishy, sky-blue comforter, Emmie's dark curls entangling with Ollie's long blonde hair.

"What happened?"

Emmie recounted between sobs how a mean group of girls had, just before recess, stolen everything out of her school desk. They had even taken the set of perfectly-sharpened colored pencils Uncle Frank had given her for her birthday. Realizing too late what those girls had done, Emmie had rushed out onto the playground just in time to watch through the chain link fence as a stack of her drawings blew away. Almost all of her pencils had rolled down the sidewalk into the storm drain, too.

"Wow," Ollie said seriously, "That was really mean."

Ollie knew all about mean girls. The girls in her class teased her because she was so smart, and because she didn't care much about clothes or boys or sleepover parties. Ollie only cared about grown-up things.

"And now my pictures —" Emmie sniffed, "I made them for Mama's birthday, and now they're all lost! I don't think I can ever make such good drawings, not ever again."

Ollie looped one of Emmie's curls around her finger and pulled it back like a spring,

"Well, if you put something on paper, you're bound to lose it eventually. And then, poof —" she let go of the curl, which bounced against Emmie's face, "it's gone."

Emmie began to sob again, but Ollie hushed her.

"Listen. If you want to make a drawing that you can't lose, one that will last forever, you need to make lots and lots of copies and hide them everywhere."

Emmie stopped mid-sob,

"But how? I can't even make two copies look the same."

"You don't draw with paper and pencil, then," said Ollie, indicating the pair of immerger gloves she had placed on her desk. Emmie frowned. She didn't understand.

Ollie sighed and said in her teacher-voice,

"Emmie, do you think that when the designers at the Lab make — I don't know — a table, a shoe, a flower — that, when they need another one, they build it again from scratch? Do you think Tomo designs every single leaf on every single tree separately?"

Emmie shrugged. Tomo could do anything.

"Well," said Ollie, "He doesn't. He designs something once, and then he stores it in a content library on the alternet. When he needs to put it in one of his domains, he takes a copy, and then when he needs another, he takes another. The alternet servers do all the hard work, making the copies. And not only that, but the alternet servers are constantly making new copies and sending them to other servers, so the only way to lose your content is if you lost *the entire alternet* too."

Emmie stared at her sister, mouthing the words *the entire alternet.*

"So," Ollie said decisively, "You should just make your drawings for the alternet. You'll be like Tomo. Now," she shooed Emmie off the bed, "Get out of here. I've got work to do."

Emmie stuck out her tongue at her sister, then dried her eyes and trotted off to her room, all the while repeating under her breath,

"The *entire* alternet. The *entire alternet.*"

∞

Emmie didn't forget Ollie's advice. She spent the next several days learning to use some of the alternet design software at the Lab. She found out that it was very easy to forget about silly girls when she could build a whole world of her own.

The night of Mama's birthday dinner, Emmie had just finished making her present for her mother — a big three-dimensional portrait of her entire family — when she heard the loud laughter of Uncle Frank. He was the first guest to arrive. Emmie dropped her drawing stylus, threw her immergers on the bed, and raced up to the kitchen.

"Uncle Frank!" she cried happily.

"Hey, little girl," he said, reaching down to tickle her and mess up her hair.

"Where's my tree?" she said, giggling and pulling at his long sleeve.

"Emmie," Mama warned, "Don't be rude."

"Oh, let her, Ana," said Daddy, "Frank likes showing off his arms to the girls." Uncle Frank's girlfriend Nora seemed to think this was very funny. Emmie didn't like Nora very much. Whenever she was around, it was hard to get Uncle Frank's attention. But now, Uncle Frank was paying attention to Emmie, and he rolled up his sleeve for her. Underneath, stretched out across his muscley arm, there was a great big tree that covered the skin from his shoulder all the way down to his elbow.

"You added more branches," said Emmie, delighted, tracing the fresh lines worked into the skin.

"Well, you just keep growing," said Uncle Frank.

"Does it hurt?" she said, looking up in concern.

"Yes," said Mama, with the voice that meant someone was about to get into trouble. Uncle Frank said seriously,

"Yes. Tattoos hurt very much. That's why you will never, ever, get one. You'll just have to be happy with your one tree."

"It's not really *her* tree, though," Ollie said, "You started that tattoo before she was even born, didn't you, Uncle Frank?"

Emmie looked up at Uncle Frank expectantly.

"We-e-ell," Uncle Frank said, "That's true, but it wouldn't be the same without the drawing Emmie made for me."

"You still have it, don't you?" Emmie said. She was proud that Uncle Frank had used her own drawing for his tattoo.

"Sure do," said Uncle Frank. He reached into his back pocket and pulled out his wallet. He took out a worn piece of paper folded many times over. He handed it to Emmie, and she spread out the paper on the countertop for Mama to see.

"Yes, sweetheart. I see it. It's very well done."

"I did it all by myself."

"Emmie," Mama said gently, "Don't exaggerate."

Emmie rolled her eyes.

"Oh, all right. I traced it from a photo of a tree in Mama's office."

Emmie saw that Mama looked a little sad about this. Mama didn't like to talk about those photographs, even though she kept them in lots of different rooms in the house. Emmie didn't understand it.

"Ah!" Uncle Frank laughed, "So our little artist is a plagiarist?"

"What's a plagiarist?" asked Emmie.

"It's someone who steals someone else's work and takes credit for it," said Ollie.

"It's stealing?" said Emmie. She pulled her drawing quickly from the countertop, embarrassed. She could feel her face turning red.

"Hey," Uncle Frank whispered, crouching down beside Emmie and putting his hand on her shoulder, "I was just teasing. Every artist steals things sometimes. Sometimes, stealing is just another word for inspiration."

∞

On the weekday afternoons over the next few years, while Ollie focused on her schoolwork in a quiet back office in the Lab, Dom followed Emmie as she roamed the floors, procrastinating. She developed a knack for slipping into the background as the Lab engineers and designers carried on their work. In this way, she managed to sneak peeks and demos of nearly every interesting gadget in development at the Lab.

The year that Emmie turned twelve, Dom watched her tireless campaign to convince her parents to install a spliner in her bedroom. Having had privileged access to the Lab spliner since infancy, Emmie had not considered that having another for her personal use might be a bit of an extravagance. Travis tried to break the news gently.

"Could I have my own identity credentials, then, instead?" Emmie said, falling back on a request that posed no great financial burden but had been frequently denied nonetheless. From where she sat curled up beside her father on the sofa, she looked pleadingly across the coffee table at her mother.

"Why do you need your own credentials?" said Anatolia, "You already have anonymous read access to every domain that could possibly be appropriate for someone your age."

"But I want to be a domain designer like Tomo," said Emmie, sitting up straight on the sofa and tucking behind her ear a strand of flat-ironed chestnut hair streaked with cobalt blue. Imitating her older sister's reasonable voice, she explained, "I can't publish my work in any of the good artist domains without my own creds, my own identity."

"Those public forums are full of unauthenticated identities, Emmie," Anatolia said patiently, "They're not safe for someone your age. There will be plenty of time for you to use those forums when you're older."

"How old?" said Emmie, not quite keeping the whine out of her voice, "Ollie already had her own credentials when she was my age!"

"Ollie needed credentials to take classes in some of her educational domains. We didn't just let her wander around any public domain she chose."

"I know how to take care of myself on the alternet, Mom! Do you think I'm stupid?"

"I think you're twelve years old, Emerald," snapped Anatolia, "You know plenty about the alternet, but I know a lot more about people than you do. You have to think carefully about what you do on the alternet. Even when you think you're doing something anonymously, securely, even when you think you're being very clever, you can leave clues. You can't even imagine what some people ..."

"What?" Emmie demanded, crossing her arms, "What some people *what?*"

Travis and Anatolia exchanged a long look.

"Emmie," Travis said, his voice uncharacteristically stern, "Mom is just looking out for you."

"What is she afraid I'm going to do?" Emmie demanded shrilly, turning to her father.

"It's not what I'm afraid you'll do," Anatolia said, more quietly now, "It's what I'm afraid *other* people might do."

"You think everyone is out to get me! I don't get it. You're not this way with Ollie. She can do whatever she wants."

"Not true!" Ollie hollered up from her room downstairs.

"Ana," Travis said, reaching out to put a hand on Anatolia's knee, "I agree that we can't just give Emmie credentials and free rein to do anything she wants with them. But unless we're going to cut her off completely from the alternet —"

"OMG, Dad," Emmie groaned, covering her face with her hands, "Don't give her ideas!"

Travis sighed, then said,

"Ana, we can't protect her from everything forever."

Ollie appeared at the top of the stairs, arriving just in time to see her mother's eyes welling up with tears. She came over to sit beside her mother.

"I have an idea," Ollie said brightly, as if addressing a class of kindergarteners, "What if you give Emmie her own credentials but only let her use them when Mom is supervising?"

"Ollie!" Emmie cried indignantly, in a voice indistinguishable from her mother's.

Anatolia cocked her head to the side, considering.

"It's an idea. I'm at the office so much that I don't get to spend half as much time with Emmie as Dad does. I just —" she looked worriedly at Emmie, "Honey, I don't want to make you hate me more than you already do."

Emmie's indignant expression melted.

"OMG, Mom! I don't hate you."

∞

So Anatolia registered an identity credential for Emmie, and Emmie resigned herself to her mother's supervision. After obsessing for days over the design of an avatar for her new alternet identity, which she named Bealsio, Emmie refocused her energy on crafting the perfect debut submission to *Emergency*, a domain where millions of aspiring alternet designers published their work in hopes of being noticed by recruiters from some of the prestigious commercial domains.

After school the next day, Emmie changed out of her school uniform into full-body immersion gear and made her way to the quiet Lab back office that Ollie had vacated weeks ago after receiving her acceptance letter from Princeton University. Emmie pushed the desk against the wall, dimmed the lights, and locked the door.

The intensity of her desire to create something magnificent woke Dom from sleep, as had happened occasionally over the years. But this time, Dom felt something different in the call, an urgency that had not been there before. The connection between them grew taut, and Dom found it impossible to resist. He cast a parting glance at the position of the stars outside the window of his sleeping quarters. He had barely four hours until sunrise. Hoping he would be able to return to his duties in time to escape the notice of the Mohirai, Dom yielded to Emmie and followed the pull through the void until he stood beside her.

She sat in a swiveling chair in the midst of the locked office, twisting a lock of her hair between the immerger-ring-encrusted fingers of one hand as she spun the chair round and round. The silver threads of her skin-tight tactile immergers glistened in the low light. Her brilliant green eyes, ringed with thick eyeliner and smoky powder, focused inward. Though the outer trappings had changed, the expression recalled to Dom a hundred thousand memories and a thousand thousand regrets.

After a while, Emmie withdrew a pair of immerger glasses from the front pocket of her loose tunic, which she wore as a concession to Anatolia's complaint that her immerger clothes were "too revealing," notwithstanding Emmie's boyish figure. A quick tap to the band on her wrist switched on the three-dimensional retinal projection functionality of the glasses and engaged the tactile feedback of her shirt, and with another few swipes of her fingers she immersed herself in *Kaisei*, Tomo's flagship domain.

Because *Kaisei* had become the final alternet testing ground for all Lab hardware prototypes, the domain was almost as familiar to Emmie as the Lab itself. Dom followed her as she chose an avatar, this time an old woman with a tranquil smile and a richly-embroidered blue silk kimono, and stepped through the red *torii* archway into the main *Kaisei* subdomain: *Minu ga hana*, a sprawling Japanese tea garden. In the physical world, Emmie reached into another pocket of her tunic to pull out an olfactory augmentation patch, which she pressed to her collar. As she moved through the simulated garden, she breathed deeply the scents of sweet grass, fresh water, rosy cherry blossoms, spicy evergreens; ran the fingers of her tactile immerger gloves over mossy stones and smooth wooden bridge railings; listened to the rustle of leaves, the splashes of frogs into the pond.

When Emmie emerged from *Kaisei* an hour later, Dom saw a chaotic flood of ideas flash before her mind's eye, vivid but fleeting. She growled at the seeming emptiness where

Dom stood beside her in the office. She withdrew a grey stylus from yet another pocket and opened the two-dimensional interface of an environmental modeling toolkit. She began painting in broad, confident strokes upon the air, colors gathering into a bright but indefinite form. Minutes later, with an exasperated sigh, she let the colors fade to nothing and switched to another tool, this time a terrain modeler, with which she had slightly better success, but still unsatisfactory results.

As Emmie's frustration grew, the pull on their connection faded somewhat, to Dom's relief. Had the pull been much stronger, he might have found it impossible to maintain the distance that had for so many years allowed him to remain hidden from her sight. The intensity of Emmie's imagination in early childhood had occasionally caused him to slip, leading to moments of contact between them. He had tried to minimize such encounters. Intruding on her awareness was a dangerous game, one that could lead quickly to madness. He had made that mistake before. As long as he could, he would keep her unaware of his presence. It was one of the few gifts he could give to her.

In the weeks that followed, Emmie established a routine of slipping into *Kaisei* after school, emerging in a burst of inspiration, scrambling to capture an idea in shape or color or sound or texture, and finally regarding the result with despair. Ava's spirit was as self-critical as ever, but still as tenacious. Some things never changed.

In her preoccupation with transforming the wild tangle of ideas in her mind into one clear form, Emmie withdrew from her unofficial responsibilities and social obligations at the Lab.

"Don't you love me anymore?" Uncle Frank wailed,

having pounded on Emmie's locked door for a solid minute in an attempt to recruit her to his team for a Nerf skirmish in the spliner. Emmie looked guiltily at the door before turning up the volume on her earbuds.

∞

One afternoon, as Dom watched Emmie examining her expensive immerger glasses for cracks after throwing them against the wall in a fit of pique, he felt the threads beneath his skin tingle. Emmie froze where she stood, and her face lit up with a look of amazement. Dom saw an image flicker through her mind that stirred up in him a swell of hope: a great tree, branches swaying in the wind. Then the image was gone. Emmie slipped the glasses on hurriedly, heedless of the distortions in the visual overlay caused by the cracks in the glasses' frame, and took up her stylus.

Over the next several hours, she sculpted into the air the great tree: roots deep in an unseen earth; branches spreading into the heavens, thick with foliage and heavy with fruit; the spicy, twisted bark and pungent, waxy leaves; the play of light and wind upon it all. Dom could not resist helping her, adding to her vision bits and pieces of his own memory, holding the vision steady in his mind when it seemed at risk of slipping from hers. When at last the vision was captured, Emmie leaned back against the wall, slipped on her backup immerger glasses to improve the quality of her visual overlay, and stared at her work in amazement.

She jumped at the loud knock on the door.

"Emmie?" came Travis' muffled voice, "Are you still in there?"

"Yeah," she said distractedly, "Can I just have a minute?"

"We need to drive home, soon, though. Nanna made dinner, and she's waiting for us."

Emmie wrinkled her nose, her eyes never wavering from the great tree hovering before her.

"Want to show me what you're working on?" Travis asked after a pause.

Emmie bit her lip, looking from the tree to the closed door.

"Fine. But I want you to be honest, if it's not any good."

She unlocked the door and opened it slowly. Travis smiled and stepped into the room, slipping on his own glasses.

"What port?" he asked.

Emmie checked her visual overlay.

"I'm on 51094," she said.

Travis flicked on his overlay and blinked to bring it into focus. He stood silent for a long time.

"Well?" Emmie asked anxiously.

"Wow," he said, a smile of intense pride spreading over his face, "Sweetheart ... It's incredible."

Emmie beamed. Dom knew this was just the beginning.

∞

Despite several clashes with Anatolia over what constituted sufficiently anonymous content, Emmie eventually managed to publish on *Emergency* an immersive portfolio containing items ranging from playful and cartoonish characters possessing basic artificial intelligence; to lifelike baby animals designed to tempt the alternet's insatiable appetite for puppies and kittens; to abstract single-sensory landscapes in visual, auditory, olfactory, and tactile modalities. It was an eclectic collection, demonstrating a burgeoning sophistication in the manipulation of the senses and a still-childlike taste for the fanciful. Emmie agonized over the question of whether to put the great tree, her masterpiece, into her public portfolio. In the end, something convinced her to keep this piece private, at least for the time being.

During sessions supervised by Anatolia, Emmie interacted through her avatar Bealsio with a slow trickle of visitors to her *Emergency* portfolio, thanking people for feedback and swapping critiques with other designers. A few months after her debut submission, traffic to Bealsio's portfolio surged when an influential alternet design commentator mentioned one of her pieces in an article about the effective use of tactile elements in domain design. Her portfolio hit all the bandwidth limits for a free account within an hour, and Emmie had to beg her mother to upgrade her to a professional account, which Anatolia did with a touch of pride.

The visitor traffic to Bealsio's portfolio continued to grow. The delight and amazement of her visitors spurred Emmie on to ever more ambitious projects. Bealsio attracted growing numbers of comments and reviews in design forums, sending Emmie through the stratosphere with praise or ripping her self-confidence to shreds with criticism.

"It's not healthy," Dom overheard Anatolia murmur to Travis after a particularly vicious comment had dismissed Bealsio's portfolio as, "A heavy-handed application of trendy multi-sensory varnish to the most tired of clichés ... Childish at best." Emmie lay listless on the sofa with the music in her earbuds blaring.

Travis, re-reading the vitriol on his visual overlay for the tenth time, spluttered, "This guy — I can't believe — What a jackass!"

"I know this is what she loves, but … isn't it a bit premature to expose her to all these crazy people?" said Anatolia, her face drawn with concern, "Look what it's doing to her."

Travis closed the article and took a deep breath, shaking his head.

"We can't do anything to stop them, and we can do even less to stop Emmie. I think we'll just have to help her ignore all the background noise."

Anatolia's lawyer instincts proved more useful than Travis' clumsy attempts to comfort Emmie. Anatolia spent lunch breaks and evenings for days digging through alternet and internet archives, even hitting the physical stacks at the Cal library in Berkeley, gathering up the historical evidence of crimes against creative people by the jaded and cynical, the self-important and pedantic, and the downright mean and stupid.

Finding Emmie swinging her legs despondently over the edge of the deck one evening, Anatolia said,

"The only way you'll become a great artist is if you learn to keep on going despite the naysayers. There's not a single great artist in history who didn't get called a hack, or worse."

Anatolia pressed into Emmie's palm the storage tablet whose contents she had so painstakingly compiled. Early the next morning, having spent a sleepless night reading every last word on the tablet, Emmie brought her mother breakfast in bed.

"I don't care what they say," Emmie said firmly, setting the tray on her mother's lap, "None of those idiots are going to stop me."

Anatolia's eyes shone.

Mother and daughter continued to bond during Emmie's

chaperoned sessions in *Emergency*, and for Emmie's sixteenth birthday, Anatolia gave her a gift so tremendous that Emmie had not even thought to ask for it: the login credentials for Bealsio.

"OMG, Mom!" Emmie squealed, staring at the coin-sized storage tablet her mother had taped to the inside of a birthday card, "I can't believe it! Thank you!"

She smothered her mother in kisses, then raced down to her room to log on to *Emergency* for her very first private alternet session.

With unlimited time now to interact with the *Emergency* community, Emmie's creative output was spurred to new heights. At the end of her sophomore year, exhausted by the attempt to keep up her real-life persona as passable high school student alongside her alternet persona as virtuoso designer Bealsio, she decided to give up the real-life persona.

When she announced her intention to drop out of high school at the dinner table that June, Anatolia and Travis turned to one another, a wordless conversation passing between them. Emmie had a long track record of winning arguments of all kinds, and the stakes were high. After an uncomfortable pause, Emmie looked from one to the other and said,

"I can still finish my diploma, if you care about that. I could even take college classes. You know how great the alternet education services are."

"Look," Travis said delicately, "I know high school isn't great all the time, but you can't just quit without a plan."

"But I do have a plan," Emmie said, "I'm going to be an alternet domain designer."

"And there's still a lot you can learn to help you do that," said Anatolia, "You could go to art school, for example. Or study computer science, or —"

Emmie shook her head.

"I've read about a lot of those programs. I visited some of the campus domains, too — at Stanford and Caltech and MIT, at RISD. I talked to students there, sat in on some classes. They don't have anything to teach me. I already know more than a lot of the professors because of all the work I've done on *Emergency* and at the Lab."

"Honey," said Anatolia, clearly struggling to keep a level tone, "You'll have the rest of your life to spend off in the alternet. There won't be that many times in your life when you can be really present with other people, in person, like you can now. To make friends who really know *you*, and not just some avatar."

"Bealsio's a real part of me, Mom," said Emmie, stung by her mother's implied disparagement of Bealsio, "not 'just some avatar.'"

They carried on the argument through the summer, Emmie developing deft responses to each new protest or concern raised by her parents. Emmie eventually recruited Ollie to her cause. Sitting in on the debate via video chat from the lab where she was doing summer research for her cognitive anthropology program, Ollie worked several compelling anecdotes from their childhood growing up in the Lab into her assessment that academia severely lagged industry when it came to emerging media. Ollie's support was the final blow to her parents' resistance, and Emmie prevailed, as Dom had known she would.

CHAPTER 4
Otaku

Emmie, now a sixteen-year-old high school dropout, set up her design studio on the bottom floor of the Bridges' house, in the room her father called the fishbowl.

"Won't you be lonely down there, Em?" he wondered at the breakfast table the morning she asked if she could take over that floor, "There's plenty of room for you at the Lab. We can give you your own office, if you want."

Emmie shook her head.

"If I stay at the Lab, I won't be able to get any work done without Uncle Frank barging in every other minute for some immerger feedback, or the interns recruiting me for games in the spliner. There's always something. And Mom can't stand going down there, so she won't bother me, either. It's perfect."

Dom was delighted by the prospect of spending time in the fishbowl, a marvel of architectural technology. A spiral staircase descended into the improbable room through a circular opening in the floor three flights below the house's street-level roof deck. The staircase let out into a small, dimly-lit chamber whose earth-colored walls and moss-green carpet gave the impression of an underground cave. Cabinets filled with artists' tools of every era — from pencils and paper to environment-sculpting knives and full-body immerger clothes — lined the dark walls. A single door led out of the dim chamber into the room beyond.

In a fit of vertigo-inducing inspiration, the architect of the Bridges' cliffside aerie had chosen to suspend the fishbowl from the underside of the cantilevered foundation supporting the three floors above. Crystal-clear panels of inch-thick synthetic glass formed three walls and the floor so that emerging from the inner chamber to the outer room gave the illusion of stepping out upon thin air. The door closing behind completed the illusion, as the rear wall became a seamless mirror reflecting the breathtaking view across the Bay.

Although Anatolia could not even look into the fishbowl without being overwhelmed by vertigo, Emmie strode out upon the glass each morning like it was the most natural thing in the world. She tended to be under full sensory immersion before she even entered the room, though, which might have accounted for her fearlessness.

Dom remained unseen even in the clear light of the fishbowl, watching and aiding Emmie's ever more ambitious creative endeavors. Unbeknownst to Emmie, their connection bound them in a dancing tug-of-war. Emmie instinctively pulled at her connection to Dom, longing for his clarifying influence as she struggled to manifest her sprawling visions in her design work. Dom in turn maintained a disciplined distance from her, extending measured responses to Emmie's creative demands with patience perfected through innumerable years working with her. Though the digital media of the alternet was new to him, it was not so different from the work he had done for her in wood and stone millennia ago.

Their collaboration ushered in a period of prolific creation for Emmie that produced a thousand gardens for the senses. For days on end, sprawled across the glass floor of the fishbowl, Emmie sketched landscapes and creatures which she later summoned into existence with sculpting gloves, texturing knife, and finishing stylus. Gazing into her visual overlay, she programmed games and outlined quests. Under the influence of full sensory immersion, she contemplated her work, animating and polishing and extending to the outer reaches of her imagination and skill. Dom watched over her through it all, witness to and participant in her waking inspirations and sleeping dreams, her every struggle and triumph in her work.

When all creativity was exhausted, she would tackle a token amount of schoolwork to satisfy her mother's requirement that she complete her high school equivalency degree. Then she would reward herself with alternet immersion, seeking in worlds shaped by other hands the inspiration for her next day's work.

∞

Having spent the entire summer convincing her parents to take her artistic aspirations seriously, Emmie felt a huge sense of satisfaction when she stepped out into the light of the fishbowl each morning. It was like being the pilot of an amazing airship. The whole world spread out before her, and she could go anywhere, with a little help from the alternet and her immergers.

She was disciplined about her work. She spent the

morning hours focused on projects for her portfolio. She was often frustrated for days and weeks on end, fighting her unruly mind into submission, searching for the one small tweak that made the difference between good and great. But it was always worth it in the end. There was nothing, nothing in the world, more satisfying than standing before a piece of her own design and knowing that it was perfect.

After she finished a piece, in the few hours or days before the itch to start something new crept up on her again, she could unwind in the alternet.

There were so many domains she wanted to see. She had spent years in the Lab peeking over the shoulders of the designers and engineers as they browsed domains that were off-limits to her without her own credentials. But now, with the unexpected boon of her mother's trust and her own alternet identity, she had expected to find every door open to her.

What she found had been disappointing. Although the public domain was still enormous, the more interesting domains were all moving behind airtight authentication protocols to avoid the scrutiny of the alternet-regulation movement. Emmie thought the movement was pretty ridiculous. Having watched the video feeds of red-faced politicians and bombastic preachers denouncing the alternet as an underworld of pornographers, tax-evaders, and black-market business owners, she wondered if any of them had ever even been immersed in the alternet.

But the owners of alternet domains seemed to take the movement very seriously.

"No one's taking any chances, after what those Luddites did to the internet," Uncle Frank had said.

Unfortunately for Emmie, this meant that most of the

domains she had so longed to see were now wrapped in nearly impenetrable layers of security. Foremost among these domains was *Mysteries of Eleusis*.

She had heard of *Eleusis* for the first time when Uncle Frank stumbled from his office bleary-eyed and grinning one day after playing the game for twelve hours straight.

"The most addictive game ever!" he raved to the engineering team.

"Isn't it just a glorified game of capture the flag?" one of the younger guys had asked skeptically.

Eleusis was both, in fact. Though the gameplay was simple — work with your army, either Zeus' or Hades', to maintain or obtain possession of the Persephone avatar — and the audiovisual quality only decent, at high levels of the competition there was an exciting degree of improvisation and skill required. The game quickly became the national pastime at the Lab, with a majority of the engineering team spending the evenings utilizing the Lab's high-speed alternet connection to play the game together.

The gameplay itself was not what Emmie wanted to see. She had never fully understood the appeal of combat games. Of more interest to her was the fact that *Eleusis* was the preferred hangout for a number of influential alternet personalities, along with a diverse yet close-knit community of players: tech-savvy screen-watchers whiling away shocking stretches of time on the clock; multi-tasking jet-setters using simulated combat to process violent urges aroused by their work; stay-at-home parents with mythic fantasies; and the usual rabble of college students, game addicts, and the unemployed.

She wanted access to that community. If she was ever going to learn how to make her own domains popular, she was going to have to understand what users truly loved. The problem was that *Eleusis* now employed an adult identity verification system that was nearly impossible to circumvent.

She spent days searching for a possible workaround in public alternet domains, eventually posting a question on *MMORPhology*, a juvenile gamer forum, asking if anyone had ever been granted an exception to the adult credentials requirement for *Eleusis*. A number of domain members posted sympathetic comments. Many had tried, all had failed.

Then a private message popped up on her visual overlay. The message said simply,

prodigytal@Bealsio: *I've cracked half the adult authentication systems out there. Want to chat?*

Emmie read the message with a mixture of elation and apprehension. Her mom would kill her if she found out she was talking to hackers on the alternet. After a moment's hesitation, she wrote back to prodigytal,

Definitely.

She accepted a private projection request from prodigytal, and a moment later she was looking at an avatar that appeared to have been modeled on a samurai warrior: heavy leather armor covered in metal scales, an elaborate helmet with a crest that spread upward like the wings of a bird, a pair of crossed swords with gleaming rose and ebony sheaths strapped over the padded shoulders. Inside the helmet, instead of a face, there was only a shadow pierced by two blue points of light where the eyes should have been. It was a beautifully designed avatar, if a bit creepy, and clearly custom-made. Emmie was surprised. Coders were not generally known for their design taste.

"Um, hi," Emmie said nervously, "So, you've cracked *Eleusis* authentication?"

There was a long pause, and Emmie thought perhaps the projection was lagging. Then prodigytal's avatar shook with laughter.

"So Bealsio's not just underage, but a girl!" The voice was a very good computerized modulation, just enough to disguise the underlying voice without interfering with the subtleties of inflection that distinguished real human speech.

Emmie frowned. She tended to use a male avatar for Bealsio, especially in gamer forums. At the moment, she was using a pretty generic twenty-something male with sandy hair and an ironic tee-shirt, but she had not thought to disguise her voice over her private audio channel with prodigytal.

"Does it matter?" she said scornfully.

prodigytal shrugged.

"I was just curious. I've been following you on *Emergency* for a long time."

Emmie heard a hundred different alarms go off in her head, all in her mother's voice, warning of alternet stalkers. Emmie was inclined to close the channel immediately, but prodigytal went on,

"But no, it doesn't matter to me. Let's talk about authentication. I've faked *Eleusis* creds before. I could do it again. So what's it worth to you?"

Emmie was taken aback. For some reason, she had expected merely a friendly exchange of tips, as was typical in gamer forums. She hadn't expected someone hacking for hire.

"I — guess I don't know."

prodigytal was silent for a moment before he said,

"I'll do it for a thousand dollars."

Emmie laughed in surprise.

"Whoa. There's no way I can afford that."

"Well?" prodigytal seemed undeterred, "What can you afford?"

Emmie shook her head,

"I was just looking for some advice. Sorry for wasting your time."

She reached up for the end session control on her visual overlay.

"Hold on," prodigytal said hurriedly, "Why can't we negotiate something?"

"Look," Emmie said sharply, "I don't know you. It was stupid of me to even ask. Why don't you just drop it?"

prodigytal suddenly switched out of avatar form, and now Emmie was looking through the projection at a live video feed of a tall, skinny boy about her own age, with white-blonde hair and piercing blue eyes.

"Fine," he said, "Let's drop the avatar bullshit. I'm Zeke Eckerd. I can get you your adult creds. And I need the money."

Zeke looked strangely forlorn, and — Emmie realized with surprise — maybe even a little hungry. She felt a pang of sympathy for the boy.

"I'm sorry, but I really don't have any money to spend on this. I'm — Well, obviously, I'm underage. I get some ad revenue from my design portfolio, but I've spent it all on software and gear this month already."

Zeke nodded, frowning thoughtfully. After a moment, he said,

"Well, maybe we could barter for it."

"Barter what?" Emmie said warily.

"I bet you've got some some pretty killer software, based on the work of yours that I've seen on *Emergency.*"

Emmie couldn't help but feel a little flattered.

"You've been following me that closely, huh?"

Zeke nodded.

"I design stuff too," he said, "Subcontracting, mostly. I could use some better tools, maybe up my rate."

"Well …" Emmie couldn't see how it would hurt to give this boy a software license or two, "I guess I could do that."

Zeke smiled.

"Awesome. Done."

The next morning, she received an email from Zeke with her fake adult credentials attached. He hadn't even asked for payment up front, clearly a gesture of goodwill. In the message body, he wrote,

I'd love to show you the ropes in Eleusis sometime, if you want. —
prodigytal

She re-read the message three times before sending him the key code for the environment modeling suite that she had just stopped using in favor of the latest release. In the message body, she wrote,

Okay. That would be cool. Thanks for the creds. — Bealsio

∞

With Zeke's fake adult credentials in hand, Emmie logged on to *Eleusis* for the first time. She and Zeke met up in the avatar modeling entryway of the domain. Today, he had chosen an avatar of a tall young swordsman with a lean physique and shining golden armor. The avatar resembled the boy Emmie had seen previously on his live projection, although the avatar's face was less pinched and pale than Zeke's own.

"So," said Emmie, checking out the in-game avatar modeling toolkit, considering what impression she wanted to make on her first foray into the battlegrounds, "Do you play *Eleusis* a lot?"

"I don't have a lot of free time, but clients sometimes want knockoffs of *Eleusis* content, so I have to keep up with what's going on in here."

Emmie considered him thoughtfully.

"It sounds like you do a lot of paid work."

"I do okay."

Emmie smiled to herself at his obvious false modesty, then asked,

"Are you still in school, or do you work full-time?"

"Um —" Zeke looked away, "Yeah, I'm out of school now. Out on my own."

Emmie nodded.

"That's cool. That's what I want to do, too — design full-time, I mean."

"Yeah," Zeke sounded enthusiastic, "It's like the best thing. I love it."

"I'd love to check out your work some time," said Emmie.

Zeke smiled, the first time Emmie had seen him smile, she realized.

"Cool, yeah, that'd be great. Most of it's incorporated into the domains of people I sub for, but I can definitely show you."

Emmie quickly got up to speed on the avatar modeling tools available in *Eleusis*. They weren't as extensive as her usual toolkit, since most *Eleusis* players had far less sophisticated immergers than she did and proportionately less interest in avatar quality, but she could make do. She decided to continue using her Bealsio username in *Eleusis*, and while Zeke waited she quickly crafted a burly, olive-skinned male avatar based on photographs of her Papou. They were old photographs — from back in the 1990's — when Mom was about her age. Emmie even managed to create a convincing simulation of her grandfather's voice using snippets of projection videos and birthday greetings from her personal files. She polished off her work with a fabulous suit of Grecian armor and a pair of short swords.

"How do I look?"

Zeke eyed her avatar appraisingly and said,

"That'll do. So, next thing is we have to pick a server. The fastest servers are all in Asia, since there's so many players there. But unless you speak Mandarin or Cantonese, it's probably not worth it to deal with the latency issues. A local server makes the realtime gameplay smoother."

Emmie scanned the map of server locations.

"What server do you usually use?"

"I'm on the East Coast, but I work late, so Pacific time's fine with me."

"San Jose, then?"

"Sure."

She selected the server and followed Zeke through the game portal into the San Jose server recruitment grounds.

Emmie was a little disappointed by the recruitment grounds — a nondescript field of sand, literally a sandbox environment. She soon realized that no one else in the recruitment grounds was interested in environment design quality, though. This was purely a business transaction area.

"We could just go in, but you'll see more of what the game's about if we start with an army," said Zeke.

So Emmie stood waiting. Scouts for different armies combed the grounds for recruits. In the public chat channel, recruiters were posting requests for players with some demonstrated experience in other game domains. Since Emmie didn't have any experience at all, she worried she'd be waiting a long time. But it turned out that keeping her Bealsio username had been smart. A few army recruiters recognized her name and came over to chat with her, willing to overlook her inexperience in light of her identity's reputation in several respectable alternet design forums.

She and Zeke were chatting with the avatar of a grizzled bowman, an unlikely fan of Bealsio's frolicking kitten simulations, when a youthful spearman approached. He wore golden armor not dissimilar from Zeke's, as well as a large circular shield, which Emmie stared at in amazement.

"That's incredible," she said, pointing to the intricate battle scene worked into the golden shield, "Did you design that?"

"I did," the spearman smiled, "Thanks!"

Zeke frowned and continued talking, more loudly now, to the bowman, but the golden spearsman went on,

"I did some tactile simulations on the shield."

Emmie reached out eagerly and, through her immerger gloves, felt the cool surface of the delicate metalwork under her fingertips.

"Really great work."

"I'm Otaku, by the way" the spearman extended his hand.

"Bealsio," she replied, taking his hand. She felt his firm grip through her immerger glove.

"Yeah, I know. I've seen your work. It's fantastic."

The grizzled bowman passed on to another potential recruit, and Zeke stood by in silence as Emmie and Otaku kept up a long conversation about the finer points of immersive design. After a while, Zeke said,

"Hey, Bealsio, sorry, but I have to go. I've got a ton of work to do tomorrow morning. Maybe we'll go into the battlegrounds some other time?"

Emmie glanced at the time on her visual overlay.

"OMG, I totally lost track of time," she laughed, which sounded strange in Papou's Greek accent, "I have to go too."

"Oh, okay," Otaku's avatar flashed a disappointed expression, "Sure … Hey," he laughed, returning to the ostensible point of their whole interaction, "So do you want to join my guild? You and your friend, I mean," he smiled at Zeke, "We're just starting up, but I think you'll like the other guys."

Zeke started to shake his head, but Emmie smiled. "Sure. What's it called, again?"

"Amaranthian," he said, sending her an invite, which popped up as a message on her visual overlay, "We practice Tuesday and Thursday nights Pacific time, starting at eight PM. See you!"

Otaku headed off toward a small group of avatars that had just entered the recruitment grounds.

"Well, that worked out well!" Emmie said brightly to Zeke.

"Yeah," he said, looking away, "I guess. See you Tuesday."

∞

Otaku turned out to be a gifted teacher and guild leader. Emmie liked the friendly team dynamic he cultivated in the guild. He took practices seriously and made everyone else do the same. He liked to win, too. She hadn't expected how fun that could be. Under Otaku's leadership, Amaranthian accumulated an impressive win-loss record and climbed the rankings on the San Jose server.

"You know, it's good to sort of move around armies, to learn some different fighting techniques," Zeke suggested after they won a few battles with Amaranthian, "Your player stats are pretty good now. I bet we could join a more established guild."

"I'm having fun here," said Emmie, "Why don't we stay a little while longer?"

Zeke shrugged indifferently.

With all the extra hours she was spending playing *Eleusis*, Emmie had started to become active around the clock, working on additions to her design portfolio during daylight hours and immersing herself in the alternet through the night, catching a few hours of sleep at odd hours here and there. As long as she went upstairs for dinner and talked about her day with her parents, they didn't seem to notice her new schedule.

She used *Eleusis* to let off steam after frustrating design sessions in the fishbowl. The clash of swords seemed to satisfy some primal appetite for mindless physical action, and she gained a lot of alternet cultural knowledge and entertainment listening to the perpetual banter on the public channel, which ranged from trending alternet memes and real-world news to the most indecipherable arcana of every imaginable subculture. Even in the absence of combat and public channel banter, though, Emmie would have returned to *Eleusis* daily just to talk to Zeke and Otaku.

A few months after she and Zeke joined the guild,

Amaranthian was heading into battle against The Destroyers, competing for the number one ranking on the server.

"My roommate Shiva is The Destroyers' guild leader," Otaku told Amaranthian as they prepared for the battle, "Their guys are insane — I know most of them from my CS program. Every person in that guild has probably logged more hours in *Eleusis* this year than our entire guild combined. But they're disorganized. They rely on mods to counter all the common army maneuvers. But we're going to write a new playbook, and we're going to crush them."

The cheer that went up from the Amaranthian army was thrilling. Emmie started to understand how people could get hooked on this.

The battle with The Destroyers was a rush like none Emmie had ever experienced. Amaranthian, an army of men (and a few women) in gleaming gold and silver armor faced off against a shadowy, smoking, blazing army from hell. Members of both guilds put on their most elaborate avatars and pulled out their most impressive custom-coded combat effects. It was a close battle filled with screen-capture-worthy hand-to-hand combat sequences and heart-stopping turning points arrayed across the otherworldly landscape of *Eleusis'* Elysium battlefield, but in the end, Amaranthian carried the win.

In the celebratory aftermath, Otaku invited members of both guilds who lived in the Bay Area to meet up in person and celebrate over a beer. The invitation, unfortunately, proved that alternet community did not usually translate well to the real world. Members of both guilds begged off, citing family commitments and work schedules. At last, Otaku turned to Bealsio.

"Come on, man. Don't tell me you're another one of *these*

agoraphobes."

"Sorry," said Emmie, her battle high fading as she thought of the risk of revealing her minority status to anyone other than Zeke, "I can't."

"How about coffee some time? Whenever you're free," Otaku's ribbing tone became more respectful, "I'd love to get your feedback in person on some alternet content I've been working on, if it's not too much of an imposition."

"Back off, man," Zeke jumped in.

"Whoa," said Otaku, looking from Zeke to Emmie in surprise, "No problem. I —"

"No," Emmie interjected, "I'd be happy to."

What r u doing? Zeke demanded in a hastily-written private message, *He could report you to server gm. U could lose your adult creds.*

Cmon he wouldn't do that, Emmie wrote back, *Chill out!*

The blue eyes of Zeke's avatar narrowed, and he looked at her in silence for a moment before suddenly logging off the server. Emmie tried to send him a projection request, but his status said he was away.

∞

Before Mom returned home from work the next day, Emmie headed out the door, tapping the smartcom on her belt to send her father, who also would not be home for hours, a quick projection.

"I'm going to meet some friends up in Berkeley. I should be back in time for dinner."

"What friends?" Dad asked blankly, squinting to refocus his eyes on Emmie after emerging from a deep immersion session.

"Just some old friends from high school," Emmie said briskly, "I'll be back soon. Love you!"

Dad raised an eyebrow but nodded.

Emmie took the bus to Berkeley. In the designated coffee shop, she flicked on her visual overlay and skimmed the list of public identities checked in at the café. Otaku was there, among a dozen other usernames. She looked up and scanned the room, spotting him at a small table by the window: an athletic young man with short-cropped dark hair wearing a neatly-pressed collared shirt tucked into khaki slacks. She caught his attention and gave a little wave.

Otaku's eyes widened, and he glanced quickly at his smartcom, whose display of café check-ins confirmed the identity of his coffee date. When he looked up again, Emmie was already making her way toward him through the clutter of tables. He scrambled up to greet her. She stopped a few feet away, gauging his embarrassment.

"Are you …?" Otaku began uncertainly, clearing his throat as his eyes ran along the form-fitting silver threads of her neck-to-ankle tactile immergers. It occurred to her belatedly that she might have thrown on one of her tunics to cover up a bit.

"How old are you?" he finished at last, revealing a trace of a Southern accent.

"Sixteen," she said, daring him to make something of it.

He inhaled slowly, then chuckled,

"Sorry. I'm being rude. This is my fault."

"So … what?" she shrugged, her voice cool, "Does that mean you'd rather not be friends outside *Eleusis*?"

The young man glanced around, considering the other café patrons, who appeared decidedly inattentive to them.

"Can we start over?" he said at last, extending his hand.

"I'm Owen Cyrus. It's great to finally meet you in person."

"Nice to meet you, Owen," said Emmie, shaking his hand. "I'm Emmie Bridges."

After a few minutes of awkward preliminaries, they latched on to the familiarity of some of their more recent in-game conversations: the latest expansion of Tomo's *Kaisei*, the widely anticipated opening of the first-of-its-kind stadium spliner installation in San Francisco, the controversial attempts by various national governments to impose identity registration requirements on the alternet. The easy repartee of Bealsio and Otaku at last returning, Owen was emboldened to turn to new subjects.

"So you're in high school?"

Emmie took a sip of her black coffee. She had ordered it mostly because Mom would never have allowed it, and, despite the bitterness, she could see the appeal of the flavor. She set down her mug carefully, unsure whether she wanted to get into this part of the conversation.

"Does it really matter?" she asked.

"Come on," he cajoled, "What's the point of meeting in person if we can't talk about normal stuff?"

"It's just going to make you feel more weird about me."

"Okay," Owen laughed, "I admit I wasn't expecting you to be a teenage girl, but it's not like you're an extraterrestrial or something. Hopefully."

She rolled her eyes at the feeble humor but still had to suppress a giggle.

"No. But I'm not in high school, either. I dropped out."

He frowned.

"What do you do all day, then?"

"You've seen it," she shrugged, "I design alternet content. I play *Eleusis*. I surf the alternet. I design some more. I study on the side, but mainly I'm working on becoming a designer."

He considered her appraisingly.

"Pretty ballsy," he said, "Dropping out, pursuing your dream."

"There's nothing else I want to be doing. *Carpe diem,* right?"

Owen looked down at the table, rotating his espresso by the edge of its saucer, his eyes distant.

"Yeah."

Emmie waited for him to go on, then prompted,

"So how about you? You're studying CS at Cal, right?"

Owen's eyes refocused on her.

"Yep. Senior year."

She cocked her head to the side. "So you're, what, twenty-two?"

"In a couple of months."

She nodded slowly.

"Too old for me, then."

Emmie smirked as Owen said, with a slightly alarmed expression,

"*Way* too old."

"Come on, I'm just kidding. So, what do *you* do all day?"

"I'm supposed to be working on my senior project, but I'm procrastinating," he smiled sheepishly, "So I surf the net, I play *Eleusis,* evade my TA duties to go on long weekend camping trips out of town. I ... guess I've gotten a little side-tracked."

"By what?"

He rubbed his chin ruefully,

"Delusions of grandeur. I always dreamed of becoming some breakout alternet phenomenon, designing games or something. Like Tomo, you know? Rags-to-riches. But ... I always knew that was a dream. My designs are primitive at best. When I managed to get into the CS program here, I realized I'd better do something practical. Accounting and software development are pretty much the only prospects in this crappy job market."

"Sounds practical. And boring."

Owen's eyes twinkled, and they sat smiling at each other. Emmie felt a little flushed, then said quickly,

"So … What did you want to show me?"

"Damn," said Owen, hanging his head in his hand, "This is even more embarrassing now that you turn out to be a little girl."

"Watch it," she said, slipping on her immerger glasses and a pair of gloves, "So, what modalities are we talking about?"

"Oh," Owen looked surprised, "Sorry. I don't actually own any immergers myself, other than a total crap pair of single-overlay glasses. I usually check out gear from the university library. I thought we could go over there."

"That's okay," Emmie said, reaching for her bag and rummaging around, "I've got some spares. The shirt's probably — no, definitely too small. You could squeeze into the gloves, though. They're an old pair of my dad's." She emptied the bag's contents onto the table. "Anyway, you probably just need glasses and gloves to access whatever you want to show me, right? I'm wearing enough gear to do audio, visual, olfactory, and tactile. Everything but environmental."

Owen stared at the pile of expensive electronics on the table.

"Wow."

"Go on," said Emmie, "Suit up."

Owen pulled on the gloves, flexing his fingers to test the fit, then slipped on the glasses. Emmie tapped her smartcom to sync their gear.

"Where's your content?" she asked, "Remote? Storage tablet?"

"It's remote, hold on —" he tapped a short sequence on the table with his gloved hand to download his files to a local directory on Emmie's smartcom.

"Okay, don't laugh," he said, "I wasn't kidding when I said my stuff's primitive. Especially compared to yours."

"Look, you asked for my opinion. I'm not gonna sugar-coat anything, but I'm not going to laugh at you."

"Thanks," he said wryly.

He tapped out another sequence on the table, launching the content compiler on Emmie's smartcom. As the compiler churned away, the log messages scrolled up the screen. Emmie let out a low whistle.

"You're working really low-level, huh? Hardcore."

"I wouldn't, except I don't have access to any decent high-end tools. The open source toolkits are okay, but all the effects in those are pretty run-of-the-mill. When I've got some basic presentation to do for a class, I can do something quick and dirty, but it's hard to make anything that seems new or exciting."

Emmie nodded. She had a major advantage over Owen in this regard, having access through the Lab to software more sophisticated than anything available in the open source community or on the consumer market.

"You've got an excuse to have primitive stuff, then. It would have taken me a hundred times as long to build anything in my portfolio if I had to work like this."

"Well, in any case, you still don't have to sugar-coat anything. Go ahead."

Emmie turned her attention to the collection of items in

the simulator. She reached first for a spiky, spherical object about the size of a softball. The spikes on the outside of the object brushed her palms, stiff but pliable, like feathers.

"You can shape the stems," said Owen, "Just touch your fingertips to them."

Emmie proceeded to draw out individual stems, elongating them. At intervals along the stem, she drew out new tendrils of material, twirling and kinking them around her fingers, flattening them out to form broad, leafy shapes, shaking the tips of the stems to soften them, or twisting them to make them stand up straight. Several café patrons looked up to stare at her. She tried for a moment to be less conspicuous, then decided to give it up. This was an amazing simulation, and she wanted to fully experience it.

"Try setting it down," Owen said, grinning.

She did, and now the object began to grow, each frond she had shaped with her fingers stretching out into the room. As she watched, smaller fronds sprouted from the larger ones, each smaller frond a miniature image of its parent. The object grew ever more intricate as the original fronds grew larger and ever-smaller fronds unfurled. The object finally stopped growing when it had filled the height of the café. Emmie turned to Owen, impressed.

"That was cool. Some sort of fractal algorithm?"

"Yeah."

"Your object physics are fantastic." She brushed the fingertips of her immerger gloves over a fern-like plume stretching across the table between them, feeling its feathery texture on her palm and watching it spring back from her touch. "The tactile simulation, too. Is that from a texture library?"

"I wrote it myself," Owen said with a touch of pride.

"It's really good."

"Thanks."

"The visuals are pretty simple, like you said," she went on, "But your lighting is great. I'd love to play around with your source, if you'd let me. I bet I could add some visual polish."

Owen nodded,

"Yeah. Absolutely. I'd love that."

She reached for the frond again, gripping it in her hand and shaking it, watching the effects of the movement ripple through the rest of the object.

"No audio?" she said.

"I hadn't gotten to it yet."

Emmie moved on to the other items Owen had put on display.

The first was a sort of semantic association game. A shape selected from a standard content library, when seeded with a single word she provided, crawled the alternet for a series of concepts to connect the starting shape to the final shape. It then rendered a slow animation of one object morphing smoothly into the next.

A collection of flasks allowed her to pour and toss multicolored liquids against the walls, ceiling, and tabletops of the café, simulating the fluid dynamics in such slow motion that she could walk leisurely through a flock of colorful undulations and watch from different angles as they touched ground and languidly rebounded in arcs of jewel-like droplets.

After half an hour of Emmie ooh-ing and aah-ing over Owen's portfolio, the barista came over and asked them if they could make a little less of a scene. Only slightly abashed, Emmie took her seat. Owen leaned over and whispered.

"Okay, this one's a little experimental. You have full

surround audio, right?"

"Most definitely."

"Great. So, you might want to hold on to your seat. Literally. If it works right, you'll be a little disoriented, but if something goes wrong, you'll be *extremely* disoriented."

"Sounds exciting," said Emmie, gripping the seat of her chair.

"I'll map the manual escape to your thumbs, so if you need the simulation to stop, just press either one or both of your thumbs onto your chair, okay?"

"Got it. Fire away."

Owen swiped his fingertips over the tabletop a few times, and Emmie heard the noise cancellation in her earplugs wipe out the ambient noise of the café. Her visual overlay flickered, and she found herself in the empty cubic room that was the default starting point for most simple environmental physics testing. She looked around and found that her body had been replaced by something rather like a large blue beach ball.

She began drifting upward in a compelling simulation of weightlessness. After she was several yards off the ground, gravity re-exerted itself, and she began to fall toward the floor, rather slower than she would have under the influence of Earth gravity. She bounced softly off the floor, and she inadvertently leaned forward in her seat, which sent her spinning slowly end over end through the room until she bounced against the far wall.

"Ha!" she laughed, "That's amazing."

She pressed her thumbs to her chair, and the simulation ended. The café flickered back into view. She pushed back her immerger glasses and said,

"I've never felt anything like that done with just

audiovisual feedback. Where did you learn how to do that?"

Owen smiled, gratified.

"That was my sophomore year final project, although I've tweaked it a bit since. I spent a fair amount of time on a trampoline doing physical therapy after a football injury in high school, and, thinking back on it, I thought that sensation could make a pretty cool immersion."

"It definitely does," said Emmie, drumming her fingers against her lips. After a moment, she said,

"Hey, listen. I've never really done any collaborative work before, but I think between your physics programming skills and my visual design concepts, we could put together a pretty killer domain."

Owen straightened up and leaned forward in his seat.

"Really? You'd want to do that with me?"

Emmie nodded.

"I could show you some pretty cool tools, too. My dad runs the Emerging Media Lab in Oakland."

"O-o-o-oh!" Owen said, suddenly making the connection, "You're one of *those* Bridges, huh?"

Emmie nodded again.

"Ha!" Owen scratched his head, "Well, I guess I lucked out when I met you, Bealsio. So, when can we start?"

∞

Owen and Emmie soon found themselves meeting almost daily — in his computer science lab, in the downtown Berkeley cafés, in the Cal libraries. Their camaraderie on the *Eleusis* battlefield translated surprisingly well to their creative collaboration. Gradually, both of them began to withdraw from Amaranthian guild activities, until at last Otaku passed on guild leadership to his second-in-command.

"You're just going to quit, huh?" Zeke said angrily to Emmie the day she told him she was leaving the guild.

"Hey, we'll find another game," Emmie soothed, surprised by the heat in Zeke's voice, "I've just got a lot of other stuff going on right now."

"Yeah," Zeke huffed, "Well, I'm pretty busy, too, anyway. I guess I'll see you around."

Emmie was upset by the exchange, but her thoughts eventually turned to other things. She and Owen were working on a joint portfolio on *Emergency,* new work that showcased the best of both their skills.

Not long after they began working on their joint portfolio, Owen insisted that Emmie introduce him to her parents.

"As long as we're going to be spending so much time together, I want them to know I'm a perfect gentleman. Also, based on what you've told me, I don't think I can afford to get on the wrong side of your mother."

After much protest, Emmie nervously invited Owen to dinner at her parents' house. Apart from asking several leading questions about how Owen and Emmie had met, Dad remained distant throughout the meal. From Mom, however, Owen received a warm reception, and Emmie gaped as her mother kept up a steady stream of friendly conversation with Owen throughout dinner.

"So before you came out to California for college, where did you live?"

"I grew up in Keller, Texas, ma'am. Outside Fort Worth."

"And does your family live there now?"

"Yes, ma'am. My parents still live there. Most of my mother's family, too."

"Do you come from a big family?"

"Well, I have an older brother, Wendell, and my little sister, Marybeth. Loads of cousins. My mama has four sisters, and they all live in Keller."

"Is it hard for you, being so far away?"

"It's good to see them, but, to be honest, my father and I were never very close. He was a Navy officer, and I didn't get to see him much while I was growing up."

"It sounds like that was difficult for you."

Owen shrugged, looking down at his plate for a moment before saying,

"We were lucky in a lot of ways. We only had to relocate once, and just for a couple of years. Other than that, my mama's family was always around to help her out. And my dad came home safe and sound, in the end."

Mom nodded slowly, and after a moment she asked,

"So, what do you think of California?"

"Love it," Owen said promptly, his eyes lighting up, "I spent my whole life wanting to get out of Keller, to move out west. Once I got that acceptance letter," he smacked his palms together, "I was out like that. I drove my car out, hit all the National Parks along the way. And when I came through the tunnel and saw the Bay, the Golden Gate," he let out an appreciative whistle, "I knew I was home. I can't imagine living anywhere else."

"You sound just like my husband," Mom smiled, patting Dad's knee. Dad cleared his throat, narrowing his eyes a bit at Owen as he said,

"It may have its problems, but it beats any other place I've been."

"Yes, sir," said Owen, shrinking back slightly in his chair. Emmie, indicating her father with a slight jerk of the head, mouthed across the table to Owen, *Sorry!*

"So," Dad said brusquely, pushing back from the table, "Can I offer you some dessert before you go, Owen? We don't want to keep you too late."

"Travis!" said Mom, "It's only seven o'clock."

Half an hour later, after Dad had ushered Owen out the door and retired to his office, Mom turned to Emmie and said,

"What a charming young man."

Emmie shook her head, amazed.

"Seriously? You're less worried about me hanging out with a college guy you've never met before than you are about letting me drive the car."

"Well," Mom said, flushing slightly, "He seems perfectly nice. And it's good for you to have a real-life friend besides your sister."

"I have other friends!" Emmie protested. Her mother cocked her head doubtfully.

Despite her approval of Owen, Mom nonetheless insisted that his future visits be chaperoned. Emmie complained, but Owen was meticulously respectful of her mother's wishes, so he and Emmie began to meet regularly at the Lab. The arrangement vexed Emmie almost as much as her father. Dad now had to see Owen and Emmie together constantly, and Emmie had to endure merciless ribbing by Uncle Frank whenever Owen was out of earshot.

"He's *not* my boyfriend," she insisted, "We're just friends. Anyway, that would be practically illegal."

"Oh, come on," Uncle Frank winked, "He seems perfectly nice."

"I wish everyone would stop *saying* that!"

∞

Except for Uncle Frank, Emmie had never found anyone as enthusiastic as she was about immersion gear, but the first time she took Owen to visit the Lab, she saw mirrored in his eyes the same delight she felt whenever a new gadget came off the lab benches. Owen had never had access to such high-quality technology, and she realized how privileged she had been to grow up in a place with so much access to the tools she needed for her work.

Uncle Frank was happy to give Owen the same privileged access that she had to the resources of the Lab, although Dad grumbled about it at first. Owen took full advantage of all the new tools at his disposal, and he soon impressed the engineers with his remarkable fluency in environment design. He rapidly prototyped a variety of domain physics, from the meticulously realistic to the fanciful. Emmie found in Owen's foundational environment frameworks the perfect context for her own content, and their collaboration took both of their skills to a new level. Owen eventually earned even Dad's begrudging admiration.

Over the next year, Owen's undergraduate studies fell by the wayside as he and Emmie produced a series of domains together. Anatolia scolded him about this, and Owen was loathe to disappoint her, so he kept up the bare minimum of work to scrape by his graduation requirements.

Owen and Emmie's work together resulted in a portfolio of simple but addictive game concepts, foremost among them *Fractal Sphere*, an evolution on the first portfolio piece Owen had shown to Emmie the day they met.

In *Fractal Sphere*, two players entered an empty arena, each with a fractal seed of their own design, and over a series of turns extended these seeds into ever larger and more complex fractal forms. The object of the game was to be the first player to completely enclose the fractal of the other.

The game initially attracted only a small, unsurprisingly geeky subset of the alternet gaming community. However, the mesmerizing quality of the game replays, in which enormous works of fractal art unfurled from the simplest beginnings, eventually caught the attention of game commentators and critics, who compiled libraries of the best *Fractal Sphere* matches as judged on various artistic, mathematical, and entertainment criteria. Communities of fans sprang up around individual *Fractal Sphere* players, and alternet entertainment forums began hosting *Fractal Sphere* competitions and tournaments that drove sales of the game skyward. The game won several design awards and became a bona fide commercial success within six months of its release, pushing Bealsio and Otaku into the mainstream spotlight for a short time.

Even after the spotlight had moved on, *Fractal Sphere* continued to produce a significant stream of income. Awash with cash, Emmie found herself contemplating the benefits of moving out of her parents' home, heedless of her mother's desire that she remain living with them forever. Emmie gladly delegated the task of finding a suitable place to Nanna, who approached the task with the relish of a real estate connoisseur, applying decades of experience remodeling area homes to choosing the perfect location, architectural style, and floor plan for her granddaughter's needs. That place turned out to be a three-bedroom cliffside cottage just down the road from Emmie's parents' home on Skyline Boulevard, to Anatolia's evident relief.

For the first time in her life, Emmie enjoyed the privacy

of a space she could truly call her own, beyond the confines of her parents' house and the Lab. While she had never lacked access to immersion gear growing up, her considerably improved income now allowed her to indulge more extravagant tastes. She kept herself in fine style as far as immersion tech was concerned, filling her closets with every new gadget and stocking her software library with only the most sophisticated new tools of her trade. Although the basement of her new home could not rival that of her parents, Emmie at last had the space and the means to install a small spliner for her personal use, and she did so with glee.

While Emmie spent her *Fractal Sphere* earnings, heedless as a child who had never worried about money, Owen saved religiously, expressing a desire to someday accumulate enough to travel the world. Long after the trip was financially feasible, however, he remained rooted in the Bay Area, either unable to give himself such a luxurious gift or unable to part for such an extended period of time from the Bridges, who had become his foster family.

∞

Owen, possessing a more outdoorsy inclination than Emmie, dragged her out of her new house as frequently as possible. ("Your mom is not kidding when she calls that spliner a death trap. You'd rot in there if it weren't for me!") He led her on daily hikes through the redwoods and eucalyptus groves in the surrounding hills, which Emmie eventually came to love almost as much as he did, and taught her to ride a bike on the scenic shoulders of Skyline Boulevard.

For Emmie's eighteenth birthday, Owen persuaded her

entire family to go on a camping trip in Yosemite on one of Ollie's too-infrequent visits home from graduate school. This was an ambitious maneuver, but Owen rallied three generations of Bridges with charisma and fearlessness born of the *Eleusis* battlefields, overcoming in the course of the five-hour journey the grousing alternet access withdrawal of Emmie, Dad, and Uncle Frank; the recurring interruptions of Nanna's loud smartcom conversations with her assistant; and the constant bickering of Nora and Uncle Frank's two little boys, six-year-old Luke and eight-year-old Nick. Despite all this, Owen successfully conducted two cars, ten Bridges, and all the attendant camping gear from the hills of Oakland into the heart of Yosemite Valley, whose awesome beauty instantly rewarded all the trouble taken to witness it.

Understandably exhausted by the trip, Owen gladly deferred to Mom's expertise pitching camp. To Emmie and Ollie's surprise, their mother managed in short order to identify the driest sites on the still-snowy campground, demonstrate to Luke and Nick how to raise tents, teach Uncle Frank and Emmie how to build a campfire, and set Ollie, Nora, and Nanna to work prepping dinner. Dad and Uncle Frank eventually reconciled themselves to their isolation from civilization by setting to work recording sights, sounds, and smells from the campground to upload later into the Lab content database.

"It's unending with those two," grumbled Grandpa as he loaded food into the bear locker, "They can't experience anything without the aid of their damn recording devices."

"Oh, hush, Patrick," said Nanna, chopping vegetables at the cook station, "When did you get to be such a cranky old man?"

"Was he ever *not* a cranky old man?" Emmie whispered to

Uncle Frank.

"So where did you learn to be so handy around a campsite?" Owen asked her mother, as they wrapped up spare tent pegs and rope.

Mom smiled wistfully.

"My sister and I practically grew up in a tent. I spent many, many summers with my parents at their archeological digs when I was growing up."

"That sounds exciting! Where was this?"

"Oh, so many places. I'm not even sure I could remember them all, now. My parents studied the ancient history of the near East, so it was mostly places around the eastern Mediterranean. Beautiful country. Some of my favorite memories are of the Greek Isles, Turkey, Lebanon. Just wonderful."

"I didn't know you have a sister," said Owen, "Where is she now?"

"Yes. Nazanin," Mom said softly, "She passed away."

There was a sudden lull in the campground chatter as many of the adult Bridges glanced toward Mom. Emmie widened her eyes at Owen in warning before looking back down at the vegetables she was slicing for kebabs. The moment passed, and conversations resumed, a bit more loudly than before.

"Oh," Owen said awkwardly, "I'm sorry."

Mom shook her head, stuffing the last of the gear into a tent bag.

"It was a long time ago."

"Do you mind if I ask what happened?"

Emmie set down her knife and looked up again. She had never actually heard the story of Nazanin's death firsthand. Ollie had long ago warned her not to ask their mother questions about it. Emmie knew only the general outline: there had been an accident, a fall, and Nazanin had been badly injured.

"I can't believe it still seems so hard to talk about it," said Mom, "Even though it was — goodness — could it have been thirty-seven years ago now? I spent so long feeling like it was my fault. I was the only one with her when it happened. I should have ..." she trailed off, shaking her head.

"Well. I was fifteen. Nazanin had just turned fourteen. Our parents were working on a dig near the Euphrates River, and we took a day trip up to Lake Van."

Mom's eyes grew distant, and she smiled.

"Nazanin loved taking photographs, and she spent the whole drive up there begging our parents to take us on the ferry, out to a little island called Akdamar, so she could take pictures. There's an ancient Armenian church there, and some of the most beautiful views of the mountains.

"My mom and dad had a day hike already planned with the graduate students, and they wanted us to come with them. But Naz kept nagging and nagging until at last our dad said she could go, as long as I went with her. I didn't mind, so they dropped us off at the boat launch, and we left with a little group of tourists.

"We spent all morning walking around the island. I was glad we had come. I remember how wonderful everything smelled. Flowers everywhere — on the bushes, in the trees. Nazanin must have taken a thousand photos." Mom smiled over at Emmie. "You've seen them, remember? All those black-and-white photographs in my office that you used to trace when you were little? Well, anyway, it started to get quite warm, and I told Nazanin I wanted to go rest in the shade beside the church. She said she just wanted to take a few more pictures of the stonework on the other side.

"So I sat down in the shade, and the next thing I knew, the ferry boat captain was waking me up, telling me that it was time to go back to shore. I got up and started looking for Nazanin, but I couldn't find her anywhere.

"I told the boat captain, and he started looking for her with me. Soon everyone was looking — the tourists, the tour guides, the priests."

Mom swallowed, and she closed her eyes.

"I remember one of the priests told me not to worry, that we were going to find her. He was so kind, and I really believed him, right up until the end. We searched up and down the island for an hour. I was heading up toward the cliffs on one side of the island when I heard shouting down below, near the church.

"They had found Nazanin's camera sitting on a rock on the east side of the island. We all started looking around there, and soon a couple of the other tourists spotted the hole in the ground, almost concealed between the roots of an old almond tree."

Her voice grew quiet, and her eyes welled up as she said,

"Later, the priests said the underground spring on that side of the island must have washed out the earth beneath the tree. It looked like the ground had given way when Nazanin walked across it. There was a long drop, more than twenty feet. They were able to pull her out, but …"

There was a long silence. Everyone had stopped what they were doing, listening to the sad story.

"I'm sorry," Owen said at last, leaning down to give her mother a hug. Emmie felt a surge of affection for Owen, and of pity for her mother. Mom dabbed her eyes and smiled, looking from Owen to Emmie to the rest of her family around the campsite.

"Life's strange, isn't it?" she said, "The terrible and the beautiful all mixed up together."

∞

They had only just finished eating dinner, and they had not yet begun the marshmallow roast that Owen had repeatedly promised to Luke and Nick, when the rain started to fall. Over the protests of the little boys, everyone retired to their tents. Emmie fell asleep before Ollie had even settled in to the sleeping bag beside her.

In the middle of the night, Emmie woke when the white noise of the rain stopped suddenly. Hearing a soft scrabbling at the tent flap, she sat up with a start. Emmie reached for Ollie's shoulder to wake her but stopped when she heard Owen whisper,

"It's me. You've got to see this."

Emmie relaxed and unzipped the tent, poking her head out to find Owen's excited face in the vestibule.

"Where are my shoes?" Emmie whispered.

Owen looked around.

"You forgot to pull them into the vestibule," he chuckled, lifting up one of her boots and pouring a stream of rainwater out of it.

"Ugh. Well, I'm not putting *those* on, for sure," she said, withdrawing into the tent and starting to zip it up again.

"Hey, wait!" Owen reached in to stop her, "Come on. I'll keep your feet dry. Here —" he crouched down beneath the vestibule, "I can carry you. It's not far."

"No way. You'll drop me in the mud!"

"Come on. You're tiny."

"I may be small, but I am fierce!" she scowled in mock indignation.

"It'll be worth it," he coaxed, "I swear."

Emmie looked doubtfully from the cold, wet campground outside back to the inside of her warm, dry tent, but, seeing the eagerness in Owen's eyes, decided to risk it.

"Oh, fine."

She climbed out of the tent and zipped it closed behind her. Owen crouched under the vestibule and looped her arm around his neck, lifting her easily.

He carried her down a short path leading out of the grove of redwoods surrounding the campground. In a meadow beyond the trees, Owen found a rocky outcropping that, if not exactly dry, was at least free of standing water. He set Emmie on her feet atop the rock and climbed up beside her. The stone felt like ice through her thick woollen socks, and she could see the pale wisps of her breath and Owen's mingling in the darkness.

"Look," he said. Emmie felt the slightest pressure of his hand on her shoulder.

Above them, the massive stone walls enclosing Yosemite Valley held up a glittering vault of stars, stars that put to shame the artificially obscured night sky of the city.

"They look so close," she breathed.

Owen nodded. After a while, she turned to Owen and said, her voice full of awe,

"I guess immersion still has a long way to go."

Owen smiled down at her, and the air around them seemed to grow warm. Emmie felt his fingertips brush her cheek ever so softly as he leaned down and kissed her.

Four days later, the caravan of Bridges, begrimed with earth and smelling of woodsmoke, returned to the Oakland hills. Emmie spent the long drive smiling vaguely out the window. Amidst the grandeur of Yosemite Valley, she had found the inspiration for her next project.

∞

Emmie's longing to recreate the sense of awe she had experienced in that moment beneath the stars pulled on Dom day and night, so insistent that he found himself dodging into alleyways and empty rooms in the Temple City, unable to resist her call long enough to hide himself in safer quarters. He knew the time of Emmie's obscurity was fast drawing to a close, and he prepared himself for the dangers to come.

She flipped through the portfolio of work she had created over the last few years, searching for a starting point from which to build something of true significance. As she sketched and modeled and discarded, Emmie frequently called up the great tree from her private content library, contemplating it for hours on end. In all her years displaying her work to the public, Emmie had never been able to bring herself to publish this work. She had shared it only once, with her father, in the momentary euphoria that had followed her first collaboration with Dom.

The tree became the axis around which all Emmie's creative work revolved, and with the focus born of their years-long collaboration, she now grasped Dom's every hint, every vision, weaving a landscape around that tree drawn from a memory that was more real to Dom than either of the worlds through which he now drifted. She utilized her experience with every technology she had ever used in the Lab, every technique she had ever learned for immersive design, to create a domain that pushed the limits of multi-sensory immersion. She worked with Owen to perfect the physics of atmospheres and oceans, the movement of stars, the change of light from morning to evening. This was *Eden*, and even endlessly self-critical Emmie saw that it was good.

When Emmie finally launched *Eden*, she attracted enthusiastic reviews and design accolades from many influential alternet cognoscenti. Reviewers described their experience of *Eden* as transformative, comparable to, perhaps even transcending, the experience of Tomo's *Kaisei*.

It was mere days after *Eden*'s public launch that Emmie received an email from Tomo Yoshimoto asking if he might take her out to dinner. Emmie stared in shock at the message for several minutes, as did Dom, before she fired off a projection to Owen to break the news.

"WHAT!?!" he bellowed, "You're joking!"

"One hundred percent serious."

As Emmie and Owen stared dumbstruck at one another through their projections, Dom withdrew to Dulai, where, in the dark of his sleeping quarters, he let the enormity of what was to come sink in. At last, he realized what the place and time of Emmie's birth might mean.

∞

For a few days, the anticipation of her dinner with Tomo injected an ecstatic mood into Emmie's visits to the Lab, her weekly dinner with her parents, and every moment with Owen, but as the appointed time for the dinner approached, terror set in. Having regarded Tomo with an almost idolatrous awe since childhood, having considered him her single greatest artistic inspiration, and having judged all of her work against his, Emmie found herself petrified by the thought of standing in his presence.

Emmie practiced what she would say and speculated about why Tomo wanted to meet her, what Tomo might ask her. Faced with the prospect of a real-world meeting, she fretted with uncharacteristic angst over her choice of clothes and shoes, handbag and hairstyle. She was so accustomed to complete control over the appearance of her avatars that the prospect of being limited to her own un-augmented features and neglected wardrobe deeply distressed her. Finding Owen an unbearable tease when she sought his advice, she called her older sister instead.

"But you look gorgeous!" Ollie insisted over the loud background noise of her flatmates at the graduate school housing in London where she was now on a postdoctoral fellowship studying the emergence and evolution of alternet subcultures.

"Don't lie," Emmie moaned, looking longingly at Ollie's perfect blonde hair and stylish clothes, "I look terrible. Can I just steal your face for a night? You could fly over here and sit in for me. I'll tell you what to say."

Ollie rolled her eyes.

"The dinner's in two hours. And anyway, you need to learn how to be as comfortable in your own skin as you are in all your avatars. You'll do great. Remember, he wants to see you. He doesn't care how you look. He cares what you can do. But you really do look great, so don't worry about it."

"All right. All right," Emmie took several deep breaths and checked her hair once more in the video feed, "You're right. Thanks, Ollie."

She left for Berkeley too early and so arrived at the restaurant over an hour ahead of time, before it had even opened for dinner. The host took pity on her and let her inside, and she waited at the reserved table. She sat, periodically tugging the hem of her skirt, flipping her visual overlay on and off, glancing at email and news feeds, unable to focus on anything.

Tomo arrived promptly at five thirty. He was a compact, vigorous man, though well past middle age, his thick black eyebrows and dark eyes framed by square-rimmed glasses, thinning silver hair speckled with black. He was dressed in a surprisingly trendy fashion, unconsciously absorbed from the current of youth that flowed perpetually into the alternet domain design space. When Emmie turned and saw him, her mouth fell open and her eyes grew wide. She stood so quickly that she nearly overturned the table. She felt her face grow hot and tried to rearrange her features into a semblance of composure. Tomo came to her aid, steadied the table, and reached out to shake her hand.

"It is so nice to meet you in person, my dear," he said, a beatific smile alighting on his features.

"Yes," Emmie said breathlessly, "So nice to meet you, too!"

Tomo pulled out her chair, and Emmie sat down. Tomo did his best to put her at ease. He steered the conversation expertly through subjects of mutual interest, discussing domains and domain designers they both loved, the latest developments in immersion technology, speculations about what might be the next hot alternet trend. Gradually, Emmie loosened up, and at last Tomo decided to reveal his purpose in meeting.

"I will soon start work on a new domain, the first domain to be released by Augur, a company I recently co-founded with two young friends of mine," he said, swirling the remaining bit of red wine in his glass, "I wonder if you might enjoy working with us on the company's first project."

Emmie gaped.

"Really? I — I —"

She closed her mouth and nodded, beaming.

"Yes," she said, "That would be awesome."

CHAPTER 5
One Year Later

As was his habit, Tomo rose from his desk well before sundown, put on his coat, and tended the greenery of his corner office. The ritual conveyed him to a bonsai tree that grew in a blue ceramic tray atop a heavy Japanese cabinet. Tomo pulled a small pair of shears from the top drawer of the cabinet and ministered to the minute leaves and branches. When he was done, he brushed the dusting of leaves into the wastebasket and returned the shears to the drawer.

But today, as Tomo straightened up, he slid his right hand down the side of the cabinet, until he found a catch concealed in the dark wood frame. A small compartment slid open beneath his fingers. He withdrew a square jade box the size of a cigarette lighter and slipped it into the breast pocket of his coat.

Tomo stepped out of his office and made his way through the maze of cylindrical projection chambers, modular workstations, and young men and women arranged singly and in clusters about the room. He passed unseen before most of them, who were immersed in the internal Augur domain where the first *Temenos* expansion was slowly taking shape. But one young man with white-blonde hair and blue eyes ringed with bruise-like shadows looked up as Tomo passed. He pushed back his immerger glasses and said,

"See you tomorrow, sir."

Tomo waved and nodded cheerfully in response,

"Don't forget to go home tonight, Zeke. Even God couldn't create a world in one day."

Zeke gave a half-hearted laugh before re-immersing himself in *Temenos*, where he would likely remain long into the night. Tomo was no stranger to energetic obsession with work, yet he worried about that boy. He had hired Zeke on Emmie's recommendation, but it had not escaped his notice that Zeke was becoming isolated from the rest of the team. Though all Zeke's work thus far had been beyond reproach, the boy seemed unable to shed his loner mentality.

Tomo stopped at an empty desk near the center of the room and looked around for its usual occupant. His gaze settled on Emmie, standing by the lounge coffee machine, deep in conversation with Owen, now her associate creative lead. He had never thought twice about hiring Owen; he and Emmie were nearly inseparable. Tomo watched them for a moment, his fingertips brushing the outside of his breast pocket thoughtfully. Then he continued on his way.

A bit more than three miles separated Tomo's office overlooking the San Francisco Bay from his home overlooking Oakland's Lake Merritt. He enjoyed the walk almost as much as the wonderful diversity of urban landscapes it encompassed.

He made his way through the spacious lobby of the recently-constructed central office building and out across the well-manicured lawns of the Augur campus. A winding path through fruit trees and over little man-made hills — modeled on a location in *Kaisei* that was particularly dear to his heart — led at last to the east pedestrian gate. He palmed the door, casting a disapproving look at the spiked wrought-iron fence as he passed through it. He had complained frequently to his co-founders that the fence was an eyesore, as well as entirely unnecessary, but they had insisted that it remain in place. In all the years Tomo had lived in America, he had never come to understand how a culture so fearlessly inclusive could yet be so fearful of its own people.

He stepped out onto the gritty sidewalk of the West Oakland neighborhood that surrounded the Augur campus. Soon after he had hired Emmie, her father had convinced Tomo of the merits of the re-emerging manufacturing district here, and Tomo had been pleased to add Augur's weight to the community revitalization effort. He, like Emmie's father, saw just beneath the urban decay the prospect of renewal.

Tomo walked through blocks of shabby Victorian homes and chic mixed-use developments, which merged gradually into the high-rise offices of the financial, governmental, and commercial district. Downtown was fast emptying of a workday population heading home toward the lake or over the bridges or through the tunnels, leaving behind only the permanent inhabitants of the street. Charmingly-renovated historic buildings came to life as cafés and tapas bars opened their doors, drawing foot traffic from the tentatively gentrifying blocks nearby.

A bright red and yellow floral motif worked into the dark asphalt of the crosswalk marked the edge of Chinatown. Mouthwatering scents of baking pastries and savory meats wafted from the open doors of restaurants and bakeries, interrupted here and there by the sweet and pungent smells of fresh fruit and green vegetables piled before grocery stores. Tomo lingered here, where details of the streetscape evoked memories of his youth in Kyoto.

He paused at one restaurant window to examine an enticing display of dumplings, considering whether to cook for himself tonight or take a table and watch the world go by. Someone a few steps behind him came to a stop before the window, as well. Tomo's eyes refocused on the glass. Behind him stood another man, watching him in the reflection. Tomo narrowed his eyes, puzzled. There was something vaguely familiar about that face.

When the recognition hit him, a chill ran down his spine. Tomo turned slowly to face the man.

He was tall and well-built, dressed in an impeccable suit, silk tie, and shiny shoes. His mane of white-blonde hair contrasted strikingly with his smooth, deeply tanned skin. He would have been quite handsome were it not for the predatory look in his pale blue eyes.

Tomo stood transfixed as the man withdrew from his jacket a slender silver cylinder that gleamed in the warm light of sunset. Although he did not recognize the object, he knew instinctively that it was a weapon. Tomo backed away slowly until he stood pressed against the restaurant window. The man pointed the weapon casually at Tomo.

"You were duly warned," said the man, his genial Southern accent incongruous with his threatening words, "It's most unfortunate things had to end this way. I do apologize."

Tomo felt a pinprick in his chest, followed by a spreading numbness. He looked down in surprise and saw a fine needle, almost invisible to the eye, protruding from his coat lapel, just over his heart. He felt dizzy, then staggered and fell heavily to the ground. He gasped as icy fingers gripped his chest. He was unable to cry out, unable to move. The man knelt over him, calling loudly,

"Sir? Sir? Are you all right? Sir!"

The man leaned in close to Tomo, blocking him momentarily from the view of the gathering crowd. A heavy gold ring bearing the sign of the cross gleamed from the man's right ring finger as his hand passed over Tomo's eyes. The last thing Tomo felt was the light touch of the man's fingers as they slipped inside his breast pocket and withdrew the small jade box.

∞

"You're awfully quiet tonight," said Owen, handing another soapy dish to Emmie, who loaded it slowly into her parents' dishwasher. She heard his words from a distance, and it took her a moment to refocus on him. Her mind had been wandering a lot lately.

"Yeah," she smiled ruefully, shaking her head, "It's just *Atlantis*, you know? I can't even look at the concept sketches without feeling this ... frustration? confusion? revulsion? Something. I know there's something wrong with it. I feel really bad for holding up the team, but I just can't let it go. I went to talk to Tomo about it this evening, since we've had nothing to show for weeks. Tomo's patient, but I know Ty's been bugging him for a review. Just my luck, though. He left early."

"You should take a page out of his book. Didn't you spend last night at work?"

"Um."

"And I bet you're planning to go back after dinner, aren't you?"

"Judgey, judgey, judgey!"

"Balance, girl. The stress is prematurely aging you."

She huffed and flicked water onto his shirt.

"Seriously, though," Owen said, brushing himself off, "Sometimes you act like you have to do everything all on your own. Don't you think you can count on any of us? At least on me?"

"Come on! Of course I do. I just —"

"Hey, you guys!" Ollie shouted down the stairs, "Are you coming back up here?"

"Let's talk about this later, okay?" Emmie said to Owen, stuffing silverware into the side basket of the dishwasher and closing the door. She wiped her sudsy hands off on her jeans and hustled up the stairs to her parents' rooftop deck, "I can't stand having Ollie analyze our shop talk."

They resurfaced from the kitchen and found that Emmie's twentieth birthday dinner party had migrated to the bridge table. Mom and Dad were dissecting a hand of bridge for Uncle Frank and Nora's benefit, part of their indefatigable campaign to teach them the game ("How have you never learned to play bridge after all these years, Frank?" Mom demanded. "How have you never learned to play *Eleusis*, Anatolia?" he had countered, laughing.) Dad was making a gallant effort to translate Mom's bridge jargon, but Mom hardly paused for breath and didn't seem to realize how confusing the phrase "getting your kids off the street" sounded to a novice player.

Emmie retrieved her wine glass from the dinner table and walked up to the railing at the cliffside edge of the deck, Owen close behind her. She turned to him, watching the sunset transform his face into a kaleidoscope of golds and crimsons. Not long ago, she had seen Owen as merely a friend and business partner, but in the weeks after their trip to Yosemite, she had started to think perhaps romance had been inevitable from the start. She was just beginning to reconcile herself to her family's teasing.

Owen smiled at her, and they leaned out over the railing, watching the warm light play out over the Oakland flats.

"I never thought I'd say this," she said, taking a sip of her wine, "But I need a vacation. Want to come with?"

"I thought you said you couldn't do anything until your next review with Ty?"

"Yeah, I probably shouldn't," she grumbled, slumping dispiritedly over the railing and propping up her chin on her hand. She dreaded her next meeting with Ty. She could never seem to see eye-to-eye with Tomo's cofounder.

"Hey, no, that's not what I meant. If you want to go, let's do it. I have a list as long as my arm of places I'd love to see. Where are you thinking you'd like to go?"

"I don't know," she said, swirling the wine in her glass, "Some place I've never seen before. Some place new."

"Hmmm. That's a tough one. I'd guess you've already visited every rendered place on Earth."

"Isn't that awful? It's like the only places left to discover are on the alternet."

"There must be *some* uncharted territory somewhere out there," he said, wrapping his arm around her waist, "I bet we could find it."

∞

The next morning, Dom stood behind Emmie on the fore deck of a ship surrounded by swirling fog. At eye level before her hovered a bright stack of windows, each displaying an aerial view of a topographical map. She flicked through these with her fingers, occasionally pulling one down to scrutinize it from multiple angles as it morphed from a two-dimensional image into a three-dimensional terrain in miniature. Beside her, Owen alternated between squinting into the impenetrable mist before them and peering over Emmie's shoulder at the renderings, making quick tweaks here and there as he noticed mistakes in the environment presets.

Dom struggled to hold for Emmie the vision of the Temple City, which Emmie had somehow plucked from Dom's own subconscious and now seemed determined to use as the basis for the *Atlantis* subdomain design. Dom would not have chosen to have the Temple City occupy both his attention in Dulai and in Emmie's world, but Emmie's mind brooked no argument. The only sound was the muffled splash of waves against the creaking hull of the ship, until Emmie said,

"Let's see this one again. *Atlantis* concept 42."

Owen glanced at her sidelong, saying softly, off the microphone,

"Are you sure?"

She shot him a cool look, and Owen backed off cautiously, mouthing, *Okay, okay*, before tapping a short sequence onto the forearm of his immerger sleeve. As Owen muttered commands quietly into his patch mic, Emmie cast the terrain maps away with a sweeping gesture and leaned forward against the railing.

After a minute of back-and-forth between Owen and the spliner control room, the fog dissolved, revealing the distant shape of a mountainous island, which the boat now approached at speed. Emmie grasped the railing more tightly as the ship pitched and rolled, unconsciously brushing away from her cheeks the sensation of cold ocean spray created by the electromagnetic tactile simulator on her headset.

"Shiva!" Emmie said sharply. In the wave of new hiring that Augur had done when Emmie first joined the company, a number of friends of hers and Owen's had signed on as well, including Shiva Mehrotra. To Emmie's perpetual annoyance, Shiva lived up to the reputation for laziness he had earned as Owen's *Eleusis*-addicted roommate, but he was undeniably competent and one of the best coders on her team. "What's with these waves?" she complained, "Sound design sent you the rest of that library like a week ago."

"Oh, yeah," Shiva's disembodied voice drawled through her earbuds, "Hold on."

A moment later, the muffled splashes, which had been incongruous with the ship's speed, escalated into crashes. Emmie, at last satisfied by the auditory details accompanying the ship simulation, focused once more on the island, which was now crisply silhouetted against a clear blue sky. The ship sped onward until they were within swimming distance of the dramatic cliffs that formed the shoreline. Unable to draw closer, the ship slowed to a stop and rolled gently in the waves. Emmie contemplated the cliffs uncertainly for several minutes, her head cocked to the side. Dom's own antipathy toward the Temple City seemed to have cast a veil over the island that even Emmie's most determined concentration could not lift.

"No," she said, furrowing her brow, "It's close, but there's something ... Something ..."

A long silence elapsed. Owen suggested tentatively, again off mic,

"We've been at it for hours, Emmie. The team needs a

break. We should —"

"Tsch!' Emmie cut him off, her eyes still locked on the cliffs, her fingers gripping the rail. Owen sighed. A moment later, she shoved back angrily and growled, mussing her short hair violently until it stuck out in a dark halo of chestnut streaked with cobalt blue.

"You haven't slept in two days, Emmie," Owen said, more firmly now as he saw her resolve weakening, "You need to take a break. Or," he laughed, looking at her greasy hair, "at least a shower." On mic again, he said,

"I'm sure *everyone* could use a break."

The disembodied murmurs of the control room operators agreed from every direction. Emmie nodded reluctantly. Casting a final reproachful glare at the unyielding cliffs of the island, she said with strained politeness,

"Thanks for your patience, guys. Really great job with the ship simulation. I'm releasing the spliner to the other teams for the rest of the day. I'll let you know our next call time when we meet tomorrow. Lydia, could you shut down, please?"

"Sure thing, boss," a cheerful voice promptly replied.

The island flickered and disappeared, and the deck of the ship sank slowly, lowering them several yards as it melted into the smooth grey floor of the spliner. She and Owen stood now in a cavernous space. Sound-dampening floors stretched away to meet distant, windowless grey walls that rose over a hundred feet. Owen stretched and yawned. He slipped off his immerger headset, tapped off his patch mic, and peeled off layers of immerger gear until he stood naked to the waist in the flat ambient light. Emmie continued to gaze at the space where the cliffs had stood a moment ago.

"You coming back for lunch?" Owen asked, pulling a

thin cotton shirt out of his pocket and over his head, then rubbing his skin to remove the tingling sensation left behind by the tactile immerger gear.

"Hmmm," Emmie murmured.

"Em?"

She nodded vaguely,

"Oh, yeah. Yeah, I'm coming. I'll be right behind you."

Owen opened his mouth to say something, then changed his mind and only nodded. He walked back to the east wall and exited through a sliding door. A beam of golden midday sunlight and the chattering of the rest of the crew momentarily pierced the grey silence of the spliner. Then the door closed.

Emmie bowed her head. Dom knew she could not bear up indefinitely under the weight of all these expectant, invisible observers with their expensive, idle hands. If he could have helped her, he would have done so, but neither of them as yet could find the clarity required to complete the Temple City.

Emmie pulled off her headset and looked out into the empty grey space. She swallowed and said softly,

"Please, show yourself. Please —"

From the distant western wall of the spliner where Dom stood, he felt the words resonate.

The desire to stand before her burned with an intensity Dom thought he had long since learned to resist. He saw Emmie stop short, her eyes widening in the half-light. Fear replaced all desire, and Dom hid himself once more. But he knew that she had seen him. He only hoped he had been quick enough that she would not believe it.

"Shiva?" Emmie said on the public channel, her voice rising. There was no reply. Everyone else had already left the building. Or so she thought. Dom saw Emmie hesitate before walking slowly toward the place where she had glimpsed him.

Up close, she found nothing but a uniform grey expanse of floor merging with the wall. She took a deep breath and forced a laugh. Programming glitches were a normal part of domain development and could easily cause a momentary extrusion of the spliner's floor or wall during the shutdown sequence. She tapped out a quick bug report on the forearm of her immerger sleeve and submitted it to the ticketing system.

She left through the east door, her footsteps swallowed up by the muffling walls and springy floor of the spliner. Relieved, Dom watched her go.

∞

Emmie emerged from the spliner, squinting until her eyes adjusted to the dazzling sunlight that saturated the brick paths and buildings, the flowering shrubs and trees, and the rolling lawns of the Augur campus.

She headed toward the main office cafeteria, but as the gleaming glass building came into view, she slowed, then stopped. The campus seemed strangely empty. On a beautiful spring day like this, the grounds would usually be filled with people on lunch break. Emmie flicked on her visual overlay and scrolled through her email to check whether someone had called a last-minute meeting, but she found no such messages. Someone must have made an announcement over the campus-wide audio channel, forgetting that the spliner was shielded from wireless signals. She hurried on.

She saw no one in the main cafeteria adjacent to the lobby, and she had nearly reached the elevators when she noticed the bright red light shining above the door of the video screening room. Normally she would not have interrupted a screening in progress, but now she walked to the double doors and pressed her ear against the crack between them. She heard the inarticulate murmur of a speaker's voice, almost entirely muffled by the room's first-rate soundproofing. She pushed open the door softly and stepped inside.

The screening room had never been so crowded, standing room only. A few months ago, the entire company would have occupied less than half this space. Emmie took in the stricken faces around her and frowned, stretching onto her tiptoes to peer over the shoulders of those before her. She could just make out Ty Monaghan and Ahmet Harani, Augur's CEO and CTO, standing at the front of the auditorium. Ty was speaking slowly, his usually ruddy face drained of color,

"... has been notified, and they will be arriving Thursday from Kyoto to attend a private funeral service. His sister has arranged a memorial service for the Augur community to take place this Sunday evening at seven o'clock at the Buddhist Church of Oakland on Jackson Street."

Emmie's eyes widened, and her hands flew to her mouth. Ty took a deep breath and continued,

"Tomo was a close personal friend for the past fifteen years. Meeting him was a turning point in my life, and I am thankful to have known him. Even though he is gone, his work will live on. His creativity and craftsmanship have shaped the heart of Augur and touched millions of people who have experienced his domains and games."

Emmie felt her face turn cold, and she staggered backwards into someone.

"Careful!" came a surprised voice. Before she could turn around, Owen appeared from somewhere nearby, and he reached out to steady her, grasping her by the arms.

"Lay her down flat," someone warned, "She's going to faint."

Several hands lowered her gently to the floor. She felt the blood rushing back to her head. Owen hovered over her, and she grabbed his hand.

"Yikes," he said, "Your fingers are like ice."

"Owen," she whispered, holding back tears, "What happened to Tomo?"

He pressed her hand in both of his.

"He's dead, Emmie. He fell down in the street while he was walking home last night. The medical examiner says it was a heart attack."

CHAPTER 6
Mementos

Dom stood unseen beside Emmie as she sat on the stone bench inside the circle of redwood trees shading her driveway. She seemed oblivious to the misty rain that had started to fall, focusing instead on skimming the toes of her black shoes back and forth across the lush spring grass. Dom, however, scanned her surroundings vigilantly. Since Tomo's death, he had spent every spare moment with Emmie, knowing that his long-awaited moment was fast approaching.

Tires crunched on loose gravel, and Owen's dark grey electric sports car pulled quietly into the driveway. He drew up beside her and climbed out of the car, an enormous black umbrella in his hand.

"Aren't you cold?" he asked, loping toward her. He opened the umbrella over her and tried to remove his jacket with one hand, managing to splash them both in the process.

"No, no," she said, tugging at his lapels to straighten his jacket, "Really, I'm fine." She flicked small droplets of water off her black skirt and stretched onto her toes to brush the rain out of Owen's dark hair, which he had carefully parted and combed.

"You look nice," he said, crouching down to keep the umbrella close to her as they walked to the car.

She shot him a small smile.

"You're sweet," she replied, "You look nice, too."

They climbed into the car, and Owen drove slowly down the steep, winding road into the Oakland flats. Dom watched Emmie from the back seat as she gazed listlessly out the window at the familiar trees and houses sliding by.

"I can't remember the last time I wasn't wearing immersion gear. It makes everything seem so quiet ... so still."

Owen glanced at her.

"You sound like that's a bad thing."

Emmie shrugged.

"Tomo never wore immergers outside of work. He'd say," she switched into an imitation of Tomo's most earnest tone, "'We must never forget how to be present in one world at a time.' I guess he knew I had trouble with that."

Owen smiled wryly. They drove in silence until he pulled into a parking space on Fourth Street across from the Buddhist church.

"I feel ... all disconnected," Emmie said, watching the twilight gather outside the car, "But not sad. None of this seems real."

Owen settled his hand on hers, and she glanced down at their intertwined fingers, half smiling as she said,

"He was my idol when I was a kid. I totally worshipped him. And then when I met him, he was so ... I don't know. I never expected it to be like that. I thought he would be a teacher, a mentor, maybe, if I was lucky. But he was much more than that to me. I felt — as soon as I met him, right away — like I'd known him forever. Has that ever happened to you?"

Emmie looked back up at Owen, expecting a reply, but he was staring through the rain-smeared windshield. Emmie and Dom leaned forward, following Owen's gaze. A small group of people carrying signs lined the wrought iron fence separating the Buddhist church from the sidewalk.

"What are they doing?" said Emmie.

Three people unfurled a huge banner across their chests:

TECH TYCOONS BURN

Emmie's mouth dropped open, and she reached for the door handle, her face livid. Owen grabbed her arm before she could step out onto the sidewalk.

"Look," said Owen, pointing. Through the rapidly-fogging windshield, Dom saw a flashing blue light rounding the corner. "Someone already called the police. Let's stay out of it."

Two officers climbed from the police vehicle and began arguing with the group standing in front of the church. Eventually, after some wild gesticulating, the group dispersed. When the sidewalk was clear, Owen squeezed Emmie's hand.

"Come on. Let's do this."

The rain had started to fall harder. Dom followed Emmie and Owen as they hurried up the steps and through the red front doors of the church. A flock of wet umbrellas dripped onto the worn red carpet covering the wood floor of the entryway. A small sign indicated that the memorial service for Tomo Yoshimoto would take place in the main *hondo* on the second floor of the church. Emmie murmured hello to a few Augur employees coming in behind them before proceeding with Owen up the stairs.

Religious objects lined the hallway on the second floor. The gleaming metals, bright paints, and rich fabrics of altars, shrines, and statues created a festive atmosphere, an incongruous backdrop to the somber stream of people headed to the memorial service. The door to the *hondo* stood open, and beside it sat a carved cedar sculpture of the Buddha, smiling serenely. Emmie looked down at the statue as she passed, briefly smiling back.

Dom, scanning the faces of the crowd hopefully, recognized with a jolt of excitement the familiar face of a sprightly Asian woman with stylishly-bobbed silver hair entering the *hondo* just ahead of them. The woman bowed slightly toward the altar at the front before proceeding at a dignified pace into the room. Emmie and Owen exchanged a look, then imitated her.

The *hondo* was quite full. Owen, surveying the room, spied an empty space in the pews to the left of the altar. He led Emmie toward it by the hand. Once seated, Emmie glanced back at the door each time someone entered. A few minutes later, Ollie appeared, followed by Anatolia and Travis. Ollie murmured something to Anatolia and bowed smoothly toward the altar. Anatolia followed her lead, while Travis, following behind, crossed himself. Emmie, biting her lip to suppress an inopportune giggle, caught Ollie's eye with a small wave and slid toward the center of the pew to make room for her family. Dom sat between Emmie and a pale, overweight young programmer with thick glasses and a wrinkled black shirt.

Ollie worked her way slowly through the crowd, edging around Owen's knees to sit beside Emmie. She smoothed a few locks of Emmie's hair away from her eyes and brushed a smear of eyeshadow from her sister's cheek before wrapping her in a hug. Anatolia reached over to give Emmie's hand a squeeze before turning to chat with Owen in an undertone.

"Did you see the protestors?" Ollie asked softly. Emmie nodded, and Ollie let out a long sigh, "I don't even know what these people are trying to accomplish any more."

Emmie leaned her head on Ollie's shoulder wordlessly and looked forward to the altar.

"What a beautiful shrine," said Emmie. A broad, dark lintel inlaid with panels of gold relief and supported by round gold columns framed the wide rectangular recess housing the golden shrine to the Buddha. A low, glossy altar table stood before the shrine, draped with fabric woven in a stylized floral pattern. Two wreaths of gleaming silver hung from the ceiling on either side of the shrine, and below each one sat a dark urn of incense. A large photograph of Tomo stood on the altar beside a vase of flowers. The serenity of the old man's smile in his portrait was quite different from the intensity of the gaze Dom remembered from Tomo's youth.

"A bit gaudy for my taste," Ollie whispered, "But I guess I can see what you mean."

As the crowd finished settling into the pews, a middle-aged priest with a shining bald head and a grey robe walked down the center aisle. He stood behind a plain wooden lectern to the right of the gleaming shrine and pulled the microphone down a few inches. The room fell quiet.

"Welcome to the Buddhist Church of Oakland," he began, speaking in precise English with a Japanese cadence, "Thank you all for coming. Today we memorialize the life of Tomo Yoshimoto and celebrate his passage into the next." He looked out across the sea of faces, and his eyes settled momentarily on Emmie before he said, smiling broadly, "I see Tomo was a man fortunate to have many friends.

"Throughout the memorial service, we will perform rituals of spiritual significance. We perform these rituals both in memory of Tomo and for those of us left behind who mourn his departure. We have many visitors, so, before we begin, I would like to tell you what to expect. ..."

∞

After the service, the Bridges filed out into a side room lined with round tables, chairs, and a long table laid out with food and drink.

"I'm thirsty," Emmie said, "My head is swimming from all that incense."

Owen offered to get drinks for everyone, and Ollie found them an empty table in a corner. Emmie took a seat and looked around. Dom waited impatiently, until at last Emmie's eyes fell on the silver-haired woman, who stood by the door leading back out into the hallway. People walked up to her, shaking her hand and nodding quietly. Several dropped small black and silver envelopes into a basket set out on a low table beside her.

"She must be a member of Tomo's family," said Emmie, "I'm going to go over." The others nodded. Dom followed.

A middle-aged woman wearing a pitch black dress and soft black slippers stood before her in the line. Emmie asked if she knew how the other woman was related to Tomo.

"Oh! Ayame is — well, was — his sister," she replied, "She lives in Oakland, not far. I met her here at the temple, well, it must have been just six months ago, now. It's sad, isn't it? He was the last living member of her immediate family, and her only family here in America, I think. She told me they were close."

After the woman in front of her had spoken with Ayame a while, she left through the hall door, and Emmie stepped forward.

"I'm so —" Emmie's voice broke, and she stopped to regain her composure, "So very sorry for your loss."

Ayame reached out and touched her arm.

"Thank you, thank you for coming. No need to be sorry, though. I will miss my brother very much, but death is a part of life. And it's not so great a tragedy when an old man dies."

"Well, even so ..."

Ayame smiled at her kindly.

"You know," she said conspiratorially, leaning toward Emmie and lowering her voice as she looked at the people milling about the room, "He would laugh to think of you all coming here to remember him."

"Why?" Emmie asked in surprise.

"I can't remember the last time he set foot inside a temple. He drifted away from spiritual practices as he grew older." Her eyes returned to Emmie, "He was quite different as a boy — fascinated by Buddhist teachings. He loved to talk about the existence of many worlds, of life after life. But then —" she waved her hand vaguely, "Life happens. I think he forgot the joys and felt only the pain."

"He never seemed that way to me," Emmie said, drawing back a little.

Ayame raised an eyebrow. After a moment, she said,

"No. No, I suppose that's right. Moving to America, this was a fresh start for him. When I finally moved here to be closer to him, I could see that he had changed. He had grown happy again."

"Well," Emmie said, her voice rising with conviction, "He had every reason to be happy. He spent his life doing extraordinary work, work that he loved."

Ayame scrutinized her closely.

"You must be Emmie Bridges," she said.

"Yes," said Emmie, surprised, "How did you know?"

"Tomo told me about you. He meant to introduce us. He said you reminded him of someone we knew when we were children. I see now what he meant."

"Oh ... Well. I'm pleased to meet you, too, Ms. ..."

"Yoshimoto. But please, call me Ayame."

"Pleased to meet you, Ayame."

"Yes, I am glad we have met at last."

They smiled at each other. A couple stepped up behind Emmie, so she said,

"Well, goodbye, Ayame."

Emmie started to leave. Dom watched Ayame anxiously, and, much to his relief, she reached out and touched Emmie's arm.

"He left something for you," Ayame said quietly, "I just heard it from his lawyer."

Emmie stopped short. Dom listened closely.

"For me?" said Emmie.

"Yes. I'm not sure what, exactly. Tomo left instructions for me to retrieve it. Perhaps we should meet later so I can give it to you?"

"Um ... sure. Of course. Whenever you like."

CHAPTER 7
Bequest

Six months later, the nine o'clock alarm buzzed on Emmie's smartcom, and she swung her arm toward her nightstand, knocking it to the floor, where it continued to buzz. She tried to reach the floor to turn it off. Failing that, she rolled heavily out of bed and shuffled toward the bathroom. She ran the shower hot, waiting for the room to fill with steam before slipping out of her pajamas and into the water.

Forty minutes later, she pulled into a space in the Augur campus parking lot. Coworkers climbed out of cars around her, waving hello and chatting with one another. The majority followed the tree-lined walkway toward the main office, but a few peeled off toward the enormous studio warehouses at the campus periphery: the sound effects studio, the tactile and olfactory studio, the music studio. Beside the window-lined walls of the studio spaces, the mammoth, windowless spliner looked ominous, belying its status as the most sought-after workspace on campus.

Emmie trudged wearily after the stream of people headed to the main offices. She flipped on her visual overlay to scan her work email, inadvertently pausing in the middle of the walkway. She nearly fell to the ground when someone rammed her from behind. She wheeled around and found herself glaring up at the tall, blonde figure of Zeke, who was flanked by two of the design team's new hires. A pained look flickered across his pale, handsome features before disappearing behind a mask of dutiful apology.

"Sorry, didn't see you down there," he said. Taking in Emmie's mussed hair, still damp from her hasty shower; the rumpled tunic she had thrown over her immerger clothes before leaving the house; the dark circles beneath her eyes, Zeke added, "Been pulling some all-nighters?"

Emmie was painfully aware of the barb inside Zeke's ostensible apology. Zeke had a special talent for discerning other people's personal hangups, and he knew Emmie hated being so short. She turned wordlessly from him. She had been so excited to tell Zeke that she had gotten him a job offer from Augur, but in the year and a half since then, she had often wondered if that had been a mistake. Zeke had been distant and cold to her since his first day here.

Emmie still might have tried to maintain some semblance of a friendship with Zeke, but in the months since Tomo's death, as Emmie had struggled to make progress on the next *Temenos* expansion, Zeke had started telling other people on the team that Emmie's design reputation had been inflated by her close collaboration with Tomo. On her own, according to Zeke's rumor, she was no longer capable of producing the quality of work she had done as Bealsio. After months of delays, even Emmie had started to wonder if there might be a kernel of truth to Zeke's lies. She would not deny that she had worked more closely with Tomo than anyone else at Augur, and she recently wondered aloud to Owen whether perhaps she had come to be dependent on Tomo in her creative work.

She pushed through the office doors, and as she was crossing the lobby toward the elevators, she saw Lydia Winner, the head *Temenos* project manager and the creative team's liaison to Ty and Ahmet. Looking harried but cheerful, Lydia waved at Emmie, bobbing and weaving toward her through the morning foot traffic.

"Good morning, Emmie. Got a minute?"

"What's up?"

"I just wanted to check in about how the work's going in the spliner."

Emmie came to a stop and sighed,

"I'm not ready to schedule a showing, yet, Lydia. I thought we had talked about this?"

"Yes, we did. A week ago," Lydia said pointedly, then, more sympathetically, "I know you all are working hard. I'm not trying to put you on the spot. But I do need to give Ty and Ahmet some sort of update soon."

"Okay. Okay. I'll get back to you. Soon. I promise."

"All right," Lydia nodded, "Thanks, Emmie."

Emmie started again for the elevators, but, seeing Zeke waiting for the next one, she changed course and headed for the stairs instead. As she neared the creative team offices on the third floor, she pulled on her headset and joined the team's public audio channel.

"Go-o-od morning!" Shiva's radio announcer voice blared as she stepped onto the floor. Emmie flinched and adjusted her headset volume with a few taps to her wrist. She scanned the open room, which was slowly filling with her teammates, until she found the projection cylinder displaying on its exterior status screen Shiva's default avatar: an exquisitely-muscled, bare-chested brown man with eight flexed arms wielding lightning bolts, dressed in little else but chains of tiny skulls. She worked her way over to his cylinder and knocked loudly on the door. It slid open to reveal Shiva in full immersion gear, facing the blank grey curve of the main display area on the cylinder's inner wall.

"Hey, boss," he said cheerfully, without turning around.

"Hi," she said hoarsely, clearing her throat.

"Late night, eh?" he said, peering back at her with eyes far more bleary than her own.

She yawned, nodding, and slipped on a pair of immerger glasses from her bag, tapping the edge of the frames to sync her visual display with the projection cylinder's. When the image came into focus, she found herself looking around Shiva down the steep drop of a promontory. Below them churned the crashing grey and white waves of a hungry sea. A dark, slick, sinuous form arced smoothly above the water, revealing several yards of scaly back. Emmie shuddered, her face a mixture of revulsion and delight.

"That's new. Looks fantastic!"

"Just in from the new guys on the creatures team. Want to see the whole thing?"

"Yeah!"

A display appeared before Shiva, hovering at shoulder height, showing a small line rendering of the serpentine creature now obscured by the waves. Shiva swiped his fingers over a few controls, and a more detailed, colorful rendering replaced the first. He rotated the creature for her to see, and Emmie pulled it closer to her, tapping another control to animate it. For a moment, they admired the creature undulating and snapping its toothy jaws.

"Fantastic!" she repeated, "But I don't remember

ordering that."

Shiva turned toward her and pushed back his glasses. She did the same.

"What?" she asked warily, "What's that look?"

Shiva glanced around outside the cylinder.

"I thought you would have heard by now."

"Heard *what*, Shiva?" she said, trying to suppress her impatience.

"Ty has Zeke working on a backup version of *Atlantis*," he said sheepishly, "You know, in case ... in case you can't wrap yours before the next review deadline."

"*What?* When did this happen?"

"Last month, maybe? I just heard about it a couple days ago. I guess Ty gave Zeke some of the creative department new hires and is letting him use the night shift on the spliner. We're just hearing about it now because Zeke's far enough along that he needs someone from the core creative team to start integrating the new expansion with the old domain. And since I'm being a bit ... underutilized on your concept lately, Ty's having me split time between you and Zeke."

"And you didn't think to tell me this until now?" Emmie said, shaking her head in disbelief.

"Sorry, Emmie. I didn't think it was my job to tell you."

She suppressed a few choice words. She knew he was right.

"Yeah. Thanks, Shiva."

"Sorry, Emmie."

She stormed off toward the lounge and poured herself a huge mug of coffee, her head spinning. She walked back slowly to her desk and leaned heavily against it.

"Good morning," said Owen, coming up behind her with his morning brew of vegetable sludge and dropping a kiss on the top of her head.

"Is it?" she said darkly, wrinkling her nose at Owen's drink and impossibly chipper morning demeanor. Owen took in her exhausted face and sloppy appearance and shook his head.

"Why do you do this to yourself? We're still weeks away from the review deadline."

"You haven't heard either," she said flatly.

"Haven't heard what?" he said, taking a swig of his far-too-green juice.

"That Ty authorized Zeke to start working on a backup release concept."

Owen gagged.

"Are you serious?"

"I just heard."

Owen looked over Emmie's head toward Zeke's workstation, where Zeke was in conversation with one of the new hires. Zeke looked back coldly, and Owen said in an undertone,

"You'd think Ty would have a little more faith."

They sipped their brews in silence a while.

"I haven't been at my best lately," Emmie said softly, "Not since Tomo died."

Owen raised his eyebrows sympathetically.

"Look, Emmie. It's going to take time. No one expects you to just plunge back in like nothing happened."

"Yeah, but ... what if I'm just no good without him?"

Owen put his hand on her shoulder and looked straight into her eyes.

"You and Tomo were a great team, but you were great before you ever met him. I was there."

"I remember," Emmie smiled, stretching onto her toes to

peck Owen on the cheek. Over Owen's shoulder, she saw Zeke looking at them. When she caught his eye, he looked away.

∞

Later that morning, Emmie sat hunched over a stack of erasable printouts of the *Atlantis* 42 map, reworking the contours of the island with a pencil and an eraser, taping on transparent overlays to sketch cities and forests and villages, tossing one sketch after another onto a discard pile beneath her desk. *Atlantis* was supposed to have been the company's major product announcement this year, an expansion of the *Temenos* domain that had launched so successfully eighteen months ago, but Tomo's death had left a void in the heart of the team. Since then, the design and development efforts on the new subdomain had been wandering at best.

Now she was reduced to working on physical media to maintain any semblance of privacy from the prying eyes of a management team that was anxious for progress and increasingly inclined to monitor any work she performed using the company servers. As the weeks of delays had stretched into months, the speculation about who would be chosen to fill Tomo's Creative Director position had intensified. Before Tomo's death, Emmie would have been the obvious choice, but her erratic performance of late had eroded her credibility.

Emmie removed her headset to tune out the cheerful banter on the shared office channel. The Friday atmosphere was doing nothing to brighten her mood. Out of the corner of her eye, she saw Zeke pass by several times, sneaking glances at her desk. She looked down at her sketches sardonically. She should just invite him over. He couldn't possibly find anything useful here.

A few hours later, Emmie pushed back from her desk and flexed her hands painfully, scowling at her heaping stack of discards and her sketch in progress. She grabbed her coat and bag and made a beeline for the elevators. She avoided as many occupied desks as possible.

The late lunch crowd was gathering in the first-floor cafeteria, and Emmie gave it a wide berth as she hurried toward the front door. Outside, she pulled on her immerger glasses, which tinted in response to the bright sunlight. She flipped on a visual overlay and called up a short list of the nearby lunch spots where she might bump into people she would rather avoid. She jogged off toward the parking lot, found her car, and slipped inside.

She started the car and leaned her head back. The tinted windows and her glasses nicely dimmed the bright light outside. She was for the moment shielded from the view of everyone on campus.

She tapped the smartcom clipped to her belt, pulled up Ollie's number, and looked at the time. She was almost certain to interrupt her sister in the midst of some important doctoral-dissertation-related task, but Emmie decided to risk it. She needed to talk to someone.

She was about to dial Ollie when her smartcom rang, an unrecognized number. She waited a couple of rings, then answered the call.

Ayame Yoshimoto's projection appeared before her.

"Hello, Emmie."

"Oh, hi, Ayame," said Emmie, surprised. She hadn't thought of Ayame in months. "How are you?"

"Fine, fine, I'm doing well, thank you. Is now a good time

to talk?"

"Yes, now's fine."

"Well, I'm afraid it's taken me much longer to call than I expected. Do you remember, when we met at my brother's memorial service, I told you he left you something in his will?"

"Yes, I do remember," Emmie said. Well, at least, she remembered now. She couldn't believe she had forgotten. She really had been out of it since Tomo's funeral. "What exactly is it?" she asked curiously.

"It took me a while to find that out, actually. I had to return to Japan to retrieve it, and I just arrived home this morning."

"Oh!" Emmie said, now intrigued, "Thank you for taking so much trouble to get it for me."

"No trouble, no trouble at all. It was very important to my brother. I would like to give it to you in person, if you don't mind."

"Of course. Could I take you to lunch? It's the least I —"

"That's very sweet, very sweet. But I think it would be better if we met somewhere in private. Could we meet now, perhaps? I've asked the minister at the temple — you remember, where Tomo's memorial took place — and he would be happy to lend us his office."

Emmie looked at the time again.

"Sure. It should only take me a few minutes to get —"

"Wonderful, wonderful. I will wait for you here."

∞

Although she passed through downtown Oakland often, Emmie had avoided the temple in the months since Tomo's memorial service.

Emmie pulled into a street parking space across from the building and climbed out of her car, tapping her smartcom to the parking meter to charge it up before crossing the street. Outside the locked gate, she peered up at the curtained front windows, unsure what to do next.

The front door opened, and Ayame hurried down the steps. She glanced up and down the street before opening the gate. Emmie wondered if the angry demonstrators she had seen the day of Tomo's memorial service frequently harassed people at the church.

"Hello, my dear," Ayame said, ushering her through the gate.

"Hi," Emmie said, "Thank you again. I hope you didn't feel obligated to rush to meet me. You must be tired after such a long —"

"No, no," Ayame dismissed the suggestion with a wave, "Not at all. Let's go upstairs."

Emmie followed her into the building and pulled the heavy red doors shut behind them. Ayame led her up the stairs to the second floor, down the hallway, and through the open door at the end of the hall. Inside, the robed priest with the shaved head whom she remembered from Tomo's memorial service sat behind a tidy desk. He rose slowly and bowed to each of them in turn. Ayame bowed back, and Emmie tried awkwardly to imitate her.

"It's so nice to meet you, Emmie," the priest said in his careful accent, "I'm Reverend Naoto Kimura."

"Yes!" Emmie said, "Nice to meet you, too."

"Please," said Naoto, pulling a couple of chairs toward his desk, "Please, have a seat."

When they were all seated, Ayame turned to Emmie.

"You must think it's strange that I have asked to meet you like this," she began, tucking a loose strand of short silver hair behind one ear, "And I'm afraid it's a bit of a long story.

"When I met you at Tomo's memorial service, I had just learned from Tomo's lawyer that my brother had designated me the executor of his estate. Not a small responsibility, it turns out! He left most of his money to endow a foundation that will invest in the startup companies of young people working in the emerging media fields. It took me nearly five months to make all the necessary arrangements, before I had a chance to turn my attention to the other items.

"You were one of the few individual beneficiaries named in the will. The first part regarding your bequest was straightforward enough. Tomo wanted you to have his bonsai tree."

"His baby," Emmie said, remembering how lovingly Tomo had tended the beautiful, twisting branches.

"Yes," Ayame said vaguely, momentarily lost in memory, "He started caring for it when he was still just a boy."

Her eyes refocused on Emmie, and she smiled briskly.

"Yes, yes, well. He also left a rather unusual set of instructions. The will said I was to visit the Enryaku-ji Temple, not far from where we grew up. There, I was to ask for a priestess named Amaterasu Nagato.

"When I finished my work here, I left for Japan, and when I arrived at Enryaku-ji, I told the nuns there that I had come to visit Amaterasu Nagato. They told me she was ill, too weak to see any visitors. However, one of her attendants took my message to her, and that same day she brought back a reply. Amaterasu promised to see me as soon as she was able.

"So I waited until she called for me some weeks later. I

visited her in her quarters at the temple. She dismissed her attendant to speak with me privately. She seemed quite frail, and I could not imagine how ill she must have been before if she considered herself strong enough to see me now.

"I sat at her bedside, and she was quiet for a very long time. She seemed to be examining me. And then, quite suddenly, she asked if I could tell her the place where I had met Midori Shimahashi.

"Well, the question surprised me. I had not thought of Midori in decades. But it was easy for me to remember meeting her for the first time, and so I told her.

"I had just turned twelve, and Tomo was thirteen. Our mother had decided to take us on a day trip from our town in the mountains to visit Kinkaku-ji Temple in Kyoto. It was autumn, and the leaves had just started to change.

"We explored the temple complex together, until at last we came upon the Golden Pavilion and its reflection pond. It was very beautiful, and we sat down at the edge of the water for a while. Tomo pulled out his sketchpad — he was an aspiring manga artist at the time — and started to draw. I remember Tomo saying to me,

"'I wish I could live here forever.'

"And then, behind us, a girl said,

"'It's a bit like heaven, isn't it? But I think I would get tired of it, after a while.'"

"We turned around, and there stood Midori. I was annoyed by her comment. She sounded so superior! But when I looked at Tomo, I could see that he was quite taken with her. She was a little older than us, about seventeen, and quite beautiful. This annoyed me even more, and I said,

"'Really? Could anyone ever get tired of heaven?'

"Midori smiled at me. She said,

"'Well, I guess it would take a very long time.'

"That seemed to break the ice, and so we kept talking. She turned out to know a great deal about the history of the temple, and Tomo took advantage of this to keep talking with her, asking question after question.

"We spent the rest of that day together, and it was evening when at last we said goodbye to Midori and returned home with my mother.

"I couldn't imagine why Amaterasu was interested in this story, but she seemed satisfied and said,

"'Thank you. I needed to make sure there was no mistake. I am glad you have come.'

"Then she told me that Tomo had left a manuscript in her care, many years ago, the beginning of an academic text on creation myths in various world religions."

"Why would Tomo have been working on a book like that?" Emmie asked, "Didn't you say he had lost interest in religion?"

"Yes. Yes, as far as I knew, that was true. But you misunderstand — it wasn't Tomo's manuscript. It was Midori's.

"You see, Midori and Tomo exchanged contact information, that day we met at the temple. In fact, a few days later, I found him writing her a letter — so old-fashioned, very romantic. I teased him about his crush, but he just ignored me.

"They kept in touch for years after that, but Tomo was very private about the relationship. When it came time for him to go off to university, Tomo enrolled at the university in Kyoto to study architecture. Midori was a graduate student there at the time, in the department of Indian and Buddhist studies.

"He and Midori began to spend a lot of time together. I could see that Tomo was in love with her, but unfortunately Midori did not seem to feel the same way about him. She was so wrapped up in her doctoral research. I thought she didn't realize what was happening.

"When Midori received a grant to travel to Buddhist monasteries across Asia to gather source material for her dissertation, I was relieved. I thought that Tomo would at last have some distance from her. But Tomo decided to take a leave of absence from the architecture program to travel with her. My parents were devastated, and I was furious at Midori. I confronted her, accusing her of ruining my brother's life. I expected her to defend herself, but instead she tried to persuade me that Tomo was making the right decision. She said,

"'The teachers we will meet on this journey have preserved knowledge accumulated by spiritual masters over centuries. This knowledge is precious, and we will be helping to ensure it survives for centuries more. Tomo is lucky to have the opportunity to do such important work in his life.'

"I didn't know what to say to that. Although I still didn't approve, I kept my mouth shut as my brother prepared to leave.

"I heard nothing from him for six months after he left, despite trying to contact him repeatedly. I had only the vaguest idea of where he might be. My mother was sick with worry, and from time to time I felt furious at Midori for this.

"Occasionally, we received a letter from Tomo. He wrote that he was very busy, and that we should not worry about him. He apologized once or twice for being out of touch, saying that the places they were staying were quite remote, without even a telephone."

Ayame chuckled at Emmie's surprised expression.

"Yes," she said, "This was 1980. Long before smartcoms, before even mobile phones had become widespread."

"But then one day," Ayame sighed, "Tomo did call. It was the first time we had spoken in almost two years. I was so delighted to hear his voice that at first I didn't understand that something was wrong. I chattered away, berating him for not calling sooner. He was silent for a long time, and then he said,

"'Midori is dead. I'm coming home with her body.'"

Emmie gasped, as distressed by this turn of events as if they had just occurred.

"Yes," Ayame nodded, "I was shocked, as well. Shocked. I didn't know what to say. Tomo told me when he would return, and then he hung up. A few days later, he was home.

"There was a funeral for Midori, and Tomo moved back in with my parents. After a few weeks, my parents told me that they were worried about him, that he hardly ever left his room. So I started to come home more frequently from university to spend time with him. Usually I just sat in his room as he lay on his bed staring at the ceiling. I asked him questions, trying to talk with him, but he barely spoke.

"This went on a long time, but I was persistent, very persistent. I was terribly worried about him, but, I'll admit, I was also very curious to know what had happened during his trip, and how it had all ended. He seemed deaf to my questions most of the time, but gradually he began to open up about the things he and Midori had seen and done during his long absence. One day, he finally answered my question about how Midori had died.

"He told me they had been in the New Delhi airport, on their way to Tibet after spending time in various monasteries in India. They had just checked in for their flight, and they were walking together toward their gate. It was very crowded in the terminal, and swelteringly hot, as well, because the air conditioning system had broken down. When they reached their gate, Midori said she wanted to go find some bottled water, so Tomo stayed behind at the gate with their luggage. She was gone for a long time, and when their flight started to board, she had still not returned, so Tomo went looking for her.

"He found her surrounded by a small crowd a few gates away. She was on the floor, unconscious. An American preacher they had met on the bus ride to the airport had called airport security, and he was trying to resuscitate Midori. A few minutes later, emergency workers arrived and took her to an ambulance. Tomo followed them to the hospital, but Midori was pronounced dead on arrival. The doctor who examined her said it was a ruptured brain aneurysm."

"How awful," Emmie said, her eyes glistening, "Poor Tomo!"

"Yes. Yes, he rarely spoke to me of Midori again after that, and I never could bring myself to ask. I'm not sure Tomo ever truly recovered from the loss.

"About a year after Midori's death, Tomo dropped out of university and got a job in a manga shop in Kyoto."

Emmie nodded. The story of Tomo's gradual ascent from lowly store clerk to international alternet sensation was familiar to every aspiring domain designer.

"And that was how things were, for nearly thirty years. He was — goodness, he must have been over fifty when he decided to go to Silicon Valley. He said the alternet was going to change the world. Amaterasu told me that was when Tomo came to see her, just before he left for California.

"Tomo knew Midori had always felt indebted to Amaterasu for her philosophical writings and commentary on various Buddhist texts. I suppose that's why Tomo went to her. Even though his whole life had been given over to manga by that point, I suppose he never stopped feeling responsible for the unfinished manuscript. It was all that was left of Midori's life's work.

"Amaterasu told me that Tomo asked her to keep the manuscript for him, until he found someone to continue the work."

Ayame turned to Emmie.

"What?" said Emmie, "Not me?"

"Well," Ayame said thoughtfully, "Well, Tomo seemed to think so."

"But I really don't know anything about writing a book," Emmie said apologetically, surprised that Tomo would ever have thought her capable of such a thing, "I've hardly ever written anything longer than an email. I've spent my whole life designing domains."

"You might find that more useful," said Naoto, who had been listening quietly, eyes half-closed, the whole time.

"What do you mean?" said Emmie, turning to him.

"Well," he opened his eyes wider and smiled at her, "Amaterasu once showed me the documents. They are very visual. Many illustrations. Maybe that is why Midori wanted to work with an artist like Tomo. Maybe that is why Tomo left the manuscript to you."

"Good, good," said Ayame, nodding at Naoto, "I see why Amaterasu suggested I introduce you two. She thought you might have some ideas about it."

"You know Amaterasu?" Emmie asked Naoto.

"I lived with the monks in Enryaku-ji for some time. Part

of my ..." Naoto smiled to himself, "youthful wanderings. Amaterasu is a very great teacher, very —"

"Oh, oh," Ayame interrupted, holding up her hands, "I almost forgot. Amaterasu said it was very important for me to tell you. She said that the information on the manuscript is very sensitive, that you should only discuss it with someone you trust."

"Someone I trust?" said Emmie, puzzled, "What did she mean?"

"No idea. No idea at all!" said Ayame cheerfully, "But now I've told you everything. So here is the manuscript."

Ayame reached over to the corner of Naoto's desk and picked up a carved wooden box about an inch square. She slid open the top of the box with her thumb and held it out for Emmie to see. Inside, the emerald-colored ceramic of a round storage tablet gleamed against the maroon velvet lining of the box. Ayame slipped the box shut again and handed it to Emmie.

Emmie looked down at it, surprised.

"All this time I was imagining some big dusty stack of papers."

Ayame laughed.

"Oh! Oh, my dear, my brother wasn't quite *that* old."

∞

Emmie's hand strayed to her coat pocket several times during the drive back to Augur, but she had no chance to look at the contents of the storage tablet, because her smartcom buzzed as soon as she pulled into the parking lot. It was a text message from Owen that read,

where are you??

my car, Emmie wrote quickly, *what's wrong?*

ty called an all-hands meeting that started fifteen minutes ago, and you are conspicuously absent.

Emmie swore, burst from her car, and set off running toward the office.

CHAPTER 8
A Proposition

Zeke emerged from the conference room with triumph blazing in his eyes. Owen followed, looking more subdued as Emmie carried on at his side in an aggrieved undertone.

"… and I even gave him a glowing recommendation to Tomo. That's the only reason he hired the jackass in the first place! And what the hell is Ty thinking, anyway, splitting the creative team into two camps? It makes no sense! It's counterproductive. Pick one of us or the other and just be done with it! Tomo would never have —"

As they entered the relative privacy of the projection cylinder maze, Owen turned to her and cut her off.

"I think we should grab a greyroom and do this in private."

Emmie sighed and nodded. It wouldn't help her or anyone left on her team to see her flipping out like this. She trudged after Owen toward the elevators. The doors opened to reveal Lydia Winner, tapping a gloved hand against her hip, eyes rapidly scanning left to right, clearly immersed in some reading. She blinked and refocused on Emmie and Owen as they stepped into the elevator.

"What floor?" Lydia asked.

"Sixth, please," said Owen.

The doors closed, and Lydia heaved a sigh.

"I'm just reading the meeting notes now, Emmie. I thought you should know that you're not the only person who's going to get screwed by this. Everyone from creative to development is going to feel the squeeze. I'm looking at these schedules, and I'm going to have to rework everything. The sprints this week are going to suck."

"Yeah, but it wouldn't suck nearly so bad if I weren't so far behind in concept already," Emmie said glumly.

The doors opened on the sixth floor and Emmie and Owen stepped out. Lydia stuck out her arm to hold the door, looked up and down the empty hall, and said,

"I don't know what Ty's thinking, moving up the next review deadline. He's rigging the game so it's almost guaranteed that Zeke will step in and save the day with his backup concept. Sure, the guy's talented. But he would make a lousy Creative Director."

"You don't seriously think Ty's considering making him Creative Director?" said Owen.

Lydia glanced at Emmie and said,

"Who knows? The shareholders have probably been breathing down Ty's neck since Tomo died, wondering whether we're dead in the water without him. Appointing a new Creative Director would at least give them some confidence."

Emmie sighed. She could use some confidence right now, too.

"Well," Lydia said briskly, "Emmie, if there's anything I can do to help you, anything at all, I hope you'll let me know. We're all in this together."

"Thanks, Lydia," said Emmie, anxious for her to leave so she could vent to Owen.

"Okay," Lydia stepped back into the elevator, "Well, I'll let you two get to it."

"Come on," Owen said as soon as the door closed, steering Emmie toward one of the empty greyrooms. He palmed the door, followed her in, and set the lock.

She turned and looked up at him.

"Owen, I'm really sorry about all of this. I know your reputation is on the line, too, here."

He rolled his eyes.

"Do you think that's what I came here to talk about? Look, I know the deadline change works in Zeke's favor, but that doesn't mean we just roll over and let him steal the show."

"I saw a bit of his expansion concept today," said Emmie, "It looks really good, and it sounds like it's way further along than mine." No matter how angry she was at Zeke, she prided herself on providing fair design criticism. "Maybe it's better for the whole team if we just go with it."

"Look, Em, I know that would take the pressure off for the next few weeks. But that's not the point. What if Ty *is* going to decide who gets the Creative Director position based on the next release? That should be your job, Emmie. Everyone knows Zeke's a kick-ass designer, but he's also arrogant and divisive. He's not a team player. Even if the next release would be easier if we went with his concept now, every release after that would be much harder with him in charge."

"Ugh," Emmie groaned, raking her hands through her hair, "I know, I know. I don't want him as a boss either. The thought of him sitting in Tomo's office makes me sick. But I am so stuck, Owen. I can't put my finger on it, but there is something just wrong about the *Atlantis* we've been working on, and I can't figure out how to fix it. I can't let it go to development like this."

"This is what I wanted to talk to you about," said Owen, "I think you're making this unnecessarily hard on yourself. I think you're holding yourself to some impossible standard, second-guessing everything because you think Tomo would have expected something better. But, Emmie, your concept doesn't have to be perfect. It just has to be good enough to release."

Emmie crossed her arms, shaking her head.

"Tomo would never let a subpar release go out."

"If Tomo were here, Ty wouldn't have had to move up the deadline, either. Tomo had the luxury of picking his own deadlines, or throwing them out if he wanted to. You can't expect to put out the same product Tomo would have without the same resources."

"Ugh," she groaned again, "I hate this."

"You know I'm right."

"Still hating it."

"Look, Emmie. You can't be perfect, not all the time. Let go a little. The team's not going to give you crap if this release has some bugs, but I don't think they'll ever forgive you if Zeke becomes Creative Director."

"Great. So my options are: put out a subpar release, or have everyone hate me and end up with Zeke as a boss."

"Sounds pretty simple to me. Go for the subpar release."

"Ugh."

"You need to relax, Emmie. Why don't you step back for a bit? We can cut out early this afternoon, get an early start on our dinner date."

"Are you kidding? I'm not leaving early, not after that meeting. I need to go to *Temenos* and figure out what the hell I'm going to do. When inspiration fails, crowdsource."

∞

Owen left Emmie alone in the greyroom, and a few minutes later she was bouncing down the ferry gangway toward *Athenai*, the subdomain that served as port of entry for all new users of *Temenos*. She had assumed a default avatar popular with new users: a blushing strawberry-blonde wearing a fantasy-genre peasant dress that showed off an ample bosom and shapely arms to full advantage. Had she used her primary avatar in this densely-trafficked area, she would have been mobbed by users eager to take a screen capture with her to show to their friends, or berate her for going corporate after her indie success, or complain about a bug in some obscure part of the domain. Her anonymous avatar would allow her to experience the *Athenai* subdomain of *Temenos* as any new user might.

Emmie had taken to wandering the subdomains of *Temenos* more and more in the months since Tomo died. *Temenos* proved a reliable source of both pleasurable escape and raw material for creativity. Here, if only for a few hours, she could forget the world and all the troubles weighing on her.

A perpetually bustling open-air market filled the half mile of sandy plain separating the ferry loading grounds from the city's central square. Emmie had chosen a *Temenos* branch hosted at a data center in New Jersey, so the air was filled with voices speaking primarily English. Emmie meandered through the sea of stalls, browsing for new content. Much of it was predictable variations on the basics most users wanted: clothes, vehicles, communication clients, and navigation mods for every budget; avatar customization and animation services; *Temenos* visitor guides and news feeds; tickets for every sort of live performance, from the most highbrow to the most unsavory; booths for fortune-tellers and matchmakers; meeting grounds for quest-givers and quest-goers; environment access codes for popular solo and team games.

She slowed to examine a vendor she had not seen before. A peacock-blue kangaroo with darkly fringed golden eyes stood before a white pavilion offering passersby their choice of colorful butterflies from a fluttering rabble tethered to the ground by silver threads. Inside the pavilion, floating bubbles of all sizes hovered at optimal viewing heights to display a twittering, grunting, barking, purring, hissing menagerie. The bubble-bound creatures filled the spectrum from the most prosaic felines and canines to the most astonishing winged, scaled, and furred creatures she had ever seen.

"My daughter would *love* this," said a brawny man in a leather jerkin to another buxom strawberry-blonde in a peasant dress. He pointed at a cat-sized, white winged horse with turquoise eyes and a coral mane. As he pointed, the price of the creature appeared in an overlay on the bubble.

"Ninety-nine temens?" the man exclaimed. He gave a low whistle, considering for a moment, then shrugged and initiated a purchase transaction. The bubble disappeared, releasing the horse and a complimentary jeweled saddle into his custody. He laughed as the horse kicked off the ground, flew to shoulder height, and hovered before him.

"Oh, well. How often does your daughter turn six, right?" he said.

Emmie pulled up a search interface on her visual overlay to locate the vendor's contact information. The search interface flattened the entire three-dimensional scene into a single structured document that concisely described every object she could see from her current point of view. The contact information she wanted turned out to be embedded in the markup of virtually every object in the pavilion, an inelegant but common technique used by designers without much coding experience. She swiped her hand over her visual overlay to copy the vendor's email and smartcom number to her to-do list, along with a screen capture of the winged horse. Every once in a while, she picked up a talented addition to the creative team this way.

She walked on until the sandy ground of the open-air market gave way to the paved streets of the commercial district, which she followed for several blocks until she reached the central park at the heart of the city's downtown. Just over a year ago, the city kernel was a mere three blocks square. Before the very first launch, she and Tomo had seeded the original content. They had decided to arrange the storefronts of *Temenos*'s first launch sponsors around the park, with the Augur-managed community center at the east edge. There, the users would be able to socialize, speak face-to-face with the *Temenos* support team, and explore domain maps and wikis in immersive multidimensional renderings. They had placed the buildings for *Temenos* commercial transaction services and subdomain zoning in the three blocks behind the community center.

To Emmie's great dismay, Ty had forced them to fill the remainder of the original city kernel with a random patchwork of empty lots for lease and nondescript buildings where users could rent private meeting rooms and anonymous storage lockers to conduct business transactions of any kind in a completely secure environment. Emmie lost a shouting match with Ty about this, furious that the slipshod amalgam of buildings at the city perimeter would be users' first impression of the domain she had worked so hard with Tomo to perfect. Ty insisted that the ugly patches would stimulate user investment in city improvement and thus solidify the user base. Tomo spent days convincing Emmie not to quit Augur after the argument.

Emmie begrudgingly admitted to herself that Ty had been right. Early users completely made over the city kernel in a matter of weeks and proceeded to push the city limits out across the plain toward the surrounding hills. Now all that remained of the original heart of the city was the central park and the community center. Within six months of *Temenos*'s initial launch, *Athenai* had expanded to the outer reaches of the subdomain real estate permitted for development by the Augur zoning committee, and users were clamoring for more space.

Emmie headed across the park toward a genteel grey stone façade with a green awning that read, "The Founders Club." The building gave an overwhelming impression of exclusivity, although the building's architect had so meticulously designed the exterior to blend in with the surrounding neighborhood that most passersby never noticed an unusual feature of the building: the rows of large mullioned windows on the building exterior were completely opaque.

Everyone who was anyone of consequence in alternet circles knew that only the *Temenos* elite could walk through the mahogany doors of this building. The Founders Club's invitation-only membership extended primarily to politically or commercially influential individuals, most of whom possessed in-domain assets worth over one hundred million *Temenos* dollars, called temens, or annual net incomes from in-domain business activity of over ten million temens. Emmie had been invited to the club in its early days because of Bealsio's minor celebrity status, as well as her reputed influence with Tomo.

Emmie sent an entry request to the door. A second later, she received an identity verification request, which she promptly authorized. The door swung open, and she stepped into an elegant reception room with shining dark wood floors covered by an expanse of Persian rug. A uniformed receptionist behind a gleaming desk smiled brightly.

"How may I help you today, Anonymous Member?"

"Just the salon, thanks," Emmie replied.

The receptionist nodded. Emmie quickly switched into another avatar, this one a slim, sleek-haired thirty-something in an expensive business suit and dark glasses. A second pair of mahogany doors behind the receptionist swung open to admit Emmie into the salon. A cylinder of floor-to-ceiling glass in the center of the salon surrounded a large interior courtyard, channeling into the room the golden light of *Temenos*'s late afternoon sun.

It was about seven o'clock pm Eastern Standard Time, a popular hour to socialize for club members doing business in this time zone. Emmie browsed the discussions on the public channel. In the courtyard, a man and woman examined an exquisitely detailed miniature rendering of the entire *Temenos* domain that hovered at waist height and filled most of the courtyard. They turned on a heat map visualization of user traffic patterns through *Temenos*'s public areas and commenced an animated discussion about the best locations for several new clothing retail storefronts, gesticulating at various hot spots on the map. A backlit cluster of zoning committee members debated the relative merits of two competing lease applications for a city block whose former tenant had gone bankrupt. A trio of open standards wonks griped about the incompatibility between a recently-released content development widget and an older suite of widely-used tools. A couple wearing flight suits gushed to a small audience about a new space shooter game that had just been released for the *Astral Plane* subdomain.

Emmie made her way toward a pair of avatars deep in conversation: a broad-shouldered, silver-haired man in a whimsical space cowboy outfit seated in a leather armchair, and a skinny adolescent in a trucker hat sprawled across a chaise. These were Gygax and Didactix, two influential domain users. Gygax operated a popular fantasy roleplaying game in the venerable tradition of Dungeons and Dragons. He had been an early adopter of Augur's game development framework and had maintained a substantial first-mover advantage in *Temenos*'s games market ever since. He was a frequent and thoughtful voice on the *Temenos* developer forums. Didactix was a freelance alternet developer who often worked on projects for Gygax but also earned a substantial stream of income from sales of easy-to-use domain navigation and transaction reporting tools. He was an avid gamer and an outspoken alternet commentator on gaming. Their public chat log showed that they had been discussing the upcoming *Temenos* release for the past half hour.

They turned to Emmie as she approached.

"Hello," she said, "May I speak with you on a private channel?" The three of them exchanged perfunctory identity verification requests. Emmie used a partial profile to reveal her status as an official Augur representative without her name or title.

Gygax and Didactix would have recognized Emmie had she been using her usual avatar, but for her purpose today it was better that she remain anonymous. It was somewhat impolite for a user to enter a private channel without providing the same level of profile information as everyone else on the channel, but Gygax and Didactix made allowances because of her official Augur status.

"Greetings, Anonymous Member," said Didactix on the new channel.

"Hello, Didactix, Gygax. Would you mind if I picked your brains about the upcoming expansion?"

"Any chance you're going to tell us just how upcoming we're talking about?" Gygax asked. Didactix perked up from the chaise.

"Sorry, guys," she said. Anything she said here was almost certain to end up on Didactix's blog. She would have to watch what she said.

Gygax smiled and shrugged.

"That's okay. Gotta ask. So, what do you want to know?"

"How do you think Augur's been doing supporting the content developer community in the past few releases? Is there anything that we could focus on in the next release to keep us ahead of our competitors' platforms?"

Gygax considered for a moment. He tended to be more deliberate than the typical user during feedback requests like this. But Didactix jumped right in, speaking rapidly,

"Look, the price point of high-end immersion gear is coming down, like incredibly fast, and user expectations for content quality are just going to keep going up. We have to expect ultra-high-resolution full-sensory immersion is gonna be the standard in twelve, eighteen months tops. I mean, spliner technology still isn't going to be widely available any time soon, but you're definitely seeing a larger proportion of users, even, like, casual users and kids, with super sophisticated tactile immergers, olfactory, motion-simulation-capable audiovisual."

Emmie nodded. She knew better than anyone how quickly the price of immergers was coming down. The Lab was constantly struggling to add new features to their immergers to maintain a quality premium over the copycat immergers now flooding the market.

Didactix went on, hardly pausing for breath,

"*Temenos*'s tools for visual content creation are fantastic, audio less so but still better than you get elsewhere, but the tactile tools in your public toolset are, like, primitive, and lagging your competition. I mean, you guys must be using better tools yourselves, because the *Temenos*-authored games are still like the highest quality immersive experiences out there. Tomo was such an artist on that front, wow."

Emmie smiled to herself. Didactix was as much of a Tomo-worshipper as she had been.

"Thanks," she said, "I'll talk to our tools team about that. And I'd be happy to put you directly in touch with the team lead if you ever want to quit the freelance scene. Your reputation precedes you."

"Tempting, but I only do business over the alternet. If I had to come into an office, I'd lose at least an hour a day commuting that I could be gaming."

Emmie had had this conversation with him and many other talented developers before. The creative and technical talent of her generation was becoming increasingly unemployable, as the ease of entrepreneurship and the perception of face-to-face interactions as onerous made them hard to lure into a real-world work environment.

Gygax resurfaced from his thoughts and said slowly,

"I agree with Didactix. A year ago, you might have gotten away with an inferior developer toolkit versus your competition, because Ty Monaghan made the decision that the core of *Temenos*'s development platform would be secure transactions, identity verification, reputation tracking, and dispute adjudication. The quality of those platform features is the reason I built my content here, and doing business in temens is the best decision I ever made. But the commercial exchange ideas you guys pioneered are being used by everyone now. The name of the game today is quality content creation. If users start wanting more immersion than I can easily develop in the *Temenos* framework, I'll have to choose between losing market share to other gaming domains or moving my business to a new platform."

"I hear you," said Emmie, copying the automated transcription of their comments onto a scratchpad with a few notes of her own, "Other pain points?"

"Platform security," said Gygax, "I know I'm not the only domain content owner spooked by these ongoing server attacks. You haven't been hit as hard as some of your competitors, but, still, I lost a week of game revenue in my West Coast region this quarter when all your local server farms went offline. And my user base might not recover from it — you know how short attention spans are with these kids. I had whole guilds switch to games on other platforms in protest when they lost rank data."

Emmie nodded sympathetically. Augur's security department had barely managed to contain the data corruption virus Gygax was referring to, and she herself had lost several days' worth of work when her local sever wiped out before its automated backup to a redundant site occurred. Considering the sophistication of the attack, it was remarkable more damage had not been done.

"I'm using this private security consultant to try to keep ahead of it with some custom-designed defensive strategy," said Gygax, "But rolling your own system security is expensive. Augur could do its whole developer community a favor by offering some additional server redundancies or data backup services or something."

"I'll pass that on," said Emmie, scribbling more notes on the transcription of Gygax's comment and firing off an email to the systems engineering and developer support team leads, "Anything else?"

"Hey, do you mind if I ask you something?" Didactix interjected.

"Sure. Anything that won't get me blacklisted by Augur legal," Emmie said pointedly.

"Well, I guess you probably won't be able to answer this, then, but anyway ..." Didactix sounded a little reluctant now, "It kills me to ask, since I am like a complete Augur fanatic, but there's a rumor going around that there are big problems with the latest expansion. I'm hearing that the current creative lead has just completely dropped the ball since Tomo died. I guess I'm maybe just the tiniest bit concerned about Augur's prospects now that he's gone. I'm not giving up on *Temenos* anytime soon, but — well, you know. I own like a lot of Augur stock, not to mention all my business here. Do you think it's time for me to diversify my risk? Sell some stock, get some stuff going in other domains, maybe?"

In the greyroom where Emmie was immersed in *Temenos*,

she flicked an override patch near her hip to decouple her facial and auditory input from her avatar. Then she swore, loudly.

On the design team public channel, Owen's voice said, "Everything okay in there, Emmie?"

Emmie bit her lip. She had forgotten that she was automatically logged on to the public audio channel when she logged off her immersion audio channel. Her entire team must have heard her.

"Yep," she said, trying to keep her voice level, "Sorry, guys. Just tripped on the treadwheel."

Recovering her composure, she refocused on Didactix.

"Sorry. I definitely can't comment on anything related to unannounced releases."

∞

Ten hours later, Emmie decided that she had entirely exhausted all sources of possible inspiration for the following day's work, so she logged off of *Temenos*. She pushed back her headset and massaged her eyes before palming the door of the greyroom and making her way back down to the third floor. In the lounge, she switched on the coffee machine, and a moment later she stood enjoying the gurgle and hiss of the boiling water.

As she waited, she withdrew from her pocket the small wooden box that Ayame had given to her yesterday afternoon. She considered it thoughtfully, wondering what Tomo could possibly have expected her to do with a manuscript about ancient religious texts. She would have to find some time tomorrow to take a look.

A last bit of boiling water chortled up from the reservoir,

and the machine clicked off. The sudden silence startled her. She looked out at the office floor, struggling to bring into focus anything father than three feet away, hopping a bit on the balls of her feet to peek over partitions and scanning the floor for cots or sleeping mats beneath the desks. It was late, and she should not have been surprised to find the place empty. The next review was weeks away. She stuck one of her earbuds back in and spoke on the public channel,

"Shiva?"

"Yes, ma'am," he drawled.

She slipped on her headset again and sent him a chat request. A second later, his projection grinned and waved at her.

"What are you up to?" she asked.

"QA," he said with a wink.

"Right. Can I see?"

He switched to a streaming video of the active workspace inside his projection cylinder, and she saw a low-resolution, two-dimensional mage avatar, assisted by a raging water elemental, battling zombies in the midst of a forty-man dungeon raid.

"Old school," she laughed, "Don't let Ty know you'd rather spend time in an internet RPG than *Temenos*."

"Lots to learn from the classics, boss."

"Well, don't stay up too late."

"Yeah, right," he said. Then, in a stage whisper, "Hypocrite."

She glanced at the clock on her visual overlay. It was nearly half past one o'clock in the morning.

"'Even God couldn't create a world in one night,'" she said to herself, quoting Tomo. She glanced across the floor toward Tomo's old office. The privacy that its four walls afforded made this space prime real estate, but in the six months since Tomo's death no one had suggested clearing out his things. His office remained untouched, a tidy memorial to their fallen leader. The custodians still watered his plants.

An insistent buzz, followed by three more buzzes in quick succession, sounded softly across the room. She patted the slot on her immerger belt where she usually kept her smartcom. Finding it missing, she hurried off toward her desk. Halfway there, she stopped and returned to the lounge coffee machine. She reached up to the shelf for an oversized mug that proclaimed "GEEK" in large letters, poured about three cups of coffee into it, and proceeded to her workspace with the hot liquid balanced between her hands.

She set the mug down on the floor beneath her desk, which was currently covered in a mess of papers and sketches, and riffled about in search of her smartcom. The ping of a new work email distracted her, and she flipped on her visual overlay to check the message.

A developer from the Ukraine office had just responded to a question Owen asked a few hours ago: would it be difficult to add a simplified artificial intelligence and personality modeling tool for game-generated characters? Despite all the difficulties she had been having with the terrain design for *Atlantis*, Emmie and Owen had managed to make headway with several quest and combat games geared toward *Temenos*'s large population of immersive roleplaying adventure gamers, who had been demanding new content for several releases now. Emmie would not have time to flesh out all the new game characters she hoped to include in the next release if she needed to repeat the time-consuming process of custom coding the AI and personality characteristics of each one. A few basic parameters were all she really needed to edit from character to character. She sat down to read the message.

Another buzz issued from somewhere on her desk, a second notification of the already forgotten smartcom message. She found her smartcom this time, wedged between pages of *Wired* magazine as a bookmark. She snapped it onto her immerger belt and was surprised to see, scrolling across her visual overlay, not just one message notification, but ten. Two were from Ollie, one was from her mother, and everything else was from Owen. She frowned as she read the latest message from Owen.

Starting to get worried about you. Thought we were on for dinner. Are you still at work? Call me.

She grimaced, closed the message, and pulled up Owen's number. He picked up after one ring.

"Hey …" she said sheepishly.

"Em! Jesus. Are you still at work?"

She wrinkled her nose, kicking her toes into the floor to rock back in her chair.

"Yeah. I'm sorry I ruined our dinner plans."

"It's okay —"

"No, it's not. You reminded me, we talked about it. I am super lame."

"Hey, don't worry about it," he exhaled audibly, "But you've seriously got to stop with these crazy hours. I hate imagining you driving around down there after dark, with —"

"Thanks, Mom!" she cut him off, annoyed.

"Sorry," Owen laughed, "Hey, there's still time for a 2 am pizza run. What do you say?"

Emmie chewed her lip, glancing back at the email, drumming her fingers against the coffee mug.

"I still have a little bit of work I want to wrap up tonight. Let's do dinner tomorrow."

"Okay," said Owen, sounding disappointed, "Love you, babe."

"Love you, too."

∞

Dom did what he could to keep Emmie awake at the wheel on the winding drive back up to her house in the hills. It was nearly four o'clock in the morning when Emmie pulled into her driveway. She parked the car, her eyelids drooping, yielding to exhaustion after two days of nearly uninterrupted artificial light. She tipped her head back against the headrest. The car door and the length of the path to her front steps were all that stood between her and bed. But now that Dom had her alone, safely beyond the reach of Augur's security guards and cameras, he could not let her go just yet.

Emmie started to reach for the car door handle, but Dom pulled at his connection to her. In Emmie's weary state, her awareness let go of her body easily. Her head rolled a bit to the side, her eyes closing, and she twitched with the onset of sleep.

Emmie's awareness entered the grey void where dreams begin, which in her mind appeared to be merely another cavernous spliner. She awaited the familiar flicker that signaled the start of a spliner session, and Dom obliged, filling the space with his own vision. A soft light glowed around Emmie, and the grey floor rippled as the shape of a ship extruded smoothly beneath her feet, changing color and texture until it solidified into the broad boards of the ship's deck. The prow of the boat cut across choppy waves, approaching the indistinct form of an island through the fog, the island Emmie had come to know as *Atlantis*.

As it had so many times before, the fog dissolved to reveal the dramatic silhouette of the island. Dawn broke behind the ship, illuminating the dark shoreline cliffs, which glistened wetly in the daylight.

But this time, drawing on every ounce of willpower he had cultivated across thousands of years, Dom centered his awareness on the Temple City, determined that Emmie should see it fully.

To Dom's relief, an inlet appeared between two cliffs, almost imperceptible amidst the craggy rock faces. Emmie's boat found the path through the imposing volcanic walls, emerging on the still, indigo waters of the Temple City harbor. The morning light blazed pink and gold upon the bright stones of the city, the great central staircase, and the domed white form of Musaion.

The boat pulled forward smoothly to the broad white steps that led up from the water, and Emmie leapt ashore. Dom strained to give her a moment to take in the landscape, but at last the strength of his concentration began to fail.

The sunlight, the harbor, and the city all flickered.

"No!" cried Emmie, desperately raking her eyes over the landscape as the entire scene seemed to rewind: the hills receding, the harbor expelling her through the inlet, the cliffs disappearing into the fog.

She awoke. Whether the memory of the dream remained with her, Dom could not tell. He watched her eyes refocus slowly in the darkness of her car, first on the steering wheel, then on the dashboard, then on her house outside. She yawned and tossed her head. She pushed open the door, grabbed her bag, heaved herself from the driver's seat, and trudged sleepily toward the house.

In the shadows of the ring of redwood trees beside the house, Dom sat waiting on the stone bench. Tingling with the accumulated anticipation of twenty years, he called to her softly,

"Emmie."

She froze. Eyes wide, she scanned the shadows ahead of her until she saw him sitting there. Her body tense, she called out,

"Who are you?"

He stood slowly and replied,

"My name is Dom Artifex."

He took a step toward her, into the pool of light cast by a lamppost, and pushed back the hood of his traveling cloak. She backed away in alarm.

"Don't come any closer," she cried, "I have a taser."

She rummaged in an outer pocket of her bag until she found the weapon that Owen had insisted she carry as insurance against mishaps during her daily and nightly solo treks through Oakland. She pointed the taser at him, and he put up both hands. It would not do for her to fire. If the taser electrode shot straight through him, it would be difficult to explain.

"I thought you would see me better in the light," he said calmly.

He watched her take in his appearance, and a strange look came over her. Dom wondered whether that might have been a flicker of recognition. He certainly had not changed, in all the time that she had known him. Short, dark curls still framed his high forehead and cheekbones. Thick brows overshadowed his deep-set eyes. His long, straight nose led down to lips with the unfading blush of the undying. He was clean-shaven, his olive skin unlined. His appearance gave a deceptive impression of youth. Emmie's gaze traveled the length of his cloak, which fell in loose folds from his shoulders to the ground. Her eyes lingered on his broad, callused hands.

Her expression hardened, and she squared the taser at his chest. Dom extended his arms upward a bit more, the sleeves of his dusty tunic falling back from his forearms, revealing the faint pink lines of deeply-embedded scarlet threads.

"What do you want?" she said, her voice steady despite her trembling hands.

"I want to help you," he said softly.

She struggled visibly against exhaustion as she tried to respond to this, her eyelids drooping as she said,

"Help me how?"

"There is a domain called Dulai," he said, "And an island in Dulai that I think you should see. An island that could be your *Atlantis*, if you wish it."

This grabbed Emmie's attention. Dom knew she could name every single Augur employee who had access to the name of the next *Temenos* expansion. Dom also knew Augur had a zero-tolerance policy for information leaks about product development. A leak like this could cost someone's job.

"I don't know what you're talking about," she said.

Dom chose his next words carefully. So much depended on him gaining her trust. Now that Emmie had Midori's manuscript in her possession, he had to work quickly, to accomplish his purpose as much as to protect her.

"You have a gift, Emmie Bridges," he said, "An

extraordinary kind of vision that led to many of your early successes. Vision that brought you to the attention of Tomo Yoshimoto. Vision that led to the success of *Temenos.*

"But something has changed. Your vision is gone. All you see now are the missing pieces."

Emmie opened her mouth and closed it again. Dom went on, watching her closely,

"It has taken a toll on you. Hours spent in fruitless brainstorming sessions. Falling asleep night after night at your desk on top of stacks of incomplete sketches. Uncomfortable silences in status meetings when you tell your team you have nothing yet for them to work on. Anxious questions from project managers about the mounting cost of man hours logged in the —"

"Who told you that?" she interrupted angrily. He fell silent, wary of her temper. He needed to use her anger to draw her to him, not push him away.

"Right," she huffed, "This is starting to make sense. Let's see … You heard a rumor on some game leaks forum that the next *Temenos* expansion is at a standstill since Tomo died. You've been stalking Augur employees, tracking them on the public alternet, following them home from work like this, figuring out how best to persuade someone to give you some insider information. And then you found Zeke Eckerd, who was only too eager to pump you full of his nasty rumors about me.

"Look, I get it. There's always a market for dirt on a big company like Augur. Or maybe you're just looking to blackmail someone for the chance to pitch a potential acquisition opportunity or game content concept to one of the higher-ups. But cornering the *Temenos* creative lead alone in the middle of the night in a dark driveway is just not the way it's done."

"Well, at least you have that right," he interjected smoothly, "The dark driveway is not ideal. But I wanted to speak to you alone, and you have been surprisingly difficult to find alone away from Augur lately. Will you hear me out?"

"I don't need to hear any more of your creepy insights into my work life."

"I only want you to see that I understand your situation."

"What situation, exactly?"

"You need a new partner."

Emmie's finger twitched on the taser trigger. Dom drew his hands up a bit farther.

"I am offering to help you," he said again.

"Why do you want to help me?" she demanded.

Dom knew his work was done for now. Emmie was curious. Her fear was somewhat diminished. Not wanting to push his luck further, he backed into the shadows, stepping behind one of the great redwoods and withdrawing from her view. Impulsively, Emmie rushed after him into the ring of trees.

"Hey! Stop!"

But she found only an empty stone bench.

CHAPTER 9
Caught Off Guard

Emmie woke with a start and found herself alone in her bedroom. She squinted at the bright light streaming through the window. She must have been asleep for a long time. She had definitely been having some weird dreams.

She reached for the headset on her bedside table to check the time. Her hand swept by the small wooden box containing Tomo's tablet, knocking it onto the floor. She started to reach for the box, but, unable to reach the floor without leaving the bed, she gave it up. When her fingers at last found her smartcom, she saw that it was half past noon. She yawned and fell back on the pillows, relieved that it was Saturday. She pulled up a visual overlay to scan her email.

Owen had logged on to her smartcom remotely using her password and had left a sticky note at the center of her visual overlay, where she could not miss it.

Figured you needed your rest, so I went ahead on the bike ride with Frank, Nora, and the boys. Call me when you're up. DON'T FORGET we're on for dinner tonight, okay? You PROMISED!

Emmie smiled and dialed Owen's number.

"Wow," he said, his projection looking down at her where she lay on the bed, "I think that might be the first time you've gotten a decent night's sleep in a week."

"Yeah, yeah, yeah," she said, swiping a pillow through Owen's hovering projection. He laughed.

"Well, you look like you're in a much better mood."

"I am."

"Good. We missed you on the ride. The boys are starving now, so we were just about to grab some lunch in Berkeley. Do you want to meet us?"

Emmie chewed her lip.

"Actually … I was thinking of going in again for a few hours, just to —"

"No," Owen groaned, "Emmie. Weekend. Come on."

"Just a few hours. I swear. I have storms in the brains."

"Well, then I'm coming over there with you, and I'm going to drag you out myself at five o'clock whether you like it or not."

"Fair enough. I'll see you there."

An hour and a half later, Owen and Emmie met in the Augur parking lot. Campus was nearly empty, except for the security guards and a few of the developers who never seemed to leave.

Emmie went up to pick a greyroom on the sixth floor, and Owen brought up the stack of sketches she had been working on yesterday, along with a thermos of coffee. As they reviewed the sketches, Emmie gradually descended into the same inexplicable frustration that had been plaguing her all week. There was something wrong, and she could not see what it was. She had to suppress her desire to rip each sketch to shreds as Owen patiently compiled a list of the few strong points they decided could be salvaged from her week's work.

At five o'clock, Emmie pushed back her headset and rubbed her eyes.

"No more. I need a break."

"Great," Owen said brightly, "Let's go home."

Emmie wrinkled her nose. She wanted to leave, but that itch of something just beneath the surface of her awareness would not go away. Contemplating the scattered sketches on the floor, she said,

"Is there any chance I could convince you to go ahead? I think I just need some time alone to think. Just an hour. One hour."

"Emmie," Owen cajoled, leading her toward the door by the hand, "You *promised.*"

"I'm not going to break any promises!" she said, with a twinge of impatience, "I just need a little time alone, okay?"

"One hour," he said sternly, "Promise?"

∞

Dom had been waiting impatiently for Owen to leave, and now he seized his chance.

"Emmie," he said.

Emmie started, then quickly pulled on her headset to check whether she had accidentally switched the projection room audio onto a public channel. If she and Owen had been on live mics, their entire conversation, in particular her despairing evaluations of her latest *Atlantis* concepts, could have been overheard by anyone on campus.

"Do not worry," Dom continued, "This is a private channel."

"Who is this?" Emmie demanded, standing up and

glaring fiercely into the empty space of the greyroom.

Dom stepped out of the wall in front of her.

"We met last night. Well, early this morning, to be precise. Do you remember?"

Emmie stared at him. He expected her to be startled, but not as frightened as she had been last night. He had been careful to choose the circumstances so she could believe he was merely a visual projection, albeit an unauthorized one.

"How — How did you get in here?" she stammered, "This is a secure office network."

"I know some tricks," he replied.

"I'm calling security," she said, her hand moving to her immerger belt.

"Wait," said Dom, pulling as hard as he dared on their connection, willing her to listen to him, "Will you not hear what I have to say, first?"

She held the tip of her tongue between her teeth, considering him more shrewdly now that her surprise had subsided.

"So? What do you want?"

"Do you remember what I said last night?"

Emmie crossed her arms.

"Let's see. Oh, right. It's all coming back to me. I have no vision ... I'm wasting company resources ... I'm no good without Tomo ..." she said, ticking each item off on her fingers, "Does that about sum it up?"

"Well, actually, you forgot the one I meant. I want to help you."

"Ah, yes. You want to help me. Very noble of you. And I know this isn't some kind of blackmail or political maneuver orchestrated by one of my dear colleagues because ...?"

"You cannot know unless you give me a chance to show

you. There is no risk. You are in a locked room, after all. Entirely secure."

"Right. Except for some crazy dude who's hacked into my private network."

"Yes. Except for that."

Her fingers hovered over the security call button on her immerger belt again, and for a moment Dom held his breath. To his relief, Emmie lowered her hand.

"Fine," she said tensely, "Show me whatever it is you're so anxious to show me. But I need to get out of here in exactly one hour."

"We will need to be quick, then," said Dom, "Sit back down."

Emmie crossed her legs and sank to the floor. Dom sat facing her, thrilled by the sensation of being seen by her.

"Well," she said expectantly, interrupting his moment of elation, "What do we do now?"

Dom exhaled softly, focusing on the task at hand.

"Open a blank canvas," he said.

She tapped a few keystrokes on her forearm, and the room brightened. She stretched out her hand in the space between them, and the grey floor changed to a matte white surface.

His success from the night before seemed to make summoning up the image of the Temple City easier, and when Dom focused on the canvas, a dark curve appeared easily, followed by another, then another. The lines resolved into one of the sketches Emmie had started working on yesterday.

"How are you doing that?" she said, "I never scanned that sketch, or any of the others, either."

"Just watch."

So she watched as the lines spread across the page. But where the unbroken line of the cliffs had been before, the outline now turned inland, forming a winding channel that opened into a central lagoon. She looked at Dom wide-eyed.

"I remember that now. I was standing … there, at the edge of that lagoon. And there," she reached for a compartment on her belt and withdrew a fine-pointed stylus, with which she began to sketch on the canvas, "there was a city."

She leaned forward on hands and knees, shading the steep incline that led from the lagoon to the white city, tracing the lines of the terraced city footprint. Dom sat back to observe, nodding from time to time, correcting a misplaced line here and there.

Her hand moved quickly as she fleshed out the sketch, completely absorbed in the work. Without pausing, she pulled a sculpting tool from her belt and began to layer upon the sketch a rough three-dimensional terrain model.

She was fine-tuning the model when her smartcom buzzed. She leaned back on her heels and answered the call. Owen's projection appeared.

"What?" she said impatiently. Owen raised an eyebrow, glancing around at the sketches scattered all over the floor.

"Oh, no," she groaned, standing up and cringing as she rolled her stiff shoulders. "Owen, I totally lost track of time."

"Really?" he smirked.

"I'm leaving right now!" she said, stuffing gear into her bag as Owen's projection wagged a finger at her, "This instant. Bye!"

After the call ended, Emmie turned toward the place Dom had been sitting.

"I have to go —"

She stopped, shaking her head. Dom had hidden himself once more.

∞

A spicy aroma and the cheerful strains of 2000's power pop washed over Emmie when she opened her door. She dropped her bag, kicked off her shoes, and padded into the kitchen, where Owen stood before the stove sprinkling fresh cilantro into a pot of steaming curry. A pan of sautéed vegetables and a covered casserole dish filled with a fluffy pile of saffron rice sat on the back burner. A pile of vegetable trimmings littered the counter. Owen two-stepped toward her, singing along with the home audio system,

"Hey, Emmie, look what they're doing to me,
Tryin' to trip me up, tryin' to wear me down.
Emmie, I swear, it's so hard to bear it,
And I'd never make it through without you around."

"OMG, you are such a dork!" Emmie laughed over the music as he completed his two-step circuit around the kitchen. She followed her nose to the stove.

"That smells amazing," she said, giving the pot of lamb curry a stir, "Thanks for cooking."

The song ended, and Owen turned down the volume.

"I was starting to think I'd be eating alone."

Emmie grimaced.

"I really tried to come back earlier. The universe does not want us to have dinner together ever again."

"Seems like it," said Owen, turning off the oven burners and grabbing a pair of plates from the sideboard, "What's been up with you lately?"

Emmie leaned against the counter and looked out the

window toward the driveway, chewing the inside of her lip. Somehow, she couldn't bring herself to tell Owen about Dom.

"I don't even know where to begin," she said.

Owen opened the oven and pulled out a plate of naan that had been warming there.

"Wow! You really did it up nice," Emmie said. Owen plated the food, and she started to head toward the kitchen table, but Owen said,

"Wait. Let's eat in the dining room tonight."

Emmie glanced at him curiously, and she noticed for the first time a warm glow emanating from the dining room. Owen steered her toward the room, where she found the table set for two, a low centerpiece of large white candles, and a pair of stemmed glasses beside a decanter of red wine.

"Whoa. Fancy. What's the occasion?" she asked.

Owen shrugged mysteriously.

"You know … We've been so slammed at work. It's been a while since we had a nice dinner together."

He pulled out a chair, and she sat down. He poured her a glass of wine before returning to the kitchen to retrieve the food. Emmie poured him a glass of wine while she waited, wondering what all the fuss was about.

"It's too bad," Owen said, looking out the window as he set down their plates, "We just missed the sunset."

"It's still pretty, though," Emmie said fairly, "The stars are coming out, and the moon is so bright."

They ate in comfortable silence, admiring the view and listening to the music playing from the living room. Emmie leaned back in her chair.

"Well, that was delicious."

"Good," said Owen, pouring them both a little more

wine. He lifted his glass, and Emmie followed his lead. They smiled at each other and touched their glasses, which rang out softly. They both sipped the wine. When Emmie set her glass down, Owen reached out and placed his hand on hers.

"Emmie," he said, "I've wanted to ask you for a long time. But it's been hard to find the right moment."

She watched in shock as Owen went down on one knee. She thought her heart was going to pound out of her chest as he fished a small black box out of his pocket and opened it. Inside, shining on a black velvet cushion, lay a silver key attached to a prosaic steel key ring.

"Emerald Isadora Bridges," Owen said solemnly, "Will you move in with me?"

CHAPTER 10
Seeking Counsel

The next morning, Emmie and Ollie stood waiting in a small crowd outside *La Note*, a Provençal restaurant in Berkeley.

"We seriously need to find another place to do our Sunday brunches," said Ollie, crossing her arms.

Emmie murmured her agreement, but her gaze was elsewhere. After Ollie had emerged from the restaurant with the disheartening wait time ("Forty-five minutes!"), Emmie had surreptitiously turned on a visual overlay of a popular domain, *Calchan*, that wrapped the university campus and its surrounding neighborhoods. Through her tinted immerger glasses, she observed the spectacle of a motley crowd of avatars superimposed on Shattuck Avenue.

From where she stood, she could listen in on overtly sexualized hookup negotiations, insubstantial social exchanges, gratuitously argumentative collegiate discussions on technical and philosophical subjects, and all variety of adolescent capering and mischief. When the scene grew repetitive, she logged off *Calchan* and opened a two-dimensional overlay to skim her work email. Switching on her fingertip keyboard sensors, she discreetly tapped out against her thigh a few short responses to some of her team's questions about the assignments she had sent out last night after her revelatory work session with Dom.

"You're immersed right now, aren't you?" said Ollie, shaking her head, "It's an addiction, Emmie. It really is."

"You should check this out, Dr. Bridges," replied Emmie, tossing her sister a spare pair of immerger glasses from her bag and logging her in to *Calchan*. Ollie rolled her eyes but slipped the glasses on nonetheless. A minute later, having taken in the virtual world overlaid on Shattuck Avenue, Ollie laughed,

"Sometimes I can appreciate why you passed on college. Based on this, I guess you figured it's nothing but a four-year frat party with a pricey cover charge."

"Or a holding tank for insecure posers."

"That's not very nice. This is your prime demographic."

"Don't be so vulgar, Ollie!" Emmie said melodramatically, "I create for an audience of alternet art aficionados."

Their conversation devolved over the next half hour into a competition to find the most hilarious public channel chat exchanges in *Calchan*, until Emmie's stomach rumbled in protest.

"Do you think it's lame to order delivery while we're waiting?" said Emmie.

"Ha ha. You'll survive another fifteen minutes."

Emmie smirked at Ollie and resumed watching the virtual tableau overlaid on Shattuck Avenue. A moment later, she turned back to her sister.

"I —"

She stopped. Right across the sidewalk, she saw a man with dark, curly hair dressed in a belted, knee-length linen tunic and heavy leather boots, leaning against the window of *La Note*. She did a double take, and the man vanished.

"Emmie? What is it?" said Ollie, following her sister's gaze.

"There —" Emmie said, pointing, "Did you see …? Huh. He's gone."

"Who?"

Emmie pushed back her immerger glasses and shaded her eyes with her hand, taking a second look at the window without the clutter of a visual overlay. There was definitely no one there. She looked at Ollie and said in a low voice,

"I'll tell you once we sit down."

"Is something wrong?"

"No. I don't know. Just weird."

After they were seated and had placed their orders, Ollie looked at her expectantly.

"Well?"

"Where to even begin?" sighed Emmie, shaking her head, "You've got to promise not to think I'm crazy."

"Emmie, come on."

"Right, so, the other day, this guy showed up outside my place. It was really late. Totally dark. I threatened him with my taser, actually."

Ollie's eyes widened.

"He said he wanted to help me with the next *Temenos* release. And he knew all this stuff that he shouldn't have, like the new subdomain name, and … other stuff."

Ollie raised an eyebrow curiously, but Emmie hurried on,

"Then, yesterday, this guy's projection showed up on the Augur network, and he —"

"Wait," Ollie interrupted, "You mean while you were in *Temenos*?"

"No," said Emmie, "Like *at work*. On the Augur network."

"Aren't you guys supposed to have excellent security? That's what all your business services promo literature says."

"Yeah, I thought so."

"So? What did he want?"

"The same thing as before. He said he wants to help me with the next release."

Ollie shook her head in confusion.

"Why does he think you need help with the next release?"

The waitress came by to pour them coffee, and Emmie waited until she was out of earshot to say,

"Well, there are these rumors going around that I can't finish the release without Tomo."

"That's ridiculous," Ollie scoffed, "If anything, you're the *only* one who could complete the release without him."

"I'm not so sure about that," Emmie sighed, "I've been having a lot of trouble with the concept work for this release, even the most basic stuff. I'm insanely behind schedule. Nothing has been going as smoothly as it used to for me. And there's this other designer, Zeke — Ty's having him work on a backup release in case I drop the ball."

"Well, that's annoying, but you shouldn't let any of it under your skin. Of course the CEO has to have a backup plan. That doesn't mean he's lost confidence in you."

"Thanks. But I guess the rumors have legs, because this total stranger seemed to know about them."

"That's creepy, Emmie. Did you tell Augur security about this guy? Or the police? This guy sounds like a stalker. He could be dangerous. And if he's hacked your office network, I guess that makes him a criminal, too."

"Maybe. But the weird thing is … well, I don't want to tell

security. This guy has offered to help me, and he already has. He's helped me a lot. I made more progress on the release last night than I have in the last six months. If I do manage to get it out the door, I'm going to have him to thank."

Ollie leaned toward her and said,

"Emmie. Think about this. Maybe it seems like he's helping you now, but he could have a longer-term plan to blackmail you or do something damaging to Augur. He could tell someone that you stole IP from him, or … I don't even know. But this could ruin your professional reputation."

Emmie pushed her hands through her hair.

"You think I haven't thought of that? I know it's stupid, but for some reason, I — I trust this guy. I believe that he wants to help me. And, more than that, he's somehow able to see exactly what was wrong with my concept, to point out the missing pieces that I just couldn't put my finger on before. I feel like … I don't know why. Like it's worth risking my job."

Ollie considered her skeptically.

"Are you sure you're not doing this because, deep down, you just want an excuse to leave Augur? The only reason you went corporate in the first place is because of Tomo, and I could understand if you felt like leaving now that he's gone."

Emmie frowned,

"It's not like that. I've really come to love my work at Augur. But I don't know how else to get the job done anymore except with Dom's help."

"Dom. That's his name?"

"Dom Artifex. That's what he told me, anyway."

"He sounds like a stalker," Ollie said seriously, "Promise me you'll be careful? And, while you're at it, talk to Mom. This guy really could be out to get you in trouble with Augur's legal department."

Emmie grimaced, and Ollie took a sip of her coffee. The waitress came by and set an omelette in front of Emmie and a bowl of oatmeal and berries in front of Ollie.

"So was that who you saw outside?" said Ollie.

"It might just be my imagination. When I took another look, he was gone."

"Creepy."

They ate in silence for a little while, until Ollie asked, "Anything else going on in your world?"

"Isn't that enough?"

"Well, I meant anything good."

Emmie peered at her sister suspiciously over a forkful of omelette.

"Like what exactly?"

Ollie shrugged innocently.

"What!" Emmie exclaimed, "Did Owen talk to you?"

Ollie rolled her eyes.

"Everyone talks to me. I'm like the family confessional."

Emmie looked away, unable to meet Ollie's eyes, and her gaze wandered across the room. At the far booth, a middle-aged Asian man sat alone, sipping a coffee and reading the newspaper. A young couple with a noisy baby was trying to wave down their waitress for the check. Four college students were laughing at the table by the window. One of the boys at the table looked like Owen, and Emmie swallowed quickly and looked down. She pushed the seasoned potatoes around on her plate.

"Is everything okay?" Ollie asked gently.

Emmie groaned, remembering the awkward exchange.

"I didn't know what to say. I told him I needed some time to think about it. What am I going to do? We're at work together every day!"

"Calm down," Ollie laughed, "There's no rush. Anyway, it would make me look bad if you did move in together. I haven't even been on a third date since I was an undergrad."

Emmie pressed her hands to her face and looked up at her sister.

"I love him to death," Emmie said seriously, "But … the last six months —" words gave way to a growl of aggravation, "I feel like the world has been turned inside out. I feel like I owe it to Tomo to finish this project, but it's turned into a complete disaster. Everyone watching, judging, waiting for me to screw it up. And now Owen — I don't know. I'd sort of just like things to stay the way they are, you know?"

"There's nothing wrong with that," Ollie said, squeezing her hand, "You guys care about each other. Don't make things more complicated than they need to be."

∞

Over the next few weeks, Emmie started taking the bus to Augur to squeeze in an additional half hour of email and chat before the work day kicked into high gear. Deadline was fast approaching. Many members of the team had resumed sleeping at the office, creating a scene reminiscent of *Temenos*'s first launch. The frenetic atmosphere had made it easy for Emmie and Owen to avoid any direct discussion of their living situation since the night Owen popped the question.

Emmie arrived at the Augur campus a little before nine o'clock and wrapped up an email to the development team lead as she rode the elevator to the third floor. As soon as she sent it, she received a new message notification. It was an email from Owen. She opened it apprehensively.

I want you to know I'm not trying to be weird — just trying to give you some space. I know you're under a lot of pressure right now. I guess I'm hoping that's all it is, anyway.

I love you, Emmie, and I don't want you to do anything that makes you uncomfortable. I just want to be with you.

Let's talk soon. I miss you.

Her eyes glistened with tears, and she laughed self-deprecatingly and wiped them away with the back of her hand, trying not to smear the eyeliner she had hastily applied while on the bus. She tuned in to the third-floor public audio channel, usually the lifeblood of the creative team's communication. The channel was silent today. Everyone was working heads-down or collaborating on private channels. She swung by the lounge for coffee before pinging Owen.

"I'm in 601," he said, "Come on up."

"Eerily quiet today," she said over their shared channel, making her way back to the elevators, "How long has it been like this?"

"Since last night. I fleshed out the rest of the island terrain model yesterday, and Lydia cranked out the detailed modeling assignments for most of the team," he said. Outside of email, they had both been studiously restricting their conversation to business. "A lot of people saw their assignments and came in late last night or early this morning to get started before the rendering farm got swamped. Didn't help much. Almost everyone else had the same idea."

"So you've got everyone tasked with something?" said Emmie, "We can finally get to work storyboarding quests for the Temple City?"

"That's what I'm working on right now."

She stepped out on the sixth floor and palmed room 601. The door slid open to reveal a greyroom littered with empty takeout containers and large pieces of storyboarding paper. Owen stood amidst the detritus waving his hands thoughtfully and staring into empty space. She switched to the room channel and found him fast-forwarding and rewinding a crowd simulation through the streets of the white city that looked down on the harbor lagoon.

Owen turned around, pushing back his immerger glasses. They looked at each other for a long moment, Owen opening his mouth and closing it again, Emmie chewing her lip.

"Did you even go home this weekend?" she asked at last, taking in the mess on the floor. It was rare to see Owen in such a scattered state.

"Nah. I'm on a roll."

"Well, thanks for the overtime. I feel guilty for taking the weekend."

"You've put in your share of weekends. Let someone else carry the load for a while."

Emmie stood next to Owen, and they watched the crowd simulation, Emmie's eyes tracing the city footprint again and again.

"I don't know what to do about this," said Owen, pausing the simulation and pointing to the plaza before the temple at the top tier of the city. He un-pinched his fingers to zoom in closer. "There's an incredible view from up here, and the visitor traffic will be huge for that reason alone, never mind the quest-goers, even with branched servers. I can't see any way to avoid complete gridlock without making avatars permeable, and cheap tricks like that really don't belong in *Temenos*. Our users expect strict Earth adherence."

Emmie smirked, and the palpable tension in the room eased a bit as she said,

"At least as long as we still let them teleport."

They watched the simulation replay again. Owen shook his head, saying,

"We've never designed such a small city environment before. Maybe we could have gotten away with this at first launch. *Athenai* was almost this small at the beginning, but the user base was tiny back then, too, and anyway, *Athenai* had room to scale out."

"Mmm," Emmie agreed distantly.

"You know …" she began. After a minute, Owen prompted,

"Know what?"

She settled her hands on her hips and stared at the terrain rendering. She felt like there was something right there in front of her that she wasn't seeing. She looked up at Owen.

"Would you mind handing off this traffic problem to me for a bit?"

Owen shrugged.

"You don't usually go in for logistics. Are you sure you want to?"

Emmie nodded, her eyes locked on the projection.

"All right," Owen shrugged. He unconsciously bobbed toward her for a kiss, then stopped himself sheepishly and waved before leaving the room.

∞

Dom felt the tingle of the threads beneath his skin as Emmie's awareness flowed into the model of the Temple City hovering before her. She was determined to understand it, to perfect it. Dom knew it was useless to struggle against her, so he let his voice slip into her ear.

"I can show it to you," he murmured.

Alone in the greyroom, Emmie straightened up, pressing a finger to her earbud.

"Dom?" she whispered, her eyes scanning the empty room.

"Yes," he said, standing unseen beside her, "I can show you the Temple City. Is that what you wish?"

Emmie hesitated only a moment, her fingers twitching toward the emergency call button on her belt, before she said,

"Yes. Show me."

Dom did not give her a chance to second-guess herself.

"I am taking you in now," he said.

When he felt her awareness drifting from her body in anticipation of immersion, he reached for Dulai and pulled her after him.

His awareness returned to his body, sitting in his sleeping quarters in the lowest tier of the Temple City. He looked up at Emmie, who was already reoriented and pacing the room, considering the view through the windows, touching the wool blankets on his bed and the cool stone walls, listening to the voices of women calling to each other on the street outside, just as she would have done upon first entry into any unfamiliar domain. Dom marveled that she could accept the shift between two physical worlds as easily as any other immersion.

"Come," he said, striding quickly from his room. Now that Emmie was here, he wanted to plant whatever seeds of understanding he could in her mind. Soon, everything would depend on her understanding his plight.

Emmie followed closely behind him until they stepped

out onto the city street, where she began to trail behind, stopping to look at the dark blue waters of the lagoon below, the colorfully robed figures of women and girls passing by, the white facades of the temple outbuildings above.

A current of salty sea air ruffled Emmie's hair.

"Really compelling," she said, impressed, "What framework are you using to code tactile effects like that?"

"Later," Dom said under his breath, "Follow me."

Dom made his way to the steep stairs that climbed up to Musaion, cutting across the boulevards that traversed each tier of the city. They passed several more women, walking singly and in small groups, chatting and laughing. He took long strides, and Emmie, trying to take in all the sights and sounds, struggled to keep up. The stairs grew ever steeper, and Emmie began to pant.

"Doesn't this place have a nav client or something?" she complained, "Can't we just teleport to wherever you're taking me?" He did not answer, as they were walking in the midst of another group of priestesses. He could not afford to draw attention to himself during this dangerous excursion.

"Slow down! I'm going to trip on the treadwheel!" Emmie said at last.

Dom slackened his pace but still did not answer.

"Hey," Emmie said crossly, "Did I do something to offend you?"

Dom glanced at her and stepped off the stairs onto one of the boulevards, ducking into a narrow alleyway between two buildings. A black cat with yellow eyes stared at them from the stoop of a doorway that let out onto the alley.

"I am sorry," Dom said in a whisper, "You are a ghost here. I cannot let anyone see me speaking to you."

"Wait," Emmie said slowly, "Why not? I thought all of

this was your IP."

"Be patient. Let me show you what you need to see."

They resumed their hike up the stairs and at last reached the white plaza before the domed figure of Musaion. From this height, they could see over the dark volcanic ridge enclosing the smooth lagoon, to the churning waters of the sea beyond. Emmie faced Dom, leaning back against the balustrade that was the sole barrier between her and a precipitous drop to the next tier of the city.

"So," Emmie said when she had regained her breath, "What's the deal with all the women? Why is yours the only male avatar?"

"I work for the women," he said simply, "There are other men here, too, but not many."

"And what exactly do you do for these women?"

"I build. I built this city."

"Wow," said Emmie, impressed, "All by yourself?"

"Others quarried the stone."

Emmie laughed.

"But seriously, you must have a lot of time on your hands to build something this detailed."

"I do."

"And some pretty incredible content development tools, for immersion this good," she said, turning around to lean out over the balustrade and look down at the city. She glanced at Dom pointedly. "No decent domain navigation interface, though."

"The city is best experienced at walking speed."

"You sound like Tomo," she said, resting her chin on her hand, "He was never a fan of all the hyperactive teleportation that the navigation clients enabled. He wanted people to use his alternet domains to explore, to relax, to discover. He felt that his generation and all the ones coming up behind it were born in a world where there was nowhere left to explore, nothing left to discover."

Dom remembered Ava expressing the same sentiment. Had she not felt this way, she never would have left him.

"Of course," Emmie added wryly, "He lost that argument with Ty. Commercial users have places to go, people to see, yada yada yada."

She looked down at all the walking boulevards criss-crossing the city and the colorful figures moving slowly along them.

"So, what are we doing? I'm assuming we didn't walk all the way up here just for the view."

"No, we did not. But we have to wait a little while longer for the Oracle."

"The Oracle," Emmie nodded approvingly, "Nice touch."

As they waited, Emmie watched the midday light sparkling on the lagoon.

"It is beautiful, but I can already hear the complaints from the users, even if I can figure out a way to solve the traffic problem in these narrow city streets. Our users are such sticklers for realism, as ironic as that sounds. So many alternet experiences contain inconsistencies that ruin users' ability to suspend disbelief. People love Tomo's work because it feels self-consistent, alive, organic, even when it's fantastical. This place is beautiful, but it's unrealistic."

"What makes you say that?" Dom asked, amused that his own world should seem less real than one of Emmie's alternet domains.

"I couldn't put my finger on it when we were walking through, but now that I think back on it, I can see what it is. Everything is too uniform. The proportions of things. The heights of every story of every building. The widths of streets and alleys. The dimensions of the blocks of stone in the walls. The sizes of windows. It's all well-proportioned, don't get me wrong. But it's like those housing developments that are plopped down all at once by the same developer — there are variations, but even the variations look the same.

"And there are little details that seem unique at first, but then they're repeated everywhere. Like the features of the statues in the plazas — the women all have the same face, the same hair."

Dom had never realized this before. But looking out toward the nearest statue, a water-bearer carved into the central fountain of the plaza, he saw that Emmie was right. Ava's face was everywhere.

Emmie swept her hand over the city below them, tracing the line of the main boulevard that climbed up toward the temple.

"The tiers of the city are all the same height, the angles of the streets ascending the mountain exactly the same at each intersection. And, weirdest of all, the grain of the stone aligns everywhere. It looks like every building, every street, every fountain, was extracted whole from a quarry and reassembled in exactly the same position. Like the entire city was carved from a single piece of stone."

Emmie's tone implied the impossibility of such a feat. Given unlimited time, however, the task had seemed not so difficult to Dom. He had done all this in pursuit of perfection, to placate the Oracle.

"What's so funny?" said Emmie.

"Nothing," said Dom, "It does look that way."

"It's also sort of sad," Emmie said thoughtfully, "You've built this beautiful city, but it can never grow."

"What makes you say that?"

She pointed out the city perimeter,

"You're hemmed in on all sides by this ridge. You've got this city — a small city, sure, but still a city — and there are no roads to connect it with anything else on the island. If you're going to prevent people from teleporting, they're all going to need some other way to get here — how? By boat? And then hike around the city? No one's going to want to do that. The whole subdomain will just remain completely isolated. Remoteness is interesting once or twice, but in the end, it's so impractical. People are in a hurry. Time and attention are the scarcest resources of all."

Dom smiled sadly.

"Sorry for being so critical," said Emmie, "It's still really impressive. The sensory work is spectacular. Even if the city is unrealistic, the sounds and the smells and the visual detail are all amazing. I could win over the users with that alone, if their immersion tech were good enough to transmit it. But I don't know if I can replicate the sensory immersion you've got going on here. So if I'm going to use this city as is, I'm going to need a killer backstory to explain all the weird bits."

A bell clanged behind them, and Emmie turned with Dom to look up at the temple. A small procession of barefoot Mohirai in saffron robes, their shoulders draped in crimson mantles, emerged from the front of the temple and descended along the paved and winding way toward the terrace where Dom and Emmie stood.

The priestesses at the front of the procession appeared to be barely out of girlhood. Next came a line of older adolescents, followed by young women. Among these, Dom recognized the dark-haired initiate he had met in the temple twenty years ago, dressed like all the rest but carrying an empty chalice in one hand. She looked not a day older.

"Is she the Oracle?" Emmie asked in a hushed voice. Unable to communicate the somewhat complicated answer to this question without drawing attention to himself, Dom chose not to respond.

The ranks of Mohirai grew apparently older as the procession passed. The last were strong, straight-backed, and proud, but white-haired and withered by time.

When the last woman had passed, Dom turned and followed at a respectful distance, Emmie trotting behind him to keep up.

They did not have far to walk this time. The procession slowed before an unwalled circle of eight white columns supporting a delicate domed cupola of translucent blue and green stone. The structure stood atop an enormous round dais. A single flight of broad white stairs gave access to the top of the dais, and the procession stopped there.

A small group of men, the only men other than Dom that Emmie had seen thus far, approached the dais from a boulevard that led up from the lower tiers of the city. These men were dressed like Dom, in leather-belted tunics and traveling cloaks, heavy leather boots conspicuously loud on the paving stones after the barefoot procession of women. The men stopped at the bottom of the narrow path that led to the dais. Dom went down to meet them and stopped at the front of the line before turning to face the dais. Emmie stood unseen beside him, while the rest of the men stood behind.

The dark-haired Mohira with the chalice stood at the bottom of the dais stairs and turned to face the men. She raised the chalice for a moment, and the men, led by Dom, bowed slightly toward her. The other women ascended the stairs behind her in a double line, the oldest women now leading the rest, and stopped just before the two columns on either side of the staircase. The line parted, and the women turned to face each other, forming an aisle between them. As they turned, each woman pushed her mantle behind her left shoulder to reveal a sheathed dagger hanging from her belt.

The dark-haired Mohira now ascended the dais, walking through the aisle of women. At the top of the steps, she turned and looked down at the men. She called out in a voice that echoed on stone,

"Dom Artifex."

Without waiting for a response, she turned and walked toward the center of the dais, disappearing from sight behind the broad columns.

Dom made his way to the bottom of the stairs, Emmie hurrying along at his side. He removed his belt and his cloak and handed them to the two youngest girls standing at the bottom of the stairs. The two above them came down and ran their hands over his arms and down his sides. Each girl withdrew a small flask from her belt. One poured water that smelled of herbs over his hands, and the other poured a small amount of oil onto her fingertips and reached up to anoint his brow. They stepped back, and Dom proceeded up the stairs.

Halfway through the aisle of Mohirai, there was a gap of a single stair that separated the young women from the older women. All the older women standing above the gap wore belts from which one or more ornaments hung. Some were simple ornaments of carved wood or stone. Others were finely worked in metal, glittering with gems.

Dom passed the end of the aisle and stood atop the dais. A narrow trough of white stone circumscribed the eight pillars, and through it flowed a rill of clear water from an unseen source. Straight ahead, a small stone bridge led to the center of the structure. Dom crossed over the water into the cool aquamarine light that streamed through the translucent stone of the domed roof.

Inside, a mosaic of small hexagonal glass tiles in all shades of blue, green, violet, and black covered the floor. In the center of the floor was a wide circular pool of clear water bubbling up from a crack in the volcanic rock beneath the dais. The cool susurrus of the flowing water emanated from the floor.

Behind the pool, the Mohira sat on a high wooden stool. She acknowledged Dom with a nod and gestured for him to approach. Dom stood facing her from across the pool.

"Long years have passed since last you made a request of the Oracle, Artifex," said the Mohira.

"Yes, Mohira," said Dom, "So long, in fact, that I wonder whether the Oracle has forgotten me."

"The Oracle never forgets, Dom Artifex." The priestess said this as if to comfort him, little suspecting that all Dom now desired of the Oracle was to be forgotten, to be released.

"Please," he said, kneeling before the Mohira, "Tell me then what the Oracle would have me do. I have nothing left to give to the Oracle. Give me my answer, or else let me be free of this task."

The Mohira's voice grew distant as she intoned,

"If you would have your answer, you must first build a temple to the mystery of enduring beauty."

Dom felt anger bubbling up within him. The Oracle still withheld all hope of his answer.

"Enduring beauty deserves no temple," Dom spat, "The world of the enduring is a barren one, cold as stone, ever crumbling, ever shrinking —"

Dom took a ragged breath and held his tongue. He knew such words were reckless. There was no telling what the Oracle might do, if provoked. The Mohira looked upon him with pity and stepped down from her stool to kneel beside him. She spoke now as only a woman.

"Be patient, Artifex."

Rage reared up in Dom's chest at these words. He seized the Mohira's wrist and pulled her toward him.

"Ava herself offered me this knowledge freely," he growled into her ear.

Frightened, the Mohira struggled to loosen her wrist from his rough grasp. Then she paused, looking curiously at Dom's hand. His loose sleeve had fallen back, revealing the grid of scarlet threads just visible through the skin of his forearm. Dom followed her gaze and let go of her quickly, shaking down his sleeves and glaring at her with a look of defiance. But in his heart, he feared she had guessed his secret.

The Mohira considered him, her expression a mixture of compassion and bemusement. At last she stood and made a gesture of blessing.

"I wish you well on your way, Dom Artifex. Devote yourself to your task, and your answer will surely come."

Dom rose to his feet without looking at the Mohira and turned away.

∞

"What was that all about?" Emmie whispered, trotting down the stairs after Dom. The two girls at the foot of the dais returned his belt, which he fastened once more around his waist, and his cloak, which he threw over his shoulders. As he walked back down the path toward the boulevard, the Oracle's voice rang out, "Anteo Artifex," and another man passed them on his way to the Oracle.

Dom could not answer Emmie's question until they were out of earshot of the Mohirai, so he descended the long staircase to the first tier of the city in silence.

"Ugh," she sighed, trudging along behind him, "It sucks being a ghost."

When at last he re-entered the privacy of his sleeping quarters, Dom turned to her and said,

"All right. I'll log you out. Then we can talk."

She nodded, then unconsciously followed his lead back to her body in the Augur greyroom.

"So?" she said, kicking off her shoes and flopping onto the springy floor to massage her feet, entirely unaware of the true distance she had just crossed. Dom considered how best to explain what she had seen.

"The women you saw in the Temple City," said Dom, "They are called the Mohirai. They serve the Oracle, carrying out her wishes, speaking with her voice."

"And who is the Oracle?" asked Emmie.

"The Oracle," Dom said slowly, "Perhaps not a *who* so much as a *what*. She is the source of life for all that lives in Dulai."

Emmie leaned back on her hands, listening with the air of a connoisseur of worlds.

"She's some sort of goddess figure? The Mother Earth of Dulai?"

"Perhaps," said Dom, "But she is also the source of knowledge, which she reveals only through the Mohirai. Anything that is known among the people of Dulai came first from the Oracle, through the words of a Mohira."

"So if you want to know something, you ask the Oracle."

"The Oracle does not simply hand out answers, though," said Dom, "To receive an answer, you must first swear an oath ... to complete a task the Oracle gives to you. Once accepted, the task cannot be abandoned."

He fell silent, until Emmie prodded him.

"And what about that priestess, the one you were talking to at the spring?"

"That Mohira was serving as the Oracle's vessel."

"But you didn't ask her a question. Well, it didn't really sound like a question."

"I already asked a question. Now I wait for my answer."

"You don't seem too happy about it."

"I have been waiting for a very long time."

Emmie cocked her head to the side and seemed about to ask him a question when another thought popped into her head.

"So ... the Oracle gives you a shot at a great reward — the answer to any question — but she could require you to do anything, and once you agree to it, you can't get out of it."

"Yes. Exactly," Dom said through clenched teeth.

"You could lose everything trying to get your answer," Emmie said, drumming her fingers against her lips, "A high stakes gamble."

The look of realization that Dom knew so well now dawned on Emmie's face as she said,

"High enough stakes to excite the courageous and keep away the faint of heart. A fantastic premise for *Atlantis*!"

Emmie beamed at him. Dom drew back his lips in a smile that did not reach his eyes. Once again, in the moment of her understanding, he was left behind.

∞

The swish that accompanied the opening of the greyroom door startled Emmie. She glanced at Dom in alarm, afraid she might be caught conversing with a network hacker, but Dom had already vanished. Owen stepped inside, looking around at the papers and takeout containers that the spinning treadwheel had driven to the margins of the room.

"Good workout?" he said.

"I think I had a breakthrough, Owen!"

Owen took in her flushed face and bright eyes and nodded slowly.

"Well, let's hear it."

Emmie paced the room, her hands waving as she chased after her stream of thought.

"So," said Emmie, her words flowing rapidly, "We'll make *Atlantis* a secret. Secrets are the one thing people love to talk about most, right? So we'll plant some in-domain characters in *Athenai* or somewhere to leak info. Pretty soon everyone will be talking about it. And everyone who can afford it will want a piece of it. But we can control the crowds by making entry contingent on accepting a task that might cause them to lose everything. And if what they have to lose is a whole lot of temens —"

"Whoa, Emmie," said Owen, "Slow down."

Emmie took a breath, trying to think of a way to explain so Owen would understand. When ideas came to her like this, they were always just a tangle at first. But she could tell that there was something in this one, some idea just waiting to come clear, if she could coax it out into the open.

"Okay," she said, "So, the business owners in *Temenos* know the value of new subdomain real estate. Everyone's been clamoring for it for months. Tons of them would pay an arm and a leg for first development rights, right?"

Owen nodded.

"So, if we put out a rumor that Augur is going to give away first development rights to users who have demonstrated the greatest ability to put in-domain resources to profitable use, they'll all jump on it. Who would want to risk missing out?"

Owen squinted, trying to follow.

"But, why a rumor? Why not just make it a product announcement?"

"For the *buzz*," Emmie said impatiently, "It's free marketing! All the rumor forums, right?"

Owen seemed stuck on this, mulling it over, but Emmie couldn't help pushing on,

"All our big *Temenos* businesses will sink temens into their existing properties in a bid for first rights to develop new properties in *Atlantis*. We'd see a revenue bump even before we open *Atlantis* to the public. Then, the businesses who actually get the rights will sink even more temens into developing their *Atlantis* properties. And so," she paused for effect, "Once we finally open *Atlantis* to the public, all the content the chosen business owners have developed for their new properties will be ready and waiting, which will distribute new user traffic evenly around the subdomain. We solve the Temple City crowding problem and the new subdomain content sparsity problem in one fell swoop."

Emmie crossed her arms, self-satisfied. A pleasant afterthought occurred to her, and she added,

"And, as a bonus for our team, this would dramatically reduce the scope of content creation we need to complete internally before the release deadline, which might actually give us a shot at beating Zeke's concept."

Owen nodded slowly, thinking it over.

"Sounds like a plan worthy of Ty Monaghan," he said at last.

Emmie scowled. Being reduced to comparison with Ty was not something she would ever be proud of. Owen laughed at her expression.

"I meant that as a compliment. I think this could actually work," he said.

"Okay," she said, invigorated, "Let's get the word out to the rest of the team. It's going to be a mad dash to the finish."

CHAPTER 11
The Spliner

One month later, Emmie and Owen stood in the windowless corridor outside the entry to the Augur spliner. They had just finished their own immersive *Atlantis* demonstration for Ty and Ahmet, and now there was nothing left for them to do but wait for Zeke to finish presenting his competing concept. Owen paced back and forth. Emmie thumped her head rhythmically against the wall.

"They can't be much longer now. They've been in there for over an hour," said Emmie, "OMG, I'm nervous."

"That's good," said Owen, trying to sound upbeat, "You're usually sharpest when you're nervous."

"I don't think it's going to help things if I throw up on the conference table," said Emmie, wincing as she delivered a particularly vigorous thump to her head. She refocused her anxious energy on twisting the rings on her fingers instead.

"You'll be okay," said Owen, "You've had nothing but coffee for the last seventy-two hours. The worst you could do is dry heave."

Emmie giggled, giddy with lack of sleep.

The whirring sound of the spliner powering down cut

through the quiet hallway. Emmie wiped her sweaty palms on the black fabric of her immerger leggings. The east doors of the spliner slid open, and Ahmet and Ty emerged, peeling off the outer layers of their immersion gear, followed by Zeke, looking tired but cheerful. Zeke shot Emmie a self-assured smile. She surprised herself by smiling back. She could not remember the last time she had seen Zeke looking happy.

"Okay, guys," said Ty, "Let's go on up to my office, and we'll hear your final comments on your concepts before we talk about the release rollout."

Ty led them all out of the spliner building and across the grounds toward the main office.

"Great job, Zeke," Ahmet said, clapping him on the shoulder, "Those creatures ... really fantastic! I think I'll have nightmares tonight."

"And you two," Ahmet dropped back to walk between Emmie and Owen, "I was just floored by the level of detail in your Temple City. Evocative. Beautiful. And your in-game characters — just wonderful."

Owen shot Emmie an encouraging thumbs-up.

Ty led them all up the stairs to the second floor offices, where Owen and Emmie at last parted ways. Owen mouthed, *Good luck*, to her and continued up to the third floor. Emmie followed Ty through the CEO office suite and into the adjacent conference room.

Ty and Ahmet sat at one end of the conference table. Emmie and Zeke sat at the other end facing each other. Emmie could not quite bring herself to meet Zeke's eyes.

"Guys, I know that the months since Tomo died have been really stressful," said Ty, "Losing our Creative Director has been hard on everyone, especially you creatives, who depended so much on Tomo's guidance. And it's not lost on me that splitting up the team like we did for this release has put you two at odds. Pressure from the board convinced me this was necessary, and I hope you'll forgive me for all the trouble it's caused.

"In spite of all that, the work you showed us today is some of your best. You should be very proud of yourselves."

Emmie forced a smile. Zeke maintained an expression of nonchalance.

"Do either of you have any final comments you want to make before —"

Zeke put up his hand.

"Okay," Ty nodded, "Go ahead, Zeke."

Zeke stood.

"First, I'd like to thank you, Ty, and you, Ahmet, for giving me the opportunity to work with my own team to develop my concept for *Atlantis*. I think our beta feedback just underscores the fact that our users are ready for a rich, surreal fantasy environment like the one I've shown you today, to complement the … simpler concepts that have characterized our previous releases. I think any of our users would be thrilled to visit my *Atlantis*.

"Thanks again for the opportunity."

Zeke settled neatly into his seat. Emmie chewed her lip. Ever since Ty had split the design team into two camps, she had wanted nothing more than to solidly trounce Zeke's concept, but now she felt a bit deflated at the thought that one of them would have to lose this fight.

"Emmie?" said Ahmet, "Would you like to say anything?"

She stood, glancing at Zeke before saying, somewhat haltingly,

"Well, guys, this was not the smoothest project I've ever run. I definitely missed Tomo's guidance, and I've been struggling from the beginning to imagine what he had in mind for this release.

"I know that the island I showed you today isn't the flashiest environment you've ever seen. Because I had so much trouble developing the initial concept, there are large stretches of the subdomain that still need a lot of content to feel really complete. But the environment foundation is strong, and elegant, and beautiful, and I think you both saw today that the locations we did manage to flesh out fully are really compelling."

She swallowed. She seemed to hear Ollie's confident voice in her head, and she tried to imitate it, gaining more momentum as she said,

"I know there are concerns about whether the simplicity of the subdomain we've put together will drive the user traffic we need for this release to be considered a success by the board. The team and I debated this at length, and we're confident that putting out a release rumor will generate buzz and domain investment at a level that could not be achieved with a more typical release marketing strategy. I think it's the kind of thing Tomo would have loved to try.

"So," she looked from Ty to Zeke and, losing her train of thought, concluded lamely, "I — I hope you'll give it a shot."

Emmie sat down, flushing slightly. She knew she had sounded pretty weak, but still Ahmet nodded and smiled at her. Ty leaned back in his chair, pressing his fingertips together.

"Thanks, guys," he said at last, setting his feet back flat on the floor and looking from Zeke to Emmie, "I appreciate what you've said, and everything you've showed us today, and I don't want to leave either of you hanging. I know you've both been waiting weeks for this decision."

Emmie turned white and pressed her lips together. Zeke leaned forward eagerly, a bright pink spot appearing on each of his pale cheeks. Ty folded his hands on the table in front of him and turned to Zeke.

"Zeke, we were very impressed with the depth and originality of the content you developed for your concept, and I'm sure we'll find a way to incorporate it into subsequent releases. However, at this time we feel that Emmie's concept evokes a greater sense of continuity with the domain's established aesthetic. We want to demonstrate for now that we're remaining faithful to the things users have come to love about *Temenos.*

"We've decided to proceed with Emmie's concept for this release."

Emmie slumped in relief. Zeke sat rigid in his chair. Ty went on,

"Good work, both of you. We've still got a long slog ahead before this release is ready to go out the door, but I hope it'll be smooth sailing from here. Or smoother, anyway."

Ty pushed back from the table.

"I'll let you two get back to work, then."

Zeke scrambled up from his chair and rushed out the door without a word. Emmie, looking slightly dazed, rose more slowly and was turning to leave when Ty said,

"Emmie, could you come with me? I'd like to speak with you privately."

Emmie looked over her shoulder before she followed Ty into his office. Through the glass wall of the conference room, she saw Zeke stopped in his tracks, watching her. His face turned an angry shade of pink before he stormed off toward the elevators.

∞

Ty pointed Emmie to a chair that faced his expansive, glossy desk.

"Coffee?"

Emmie shook her head, and Ty made his way to the high-backed chair across from her. He pressed his fingertips together and swiveled to face the floor-to-ceiling windows looking out over the San Francisco Bay. The lights of the Golden Gate Bridge were just starting to twinkle against the deepening violet of the winter twilight.

"I want you to know I understand what a tough time you've been going through."

Emmie pressed her fingers to the bridge of her nose and sighed. She couldn't imagine that he did.

"Please don't mention this to anyone," said Ty, "But our investors and the board just about lost their minds a few months ago with all the delays we were having. Authorizing Zeke's backup concept was the only thing I could think of to buy you some more time. It's not lost on me how bad that was for your team's morale."

Emmie let out a humorless laugh.

"Yeah. Just a bit."

Ty rubbed his chin.

"You took it in a stride, though. You demonstrated real leadership, and you kept your cool despite all Zeke's posturing."

Emmie raised an eyebrow. Ty chuckled.

"What? You think I'm blind? No. He's a smart kid, but … Well, anyway, that's not what I wanted to talk with you about.

"You've probably been expecting this. Frankly, I would have done it sooner if it hadn't been for all the goddamn politics I've had to deal with, considering all the qualified candidates, doing interviews, etcetera etcetera."

Ty leaned toward her across his desk.

"I want to offer you the job of Creative Director. You were the obvious choice from the beginning, but you've really shown us through the last few months that there's no one better equipped to take over the team leadership than you are."

Emmie felt a surge of anger toward Ty. Putting together *Atlantis* had been a struggle enough on its own without Ty playing these games for the shareholders' benefit. Tomo never would have put her through that. At the thought of Tomo, she felt her eyes grow hot with tears.

"I was hoping that would be good news," said Ty, taking in her look of distress.

Emmie cleared her throat. She was certainly not going to cry in front of Ty. Still, her voice broke a little as she said,

"It just seems so final, doesn't it? That he's really not coming back."

Ty nodded and said,

"He was a good man. A good friend. I miss him, too."

They sat in silence for a while.

"Well," Ty said, straightening up, "That means you're the lucky winner of the corner office." He tapped out a quick sequence on the top of his desk. "There's the access code. It's all yours."

∞

When Emmie stepped out of the elevators, a small cheer went up from her team on the third floor. She accepted congratulatory shout-outs on the public channel and high-fives from the tired-looking designers and engineers milling about the floor until she at last reached her desk and collapsed into her chair.

A minute later, Owen's hands settled on her shoulders.

"You should see the look on Zeke's face," he said.

"Ugh," said Emmie, shuddering at the memory of his expression as he stormed out of the conference room, "What Ty did to him was just the worst. Raising his hopes like that, and then just shelving everything he's been working on." She shook her head in distaste.

"Are you actually feeling *sorry* for Zeke?" asked Owen, surprised.

Emmie didn't answer. Up until today, she would never have expected to feel sympathy for Zeke ever again, but, with Ty's words still ringing in her ears, she could not help but think that Zeke had been wronged.

"Well," said Owen, "It's not like his work just goes down the tubes. Everything ends up in the content library. Some of it might live to see another day."

Emmie nodded, rocking back in her chair. She should have been savoring this moment with Owen. Looking up, she saw in his face the same mixture of exhaustion and elation that she felt.

"I didn't get a chance to thank you," she said.

Owen crossed his arms and leaned against her desk.

"I'm all ears, boss."

"Thank you," she said, with all the solemnity she could muster.

"You're welcome," said Owen, his eyes twinkling.

They looked out over the workstations to watch the celebratory Nerf war that had just broken out in the lounge. Several people were packing up sleeping mats and pillows from under their desks and trudging toward the elevators to go home early.

"Take a cab!" Owen shouted at a few of their most exhausted-looking teammates.

"What a day. What a month!" he said, shaking his head. After a minute, he looked down at Emmie again and said tentatively, "So ... want to come over to my place for a beer?"

Emmie smiled up at him. The dark clouds of the last few months seemed to be lifting. She could think of nowhere else she would rather be.

"I'd love to."

Owen nodded slowly and said,

"So ... does that mean things are back to normal?"

A small bell chimed on the public channel, and Emmie and Owen looked up. Shiva's voice, ill-disguised by a voice modulator, said,

"The creative team would like to welcome our new Madame Director: may your reign be long and prosperous. We would also like to extend our sincere condolences to your first runner-up, Z —"

Owen cut in on the channel with his override privileges.

"Shiva! Please come and see me. Now."

Emmie patted Owen's knee.

"Go get 'im, cowboy."

∞

It was nearing midnight as Owen drove Emmie the last winding quarter mile along Skyline Boulevard toward her house. Through her window, she looked down at the city spread out below the hills, a field of white and gold light surrounding the darkness of the San Francisco Bay.

The moon had not yet risen, and the road was dark. As the trunks of the great redwoods flashed by, she saw patches of night sky studded with stars — beautiful, but nowhere close to the memory of that glittering vault beneath which she and Owen had shared their first kiss.

Her eyes turned to Owen, who was guiding the car smoothly around treacherous curves. He had insisted on driving her home. He could be overprotective sometimes, Emmie thought. Her vision seemed to sway a little as they rounded another bend. She really had meant just to have one beer, but perhaps she had gotten a bit carried away. Tonight, all she had wanted was to forget the sadness and frustration of the past several months.

Owen pulled into her driveway and parked. They sat in a comfortable silence for a while. Emmie took Owen's hand, and he smiled at her.

"Ready for bed?" he asked.

"Almost," she said.

He stepped out of the car and came around to open her door. Emmie stood up and stumbled a little.

"Easy there," Owen laughed. Emmie giggled, leaning against him.

Owen led her up the dimly-lit path to her house. At the door, Emmie dug around in her bag for her keys. Her fingers closed around them, and she looked up.

"Do you want to come in?"

Owen closed his eyes, moistening his lips.

"I do," he said, letting out a sigh. He took her in his arms and kissed her forehead lightly, "But," his voice sounded pained, "I think you need some sleep. We can talk more tomorrow."

Emmie frowned and drew back a little. The stars seemed

perhaps a little less bright as she looked up and searched his eyes. She felt her head spinning. He was probably right, she thought reluctantly.

Emmie stood on her toes and gave Owen a quick kiss, then fumbled with the door until she managed to unlock it.

"See you tomorrow," she said. She turned back for a parting look at him. Owen was squinting up into the trees beside the house.

"What's wrong?" she said, stepping out again and following his gaze.

"Did you get a security camera installed?" he said, pointing.

Emmie thought she could just make out a black box high up in the branches, but she found it hard to focus her eyes. She couldn't imagine how Owen had noticed something so small in the darkness.

"Ummm —" Emmie struggled to remember, "I don't *think* so. Maybe my mom did something?"

Owen cocked his head at the box suspiciously before saying slowly,

"Maybe. I guess that sounds like her. We'll have to ask her tomorrow." He looked back at Emmie. "Hey, drink some water before you go to bed, okay?"

"Now who sounds like her?"

Owen smirked.

"Good night, Emmie."

Emmie closed the door and flipped on the lights, dropping her bag and kicking off her shoes. She made her way to her bedroom, hand trailing along the wall, and sat down heavily on the bed. She flopped back onto the pillows, closing her eyes for a moment before rolling over and reaching for the immergers in the top drawer of her nightstand. She thought she would send Owen an email, maybe browse a few of her news feeds, before she called it a night. She had barely settled her glasses on her nose when Dom stepped out of the shadows at the corner of her room.

"Augh!" Emmie cried, leaping up from the bed.

"Calm down," he said, "We have to talk."

"OMG, Dom!" she said, pressing her hand to her chest, realizing with relief that he was just a projection, "How the hell did you open an unauthorized connection?"

"The same way I always have," said Dom, nonchalant.

She huffed. Dom was always so mysterious about everything. She knew she should have been alarmed by the fact that he could project into her room unauthorized, but ever since she had met him, her mind had always stopped just short of being frightened of him.

"What do you want?" she asked warily.

"Perhaps we could start with a small thank-you for the part I played in your success today?"

Emmie frowned. She supposed she did owe Dom something for all his help.

"Thank you," she said, as graciously as she could manage. Dom nodded.

"And I wonder if I could ask for your help on a problem I have in my own domain."

She pressed a hand to her temple, which had suddenly started to throb. She rolled her head to the side as she regarded him.

"I'm sorry, Dom," she said, "I have a contract with my employer. I can't do outside consulting. Especially for competitors."

"My problem is personal in nature and presents no competitive threat to Augur," said Dom, "No one will find out that you have been helping me unless you choose to tell them yourself."

She chewed her lip. She supposed there was nothing wrong with that.

"What do you need?"

Dom was silent a long time before he said,

"I need you to show me what is on the tablet that Tomo left for you."

Dom pointed behind her, and Emmie turned. There, just under the edge of her bed, in the place it had fallen weeks ago as she fumbled to silence her buzzing smartcom, she could see the small wooden box containing Tomo's tablet. Emmie shook her head in confusion.

"That? But why?"

"I believe it will help me complete the task the Oracle assigned to me."

"You mean in Dulai?" she found herself unable to suppress a giggle at the absurdity, "For some — some alternet game quest?"

"This is what I need from you," said Dom, looking deadly serious.

"Well, I don't know what you heard about this tablet," Emmie said frankly, sitting back down on her bed. The mattress felt extremely comfortable. "But as far as I know, it's just a bunch of ancient religious stuff. I don't think it could have anything to do with your alternet quest."

"I can only find out if you show me," said Dom, his projection stepping closer.

"But —" she yawned, "But I'm only supposed to show it to someone I trust."

"Have I done anything to violate your trust?"

Emmie thought hard, but it seemed difficult to remember

if he had.

"Oh, fine," she said, waving her hand, wishing he would just go away and let her sleep. She reached under her bed and picked up the tablet. "Let's take a look."

She was about to plug the tablet into her smartcom when Dom said hurriedly,

"No. Not here. You should view the contents somewhere secure. Someone could tap into your local network here."

Something in Dom's voice did frighten her this time, and Emmie's head felt momentarily clear.

"You mean someone besides you," she said slowly.

Dom nodded. Emmie felt any icy prickle run down her spine.

"You're freaking me out."

"Please humor me."

Emmie swallowed and closed her eyes.

"Okay. I'm going to bed now, but I'll take a look at this with you tomorrow. At work. That's the most secure place I know."

"Thank you," he said.

"And right after that, I'm going to hire a security consultant. I don't want any more hacking on my smartcom," she said sternly, "From you or anyone else."

"That is probably wise," Dom said, then vanished.

∞

Emmie rolled in to the office late the next morning. She stepped out onto the third floor, where the mood today was celebratory. The sudden drop in the office-wide sleep deficit was fueling a lot of good-natured mischief. She overheard Owen interject a few half-hearted, "Get back to work, people," directives over the public audio channel, but he was universally ignored.

Emmie made her way over to Owen's desk and waved hello. In her pocket, the wooden box containing Tomo's tablet was warm and smooth. She had been turning it over and over in her fingers for the entire drive down from the hills.

"Hey, you," he said, "That was fun last night."

"Yeah," she said, a bit sheepishly, "Maybe a little too much fun."

Owen chuckled.

"Any chance of getting some work done today?" Emmie said, looking doubtfully at the groups of chattering designers gathered around desks and solo engineers not bothering to disguise that they were playing games at their workstations.

"Nope," Owen said definitely.

"I saw on the schedule that the spliner's miraculously unoccupied starting fifteen minutes from now. I booked it. I thought I would slip in for some non-*Atlantis* time."

"Sounds like fun. Want some company?"

"Sure," said Emmie.

There was a chill breeze blowing across the grounds outside, and they hurried along the path to the spliner. Halfway there, they passed Zeke. His nostrils flared, and he brushed by without making eye contact.

"Ugh. That guy," said Owen, looking back at Zeke over his shoulder, "Has he always looked that shady?"

Emmie shrugged. She didn't feel like making fun of Zeke today.

As they approached the enormous, windowless spliner building, Emmie's fingers closed once more around the wooden box in her pocket.

"I didn't tell you, but Tomo left me something in his will."

"Really?" Owen said, impressed, "A story to tell the grandkids."

Emmie blushed slightly. They walked in awkward silence until Owen said,

"So? What did he leave you?"

"It's kind of a long story," she said slowly, "The short version is that it's a manuscript for a book that Tomo's childhood sweetheart — a woman named Midori — was writing. She died before she finished it, and then he tried to finish it, but — well, he died, too."

"And what are you supposed to do with it?"

"I'm not sure. Maybe he wanted me to try to finish it."

"Are you're going to?"

"I don't know. I haven't actually had a chance to take a look at it yet. That's what I want to do in the spliner."

"How will the spliner help? It's a book manuscript, not immersive, right?"

"Well," she didn't know how to tell Owen that she wanted to view the tablet in a secure facility, "It sounds like there are a lot of illustrations that go along with the book, and it's in all sorts of ancient languages, so I thought … some physical space to spread it all out, walk through it, you know, literally."

"What ancient languages are we talking about?"

"Actually," Emmie laughed, "I don't even know."

Owen made a doubtful face.

"It sounds like you might be in a bit over your head."

Emmie palmed the door of the spliner.

"I guess we're about to find out."

∞

Inside the spliner control room, Emmie activated the mechanical subsystems and configured her smartcom as the master controller. She and Owen would now be able to utilize far more sophisticated multi-sensory immersion, and far more physical space, than they could in a projection cylinder or greyroom.

They pulled on their immergers in the dressing room before entering the cavernous extrusion chamber of the spliner.

"So," said Owen, "Where is this manuscript?"

Emmie drew out the small wooden box and slid open the lid. She snapped the coin-sized storage tablet into a port on her belt and skimmed the contents on her visual overlay. She hoped Dom was watching, from wherever he was. This was his big moment, after all.

"Most of the files are two-dimensional scanned images, it looks like," she said, taking in the filesystem interface hovering before her, "Those must be Tomo's illustrations. Oh, and the source texts, too. And here's some stuff in document formats ..."

She opened a secure private channel and shared her visual overlay with Owen.

"Ugh. Zero organization," he grimaced, "How are you supposed to tell what's what?"

"Dunno," said Emmie. She tried to view the files in a relational format, then shook her head. "Wow — really outdated filesystem ... No surprise, I guess, if Midori started working on the manuscript fifty years ago — Oh, hey, look at this."

Emmie pointed out several files with an ACML file extension. Alternet Content Markup Language had emerged alongside the alternet, so these files couldn't be more than fifteen years old.

"Someone was working on this relatively recently," said Owen, "Who do you think added these files? Tomo?"

"No idea. There's not much metadata on the new files. When Tomo's sister gave me the tablet, though, she told me it had been in the possession of a Buddhist priestess in Japan. Maybe the priestess was working on it."

"A Buddhist priestess? You glossed over this bit."

"It's seriously a long story," she laughed.

She launched her browser and opened one of the ACML files, which rendered a network visualization of seven documents in Japanese linked to a number of the scanned images on the tablet.

"Well, that's helpful, at least," said Owen, approaching the network visualization and trying a few different display options until the open files arranged themselves in a ten-foot-high panorama hovering in the open space of the spliner. Emmie walked by his side as they tweaked the sizes and display formats of the different files until they could see everything clearly from the center of the room.

Emmie tapped a long command against her hip with her gloved hand, and beside each of the seven Japanese documents materialized a rapidly-rendered English translation. She read a few sentences aloud to Owen.

"When it was not yet named in the height of heaven,
And yet beneath the earth, does not bear the name
And the Apsu of the ancient birth to them,
And confusion, Tiamat, the mother of them both
That water was mixed with
And the field has not been formed, no marsh was not be observed.
And without God in the time it was called into
And none bore a name, what was the fate of when established

Then I created the gods in the midst of heaven
Was called into being as a Lahmu Lahamu
Age was increased —"
Emmie stopped, bewildered. Owen laughed,
"Lost in translation."

Emmie reread the lines several more times, shaking her head. She ran a quick text search on the few names in the gibberish — Apsu, Tiamat, Lahmu Lahamu — and saw search results that referenced a Babylonian creation myth from a text called the *Enuma Elish*. That simplified things somewhat. She could see that a half-dozen English translations of the *Enuma Elish* were in the public domain. She saved one of the translations to her smartcom and proceeded to examine some of the other files on the tablet.

There were hundreds of files to go through, many of them scanned images paired with Japanese translations. Emmie tried running a few more Japanese-to-English automated translations, but these were even more obscure than the first, and most of them had no discernible keywords to provide clues as to their origin. Attempting a direct translation from the source texts proved even less helpful, as the intricate characters of the ancient documents, many arranged in complex geometrical patterns, defied the character recognition algorithms of every program she tried.

"It would take me forever to sort through all this," said Emmie, overwhelmed, "And I'd need, like, a graduate degree in ancient history to even understand half of it."

Owen, looking over her shoulder, did not contradict her.

Emmie considered the problem.

"I guess I could try to use one of those human translation services. Someone already took the trouble to translate from the ancient languages to Japanese. It's probably a lot easier to get a good translation from modern Japanese to English."

She swiped a series of controls on her visual overlay to run a quick search for human translation recommendations from her social network. A friendly avatar in the domain of the most highly-recommended service she found explained to Emmie that a job this size would take several days to complete. Emmie decided to start the upload anyway and returned to examining the files on the tablet.

Having exhausted for now her patience with the source texts, Emmie turned to examining Tomo's sketches.

"His sister said he wanted to be a manga artist when he was little," she said, flipping through several landscape sketches and portraits, smiling as she recognized Tomo's handwriting on some of them.

"He would have been great at it," Owen said, pointing at a series of sketches of a pastoral village square. The images conveyed the passage of time from morning to evening, as well as the village's passage from thriving enclave to industrial decay. "There's a beautiful narrative quality to these. Surprising realism. Different from most of the manga I've seen. You can see the beginning of the aesthetic he brought to *Kaisei*, then to *Temenos*."

Emmie opened an image that, when viewed at full size, turned out to be a massive round landscape painting more than thirty feet in diameter. Owen called up from the spliner floor a bench-shaped protrusion, which carried them, seated side by side, to the top of the canvas. They examined every inch of the painting as the protrusion lowered them slowly back toward the floor.

An inky blackness pressed in from the outer circumference of the painting, fading gradually into a dark ocean wrapped around an indistinct grey shore. Faint yellow plains and washed-out blue rivers drew the eye toward the center of the canvas, through rolling grass-green hills and shadowy green forests. Owen let out a low whistle.

"And it's all just pen and ink and watercolors," he said, shaking his head in amazement, "This must have taken him forever."

Standing on the floor once more, Emmie pulled the canvas toward her and zoomed in on the heart of the scene. There, in a broad valley, was a dark-haired woman painted with the brightest color and finest detail on the entire canvas. She stood beside a deep blue pool, the source of the many rivers flowing out to the dark edges of the canvas. Behind her grew a gnarled tree bearing pomegranates. In her left hand she held one of the round red fruits and extended it to her companion, a man who looked, Emmie realized with some surprise, like Dom.

Across from the pool stood a second woman, clothed in snowy white, her eyes on the man and woman. Like the first woman, she was surrounded by a halo of color and sharp detail, but in her left hand she held a chalice over which hovered a small flame.

Other figures were arrayed across the landscape, but Emmie remained staring at the three characters at the center of it all.

"What do you think?" Emmie wondered aloud.

"Looks like a Japanese landscape painter's take on Adam and Eve," Owen offered, "It reminds me of some of the illustrations in my Sunday school books from growing up."

"But then who's the woman with the cup?"

"No idea," said Owen, "Angel? Demon? She doesn't look like the serpent, that's for sure."

Emmie's gazed drifted from the center of the painting, and she pointed to the rocky mountain range off to the left.

"Hey, does that sort of remind you of —"

A soft ping accompanied by a pulsing yellow indicator on her visual overlay drew Emmie's attention away from the painting.

"Argh," she growled, "The file upload on the translation failed. Looks like our alternet connection cut out."

She and Owen started trying to reconnect on their smartcoms. Suddenly, behind her, Emmie heard Dom's voice cry out,

"Emmie!"

Emmie wheeled around in surprise and stumbled against Owen.

"What's wrong?" he said, reaching out to steady her.

Over Owen's shoulder, Emmie saw a series of grey ripples extruding from the spliner floor, spreading toward them from the western wall. Owen followed her gaze and asked nervously,

"Are you doing that?"

Emmie tapped her fingers in a rapid sequence on her hip to shut down the extrusion subsystems, but the ripples continued moving toward them.

"No. And I'm not getting any subsystem responses. The local wireless is out, too."

"We'd better get out of here," Owen said, tugging her hand, "I don't want to be standing in here if the mechanics are glitching."

Emmie nodded and quickly shut down her visual display. The painting and the documents that had been hovering before her vanished. She and Owen were now surrounded by nothing but blank grey walls.

The ripples behind them were gaining speed. They hurried to the east wall. Owen palmed the exit door. He waited for a moment, and when it did not open, he palmed it again more slowly, glancing over his shoulder.

"Quickly!" Dom's voice urged from somewhere behind her.

"Here, let me try," said Emmie impatiently, edging Owen to the side and palming the door. When it still did not open, she turned back to face the approaching disturbance.

"We need to call security," she said slowly.

"Right," said Owen, taking a few quick jabs at the air in front of him, "Let me just …" he trailed off, then said slowly, "No radio, either. The building is shielded."

The ripples now reached them, and they both struggled to keep their footing on the shifting surface, which grew steadily more turbulent and was joined by a low mechanical droning sound. Emmie swore and said,

"This is my fault. We're always supposed to have an operator in the control room in case we need a manual override."

"I've never heard of the door palm system breaking down," Owen said, "And, anyway, the doors should open automatically if there's any kind of system failure."

"Agh," Emmie cried out in pain, having tripped over a two-foot wave and fallen to her knees. The same wave knocked Owen onto his backside next to her.

"I guess we'd better stay on the ground in case this gets any rougher," he said, flipping onto his hands and knees with agility.

"Dom!" Emmie called out in a sudden burst of inspiration, "Can you call security? You still have alternet access!"

"Did you find a live channel?" Owen said hopefully.

"I am sorry, Emmie. I cannot," Dom's voice replied.

"Why not?" she cried, "There must be something you can do!"

"Is that security?" said Owen, "Tell them to send someone to the control room."

The treadwheel engine beneath the floor whirred to life, and the floor began to move westward, away from the door. Emmie glanced at Owen in alarm. Owen's tanned face looked strangely pale in the flat ambient light. He seized her hand, and they scrambled over the roiling floor toward the exit.

A broad spike protruded suddenly from the floor between them, knocking Emmie to the ground and separating her from Owen. The floor before her shot up into another extrusion, this one a huge grey tentacle, which quivered in midair before whipping down violently toward her. Emmie slammed her feet against the side of the extrusion just in time to push herself into a trough between two waves. The waves stopped the crashing tentacle inches from her nose.

Over the churning mechanical sounds of the floor came a piercing siren, followed shortly afterwards by pounding and muffled shouting.

"Someone hit the alarm!" Emmie called toward Owen, relieved.

Owen popped suddenly into view from behind another wave, crawling toward her. He looped Emmie's arm around his neck and heaved them both to their feet.

"Come on! Let's get to the door!" he shouted over the noise, seizing her hand and running as best he could from one level patch of floor to the next, heading for the east door.

From the wall to their left, another extrusion shot out just as a wave rolled up under Emmie's feet. She jumped away, but not before the extrusion dealt her a heavy blow to the shoulder and knocked her to the floor.

"Emmie!" cried Owen, kneeling beside her.

"I'm okay, I'm okay," said Emmie, wincing.

Another tentacle rose up before them, this one much larger than the others. Emmie regained her feet, gasping at the pain in her shoulder, just as a wave knocked Owen backwards. She scrambled toward him. He tried to get up, but another wave rolled by and knocked him down again. Emmie worked frantically with her good arm to haul him to his feet, but she could only manage to bring him up to his knees.

"Behind you!" Emmie heard Dom shout.

Emmie turned just in time to see the massive tentacle whipping toward them. There was no time for her to dodge it, and the extrusion crashed into her chest, laying her out flat. Tomo's tablet crumbled from her pulverized immerger belt onto the undulating floor in a shower of glittering emerald ceramic and dull grey storage medium.

Then the deafening mechanical mayhem spun down, and the floor melted back to a level plane, lowering Emmie several feet. The east door slid open, and a dozen people burst into the room. Emmie rolled over and pushed herself up on her hands and knees, curling her injured arm around the agony in her ribs and struggling for breath.

When at last she managed a ragged inhalation, Emmie rocked back onto her heels, and her eyes fell on a crimson stream wending its way slowly across the floor toward her. A wordless scream filled her ears. Before her, Owen lay sprawled on his back, his head soaked in blood.

CHAPTER 12
Lost and Found

Emmie looked up to see Ollie pushing through the curtains around her hospital bed. Ollie dropped her briefcase on the floor and leaned over Emmie, her eyes quickly taking in the livid bruises on her arms and shoulders, her bandaged ribs, palms, and elbows.

"Oh, Emmie," Ollie whispered.

Emmie shifted in an attempt to sit up, then winced and fell back against the pillows.

"I'll be fine," she rasped. She took Ollie's hand and said, "How is Owen? No one here will tell me anything."

Ollie looked away, her eyes glistening. Emmie's face froze in shock, her fingers falling limp. She started shivering and moaned at the stabbing pain that followed. Ollie called for a nurse, who hurried in a moment later. The nurse gave Emmie two pills to swallow and held a cup of water to her mouth. She settled another blanket over her and said,

"Just hit the button if the pain gets worse, honey."

∞

A few hours later, Emmie sat dazed in a wheelchair with a paper bag of pain medications in her lap. Her father pushed her through the front lobby of the hospital while her mother and Ollie walked alongside. Uncle Frank trailed behind, his face a sickly shade of grey.

At the entry doors, Dad gave her a hand, and Emmie rose stiffly to her feet. The five of them walked slowly together to their cars. Ollie, Mom, Dad, and Uncle Frank had all driven to the hospital separately when they had received the call. Mom and Ollie settled Emmie gently into the front seat of Dad's car.

"We'll be right behind you."

Dad sat down heavily in the driver's seat, ashen-faced. He hit the button to turn on the car but did not put it into gear. He pressed the palms of his shaking hands together and bowed his head.

"Are you okay to drive?" said Emmie.

"I just need a minute," he said, his voice breaking.

Emmie put her hand on his knee, her eyes gleaming, her voice thick with emotion.

"I'm so sorry, Dad."

He grabbed her hand, loosening his grip when she winced.

"What do you have to be sorry about? I'm just thankful you weren't more badly hurt. And I'm furious," he said, the muscles in his neck growing taut with the effort to remain calm, "Some idiot made a terrible mistake with that machine. And now you — And Owen …"

His jaw worked, and he stared into the rapidly darkening parking lot. Ollie beeped her car horn softly, and Dad waved at her and put the car in reverse.

"You don't have anything to be sorry about, Em."

As the car climbed the winding road up into the hills, Emmie drifted off into a dreamless sleep.

∞

She awoke in her bed and heard the sounds of her family shuffling around in the kitchen. The sweet smell of frying onions drifted through her bedroom, and she started to sit up, then gave a small, sharp cry. Ollie appeared at the bedside instantly and leaned over her.

"What's the matter? Are you okay?"

"Yeah," she gasped, trying not to breathe, "It hurts, though."

"Take it easy. Let me get you another dose of those painkillers."

Ollie came back with a glass of water and a couple of white pills, which Emmie swallowed.

"What time is it?" Emmie said hoarsely.

"Time for you to eat," Ollie said, forcing a smile, "You've been asleep for," she glanced at her wristwatch, "Almost fourteen hours."

Emmie's head swam. There was a flash of red in her mind's eye, but she pushed it away, inhaling sharply through her nose to clear her head. She let out a small cry at the pain in her ribs.

"Remember what the doctor said," said Ollie, sitting down on the edge of the bed and pressing her hand to Emmie's arm, "Try not to breathe too deeply."

"Uncle Frank came by again this morning," Ollie continued, "Nanna and Grandpa were here too. They told us to call as soon as you're up."

"I think I need a little quiet time before all that starts," said Emmie, closing her eyes.

"Mom cooked breakfast. Do you want me to bring you some food?"

"I'd rather get up. Can you give me some help?"

Ollie hesitated.

"Come on," said Emmie, "If you don't, you know I'm going to do it myself."

Ollie smiled a little and shook her head. She put her arm gently behind Emmie's shoulders, raising her into a sitting position. Emmie swung her legs over the edge of the bed, and Ollie helped lift her to her feet.

"Okay," Emmie said, grabbing the nightstand to steady herself and trying not to breathe, "Okay. It's not so bad once I'm up." Ollie accompanied her down the hall and to the sofa in the living room, where she helped her sit down.

Dad sat on the ottoman rubbing Emmie's feet while Mom talked quietly with Ollie in the kitchen. A few minutes later, they returned with four plates. Everyone stared at the omelettes and toast getting cold on the coffee table before them. The eggs looked grey to Emmie. Everything looked grey. She felt nauseated.

Mom and Ollie kept glancing at each other, until at last Emmie said,

"Okay. What's going on?"

Mom stood up and moved next to Emmie on the sofa.

"We got a call from Ty Monaghan this morning, Emmie. He told us that what happened to you and Owen in the spliner wasn't an accident."

Emmie shuddered, then grimaced at the pain it caused.

"How do they know?" she whispered.

"Your CTO, Ahmet, spent all night poring over system logs with the Augur IT security team to figure out the source of the malfunction and to make sure there were no other security breaches. Ty told me that so far they've found only one anomaly, but it's definitely the cause of the accident.

"From what Ahmet's put together so far, someone installed an unauthorized server daemon on each of the Augur network servers some time in the last week. The daemon was programmed to activate a trojan in any part of the network where someone connected an external device containing a specific combination of characters in the file contents. Ahmet says the program mimics a sophisticated information security technique that Augur uses itself, but the trigger in this case seems totally random. They're not even sure what you might have done to trigger it, since the virus wiped out the system logs in the entire spliner subnetwork. They're worried the program might have been part of an attempt to wipe out Augur's domain content library.

"While the campus was on lockdown, one of your coworkers tried to leave through a back gate. A security guard forcibly detained him. The police came to investigate the accident, and apparently when they interviewed him he wouldn't speak to them without a lawyer."

"Who?" said Emmie, her face pale, "Who was it?"

"A young man named Zeke Eckerd. Do you know him?"

Emmie put a hand to her forehead and leaned back against the sofa. She remembered brushing past Zeke on the way to the spliner. Owen had said — at the thought of Owen, her stomach lurched.

"Zeke?" she whispered, "I don't believe it."

Mom and Ollie exchanged another look. Mom reached out to touch her knee, saying gently,

"The police need to come by to interview you about what happened, as soon as possible. As soon as you're able to receive visitors."

"Well, they can wait," said Dad, frowning, "She's in no condition to be talking to anyone right now."

"I know it's hard, but it'll be better to get it over with while the memory's still fresh," Mom said gently, "Anything you remember might be critical."

Emmie closed her eyes and nodded. Her father squeezed her foot.

"Take as much time as you need, love."

"I need to be alone," Emmie whispered, "Sorry. I don't want you to leave. I just need to be alone for a little while. Ollie, can you help me back to bed?"

∞

Ollie propped Emmie up on the pillows and spread the blankets back over her. She was turning to leave when Emmie said,

"Ollie, where are the clothes and other stuff I was wearing when they took me to the hospital?"

"Oh. Mom brought them. Do you need them?"

"Yeah. Would you mind?"

Ollie went into the hall and came back with a plastic bag.

"Thanks," said Emmie, "That's all. Can you close the door?"

Ollie left the room. Emmie emptied the contents of the bag onto her lap. Her clothes and gear were inside, along with her smartcom. One knee of the jeans she had been wearing over her immerger leggings was badly scuffed, and the other was torn. There was a smear of dried blood on the sleeve of her shirt. From her shirt pocket, she withdrew a handful of splinters, all that remained of the wooden box that had housed Tomo's tablet. Her smartcom, in its virtually indestructible titanium case, appeared unharmed.

She pulled out her immerger belt. Its small processor unit was crushed, and only a fragment of the green tablet remained jammed into its port. She tried to loosen it with her fingernail, but the remainder of the ceramic coating and the solid-state storage medium crumbled into her lap.

"Damn," she muttered, her eyes blurring.

She reached gingerly for the spare immerger headset and belt in the drawer of her bedside table, fastening the belt very loosely around her waist before slipping on the headset. She bit her lip, then whispered,

"Dom? Are you there?"

After a long silence, Emmie leaned back against the headboard. She tried to force herself to take slow, shallow breaths, but these eventually gave way to heaving sobs.

∞

Emmie drifted through the next two weeks in a haze of painkillers and grief. Christmas and New Year's Day came and went. The police came and went twice. Her parents came and went many times.

Ollie stayed in the guest room, answering calls from friends and family, arranging the flowers and cards on the table, trying to tempt Emmie's appetite with ever more ambitious culinary endeavors. Uncle Frank stopped by frequently with his boys, sitting by Emmie's bedside and entertaining her as best he could with anecdotes about the latest goings-on at the Lab.

Owen's family arrived to make arrangements for the funeral. They had been staying with her parents for three days when Ollie returned to Emmie's house after work and sat down at her bedside.

"Emmie," she said gently, "Come with me to Mom and Dad's. You know the Cyruses want to meet you."

Emmie covered her eyes with her hand, her face contorting with grief.

"I can't," she said hoarsely, "I can't. How can I look them in the face? It's my fault he's dead."

"Emmie," Ollie said, climbing onto the bed beside her sister and wrapping one arm around her shoulders, pulling her close, "Don't do this. Be strong. They've come to say goodbye to him, and you can help them. He loved you, and this place, and all the work you did together. You can show all of that to them."

Emmie started to sob, and Ollie held her, soothed her, and waited. When at last all the tears were spent, Ollie said,

"You owe this to Owen."

So Emmie went with Ollie to her parents' house. They stood above the entryway, arm in arm, and Ollie helped Emmie slowly down the stairs into the living room, where Owen's family sat quietly arranged on the big sofa. Owen's mother, Gracie, a small woman with smoothly-coiffed blonde hair, perfect makeup, and a neatly-pressed but faded cotton blouse, saw Emmie first and rushed forward to embrace her, missing Emmie's pained wince, kissing her on both cheeks. She smelled like roses.

"Oh, honey," said Gracie, brushing away Emmie's tears, then her own, "I'm so glad to meet you at last."

Owen's sister, Marybeth, a slim, elegantly-dressed young woman whose glossy dark hair stood in stark contrast to her pale face and red-rimmed eyes, followed close behind her mother. Marybeth hugged Emmie more carefully, avoiding the injured shoulder, and said, with one hand pressed lightly to Emmie's arm,

"I'm sorry we didn't meet before now. Owen told me so much about you."

Behind Marybeth stood Owen's brother, Wendell, and father, Howard. Emmie's eyes lingered on Wendell, who was a mirror image of Owen, before looking down, fresh tears running down her face. Wendell shook Emmie's hand wordlessly, as did his father, Howard.

A few days later, the Bridges and the Cyruses, along with a crowd of Owen's friends from Cal and Augur, gathered for the funeral in Redwood Regional Park, where Owen and Emmie had spent so many sunny days together. Emmie wept in her father's arms as a Baptist minister performed the service. Marybeth delivered the eulogy, and Owen's mother scattered her son's ashes over the roots of the trees with shaking hands, her tears mixing with the dust.

∞

In the weeks that followed, Mom emailed Emmie updates about the legal proceedings. Emmie deleted these unread, but in late February Mom came in person to deliver the news that Zeke had pled guilty to charges of aggravated battery and second degree murder. The judge had sentenced him to fifteen years to life in prison. This seemed to bring her mother some small measure of satisfaction. Emmie felt nothing but numbness.

One morning, a few weeks after Ollie had moved out of the guest room and back to her apartment in Palo Alto, Emmie woke early, pressed a hand to her ribs, and rose tentatively from bed, leaving her bottle of painkillers untouched on the bedside table. She showered, dressed, and walked out her front door, unaccompanied for the first time since she returned from the hospital.

She climbed into her car and drove slowly down into the flats, back to Augur.

At seven o'clock in the morning, she knocked on Ty's office door, and he swiveled around in his desk chair.

"Emmie!" he said, standing, "How are you? I wasn't expecting you in. Especially on a Saturday."

He came over and pulled out a chair for her.

"Coffee?"

She shook her head, and Ty walked back around to the other side of his desk.

"I'm so sorry about everything that happened. I never imagined ..." he shook his head. Through her numbness, Emmie felt a stirring of something, perhaps of anger. If it hadn't been for Ty, perhaps Zeke would never — She wouldn't finish the thought.

They sat in silence for a while, until at last Ty said,

"Did you stop by to talk about something?"

"Yes," Emmie said, suddenly remembering why she had come, "I'm quitting."

Ty inhaled loudly through his nose and pressed his fingertips together, contemplating his grand view of the San Francisco Bay, now blanketed in morning fog.

"I was afraid you might be feeling this way," he said, leveling a sympathetic gaze at her, "And I'd understand if you decided to leave.

"But, Emmie, we need you here. Think things over. We could give you a paid leave of absence — or as much time as you need."

Emmie rubbed her forehead and looked past him toward

the bridges crossing the Bay.

"No," she said distantly, "No, I don't think so. I won't be back."

Ty nodded slowly, and Emmie did not meet his eyes as he said,

"Take care of yourself, Emmie."

∞

Emmie took the stairs down to the creative team's offices, where the floor was empty and the public channel was quiet. The motion-activated lights came on as she walked along the perimeter of the floor toward Tomo's office. She pulled up the access codes Ty had sent to her smartcom weeks ago and pushed open the door.

The air inside the office was fresh with the scent of thriving plants. Emmie stood at the center of the room, blinking back tears, then took a deep breath and made her way to the low chair standing just where Tomo had left it. She brushed her fingers along the seat back before moving on toward the heavy Japanese cabinet, where Tomo's bonsai tree still stood. Delicate red buds were emerging on the tiny, twisting branches, and she touched them one by one with her fingertips.

Her eyes caught a glimpse of something glittering through the crown of dark green leaves. She felt a surge of adrenaline, a clearing in her head. She leaned down until her eyes were level with the base of the tree. There, half-buried beneath the mossy soil, was a button-sized disc, jewel-green.

Heart pounding, Emmie reached out to brush the soil from the tablet's hiding place.

"Wait."

Emmie jerked back her hand and spun around to find Dom standing by the window. Her alarm changed quickly to fury. She stepped toward him, trembling, balling her fists as if to strike him.

"You," she growled, "I don't ever want to see you again. Do you understand me? Never again."

"You must listen to me, Emmie. As soon as you have that tablet in your possession again, your life will be in danger."

"What do you care?" she said, her voice thick with accusation, "You had no problem letting me walk into a trap before. You just stood by, you bastard."

"I am truly sorry," Dom said softly, "If there was anything I could have done —"

"You could have told someone!" Emmie cried.

"There was no way for me to warn anyone but you."

"You expect me to believe that?" she said angrily, "After you've hacked into every network, every private channel at Augur to talk to me? No. You let someone die just to cover your worthless hacker ass."

"Emmie, I know you have no reason to believe me, but I swear to you, if there was anything I could have done to save Owen, anything at all, I would have done it."

Emmie looked at him, wanting to hate him almost as much as she wanted to believe him.

"None of that matters now — what you could have done, what I could have done," she hissed. She reached out toward the bonsai tree once more and picked up the tablet. She felt the cold ceramic warming slowly in her palm. Her mind felt sharp, for the first time in weeks, as she said,

"What I need to know is why. *Why* did this happen?"

CHAPTER 13
On the Road

Emmie decided she had better not mention where she was headed, so she told her parents she was going to spend some time in Yosemite. Ollie wanted to come and keep her company, but Emmie said she needed to be alone.

Emmie left early to avoid the morning traffic, and when she slipped the car into autopilot on the long, open stretch of 580 East, it was barely eight o'clock. She knew that Dom was there, somewhere, somehow, watching, but she did not want to talk to him. She slipped on a headset, immersing herself in *Temenos* and wandering the streets of *Athenai* in an anonymous avatar. The release rumor had gone out just as she had planned, and the public channels were now buzzing, just as she had hoped. She remembered Owen's skepticism and felt a lump rise in her throat. However skeptical he might have been at first, he had backed her up all the way, to the end.

The tears in her eyes interfered with her visual overlay, and she pushed back her headset, pressing her forehead to the cool glass of the car window. Mile after mile of landscape slipped by: the rolling hills with their white forests of wind turbines; the flat expanse of the Central Valley with its blossoming orchards of almonds, cherries, and apricots; the open fields of green and gold; the broad blue irrigation canals.

The car turned south on I-5, passing ever more arid agricultural land and exits to ever more nondescript towns. When the navigation system announced the approaching Coalinga exit, Emmie withdrew from *Temenos* and took the wheel again. She slowed to turn off at exit 325 and continued onto a country road bordered on both sides by dusty farmland. A few miles later, she passed a large hospital facility and slowed to turn through the front entrance of Pleasant Valley State Prison.

She pulled to a stop in the visitor parking lot and stored her immerger belt, smartcom, and headset in the glove compartment. As much as she wanted to ignore Dom completely, she kept her earbuds, just in case he wanted to say something. She reached for the door handle, but before she could bring herself to step out, she found herself whispering,

"I feel the same way now as I did when Tomo died. Emptiness. Not sadness, not fear. Not even anger."

"It will be better this way," came Dom's voice, as she had known it would, as, she realized, she had hoped it would, "Anger will not help you understand."

She took a deep breath. Despite his infuriatingly opaque motives, despite his unbelievable intrusion into her life, despite his suspicious involvement in the events of the past several months, nonetheless Dom's presence comforted her in a way that no one else's had since Owen died.

She steeled herself, climbing from the car to join a stream of people walking toward the processing center. She filled out the requisite visitor pass and waited for her turn to go through the full-body scanner. On the other side, she retrieved her coat, shoes, and bag.

She found her way to the room indicated on her pass and showed it at the door to the guard, who waved her through. Inside the bare, brightly-lit room, men, women, and children sat alone or in groups around small tables, some speaking quietly to prisoners in faded jeans and blue chambray shirts, others simply waiting. She found an empty table and sat down.

A few minutes later, Zeke entered through the double doors at the far side of the room. His eyes fell on Emmie, and she felt her entire body grow tense as he approached and sank into the chair across from her. He looked skinny and pale and so very young in his shapeless blue prison uniform and short-cropped hair.

"I'm surprised you wanted to see me," he said.

Emmie searched for words and found that all she could say was,

"Tell me why you did it."

Zeke pressed the tips of his long white fingers to his forehead, closing his eyes.

"I don't expect you to believe me, but I never meant to hurt anybody."

Emmie felt no pity for Zeke now — only a cold, hard knot in the pit of her stomach.

"What *did* you mean to do, then?" she said, "What were you thinking?"

Zeke opened his eyes to meet hers. His eyelids were raw and red beneath pale lashes. Across one cheek she saw a scattering of blonde stubble that his razor had missed.

"I realized as soon as Ty made you Creative Director that he had just been using me to keep the board happy. He wanted you all along. Just like Tomo.

"So I was angry. I wanted you to know what that felt like. To have all your work just disappear without anyone ever seeing it.

"I thought that I was planting an armageddon virus, that it would corrupt the content library, spread to the backup data centers, a complete wipe. But — But I didn't know what that code was going to do to the spliner. I swear I didn't."

Emmie shook her head in disbelief.

"You idiot. You couldn't even bother to take a look under the hood? Who told you it was an armageddon virus?"

"My —" Zeke's voice shrank almost to a whisper, "My father gave me the code."

"Your father?" Emmie said, confused.

Zeke's pale face managed to turn even paler. He swallowed, his eyes flicking nervously from side to side before he said,

"Have you heard of the Church of the True Cross?"

Emmie shook her head.

"It's a fundamentalist church," said Zeke, "A cult, maybe. I'm not sure there's a difference. Anyway, they believe that an apocalypse is coming, that God is going to punish the world for its sins. Pretty run-of-the-mill fundamentalist stuff, I guess.

"The church hates the alternet. Well, at least they hate pretty much everything that people use it for. Video games. Sensory immersion. 'Tuning out,' that's what they call it. They think it's this pervasive force of evil leading people away from the path to salvation.

"The Church is one of the biggest funders of the alternet regulation lobby. They know they can't stamp out the alternet entirely, at least not all at once, so for now they'll settle for doing what they helped to do to the internet and television and radio over the last several decades. But ... government works pretty slowly."

Emmie tried to understand what he was implying.

"Are you saying they're involved in cyberterrorism?" she said slowly.

Zeke raised an eyebrow meaningfully.

"Whoa," said Emmie, "So ... what does that have to do with your dad?"

Zeke's gaze turned inward as he said,

"My father is a high-ranking member of the church. A Steward of the True Cross. He heads up a church ministry called Youth for Truth, to keep young people away from all the corrupting influences of mainstream society. Including the alternet."

Emmie gave a humorless laugh.

"How did you end up being a hot-shot domain designer with a father like that?"

"I never wanted anything to do with him," Zeke said bitterly, "I left as soon as I figured out how to support myself.

"But my dad kept tabs on me. I guess I didn't make it that hard. I didn't change my name or anything. My mom did. She disappeared a long time ago."

Zeke heaved a sigh.

"I should have tried harder to stay away from him. A little over a year ago, he just showed up. He was starting a new church in Oakland, and he came to see me.

"I ... I was lonely. I started talking to him about my life, about how things at work were going. I was really unhappy. And jealous. My dad saw that. He started trying to convince me that God was giving me a sign, showing me that Augur was evil. He said God wanted me to bring about his plan by taking down *Temenos*.

"I didn't believe him any more than I had when I was a kid, but he gave me the code anyway. He said I would realize soon enough that he was telling the truth. He said he knew that I would do the right thing.

"And when Ty didn't pick my backup concept — I just didn't think. I was so angry ..."

He looked away, and Emmie pressed a hand to her forehead, feeling dizzy as she said,

"But you didn't tell this to anyone? Your lawyer? The judge?"

"It doesn't matter," said Zeke, unfocused eyes staring off into space, "I planted the code. I'm responsible for what happened."

"But you weren't working alone," Emmie insisted, unable to understand his detachment, "Why did you just plead guilty?"

Zeke shifted uncomfortably on the hard plastic seat attached at a fixed angle to the table.

"I'm safer in here."

The way Zeke said that made Emmie feel sick.

"Safer from what?" she whispered.

After a long silence, Emmie reached slowly across the table and touched his hand. It was ice cold.

"Zeke," she said, her voice low, "What the hell is going on?"

At last his eyes turned to meet hers. He swallowed and said,

"Emmie. I never meant to hurt you or Owen. I've had a lot of time to think about what I did, and I ... I remember telling my father a lot of things. About how close you and Tomo were. And I remember something he said. That you and Tomo were two of the biggest threats to the church, and that it was the will of God that you be stopped."

Emmie pulled back her hand, and a red haze crept in around the edges of her vision.

"Are you saying your father had something to do with Tomo's death?"

"I — I don't know. But my father knew what would happen when I planted that code in the spliner. Owen's death was no accident. Maybe Tomo's wasn't, either."

∞

Emmie couldn't remember how she returned to her car, but now she was throwing it into reverse, peeling out of the parking lot, narrowly missing a barrier fence on her way back to the freeway.

"Careful," Dom said softly, his projection materializing beside her. Emmie jumped, then switched the car into autopilot with a shaking hand. She focused on the horizon as the dusty expanse of the Central Valley rushed by, forcing the swirl of confusion in her mind to resolve into a single desperate thought.

"This can't be true," she muttered, launching her anonymous proxy internet browser. A moment later, she was grappling with the Oakland PD's website, an archaic internet interface typical of government services. She read through a poorly-organized web page explaining the process for requesting public records. She drafted a request for the accident report of Tomo's death using a template produced by a quick alternet search. After she submitted it, a message explained that an automated review process was checking confidentiality restrictions on the information she had requested. A moment later, the report popped up.

She examined the document. *Name of deceased: Tomo Yoshimoto. Location of incident: Webster and 8th Street, Oakland, CA.* She skimmed past the name of the ambulance company and other extraneous details. A note referenced two attached witness statements.

The first was from a man named William Chen, a short statement that explained he had been walking by when another man at the scene asked him to call 911. Chen stated that Tomo had appeared unconscious from the time he had called until the time the ambulance had arrived.

The second statement, which closely matched the first, belonged to a man named Amos Eckerd. She ran an alternet search, turning up several photos of a tall, handsome man preaching, standing in prayer circles, building houses in Third World countries. The resemblance to Zeke was unmistakable.

"Damn," she said, "That's him."

She massaged her eyes for a minute, then flipped on a visual overlay. A few alternet searches on "Stewards" and "Stewards of the True Cross" turned up surprisingly little: mostly references to legends about the physical remnants of the cross upon which Jesus Christ was crucified, and some internet websites and alternet domains that made incidental references containing similar phrases.

Emmie closed the useless search results and closed her eyes.

"I need help," she whispered.

Her eyes flickered open.

"Yeah. I need help."

∞

Emmie logged on to *Temenos* and teleported directly to the lobby of the Founders Club. The uniformed receptionist behind the desk smiled politely.

"How may I help you today, Anonymous Member?"

"I'd like to check out a secure meeting room," said Emmie.

"Certainly. Just a moment."

After her identity verification was complete, a message popped up on Emmie's overlay containing a link to an encrypted subdomain. She followed the link and found herself in an elegant gazebo surrounded by a vast English garden. A warm summer breeze carried a carefully engineered scent of flowers across the neatly trimmed lawn. Emmie inhaled appreciatively. The extravagant quality of even the most prosaic services was one of the perks of Club membership.

She realized after a moment that Dom was standing behind her, and she turned around to face him, shaking her head as she said,

"How do you do that? It's impossible to hack your way into an encrypted subdomain on *Temenos*."

Dom's face was unreadable as he sank into the cushioned seat of the white wicker chair across from her.

"What are you planning to do?" he asked. Emmie leaned against a column of the gazebo and dictated,

"Member offers temens, reputation, or favor in exchange for information on religious organization called Church of the True Cross. Mutual identity verification required."

With a few keystrokes, she broadcast the request to all Club members, then trotted down the steps of the gazebo to contemplate the calming scenery.

A few minutes later, several responses appeared on her

visual overlay. She sent polite, if perfunctory, rejections to all but the top three responses as ranked by her personal trust algorithm. After skimming the recommendations for each candidate, she finally settled on the one unnamed identity whose long list of trust network recommendations included those of several prominent Club members, including Tomo.

She initiated an automated negotiation to establish the minimum profile information required by this identity as a prerequisite to meeting in the secure transaction space. When the negotiation concluded, Emmie quickly scanned the proposed exchange and approved it with a wave of her hand. A moment later, the profile of the other party appeared on her screen.

> *Identity: Falsens.*
> *Reputation in your professional network:*
>   *High: Private alternet security*
>   *High: Corporate alternet security*
>   *High: Electronic surveillance*
>   *High: Electronic counter-surveillance*
>   *High: Cyberterrorism*
>   *High: Counter-cyberterrorism.*

The reputation listing went on and on, and Emmie stopped reading long before she reached the end to punch the "Enter meeting" prompt hovering below the profile.

A moment later, a squat avatar of indeterminate gender, race, and age appeared at the foot of the gazebo. Emmie raised an eyebrow.

"I guess your profile's not kidding about the security bit."

Falsens responded in an electronically modulated voice that morphed smoothly from male to female, adult to child, and back again over the course of a few sentences.

"Avatars give away a lot. Yours puts you at ninety percent probability female, eighty-four percent probability technology industry, seventy-eight percent probability American, etcetera. Most people don't think about it until it's too late."

Emmie sucked her teeth. Falsens might have her pegged for a techie American female, but she could already tell that she was dealing with a condescending, subtly misogynistic geek of the male persuasion. She pushed on through her irritation.

"So you know something about the Church of the True Cross?"

"That is why I responded."

"What would you like in exchange for the information?"

"Two thousand temens. Subsequent consultations will be twelve hundred."

Emmie laughed in surprise at his presumption.

"You're expecting repeat business?"

"Based on my knowledge of the Church of the True Cross, I imagine you have a specific security concern in mind. Whatever those concerns may be, I am sure you will find my other services useful. Is the price acceptable?"

A payment authorization prompt appeared on her visual overlay, and Emmie let out a low whistle. She had never been very thrifty, but this was a pretty big sum to drop just for some information.

"Fabulous," she said dryly, deciding this was her best option. She tapped her authorization for the charge. "So what can you tell me?"

"The Church of the True Cross is a regional branch of a larger organization funded by a number of religious fundamentalist denominations around the world. The umbrella organization goes by many names, but members of the central leadership are usually referred to as Stewards. The congregations directed by the Stewards have been implicated over the past several decades in a number of sophisticated cyberterrorism attacks against key communication infrastructure hubs. A number of private corporations affected by the attacks have taken legal action against different denominations related to the Stewards, but all such suits have settled out of court."

Emmie chewed her lip as she processed this information, then asked,

"Were the server farm wipe-outs that Augur experienced last year caused by the Stewards?"

"Multiple attacks on alternet domains last year, including the attack you're referencing, were attributed to the Stewards by private security analysts."

"What about killings? Assassinations? Have they been implicated in anything like that?"

"Not according to any information I have seen. Although the organization's motives for cyberterrorism are unclear, the effects of these attacks have tended toward destruction of hardware, software, and data, not human life. Why do you ask?"

Emmie took a deep breath.

"There was a hardware malfunction in the main spliner belonging to my employer, Augur, this past December. I was injured in the accident, and my — my colleague, Owen Cyrus, was killed. Another colleague of mine, Zeke Eckerd, was convicted of planting the trojan that caused the accident. I just visited Zeke in prison, and he told me that his father, a man named Amos Eckerd, provided the software that caused the malfunction. He said his father works for The Church of the True Cross. He also said his title, or something, is Steward."

"Do you believe this man, Amos Eckerd, was attempting to assassinate you? Or Owen Cyrus?"

"I don't know. But this man may have been involved in another death. My former boss, Tomo Yoshimoto."

"Do you have any evidence implicating Amos Eckerd?"

"Only circumstantial. He gave a witness statement to the police who showed up when Tomo collapsed on the street."

"And are you concerned for your own safety?"

The question caught her off guard. She had been so absorbed with what had happened to Owen and Tomo that she had not fully considered what this might mean for her.

"I don't know," she said slowly, "Maybe. Should I be?"

"I don't have enough information to advise you at this point. However, I would be more than happy to investigate the matter further for you, as well as advise you on safety precautions. Would you like to see a proposal for these services?"

Curious, but unsure what she might be getting herself into, Emmie said,

"I guess so."

"Please hold."

A moment later, an interactive presentation appeared before Emmie and responded to her touch as she navigated through a proposed list of services interspersed with a collection of well-produced short videos describing different case studies and highlighting various anonymous and signed testimonials.

"And pricing?" asked Emmie.

"Five hundred temens per day for my 24-hour personal security concierge. Ten percent discount for subscriptions lasting more than three months. Twelve hundred temens per consultation, investigation travel and meal expenses extra, as required. All charges subject to client approval at the time of request."

Emmie flipped through the proposal presentation a second time.

"Well," she said, taking a leap of faith in her trust algorithm, "My network says you're good."

"The best," said Falsens.

"All right. Let's do it."

∞

Having approved Falsens' proposal and installed the personal security concierge client on her smartcom, Emmie logged out of *Temenos*. Her car was still speeding north on I-80, and the late afternoon sun streamed in through the driver's side window. She turned up the tint on the car windows and turned down the temperature of her immerger clothing to help cool herself off. Her heart was beating unusually fast.

"Security alert," a calming simulation of a female voice spoke into her earbuds. A flashing indicator on her visual overlay indicated that this message came from her personal security concierge.

"What's wrong?" said Emmie, frowning.

"Preliminary security screening of your current location indicates a high probability that the Tesla Courant, license plate 5-SOS-101, currently two tenths of a mile behind you, has been following you since the Los Banos onramp."

"Are you kidding?"

"This is what your preliminary environment security

screening indicates."

Emmie massaged her temples, exasperated.

"Well, do you know who's in the car?"

"No. Tinted glass prevents facial recognition by our roadside security monitors."

"What should I do?"

"Please request a consultation for additional recommendations."

Emmie craned her neck to look out her back window, squinting at the cars in the distance until she realized she would not recognize a Tesla Courant even if it pulled up beside her. After a pause, the concierge prompted helpfully,

"Would you like to initiate a consultation?"

"Uh," Emmie turned around to face the front again, "Sure. Yes."

A moment later, Falsens' avatar appeared in a projection.

"Hello, Miss Bridges. How may I help you?"

"Your concierge says someone is following me. What should I do about that?"

"I would suggest maintaining your present course until I can send a counter-surveillance operative to guide you through evasive maneuvers."

Emmie gaped at Falsens.

"You can do that?"

"Yes. Perhaps you did not have a chance to review my complete list of available services." Falsens' interactive proposal appeared before Emmie again. "If you navigate to section —"

"No, no. That's okay. I want to go ahead with it."

"Certainly. All I need is your authorization."

An interface popped up on Emmie's visual overlay displaying a detailed tally of the charges incurred so far, as well as the additional charges for the latest consult and proposed counter-surveillance operation. Emmie inhaled sharply, then tapped the approval button.

"Thank you," Falsens said promptly, disappearing from view.

Emmie's stomach twisted as she imagined the cold blue eyes she had glimpsed in the alternet search results, watching her through the dark glass of one of the cars behind her. She pulled her feet up onto the car seat, hugging her knees to her chest, watching the status indicator on her visual overlay count down the seconds to the estimated rendezvous time with the counter-surveillance operative.

∞

The freeway traffic had slowed to a dead stop somewhere outside Livermore, still miles from Oakland, when the crisp voice of the security concierge said,

"Please prepare for rendezvous."

Emmie looked out at the sea of cars surrounding her, then flipped open a map on her visual overlay to check her current location and the cause of the standstill: a rare vehicle accident that had closed all four lanes of traffic.

"Where?" she said anxiously, "We're miles from the next exit."

A sudden clamor of car horns caused Emmie to flick off her visual overlay. In the rearview monitor on her dashboard, she saw a small dust cloud approaching. She turned quickly in her seat to watch through the window as a small grey sedan with opaque black windows raced up the shoulder, coming to a stop just across from her.

The car's driver's side door popped open, and a small man

with dark sunglasses and a grey fedora sprang out, weaving swiftly through the sea of parked vehicles. He tapped the glass on her window, and she rolled it down a few inches.

"Emmie Bridges?"

Emmie peered at the man curiously. She thought she recognized that voice.

"Counter-surveillance operative identity confirmed," said the calm voice of the security concierge, "Please follow operative instructions for secure vehicle transfer."

"Um —" Emmie peered up at the man. She was having second thoughts about this operation.

"Quickly," said the man, pointing at Emmie's dashboard.

Emmie looked down at the rearview monitor and felt a surge of adrenaline as she recognized the tall, fair-haired figure of Amos Eckerd running up the center of the freeway toward her car. She gasped and fumbled with the manual handle to open her door, nearly clobbering the man in the dark sunglasses, who stepped aside just in time. He took Emmie's hand and pulled her quickly to her feet.

"Hurry," he said, pointing toward his car but keeping his eyes on Amos. Emmie hurried, waving nervously at drivers as she squeezed between car bumpers. The grey sedan's passenger door swung open to admit her and quickly closed behind. She looked back and stopped breathing as she watched the man with the dark sunglasses backing slowly toward her, pointing what appeared to be a silver pen at Amos, who had stopped dead in his tracks, mere yards from Emmie's car, and now stood with his hands above his head, his face red with exertion.

The driver door of the grey sedan swung open to admit the little man, and in one smooth motion he slid into the seat, seized the wheel, and floored the accelerator. They raced off along the shoulder, provoking a cacophony of honks from the disgruntled traffic jam.

∞

"Oh my god. Oh my god," Emmie hyperventilated, staring out the rear window as the figure of Amos Eckerd receded into the distance.

"Don't worry," said the man in the dark sunglasses, steering neatly around a biker who seemed to share his ideas about the proper use of the freeway shoulder, "I think we have at least a two-minute lead on him."

A moment later, the man turned off the freeway exit ramp and pulled up to an empty port at a busy recharging station. A large white SUV pulled up at the port beside them, and the man turned to Emmie and said,

"Now we're going to change vehicles. When your door opens, just step calmly into the SUV."

Emmie nodded, heart pounding. Her door opened, and she climbed out of the car, as did her driver. Simultaneously, the doors of the white SUV opened, and Emmie stopped to stare as out stepped a small man in a fedora and dark glasses accompanied by a diminutive young woman with cobalt blue highlights in her bone-straight brunette hair.

"Come on," said her driver, ushering her past their doppelgängers and into the rear passenger door of the SUV. The door shut behind her, and Emmie looked out the window to watch the grey sedan pull out of the charging port and take off toward the freeway at speed. A few minutes later, her driver hopped in behind the wheel of the SUV, pulled out of the charging station at a leisurely speed, and headed in the opposite direction.

When her breathing at last returned to normal, Emmie turned toward her driver.

"Where are we going?"

"I'm taking you to a safe house. It's —" he glanced at a visual overlay Emmie could not see, "about an hour away. We have to take the long way to get around the accident we planted."

Emmie opened her mouth, uncertain what to say to this. At last, she said,

"Thank you. I don't know what —"

She blinked, then peered closely at the man's profile.

"You!" she exclaimed, "You're — No, you can't be … Na — Na —"

"Naoto Kimura," he said, smiling at her, "I guess my disguise isn't quite as good as I thought."

He removed his sunglasses, fedora, and a convincing wig of short-cropped black hair, revealing the shining bald head Emmie remembered from Tomo's memorial service. She shook her head, not quite believing her eyes.

"But — You were *old*."

He winked at her and stooped his shoulders subtly, creasing his face in some way that seemed to age him twenty years. He said, now with the precise, Japanese-accented English she remembered,

"Surely in your line of work you have learned that looks can be deceiving."

Before she could decide what to think of that, the cool voice of Emmie's security concierge interrupted them over the SUV audio channel.

"Status update."

"What's wrong?" Emmie asked nervously.

"Your personal vehicle's autopilot has been directed to a

secure garage facility in Livermore. You are advised to continue using the secure car service provided by your counter-surveillance operative until further notice."

"Oh. Okay, thanks."

She slumped back against her seat, saying, to herself more than to Naoto,

"It would be great if she could differentiate between, 'You're being followed,' and 'We're parking your car,' don't you —"

"Status update."

Emmie's mouth went dry. The security concierge continued,

"Facial recognition monitors have confirmed the identity of the driver of the Tesla Courant, license plate 5-SOS-101, as Amos Jeremiah Eckerd."

"You think?" Emmie snorted.

"Would you like to hear public information about Amos Jeremiah Eckerd?" asked the concierge.

Emmie looked at Naoto, who shrugged.

"Sure," said Emmie, "Lay it on me."

"Amos Jeremiah Eckerd, male, age seventy-six —"

"Seventy-six!" Emmie exclaimed, "Could have fooled me."

"— Born in Lynchburg, Virginia. Oldest son of Jeremiah Josiah Eckerd, deceased, and Miriam Fuller Eckerd, deceased. Father to Ezekiel Amos Eckerd. Married to Annabelle Abbott Eckerd, presumed deceased.

"Eckerd holds an undergraduate degree in Philosophy and Religion from Liberty University, and a PhD in Theology and Apologetics from Liberty University Theological Seminary.

"Eckerd is presently employed as senior minister of —"

"Okay, okay," said Emmie, raising her hands, "How about something useful? Like why he's following me?"

"Would you like to initiate a consultation?"

"Ugh," Emmie grumbled in disgust, "Not right now."

Naoto chuckled and said,

"Falsens sticks to protocol, doesn't he?"

Emmie wondered what Naoto might know about Falsens.

"So he is a he?" she said.

"Mmm," Naoto cocked his head to the side, "I just assumed. I should know better — I haven't actually met him. Or her."

"But you work for him?"

"I've done a lot of work for Falsens in the past, but, if you navigate to section seventeen of Falsens' standard proposal terms," Emmie shook her head at the memory of the monumental document, "You'll see that, technically, I'm working for you. Falsens likes to spread liability around."

"So who were you working for while you were impersonating a Buddhist priest at Tomo Yoshimoto's memorial service?"

Naoto's face grew serious.

"Interesting question. Normally I wouldn't be able to discuss other clients' work, but in this case, you happen to be both clients. So that dovetails nicely."

"What are you talking about?"

"Amaterasu Nagato hired me on your behalf to provide counter-surveillance and security services. Apparently she anticipated some of the trouble you would be having."

Emmie sank back into her seat.

"So what exactly have you been doing?"

"Periodic bug sweeps, personal communication channel monitoring, wireless network shielding, round-the-clock bodyguard detail. Among other things. My instructions were fairly broad. Provide you with as high a level of personal security as I can. Minimize detection by third parties and interference with your regular activities."

"So where were you when the accident in the spliner happened?" Emmie asked softly, wondering how, with all the people spying on her, she had been so utterly alone in that moment.

Naoto sighed.

"My ability to provide security on the Augur campus without detection was limited. I alerted Augur security as soon as my remote surveillance detected the disturbance in the spliner, but by then the damage was done."

"Damage. You mean Owen."

"Yes. Owen. I'm sorry."

Emmie pressed her forehead to the window, forcing herself to move on to a more pressing concern. She knew now what Amos Eckerd must be after. Her fingers traveled to the emerald tablet tucked away in the little compartment on her belt. She wished it had never come to her, almost as much as she wanted to understand why it had.

CHAPTER 14
The Anonymous Collective

Emmie stared through the tinted windows of the SUV at the bright red doors of the Buddhist Church of Oakland.

"You're kidding," she said, "This is the safe house?"

"The very same," Naoto replied, pulling the car up alongside the curb, "Now, I've keyed the door to your palm. Go inside and check our shared channel for instructions to enter the safe room. I'll be right behind you." He glanced through the rear window. "I just need to get rid of this car."

Emmie felt a renewed surge of adrenaline as she contemplated the broad stretch of sidewalk separating her from the church. She seemed unable to convince herself to open the door. Naoto squeezed her shoulder.

"You're going to be fine. Go."

Emmie stepped onto the sidewalk and faced the church's wrought iron gate. Naoto pulled away from the curb, leaving her standing there, exposed. Glancing nervously at the slow-moving pedestrians and cars moving along the block, she pressed her hand to the palm scanner. The padlock clunked, and the gate swung open. She hurried up the front steps, and the heavy red front doors swung open at her touch.

Emmie stood alone on the worn red carpet in the lobby for a while, breathing in the faint scent of incense, until she heard a ping on her smartcom. She flipped on a visual overlay, where a text message read,

Go to the hondo.

She remembered the way, and she took the stairs slowly up to the second floor. She approached the smiling wooden Buddha standing at the open doors of the *hondo*. Inside, rows of empty pews faced the gleaming altar at the front of the room. Her smartcom pinged again.

Press hand to Buddha's belly.

She reached out toward the smiling wood carving and pressed her hand against the smooth, cool cedar. A faint buzz emanated from the pedestal beneath the statue, and a pulse of warmth traveled along her palm. As soon as the buzz fell silent, another text message appeared.

Proceed to the shrine.

She hurried down the center aisle and came to a stop before the richly gleaming shrine.

Touch Buddha's foot.

She stepped around the heavy incense jars and draped altar table. She reached out tentatively toward the golden Buddha at the center of the shrine, pressing her fingertip to one gleaming foot.

She felt a rush of air as the entire wall panel containing the shrine pulled back, creating a gap on either side of the panel that led into some dark space beyond.

Take the right path ;-)

Emmie glanced nervously over her shoulder before stepping toward the Buddha and turning right. She could just make out the three bare walls of a small room before the wall behind her began to close. She was plunged into darkness for an instant before bright ceiling lights switched on.

She found herself standing in a wide but shallow room, unfurnished, with uniformly grey walls. She felt a moment of panic at the thought that she had stepped into some kind of spliner, but when she reached out toward the near wall, she felt the reassuring rigidity of drywall.

Her smartcom pinged.

Stay there. I'm on my way.

Emmie sat down against one of the narrow walls, wrapping her arms around her knees and burying her head. She felt trapped and alone inside the small grey room.

But a moment later, a warm prickle of awareness on her skin reminded her that she was not entirely alone. She wondered if Dom might be there, somewhere, and when she looked up, she found his projection seated across from her, leaning against the adjacent wall, watching her. She cocked her head to the side.

"Amos was right there," said Emmie, "Just a few car lengths away from me."

"I saw him. It is fortunate that Naoto was there. He

seems to know what he is doing."

Emmie shivered, looking around the tiny room.

"I hope so."

The lights went out. Emmie jumped to her feet in alarm, unable to back away much father as the entry wall pushed in a few feet toward her.

She sighed in relief as Naoto's small figure, now dressed in the robes of a Buddhist monk, slipped through the opening. A rush of air escaped the room as the wall closed once more, and the bright LED lights switched on again. She glanced at the place Dom had been sitting, but he had disappeared.

"Sorry I startled you," said Naoto, "I spend so much time in here that I didn't even think about the lights."

"You have to spend a lot of time in here?"

Naoto shrugged.

"It's convenient for work. Small, well-hidden, easy to secure …"

He sat down on the floor and pressed something concealed beneath the waist of his robes. The bright lights dimmed, and all four walls of the room lit up with a mosaic of two-dimensional projections.

"… A very serviceable command and control station."

He pointed toward a video feed projected on the broad wall, and it drifted toward him. Emmie knelt beside him to look at an aerial view of her house on Skyline Boulevard. Naoto zoomed in on the ring of redwood trees surrounding the stone bench by her driveway. There, nearly obscured by shadows, stood a man in a bulky hoodie and baseball cap, shifting slowly from one foot to the other.

"Is that Amos?" she asked, her hand moving involuntarily to her throat.

"No," said Naoto, "He'll be too smart for that. Still, we know you can't go back there."

"Wait," she said suspiciously, "How do you have a live video feed of my house?"

He zoomed out again and tapped a redwood in the projection.

"Tree's-eye view."

Emmie's mind drifted back to the last night she had spent with Owen. He had spotted one of these cameras. With everything else that had happened since then, she had forgotten.

"Man," Emmie shook her head, unsure whether to be grateful or furious that someone had been watching over her all this time, "I love my trees, but between the stalkers and the cameras ..." Her hand flew to her mouth, "Wait. Do you have a camera at my parents' house? Is there —"

"Yep," said Naoto, switching to another video feed and pointing out another figure in the shadows.

Emmie fumbled with her smartcom, overcome by the urgent need to confirm that her parents were safe. Naoto raised his hand.

"Don't. They still think you're at Yosemite. If you call, you're just going to worry them. Let's keep things simple. I've called in bodyguards for your family members for now. I don't think the Stewards are going to make a move on them."

"But you don't think — Shouldn't they be warned? They could be kidnapped or something!"

Naoto shook his head,

"Your parents don't know anything useful to them. It's you they want."

"Right," said Emmie, slumping against the wall, "Comforting thought. And now we're pretty much trapped, aren't we?"

"We're working on it," he said, returning to poring over his projections.

Emmie straightened up to look over his shoulder, pushing the gloomy thoughts from her mind in an effort to understand what options might still remain to her.

"What exactly are we looking at here?" she asked.

Naoto pointed to a map of the Bay Area covered in slowly-moving dots.

"These are pedestrians and vehicles that our traffic analysis suggests are performing sweeping and patrolling maneuvers. The blue ones have been there for at least six hours. The red ones have just become active within the last two."

"There's a lot more red ones."

"Yeah. Means Amos' people have probably just deployed a lot of new surveillance resources in the area. They may not know our precise location, but they think you're here."

Emmie crossed her arms, trying to remain calm.

"This is probably naïve. But can't we just call the police?"

Naoto shook his head.

"I wouldn't advise it. Not until we know who we're dealing with and what they want. Amos isn't working alone, obviously. He could have connections anywhere. And if anyone's likely to be working for the dark side, it's the government."

Emmie rolled her eyes.

"You sound like my Uncle Frank."

"Your Uncle Frank sounds like a smart guy," Naoto said distantly, absorbed in his visual overlay. Emmie watched in silence until, a few minutes later, Falsens' stumpy projection showed up.

"Miss Bridges, I have an update on your investigation request."

"Did you find Amos?" Emmie asked hopefully.

"Unfortunately, I am currently unable to locate Amos Eckerd," said Falsens, his androgynous voice slowly verging on feminine, "A construction crew near the point of your rendezvous with Mr. Kimura disconnected all our concealed monitors along a quarter-mile stretch of the freeway in a matter of minutes after we captured Eckerd's image. This is unlikely to have been a coincidence.

"Currently, all of my online monitoring networks are searching for Eckerd. I will of course report to you as soon as I have further information concerning his whereabouts."

"Damn," Emmie said softly, disturbed by the idea that Amos could be anywhere out there now.

"I apologize for this disappointing news. However, I am happy to report that I have found a new lead regarding Amos Eckerd's possible involvement in the Augur spliner malfunction.

"A review of the public records from Zeke Eckerd's plea bargain showed that Augur's IT department recovered a cached copy of the trojan responsible for the malfunction. I ran an analysis of the coding style in an attempt to identify the author, which turned up an almost ninety-eight percent match to the coding style of the public identity Didactix."

"No way," Emmie interjected, "I know Didactix. Well, I mean, he's an acquaintance in *Temenos*. But his identity's reputation speaks for itself. He would never write something like that. And if he did, he'd be smart enough to disguise it."

"I was suspicious of the match as well. Even comparisons of code samples known to belong to the same coder typically have no better than an eighty-five percent match.

"Nonetheless, I met with Didactix to show him the results of the code analysis. He was quite upset to have been implicated in the attack, both because of the death involved and because of the poor quality of the trojan code. He claims to know nothing about it, and in his defense he showed me several examples of code recovered from recent data corruption attacks. Many of the code samples match the coding styles of public identities who, like him, have no apparent motive to develop such code.

"Didactix, along with several other of the implicated coders, have offered their services pro bono to help track down the actual program designer."

"Well, that's nice of them. But are we really likely to learn anything from that? Anyone might have been hired to write that trojan, and they could have done so without knowing a thing about who was going to use it, in the end."

"Didactix seems to have something larger in mind than tracking down the coder of this particular trojan. He thinks that these mimicked coding styles could point to a single architect behind a number of recent cyberterrorist attacks."

"You're saying he thinks he can find a way to implicate the Church of the True Cross?"

"Per the confidentiality terms of our agreement, I did not mention the Church of the True Cross or Amos Eckerd. Didactix only knows what's on the public record."

"I don't like it. Didactix has no idea what he's getting himself into."

"Well, as I made no formal arrangement with Didactix, neither you nor I will be held liable for the outcome."

"That's not my point! What —"

"Miss Bridges," Falsens interjected, "I think you underestimate Didactix's ability to take care of himself. He is a well-connected, high-reputation identity. My own analysis of his public social network suggests a high probability that he is part of the anonymous collective."

"Well, even the collective hasn't managed to identify the people behind these attacks so far."

"They haven't had any real motivation to do so. Their political leanings tend to be anarchic. They typically see large-scale attacks as beneficial in the long run, as they produce adaptive innovations that increase overall system security."

"So why would they want to help with this now?"

"Because now it's personal," said Falsens.

"I really don't think it's a good idea to get them involved," Emmie insisted, "They're totally unpredictable."

"I'm afraid it's too late for that," said Falsens, "Based on public chatter I picked up, Didactix had the collective engaged before my interview with him was even complete.

"What I came to tell you is that the anonymous collective has identified a section of obfuscated code in the Augur spliner trojan that seems to be shared in common with a number of trojans that have been used in attacks linked to the Church of the True Cross.

"The purpose of this obfuscated code is to listen on a network node for any activity containing data that matches an encrypted dataset stored within the trojan. A data match triggers various programs that produce catastrophic system failure on any hardware that might relay or cache the matched data, destroying the data as well as the trojan itself.

"Essentially, the trojan is designed to stop whatever this dataset is from entering or being accessed over networked systems."

A horrible realization washed over Emmie.

"I tried to upload some files to the alternet from my

smartcom while I was in the spliner," she said slowly, "That's what triggered the trojan."

"What files were these?" asked Falsens.

Emmie hesitated, wondering if she should trust Falsens and Naoto this far. She realized then that, for all practical purposes, her life was already in their hands. And, anyway, she couldn't see how she was going to figure out what to do with the tablet without their help.

"In his will," she said, "Tomo Yoshimoto left me a storage tablet. His sister told me when she gave me the data that it was sensitive in some way. I just didn't think about it when I sent the files off for translation."

"A significant oversight," Falsens said bluntly. Emmie blinked back tears as Falsens continued briefing her on his findings.

"Because the dataset shared by these trojans is encrypted, it is virtually impossible to recover the data, even if the trojan is itself recovered after an attack. This does offer some security to the designer of the trojan — the anonymous collective itself can't tell what the data is that the trojan is intended to destroy.

"However, the anonymous collective finds it interesting that the encrypted dataset is identical, byte for byte, from one trojan to the next. A more secure method might have been to encrypt the dataset with a different key in each trojan. Given how much trouble the trojan designer has already taken to protect its identity — using code style matching, obfuscating the triggering function, designing the code to essentially self-destruct — it seems like a major oversight to leave evidence that all these different trojans are linked.

"This might mean that the program designer does not know what the dataset contains, only what the encrypted data looks like. It is possible that the program might not even recognize the data if it is in its unencrypted form, or if it is encrypted using a different key."

"But that doesn't make sense," said Emmie, "These files aren't encrypted. They opened right up on my smartcom, no authentication required."

"That is interesting. May I examine the files?"

"Uh — are you sure you want to risk it?"

"I will send a hardware analysis program to Naoto's smartcom. None of the data on the tablet will itself be transferred to me. I will only see the analysis summary."

Emmie handed the tablet over to Naoto, who plugged it into a port on his smartcom. A moment later, the analysis summary popped up.

"Ah," Falsens and Naoto said in unison.

"What?" said Emmie. Falsens explained,

"The storage tablet you have there is designed to mimic the form factor of a standard storage tablet that you might purchase from any office supply store. But the electrical impedance of the tablet surface ceramic indicates the presence of a biomaterial. This is common in devices that perform biometric authentication. This tablet seems to have been programmed to decrypt its contents only when you are the last person to touch it, and to re-encrypt the contents with a key contained within the un-encrypted data when it changes hands.

"Naoto, if you would confirm our hypothesis …"

Naoto swiped a few controls on his projection, and a filesystem browser opened up containing the message,

Device corrupted. Eject or reformat?

Naoto popped the tablet back out from his smartcom and handed it to Emmie, who in turn plugged it into her smartcom. Her filesystem browser opened to reveal neat columns of files and folders, as it had before in the spliner.

"Very interesting," said Falsens, "Whoever prepared this tablet wanted to make very sure that only you could access its contents."

"But why?" said Emmie.

"I am unable to determine that based on the current information. Do you know what is on the tablet?"

"Tomo's sister told me it's the manuscript for a book about creation myths, but I haven't really been able to decipher any of it."

"I would need to run an analysis of the tablet's contents to determine why such information may be sensitive in nature. We should now assume, however, that Amos knows you are the only person able to view this data. He has gone to quite a lot of trouble to ensure you cannot spread it widely by electronic means, and he now appears to be systematically attempting to eliminate the threat posed by you or anyone else who has seen the data."

"So you can't even look at this thing without becoming a target," said Emmie.

"Hmm," said Naoto, "Now there's an interesting idea."

Emmie raised an eyebrow.

"Interesting how?"

"We've been trying to figure out how we're going to get you out of here, with these ground operatives crawling all over the place. What we could really use is a good old-fashioned diversion."

"So ...?"

"So, what if everyone becomes a target, all at once? As

far as Amos' people know, you're the only one alive who knows what's on that tablet, so they're focusing all their efforts on you. But what if everyone knew what's on that tablet? The Stewards can't pick off everyone, at least not all at once."

"Bad idea," Emmie said decidedly, "The only way to get the information to any significant number of people is to get it out on the alternet. We've already seen what happens when you try to do that. I don't think the world will appreciate it if we trigger a cascading alternet infrastructure meltdown trying to broadcast this."

"The world might not appreciate it," said Naoto, "But I think we know just the people who would."

∞

As Naoto had anticipated, the anonymous collective had no qualms about risking the stability of the global alternet infrastructure in an effort to propagate information that someone wanted desperately to keep secret.

Within an hour, Falsens' projection returned to deliver the news.

"The collective proposes a rather straightforward distribution method. We will send encrypted video streams of the files, recorded from cameras at your current location, to a small network of crowdsourced transcription services, which will in turn send encrypted video streams of the transcribed content to a second-degree network, and so on. The electronic format of the data will change from point to point. The first group of transcribers will upload their transcriptions to a collection of video streaming server farms located in the South Bay. This is close enough to your actual location not to be suspicious, but far enough away that we'll hopefully clear out some of the operatives in our neighborhood.

"The anonymous collective will circulate the information that these video streams are a sensitive data leak and begin to vote up the streams, ensuring a general field day in conspiracy theory and rumor forums and, eventually, attention from the more popular media streams, as well.

"The collective anticipates, based on prior leak campaigns they've orchestrated, that the servers hosting the first group of video streams will be brought down by the Stewards within hours. When fifty percent of those servers go down, the second-degree transcription network will be scheduled to go live with their own streams. And so we will have rolling leaks which should be able to go on for at least a few hours, possibly more if the story gets better traction among the general public and we see small-scale data caching."

"There could be so much system damage from that," Emmie groaned, "People could even be killed. If you have alternet nodes go out, autopilot networks can go down, medical networks — it's impossible to predict."

"The collective believes that it is unlikely the architect of the trojans is prepared to trigger widespread infrastructure damage if the information leak is that widespread. It's a catch-22. If they don't destroy the infrastructure hosting the leaked information, it gets out. If they do destroy the infrastructure, they will have established the importance of the information, heightening public interest in the information and also risking scrutiny that might reveal their identity. Either way, they're going to be scrambling for at least a few hours to contain the leak with backchannel methods before they realize the scale of the leak."

Emmie raked her fingers through her hair, frustrated by

her own indecisiveness.

"I don't know. I don't know. How can the collective be sure no one else will get hurt?"

"They cannot be sure," Falsens said matter-of-factly, "You must decide whose lives you are willing to risk."

Knowing full well how many lives she had already put at risk and how many more might yet suffer for it, Emmie nonetheless longed to strike back at the Stewards. Tomo had left this tablet to her for a reason. Surely she must do all she could to keep it from the hands of those who wished to destroy it. Steeling herself for the unknown, she said,

"All right. Let's do it."

∞

Naoto slipped out of the safe room in head-to-toe night camouflage to gather the cameras they would need from the perimeter security system of the church.

"Doesn't that sort of undermine the whole idea of perimeter security?" Emmie had asked nervously.

"We'll have to risk the blind spots," he said, "Even the same-day delivery services won't be able to get us the cameras we need fast enough. Just keep an eye out on the video feeds I showed you. Give me a holler on the shared channel if you see anything suspicious."

He returned without incident, and as he set up the makeshift video recording studio, Emmie wrote a script to display each file on the tablet in succession: seven different projections for the seven different cameras Naoto had collected from the church exterior. By her calculation, the roughly ten thousand pages of documents and images on the tablet would take nine minutes to record and convert into an encrypted video stream, and another five minutes to upload to the servers of the human transcription services the collective had proposed for the first wave of the leak.

"Well," said Emmie, as Naoto dimmed the lights so the recording could commence, "Here goes nothing."

She hit the execute button on her script, and on the blank grey wall before them, hundreds of images flashed by in succession, three images per second per camera. She watched, mesmerized, as the illustrations and writings poured out on the wall, feeling an occasional flicker of recognition as something slipped by in the stream. When the recording concluded and the lights came on again, Emmie stepped back, dazed.

"Encrypting now," said Naoto. Emmie chewed her lip anxiously.

"It's not too late to stop this," she said, watching the progress bar on the encryption approaching completion.

"Look, Emmie," said Naoto, "I don't want to scare you, but I don't think we have a lot of options right now. I don't want to see anything happen to you. Why don't we just trust that the collective knows what it's doing?"

"Seems like a pretty big leap of faith."

The progress bar finished, and an upload confirmation prompt appeared before Emmie. Naoto looked at her and said,

"Falsens' protocol. You've got to do the honors."

There was no turning back now. Whatever the consequences, she was fully responsible. She closed her eyes and initiated the upload.

∞

Fifteen minutes later, alternet forums were already buzzing with news of the leak, and Naoto's surveillance monitors showed that ground operatives scattered throughout the Bay Area had started to converge around the server farm hosting the first video stream.

"We're going to leave through the rear fire exit," said Naoto, "We have to assume that all wireless communications may attract attention, so I'm going to need you to leave all your immergers, smartcom, everything with wireless capability, behind in the safe room.

"Once we're on the road, there will be time to decide where best to take you."

Emmie realized that there was only one place that she wanted to go.

"Naoto," she said, reluctantly removing her immergers to place into the bag Naoto was holding out for her, "Can you take me to Amaterasu?"

Naoto nodded. Just before Emmie took off her headset, Falsens' projection appeared.

"Of course, we will need your payment authorization first," he said officiously.

Doubting that there would be anything left in her checking account by the time this was all over, Emmie waved her hand in assent. Dom had warned her. There was no telling the price, once the task was accepted.

∞

Neither cop nor ground operative intercepted them as they sped through the streets of downtown Oakland and wove through the middling midnight traffic on the freeway. Twenty minutes later, Naoto pulled to a stop on the tarmac behind the Oakland Business Jet center. He pointed to a small airplane up ahead.

"That's us!"

Though Emmie had experienced countless flight simulations — prosaic commercial aircraft connections, thrilling helicopter tours, even whimsical bird rides — and visited much of the world through environment simulations, she had never actually set foot inside an airplane. She never would have imagined that her first trip would begin under such circumstances.

Naoto reached out his hand to open the door, then stopped and swore under his breath. Two men in dark uniforms had just stepped out onto the tarmac.

"What's wrong?" Emmie whispered.

"Someone's called in TSA screeners. I'm sure it wasn't Falsens. He uses private contractors for that."

Emmie watched the men pacing leisurely alongside the small private jet.

"Could the TSA be working for Amos?"

"Could be. But even if they're not, any body scans they take could end up somewhere Amos can find them. That would make it hard to cover our tracks."

Naoto waited for a moment, then said sharply,

"Falsens? Are you paying attention?"

"I am aware of the screener issue at the jetport, Mr. Kimura," Falsens replied curtly, "Please hold for further instructions."

Emmie wiped her sweaty palms on her jeans, chewing on her knuckle as she watched the TSA agents ambling back and forth, swinging their scanner wands beside them.

"Mr. Kimura, can you confirm that the TSA agents are wearing audiovisual sensory augmentation devices?"

Naoto squinted out into the darkness. The TSA agents were standing near the edge of a pool of runway lamplight, making it difficult to see them. Emmie said,

"There. The guy on the left just made that gesture," she imitated him, "He's listening to music. He's got earbuds on, at least."

"And the other agent?" said Falsens.

"Can't see him," said Naoto, "It's too dark."

"Miss Bridges," said Falsens, "I'm afraid that in order to get you onto that plane, we're going to have to take somewhat of a risk. Statistically speaking, there is a seventy-one percent chance that the first TSA agent is wearing some kind of sensory augmentation equipment. The second agent, who appears to be listening to music through auditory immergers, is more than ninety-five percent likely to be wearing visual immergers of some kind as well.

"In the event that both agents are in fact equipped with audiovisual sensory augmentation susceptible to the remote sensory projection program that I will provide to Mr. Kimura for this operation, your boarding process should be quite straightforward. They will never see you pass. However, in the event that one or both of the agents is entirely without audiovisual sensory augmentation, you will need to authorize Mr. Kimura to forcibly incapacitate both agents."

Naoto tapped his side, where he was evidently concealing some weapon of force. Emmie swallowed.

"That's not …?"

Naoto shook his head.

"No. Tranquilizer gun."

A liability waiver prompt appeared on the vehicle dashboard display, as Emmie was no longer equipped with her own headset.

"You're definitely not going to kill anyone?" she said to Naoto.

"Scout's honor. And, anyway," he said sardonically, "Falsens would have to get a different authorization for that."

She sighed and pressed her thumb to the dashboard to sign the waiver.

"Stay in here until I say otherwise," said Naoto, "I'll be on the car audio channel if you need me."

Naoto stepped out of the car and walked casually toward the TSA agents. Emmie saw him offer each of them a cigarette from a pack he produced from his jacket pocket. One man accepted, while the other waved him off. Naoto and the smoker stood to the side chatting for a few minutes, and afterwards Naoto stepped toward the other agent and clapped him on the shoulder before walking off to the nearby private charter terminal.

"Both of them are wearing immergers," Naoto said through the car speakers.

"Should I get out of the car?" said Emmie.

"Not yet. Costume change."

Less than a minute later, Naoto re-emerged from the terminal wearing a pilot's uniform, carrying a small briefcase, and looking about six inches taller and thirty pounds heavier.

"How do you *do* that?" Emmie said, staring at him in disbelief as he approached the plane again. She thought she saw Naoto wink at her across the tarmac.

He stopped before the TSA agents and chatted with them as they patted him down and took a full body scan followed by a scan of his briefcase. They waved him aboard.

"Wait for it," Naoto's voice came over the car speakers.

Emmie watched with bemusement as the two TSA agents continued their wand routine, this time with an unseen subject. They were now under the influence of Falsens' interference projection program.

"How do you *do* that?" Emmie said again, this time to Falsens. Again, her question went unanswered.

"Okay," said Naoto, "Just walk around behind them. Don't bump into them." When Emmie hesitated, Naoto urged, "Quickly, Emmie. Trust me."

Emmie steeled herself, opened the passenger door slowly, and stepped out of the car. The door started closing automatically behind her, and she hurried across the open tarmac toward the airplane, painfully aware of her heart in her throat, her sneakers thudding softly on the pavement, and her long shadow pointing like an arrow straight toward her. It seemed impossible that the TSA agents wouldn't see her.

But the TSA agents never even looked her way as she crept past them and climbed as quietly as she could up the gangway.

"Have a nice flight, ma'am," said one of the agents. Emmie wheeled around in surprise, almost tripping back down the stairs of the gangway. Naoto was instantly behind her, one arm around her and another covering her mouth. She felt her pulse racing as she stared down at the agents standing just feet below her. They waved into the darkness at an unseen person.

"Get in the back and sit down," Naoto whispered in her ear.

He pulled Emmie back into the cabin and started to close the hatch. Emmie gripped the arm of the first seat she found and collapsed into it.

∞

Emmie could not bring herself to open her eyes during takeoff, and they must have been miles out over the Pacific by the time Naoto came back from the cockpit with his briefcase and sat down in one of the swiveling leather recliners across from her.

"Who's flying the plane?" Emmie asked in alarm.

"Falsens," Naoto said calmly, "Remotely."

Emmie decided that it was pointless to freak out about this. They had already reached a stable altitude.

"Do you think you could sleep?" said Naoto, "It's about ten hours to Japan."

"I don't think so," said Emmie, still feeling the aftereffects of adrenaline overload, "I'm totally wired."

"Here," said Naoto, climbing out of his recliner to open a small refrigeration panel mounted on the cabin wall. He poured her a double whisky and set it down on the table beside her, "Maybe you'll change your mind."

"Thanks."

"I'm going to stay up there in the cockpit. Falsens and I need to work out some of our ground logistics, and I want to stay at the controls in case we need to switch out of autopilot."

"Do you think something might …?"

"Nope. I don't think anything's going to happen. Just being careful."

Emmie sighed. She picked up the whisky tentatively, took a sip, and promptly started coughing. Naoto grinned and turned to leave, but Emmie stopped him, her eyes still watery as she rasped,

"Hey — If it's not a security hazard now, do you have any immergers I could borrow to surf the alternet? Helps me get to sleep."

Naoto laughed.

"Oh, yeah. Falsens said to check the briefcase."

Emmie turned to the briefcase that Naoto had carried aboard and popped it open to reveal a full set of the very finest immerger gear.

"Falsens, you're the best," she whispered, holding up the headset appreciatively.

"Thank you, Miss Bridges," Falsens said over the airplane intercom, "I hope you will say so in your review."

Emmie smirked briefly. She rose from her seat and made her way into the surprisingly capacious lavatory to put on the new gear. After a few minutes spent configuring interface preferences and installing essential tools, she flipped on a visual overlay and started crawling through her alternet feeds for news on the leak.

Barely an hour had passed since the plane had taken off from Oakland when Emmie came across the first chatter about the leak. As the anonymous collective had predicted, a number of the server farms hosting the first wave of leaked video had gone offline under mysterious circumstances. This had automatically triggered the spread of the leak to the second-degree servers.

Emmie began to mentally cheer on the anonymous collective as the plan played out. Faster than the video streams could disappear, several high-reputation alternet identities, repaying or earning the favor of the anonymous collective, conveyed their loyal followers to the content with pointed commentary about the exceptional speed with which the content was spreading and disappearing. Identities inclined to conspiracy theorizing gamely picked up the story and commenced speculation as to the purpose of the leak and the significance of the covert attempts to suppress it.

The video hosting providers, perplexed as to the cause of the outages and harassed by their subscribers, sent up a hue and cry about the attacks on their servers. Emmie watched the videos as mainstream news outlets happily sensationalized the story with the generous support of alternet security sponsors promoting one-day-only product discounts.

Mere minutes after the mainstream coverage on the video server outages began, however, an armageddon virus took a large alternet currency exchange offline, handily co-opting the attention of most commentators and concluding that news cycle. The exchange meltdown rekindled Emmie's fears about the spiraling consequences of the leak she had initiated.

To Emmie's surprise, the attention of the conspiracy theorists proved tenacious. By the time the news cycle about the exchange meltdown had ended, she started picking up public forum discussions that revealed a somewhat cohesive narrative about the leak. The conspiracy theorists had dubbed the leaked content the World Tree Codex, based on the recurring symbolic references in the texts it contained.

The Codex, the conspiracy theorists claimed, was a long-lost cache of ancient mystical texts and artwork. Depending on the commentator Emmie read, the Codex proved the extraterrestrial origin of life on Earth, provided the precise location of the lost continent of Atlantis, confirmed once and for all the date and time of the apocalypse, expressed the mathematical formula reconciling quantum and relativity theory, or encoded the master plan of the Freemasons to consolidate control over world governments.

The catchy new name re-captured the attention of the mainstream news outlets, who now sensationalized the World Tree Codex story with the help of panels of renowned author-scholars from a variety of disciplines. Emmie noted with amusement that these panelists had all, most fortuitously, and seemingly only moments earlier, released bestsellers in the conspiracy non-fiction genre.

Wholly-owned subsidiary news outlets, to more fully capture the momentary surge of popular interest in the World Tree Codex story, produced their own panels of even-more-renowned author-scholars. These experts cast aspersions on the deplorable fabulists on the nominally competing news outlets, while coincidentally pitching their own newly-released bestsellers.

By the time Emmie had finished her whisky, over sixteen hundred expert contributors had synthesized their speculations into the definitive wiki article on the World Tree Codex, which was deemed a hoax perpetrated by a cabal of alternet security consultants to spur product sales. Falsens was implicated in the hoax, although a footnote conceded that this was disputed. The wiki article directed readers who wished to view the hoax videos and the virus code that had caused the cascading server outages to the offshore alternet content repository operated in an unknown, secure location by the anonymous collective.

Emmie watched through the semantic hits chart in her feed reader as the World Tree Codex story faded into the distant past of the alternet's memory. She was only mildly surprised by the speed with which it had all unfolded. She said to Naoto over their shared channel,

"All that, and still I have absolutely no idea what the World Tree Codex is about. Unless Midori was really writing a book about aliens or telepathy or something."

"I think that guy going on about the JFK prophesy might have been on to something," Naoto offered. Emmie snorted.

CHAPTER 15
Into the Mountains

Emmie drifted in and out of sleep for the next several hours, until Naoto said on their shared channel,

"We'll be landing soon, Emmie."

She blinked sleepily and stretched, leaning over the padded arm of her recliner to peer out the window. The sky was dark, but below, the bright lights of an urban sprawl illuminated broad valleys enclosed by the dark folds of forested mountains. She imagined how delighted Owen would have been to look down on an unfamiliar landscape like this, with the prospect of a real-life adventure before them.

"Where are we?" she said.

"We're passing over the Kansei region of southern Japan. We're going to land at the Itami airport."

Emmie pulled up a map on her visual overlay to orient herself to the new location. After a few attempts to guess the correct spelling of Enryaku-ji, she located the temple where they would meet Amaterasu: atop Mount Hiei, a three-hour drive northeast from the Itami airport, according to her navigation system.

"We can't land any closer?" she asked nervously, the freeway encounter with Amos still fresh in her memory.

"Sorry. Falsens doesn't have any landing strips in the mountains."

"What are we going to do about the Japanese — whatever they've got. TSA? Immigration officers?"

Naoto laughed.

"The Japanese and their immergers are inseparable. As long as we have Falsens' remote sensory projection program running, you'll be invisible to nearly everyone."

Naoto was right. Emmie easily sidestepped one airport security checkpoint after another. She watched in amazement as security personnel waved through the invisible young woman that Falsens seamlessly integrated into their experience while erasing their perception of Emmie. Emmie kept up a near-constant stream of pestering trying to get Falsens to tell her where he had acquired such technology, but he remained tight-lipped on this topic.

An autopiloted car picked them up at the curb, and Naoto took the wheel. Emmie settled into the passenger seat and stared out the window as they raced through the tangled undergrowth of narrow highways, raised train tracks, and power lines that stretched from one high-rise to the next. The concrete jungle thinned a bit as they crossed the river into Osaka and turned north into a more human-scale landscape of residential neighborhoods.

The first light of dawn began to glow on the eastern horizon, illuminating a dark green ridge of low mountains ahead. An hour later, they passed under raised train tracks, and Naoto slowed as the road narrowed. Sidewalks separated from the road by low barriers pressed in on both sides, and pedestrians walked by an arm's length from Emmie's window.

Supermarkets opened their doors, and window shades slid open on the second floors of houses facing the road. A few industrious gardeners were already at work tending patches of greenery in the alleyways between buildings.

The road passed beneath a series of brightly painted *torii* archways and through intersections marked by small stone pagodas, reminiscent of the entryways to subdomains in Tomo's *Kaisei*. As the sun rose over the mountain that both Tomo and Midori must have ascended so many years ago, Emmie experienced for the first time in many months a true sense of peace, and, inexplicably, security.

A few miles outside the city, the road entered a wood at the foot of Mount Hiei and began a winding climb toward the summit that concluded at a deserted parking lot beside a tourist bus stop.

"Is it safe to go out?" said Emmie, uncertain why she felt the need to whisper.

"Falsens and I are checking it out," said Naoto, flipping through visual overlays so quickly that Emmie could not determine what exactly he was looking at, "The marathon monks do a good job maintaining a secure perimeter here. But better safe than sorry."

"Marathon monks?" Emmie said curiously. Naoto did not seem to hear her, but she asked another question anyway.

"What do a bunch of monks need perimeter security for? Are they afraid of the Church of the True Cross?"

"No, not officially," said Naoto, "Or, at least, not specifically. It's more like tradition. A long time ago, there was a lot of violence in this area. Competing monastic orders, local political squabbles, lots of warrior monks from different sects attacking each other."

"Whoa. Warrior monks? I thought Buddhists were nonviolent."

"No religion's exempt from extremism. Even Buddhism," said Naoto, giving a last glance to a heat map of the surrounding woods before saying,

"Okay. Follow me."

Emmie hopped out of the car and followed close on Naoto's heels as he made his way up a path into the temple complex. They passed a large pagoda with a curving slate-blue roof supported by wooden pillars and carved walls painted brightly in red, white, black, and gold; a smaller pagoda housing an enormous bell; and a series of increasingly ornate halls. Naoto turned off the path to climb a stone staircase leading to two-story pagoda that formed a great gate amidst a tall stand of cedars. They passed through the gate and looked down another staircase, which led to a large temple fronted by a long colonnade.

They hurried down the stairs and toward the red wooden doors at the center of the colonnade. Naoto reached up and knocked three times.

"The temple doesn't open to visitors for another few hours," he explained, "Amaterasu sent a guide to meet us."

A moment later, the doors creaked and swung out to reveal a smiling young woman, head shaved, robed in orange. She bowed to them, then spoke to Naoto in Japanese.

"She says Amaterasu is waiting in the main hall," Naoto translated, "and that we should follow her."

Emmie looked around nervously as they crossed a small courtyard shaded by flowering trees. Before them stood the enormous main temple, raised up on a foundation of short red columns. A flight of stone steps led to a dark, carved wooden door, framed on either side by panels of wood latticework.

The nun opened the door for them and bowed once more, ushering them across the threshold and closing the heavy doors behind them, shutting out even the soft sounds from outside.

Emmie followed Naoto's lead and removed her shoes, then followed him into the heart of the temple. She paused unconsciously when she entered the great hall. A spicy smell of wood and incense pervaded the dimly-lit space. Dark, gleaming pillars of polished cedar rose to a beautiful wooden ceiling traversed by carved crossbeams. The pillars formed a central aisle leading to the main shrine.

The two of them walked in sock feet along the honey-colored wooden floor until they came to the shrine. A gleaming gold Buddha stood before a backdrop of violet, red, and green. Before the Buddha, three square paper lamps glowed softly.

"The lamplights of eternity," Naoto whispered, bowing toward the shrine, "They've been burning for over twelve hundred years."

Emmie glanced at him in surprise, about to ask him how anyone could know that for sure, when a reedy voice spoke from the shadows beside the shrine.

"Naoto-san."

Emmie turned and saw a tiny old woman in orange robes approaching, her shaved head gleaming in the lamplight.

"Amaterasu Roshi," said Naoto, bowing solemnly, "I am glad to see you fully recovered."

The woman bowed in return, her eyes twinkling. She thought for a long moment before saying haltingly, "Perhaps my work here is not yet complete."

She turned to Emmie, bowing and saying,

"And Emmie-san. How pleased I am to see you again."

Emmie blinked at the unexpected phrasing and bowed awkwardly.

"Thank you. It's, ah … so nice to meet you, too. Thank you for agreeing to see me."

"Yes, yes," said Amaterasu. She switched to Japanese, continuing to speak to Emmie but glancing at Naoto, who said,

"The roshi apologizes but asks if you would mind having me translate. She feels her English — ah — slipping through her fingers as she gets older."

"Oh, no, of course. I'm sorry I can't speak even a little Japanese."

Amaterasu chuckled, and Naoto translated as she said,

"We are so many little islands."

Emmie wondered what might be the appropriate response to this, but Amaterasu saved her the trouble by saying, through Naoto,

"Come, let us talk together a while, before it is too late."

"Too late for what?" Emmie asked, alarmed.

"You see I am not getting any younger," said Amaterasu.

∞

Amaterasu led Emmie and Naoto into one of the galleries off the center aisle. The outer wall of the gallery was formed by a series of dark wooden doors, some of which were rolled back to reveal smaller shrines or rooms beyond. Amaterasu chose one such door, and Naoto rolled it back to reveal a small, unfurnished room with smooth wooden floorboards covered by a woven tatami mat. Morning light filtered through translucent paper screens covering tall windows.

Amaterasu sat down on the tatami mat and indicated that Naoto and Emmie should do the same. She smiled at Emmie, and Naoto translated as she said,

"Emmie-san, can you tell me about the first time you met Tomo Yoshimoto?"

Emmie nodded, remembering that Ayame's interview with Amaterasu had started in a similar way. She wondered why this memory in particular might interest Amaterasu, but, seeing no reason to do otherwise, she let her mind return to that day.

"It was … almost two years ago, now. We met at an Indian restaurant in Berkeley. Saffron. You know, I didn't even think about it at the time, but that's my favorite restaurant. I have no idea how he found that out.

"Well, anyway, I was so nervous when I saw him come in, I nearly knocked over the dinner table," she laughed, "It was awful. But Tomo was really nice about it. He made it seem really funny, and it sort of broke the ice. I practically forgot how embarrassed I was. Well, almost.

"I remember that the waiter had to come back like five times to take our order, because neither of us looked at the menu. There seemed to be so much to talk about. I had so many questions I wanted to ask him. Here was the man who had created *Kaisei*, the most beautiful place I'd ever seen. Maybe the most beautiful place I'll ever see. I wanted to know everything, about where his ideas came from, the techniques he had used … It was amazing to talk with him about it all, even though I think I'd watched every single documentary about him and every interview he ever gave a million times before.

"He had a lot of questions about me, too, about how I'd grown up, and what made me want to become a designer. He was especially interested in my *Eden* domain. That was what made him want to meet me in the first place. I was really flattered by that. He asked me a lot of questions, about where the ideas for the content had come from, lots of little details. I remember thinking how I couldn't wait to tell Owen that Tomo had loved all the environment physics he'd programmed ..." Emmie swallowed, and her gaze drifted from Amaterasu.

"That was the day he asked me to join Augur. Both of us, actually, me and Owen. One of the best days of my life."

Emmie turned her eyes back to meet Amaterasu's, and she found the woman watching her closely, unblinking. Amaterasu nodded, leaning back on her heels as she said smoothly, her accent now gone,

"Yes. It was one of the best days of Tomo's life, too."

Emmie blinked, then gaped as Amaterasu's face seemed to change, years melting away, transforming her into a woman in the prime of life. Shocked, Emmie turned to Naoto, who inclined his head toward Amaterasu, grinning as he said,

"You see I learned from the best."

"What — What is this?" said Emmie, turning again to Amaterasu, "What's going on?"

"We've set up a patrol of the perimeter," Amaterasu said to Naoto, "Perhaps you can join the others for a while? We will need some time alone together."

Naoto bowed deeply to Amaterasu and slipped out of the room.

"I know this must seem a bit confusing," said Amaterasu, turning back to Emmie.

"Yeah. A bit," said Emmie, annoyed.

Amaterasu chuckled.

"I wondered if Tomo might have made a mistake. But,

no, you are so very like her."

"What are you talking about? Like who?"

"Midori," said Amaterasu, eyeing her appraisingly, "You have the same restlessness, the same impatience."

Emmie frowned.

"Well, can you blame me for being impatient? There's someone after me. Someone who killed two people I loved very much, who's probably planning the same for me. I thought maybe you could help me. Now it looks like you're just playing games with me."

Amaterasu's expression turned serious.

"I know it must seem that way. But I needed to be certain it was you."

"What are you talking about?" said Emmie, struggling to keep a level tone, "Who else would I be?"

Amaterasu raised a hand, emanating an authority that quieted Emmie.

"Listen," said Amaterasu, "There is much to tell you, and the —" she raised an eyebrow, "the so-called Stewards could arrive at any time."

"You mean Amos' people?"

"Yes. Amos Eckerd is one of them. I realized this too late, unfortunately. They, too, are learning the art of disguise.

"He came to visit me shortly after Tomo's death. He said he was Tomo's lawyer, and I believed him. Quite a charming man, I thought, actually. He seemed very interested in the temple here, and I showed him the grounds, the library, the temple of initiation. We had a long conversation about Buddhist philosophy. I should have been more on my guard. He must have been doing reconnaissance.

"He showed me Tomo's will and said that Tomo had asked me to return to his estate a collection of documents he had left in my care. That was when I first became suspicious. The wording of the will seemed a bit vague, as if Tomo himself wasn't sure what he had wanted me to return. Tomo was such a precise man. It didn't seem like him.

"I apologized to Amos and fell back on my cover, saying my memory had become so poor that I could not even remember what documents Tomo might have meant. But I invited Amos to look through the library for anything he thought might belong to Tomo's estate.

"I think Amos turned the pages of every book and looked into every corner of the library. But in the end he found nothing. He didn't know what he was looking for. So he left me his card and asked me to call if I remembered anything.

"The very day Amos left, I fell quite ill. He must have poisoned me. Clearly, I was not intended to survive. Of course, Amos did not realize who I was, just as I had not realized who he was.

"I had my suspicions about Tomo's death even before Amos arrived. After Amos left, I was nearly certain. But there was nothing to be done about it then. I imagined Tomo had been robbed of Midori's research and that I had the only remaining copy. All I could do was keep it safe and wait.

"And when Ayame came, I knew she had Tomo's true instructions. Tomo was such a careful man. He had worked out every little detail of how the tablet was to be conveyed to you at the safe house, who should be present, how the tablet should be packaged — everything.

"He had reason to be cautious. In one of our last correspondences, he told me he had gathered new information that he wanted me to keep for him. He said he had encountered difficulties trying to back up the data, that copies would become corrupted, that he was unable to send the files to me electronically. He suspected that someone was trying to interfere with his research.

"He knew about the protections at the monastery here. He had prepared a tablet containing the data he wished to send me, and we arranged to use the Oakland temple as a drop site. I sent Naoto to retrieve the tablet, but Amos intercepted Tomo first."

"Intercepted?" Emmie huffed, "Is that what you call being murdered?"

"I understand that Tomo's death was upsetting to you," Amaterasu said calmly, "But he understood the risk he was taking. He loved Midori, enough to risk his life to preserve the work that was so important to her. And he succeeded. He kept the documents safe for a very long time. Fifty years. Long enough to find you."

"But why would he take such a risk?" Emmie cried, "What did he want me to do with this information?"

Amaterasu looked at her curiously, then peered around the room, as if searching for someone in a crowd. Emmie followed her gaze uneasily.

"But the Artifex must have come to you by now," Amaterasu said at last, frowning. Emmie stared at her.

"Who?"

"The Artifex. Dom Artifex, isn't it?"

"How do you know about him?"

"I have not known you long enough to be sure," Amaterasu said carefully, "but I trust that Tomo did. He would have recognized the mark of the Artifex in you, just as I saw it in Midori. Otherwise he would not have left the tablet to you."

"I don't understand."

Amaterasu glanced around the room once more, this time reproachfully.

"I'm sorry. I see I've assumed too much. The Artifex has kept a great deal from you. Too much, I think. Is he here now?"

Emmie looked at her, puzzled.

"How could he be? There's like zero wireless coverage here. I haven't had a connection since we came onto the temple grounds."

"Perhaps he is the one playing games with you," Amaterasu said, shaking her head, "Ah, well. He must have had his reasons. But the time has come for you to understand."

∞

Dom sat unseen beside Emmie on the tatami mat. He knew Amaterasu was right. He had been playing games with Emmie, misleading her about his true nature and concealing his purpose. The time had come for her to understand.

"Call him," said Amaterasu, "He has much to answer to."

"Call him? How? Like I said, there's no connection —"

"Just call him. He must come to you."

"I don't understand."

"Like this, perhaps. 'Dom Artifex, show yourself!'" said Amaterasu, her voice resonating in the still air of the room.

Amaterasu turned to Emmie expectantly. Emmie glanced around the room, then echoed her uncertainly,

"Dom Artifex … show yourself."

Dom had known that his ever more frequent intrusions into Emmie's awareness had been awakening her to his presence, but this time, for the first time, she summoned him consciously. He felt the veil between them lifting. When Emmie saw him appear suddenly beside her, she gasped and scrambled away.

"How …?" She felt for the immerger headset that she had cast off in the car when her alternet connection cut out. She turned to the door, as if Dom might have slipped in silently while she was not looking. "No," she whispered, "that's not possible."

"Do you see him, then?" asked Amaterasu.

Emmie cast a panicked look at her.

"You don't?"

Amaterasu sighed and stood.

"Speak to her, Artifex," she said brusquely, "You owe her this much."

To Emmie, she said more kindly,

"I will wait for you in the temple. There is still much to discuss."

Before Emmie could protest, Amaterasu slipped out through the doors, leaving her alone with Dom. They watched each other in silence for a long time, until Emmie burst out,

"Who are you? How are you doing this?"

Knowing no amount of preparation could make this explanation any easier, Dom began by saying,

"I am sorry, Emmie. It became so easy to blur the line between our worlds. I should have tried to explain this all sooner.

"The first time I came to you, the night I told you I would help you build *Atlantis*, you thought I was merely a projection. A hacker, unauthorized, but still just a projection. I thought that the familiar context would make it easier for you to accept me, less inclined to wonder whether I was a hallucination."

"Are you a hallucination?" Emmie said uncertainly, mostly to herself.

"I do not know what the right word might be. No one else would find a trace of me in any server logs, on any recording device. No one else but you will ever see me."

Emmie shook her head in disbelief. Dom went on,

"Afterwards, I showed you Dulai. I let you believe that it is just another domain, like your *Eden*, or Tomo's *Kaisei*. But you will find no trace of Dulai anywhere on your alternet, just as you will find no trace of me anywhere in your server logs. Dulai is not an alternet domain."

"So what is it?"

"A world like your own, except … elsewhere."

Emmie rolled her eyes.

"So basically you want me to believe that you're from a parallel universe."

"Can it be a parallel universe if we can communicate with each other? I am not sure."

"That's crazy. You're crazy. Or maybe just I'm crazy."

"And Amaterasu as well?"

"If I'm the only person who can see you, how did Amaterasu know about you? How did she know how to … to call you, or whatever?"

"She has seen you do it before. A lifetime ago, when you were Midori."

"When I was Midori," Emmie said slowly.

"I know this will be difficult for you to accept," said Dom, "You have always found it difficult. Even as Midori, growing up in a place where reincarnation was accepted almost as easily as gravity, even then you did not want to believe me at first."

"You think I'm the reincarnation of some dead girl you knew?" said Emmie, aghast, "That's — I don't know, Dom. Totally morbid. Why would you even think that?"

"Emmie," said Dom, his voice low and soft, "You and I knew each other long before, long before your time here on Earth."

Emmie shivered, and Dom felt his awareness of her spreading across every inch of his skin. The hopeless desire to make her remember surged through him, and he pulled tightly on their connection. His mind raced back across the ages to that day beside the fountainhead, and at the intersection of his world and hers, the memory of the great tree rose up, branches stretching toward the heavens, leaves unfurling, flowers blossoming and falling and giving way to swelling fruit. Dom watched the branching form reflected in Emmie's green eyes as she stared, transfixed.

"Was it you?" she said wonderingly, "I thought I was alone, but you were there, weren't you? The first time I saw this tree?"

"I was there, but that was not the first time we looked upon this tree together."

He could feel her struggling to remember, clawing uselessly at the veil of forgetfulness protecting her from the memories of all the lives that had come before.

"You were called Ava then," he said, "I remember the first time I saw you, up in the branches of a great olive tree in a sacred hilltop grove. You were spying on the children going to the Oracle," he chuckled, "You were not old enough to go, but you were terribly impatient to learn what the Oracle had in store for you. I pretended that I had already gone to see the Oracle, and I teased you until you jumped out of the tree and threatened to tell the women that I was trespassing in the sacred grove. When I pointed out that you were, too, we made a truce.

"Afterwards, we became friends. We spent a year wandering the groves together in secret, getting into trouble with the women, going places we should not have gone, and always speculating about what the future would hold for us.

"And at last the day came when it was our turn to visit the Oracle. The Mohira who had come to speak with the Oracle's voice came to the women's colony in the great cedar forest by the sea, where all children in Dulai grow up. She gathered us up, all of the children who had come of age, and she led us to the sacred spring.

"One by one she called us to her, and the Oracle spoke. You were called to serve the Oracle as one of the Mohirai, and I was called to serve the Mohirai as one of the Artifikes. But something happened that day. You — You saw a vision of a distant land. A vision you could not forget.

"You took great pleasure in the life of the Mohirai, for ages upon ages, until at last some restlessness came over you. You could no longer be content with the life the Oracle had given to you. You had to look upon that land once more.

"I tried to make you remember the happiness we had once shared in the service of the Oracle, but I could not. I tried to convince you that there was no higher calling than this. But you had no peace, only questions and questions and more questions. Even initiation into the highest of the Mohiran mysteries could not satisfy you.

"So at last you went to the Oracle with your own question.

"The Oracle told you that to have your answer you must build a temple to all that is fertile. So you set out to wander the earth in search of a suitable place for such a temple, and you asked me to follow you, which I did gladly.

"At last you found the place, a great valley watered by an underground river. Together we worked the ground, day by day, creating a living temple the likes of which will never be seen again.

"For you, the years felt like an eternity, but for me it passed by in an instant.

"And in the end, the Oracle gave you your answer. She said you would find it in the midst of the living temple we had built together. So I followed you into the heart of the temple, and as we stood here, beneath this tree, you saw something, I know not what, only that you had found your answer at last. I had never seen such joy in your eyes."

Dom closed his eyes, remembering how lost he had felt, knowing that Ava had at last found her heart's desire and that it was something he could not share with her.

"You asked me to follow you. You offered me the gift of understanding, but I was afraid, because you said that you must cross over into Death. I have been paying the price for my cowardice ever since."

Dom looked up to find Emmie watching him with an expression of bewilderment mingled with compassion.

"What price?" she said.

Dom felt the weight of his oath upon him as he said,

"In my desperation, I asked the Oracle a question of my own, knowing full well what the price of my answer might be. I asked her to show me how to follow you.

"The task she gave me has proved impossible for me to complete on my own. I cannot satisfy the Oracle without you here to guide me. Now I am trapped in Dulai twice over, by an unending task and an undying body."

∞

Beneath the hovering form of the great tree, Emmie saw Dom as if for the first time. The clamor of protesting voices in her mind fell silent, and for a long moment she felt nothing but an overpowering awareness of her connection to Dom. But it was not a new sensation, she realized. It was as familiar as her own heartbeat.

She realized then that the wonderful dreams she had inhabited since childhood had been his gifts to her. He had been the source of her inspiration all along, a font of memory from which she had drawn so many things of beauty. She had found happiness because of him, but he had suffered because of her.

The enormity of this strange revelation made her dizzy, and she pressed her hands to her head. Dom watched her anxiously, and at last she said,

"I believe you. I don't know why, but I believe you."

Dom exhaled as if he had been holding his breath for a century. The look of relief on his face was transformative. She struggled to find words adequate to encompass the scale of what he had just told her. At last she settled on a question.

"Why would you want to give up immortality?"

Dom's gaze grew distant.

"You might misunderstand immortality to be a blessing. In truth it is a curse, to live in an undying body, bound to an unchanging world. Even a world as beautiful as Dulai … it is a world of another's choosing, a beauty as cold as stone."

Emmie shook her head in bemusement and said,

"I don't know how I can help you. Except to suggest something horrible. Throw yourself off a cliff? Drown yourself in the sea, maybe?"

"Do you think I have not tried?"

Emmie grimaced.

"Well, what then? It's not like I have some road map through death that I can give you."

"Actually," said Dom, "That is what Tomo left for you."

Emmie looked at Dom in confusion, then reached down and touched the tiny compartment on her immerger belt where the tablet was tucked away. Dom said,

"The story of how you left Dulai and came to Earth has spread throughout your world, although it has evolved through the ages as it passed from storyteller to storyteller. Midori was tracing the origin of the story back through ancient texts. She believed this would lead her to the location where the tree still grows.

"I must stand there once more, this time to face Death without fear so that I may follow you."

"But you said you've been there before. Why can't you find your way back?"

"The Oracle commands me to remain in the Temple City, and so the world beyond is closed to me."

"Then even if I find the tree, how will it help you if you can't go there?"

"I can go there with you, Emmie," he said, "I am bound to you. If you lead me there, I will see it through your eyes."

Emmie looked at Dom for a long time, feeling an unaccountable sense of obligation growing within her.

"All right," she said at last, trying to steel herself for whatever unimaginable journey she was about to begin, "All right. I will help you find this place."

∞

Emmie rolled back the dark wooden door and found Amaterasu seated in a meditative pose on the floor outside, eyes closed. Emmie stood behind her awkwardly, unsure whether it would be impolite to interrupt, but a moment later Amaterasu opened her eyes and rose to face her.

"Do you understand now?" Amaterasu asked, as if this were the most normal question in the world.

"That might be a bit of an overstatement," said Emmie, "But, basically, it sounds like I need to find this tree, and then I have to go there so Dom can … cross over into Death, somehow."

"Yes. But it's not as simple as it might sound. Otherwise, Midori might have succeeded. As it was, Amos killed her first."

"Amos killed her," said Emmie, realizing for the first time how wide a net the Stewards cast. Amaterasu went on,

"The reason it was so difficult for Midori to piece together the true story of Ava's passage to Earth is that the Stewards have been working for thousands of years to destroy all evidence of it. They have been thorough, but still fragments of the story have survived."

"What's so important about some tree that they'd be willing to kill people to keep its location secret?"

"It is not the tree they wish to conceal, but the spring over which it stands. The spring flows from elsewhere, and it brings unending life to all who drink its waters."

"Are you telling me Dom's not the only immortal kicking around?"

An amused smile played across Amaterasu's lips.

"There are in fact a few of us kicking around."

Emmie stared at Amaterasu.

"Not you?"

Amaterasu nodded.

"And Naoto?" said Emmie.

"No. Naoto is as yet a mere novice. Perhaps he will never be called to such a sacrifice. Few would wish to take on the responsibility that comes with unending life."

"Dom seems to think so, too."

"He had the misfortune to fall in love with a restless spirit," Amaterasu said, smiling sadly, "What might have been a great gift has for him become a great sorrow."

Emmie tried to ignore an inexplicable feeling of guilt and changed the subject.

"If you're ... immortal, does that mean you drank from the spring? Do you know where it is?"

"No. I came by immortality another way. There are many great mysteries in the world, not just the one you seek. But the so-called Stewards of the True Cross believe that theirs is the only such mystery."

"Why do you say 'the so-called Stewards'?"

"It is the work of true keepers of the mysteries to ensure that others don't stumble upon things for which they are unprepared. The Stewards of the True Cross were corrupted long ago by the power that came with this responsibility. They have debased the meaning of that which they were meant to protect, preying on men's ignorance of death and pretending that they alone possess the secret of eternal life.

"They have made a travesty of a great mystery, and in so doing even they have forgotten the truth. All who live possess eternal life, and few would trade it for an immortal body, if they truly understood what it is to be alive."

"Still, it seems like an immortal body could be the best protection against Amos," said Emmie.

"You must put that out of your mind. Focus on the task

at hand. You have a slight advantage over the Stewards now. They do not know where you are and they do not know what you are planning to do."

"Yeah, but neither do I."

Amaterasu chuckled and said,

"Come with me. Perhaps I can help you get started."

∞

Emmie followed Amaterasu out of the temple, through the courtyard, and out into the wooded grounds beyond. She glanced anxiously from side to side, peering into the deep shadows between the tall stands of cedars.

"Don't worry," said Amaterasu, "The perimeter is secure, for now."

Amaterasu led Emmie along a winding path through the woods, until they came upon a sunny clearing where a small pagoda stood, looking quite plain with its white-painted walls and polished wood beams after all the ornate structures Emmie had seen in the main temple complex.

"This used to be one of our rooms for visiting monks and nuns," said Amaterasu. She opened the door to reveal a sparsely-furnished space filled with sunlight.

Emmie stepped in after her and looked around. A wooden screen stood at the center of the room, separating the space neatly into two halves. The half nearer the door contained an elegantly-carved teak desk and matching stool, as well as a tall cabinet. A low altar table stood against the screen topped by a silk cloth, a wooden carving of the Buddha, and a small jar of incense. Emmie walked around the screen and found herself standing beside a low bed covered with a yellow blanket. A freestanding basin and a bedside table with a single drawer stood on either side of the bed.

"There's a hard-line alternet port behind the desk," said Amaterasu, indicating an outlet on the wall. She walked toward the tall cabinet and tapped on the door, saying, "This used to be in the library. I had it moved here shortly before Tomo passed away."

Emmie approached and examined the cabinet closely. It was a beautiful piece of furniture with elegant proportions, carved from an unusual wood with a lovely, swirling grain.

"It's beautiful," she said.

"Yes. Midori was quite taken with it, too," said Amaterasu, opening the pair of cabinet doors.

Inside were a great many deep shelves, each stacked with flat cedar boxes. Amaterasu drew one out and knelt on the floor to set it down. Emmie sank to her knees beside her, feeling like a child who had found a treasure chest.

Amaterasu opened the box to reveal a large pile of papers. She slid the box across the floor toward Emmie, and Emmie lifted the papers out carefully. She spread them one by one across the floor, forming a mosaic of beautiful drawings and paintings and handwritten pages. She could read none of the documents, though she thought she recognized characters of Hebrew, Sanskrit, even some sort of runes. There were many other characters she could not identify.

Although she could not read the texts, she appreciated the illustrations that accompanied them. Some were only symbols: crosses and circles and geometric patterns. Others were more realistic, and somehow strangely familiar: men and women amidst beautiful gardens, groves of trees filled with animals, mountainous landscapes. And over and over again she saw a depiction of a solitary tree, branches spreading toward the sky. Emmie had always been drawn to images like these, and she traced the outline of each one she came across thoughtfully, smiling at the memory of Uncle Frank flexing his arm beneath his colorful tattoo.

"I remember the first time I saw these," said Amaterasu, "I was sitting on the floor of the library with Midori, just like this.

"She was a student in one of my classes, studying with us at the temple the last summer before she went off to the university. We spent many afternoons together, walking about the grounds, discussing her endless questions. I had encouraged her to make use of the library, pointing her to the writings of many of my own favorite teachers.

"One day, she came to me, very excited, saying she wanted to show me something. She led me into one of the back rooms of the library, and there stood this cabinet. It might have been standing there undisturbed for centuries, for all I know. I had never noticed it before. But Midori had been so curious about it that she had been unable to resist opening it. I'm sure you see why she was so delighted with what she found.

"She became obsessed with these documents over the following days and weeks, and before she went off to university, she took photographs of them all. They became the basis of the research project that led to her uncovering related documents all over Asia. Only later did she tell me how and why Dom Artifex led her to the documents in the first place."

Emmie cast a sidelong glance at Dom.

"Maybe I'll hear about how he roped her into it some other time."

"Another time," Amaterasu agreed, rising to her feet and

saying, "You must use this time for the task at hand. Find out where you must go."

∞

"Good luck," said Amaterasu, bowing and withdrawing from the room.

Emmie looked across the paper-strewn floor at Dom.

"So, you've seen all of this stuff before. Any idea where I should begin?"

Dom stood over her, looking at the papers thoughtfully. He said,

"The last thing Midori was doing before Amos found her was arranging the documents according to chronology and geography. She thought perhaps the oldest references to the tree might be closer to its original location."

"Seems like as good an idea as any. Did she make any headway?"

"She had only just decided to pursue that line of inquiry," said Dom, "Before that, she had been focusing her efforts elsewhere. She spent a great deal of time traveling throughout Asia visiting descendants of the original Bodhi tree. There are quite a number of them. Buddhist emissaries carried saplings with them all over the continent as they spread the tenets of the new religion. But as far as Midori could determine, the common ancestor of these saplings was itself dead. She was convinced that the tree we were looking for was still alive."

"A living tree. Well, that narrows it down," Emmie muttered as she searched the compartments of her immerger belt for an alternet cable. When at last she found one, she plugged the elastic wire into the hard-line alternet port Amaterasu had pointed out behind the desk. Emmie bobbed and weaved a little to test her range on the wire, then flipped on a visual overlay and opened an alternet browser.

"Ah!" Emmie sighed with satisfaction, "Information."

She spent several minutes recovering her sense of normalcy by mindlessly scanning news feeds and public domain transcriptions, until Dom said gently,

"Emmie?"

"Yeah," she said, reluctantly closing her information feeds. She rubbed her hands together. "Okay. Chronological and geographical cross-referencing. Preferably without triggering any cascading equipment meltdowns."

She considered the problem for a while, thinking aloud,

"The fastest thing would be to send out a huge crowdsource request to parse out geo and historical data from the source texts. But any single request like that could trigger a disaster for the recipient, since the Stewards could just focus in on them with a single cyberattack. The anonymous collective did a good job diffusing the Stewards' attention across tons of server locations before, but I don't have that kind of reach on my own, and I have nowhere near enough favor with the collective to ask them for help like that again.

"Even little requests routed along different paths to different crowdsourcing services could be a problem. I have no idea how much of the alternet infrastructure between me and the recipient might be surveilled by the Stewards. They might be able to trace the request from point to point to figure out where I am, if they don't already know I'm here.

"It seems like the only safe analysis tools are going to be ones that I can download to my smartcom and run locally. But pretty much any tool powerful enough to do decent analysis is going to be proprietary, and hosted, and therefore possibly traceable to me.

"The only stuff I can think of that's safe to use is static data in the public domain and open-source tools that don't rely on external databases to work."

"There is still a great deal of information in libraries," Dom suggested, "That is how Midori did her research."

"OMG, Dom," moaned Emmie, "Are you serious? How did she get anything done with just a —"

She paused.

"Huh. You know, actually ... There is a lot of information in libraries," she said begrudgingly, "Practically no one ever looks at it anymore, since all the information that pre-dates the alternet has been rehashed in a billion more user-friendly forms by now. But it's a place to start. I could download the national libraries to my smartcom — I remember doing that for my information science class in elementary school. A download like that would probably be a complete non-event for anyone scanning data traffic."

Emmie made her way to the stodgy alternet domain for the international not-for-profit devoted to preserving libraries and library collections of historic significance. The domain did not appear to have changed much since she last visited in elementary school. She pulled a copy of each of the national library collections onto her smartcom.

When she opened the files on her smartcom, she grimaced.

"I forgot that this stuff even pre-dates hyperlinks."

She massaged her eyeballs, willing herself to be patient. She opened the clunky scripting environment that had come by default with her smartcom operating system and dusted off some long-neglected programming skills to write a slow but serviceable semantic parsing tool. While the script churned through the library data, making it more amenable to keyword searches, she flipped off her visual overlay and lay down on her belly to further examine the papers on the floor.

After a while, a question popped into Emmie's head. She turned to Dom and said,

"Why were you following Midori around? I mean, before she found the documents. What use could she have been to you if she wasn't even looking for this tree of yours?"

"What use was she to me?" Dom seemed stung by the words. "Do you think I have used you as a mere tool for my purposes? No. No. We are bound together, but you do not merely serve me, and I do not merely serve you. Can you not see this, after all the work we have done together?"

Emmie bit her lip uncertainly, remembering the first clear vision that Dom had given her and all the gifts that had come since then.

"I'm sorry," she said, "That's not what I meant. I just — I don't see why you would have bothered with her if you didn't know she would find this stuff. It just seems like an accident."

Dom smiled.

"I think there have been no accidents. There has been a common purpose across your lives, Emmie, although perhaps only I can see it. You seek the high mysteries, and as you have learned, so you have taught me."

"I don't know, Dom," said Emmie, shaking her head, "Maybe this life is different. I don't know about any mysteries. I'd tell you if I did."

A small ping emanated from Emmie's smartcom, announcing that her semantic parser had finished indexing the library content. She flipped on a visual overlay and typed in a few keyword searches to get a sense of how well the parser had worked. In deference to the name the alternet had given to the tablet information leak hoax, she decided to start her search with the phrase "world tree".

A long list of hits appeared on her visual overlay. She picked the top result, an article from the impressively-titled book *A Cross-cultural Exploration of Myths and Legends*, and read an excerpt.

The Christian cross is one of the most widespread examples of the world tree symbol, a stylized version of the tree that has since ancient times stood as a symbol of life and resurrection. The origin of the cross in the pagan tradition of tree worship can be seen clearly in the traditional style of the Armenian eight-pointed cross, pictured left. Note the leaves and flowers worked into the forked crossbeams. This rendering of the world tree symbol emerged in the Oriental Orthodox Church near the end of the first millennium AD.

From the sacred groves of the pagans to the Hebrew's Tree of Knowledge, from the Buddhist's Tree of Enlightenment to Native American cosmologies, the world tree —

Emmie stopped to examine the black-and-white photograph of the Armenian cross pictured beside the text. The photo appeared to be of a weathered stone carving on a great slab standing in the middle of a field, like a headstone. It looked familiar. She drummed her fingers against her lips, but, unable to remember where she might have seen the image, she clipped it to the top corner of her visual overlay and moved on.

She pulled open several image scans from Midori's source documents and fanned them out across the air before her.

"Well. I'm not going to be able to write a translation program for these. The best I can probably do is pick out the languages."

She found a few library books on ancient languages and

began comparing writing systems. She quickly realized that she was out of her depth. Even the character sets she had at first thought she recognized proved difficult to identify for certain. What seemed at first to be Hebrew might in fact have been Aramaic or some related language. A collection of images that appeared at first to be Old Babylonian cuneiform might in fact have been Old Persian.

She resigned herself to ever broader generalizations. This was probably some form of Egyptian. That looked like Mayan glyphs. Old Norse runes seemed fairly distinctive, but perhaps they were an Anglo-Saxon form. She swept an entire pile of obviously unrelated Asian character sets into a single pile.

"Wow," she said, lying down on the floor and staring up at a projection of a world map, where she had placed a counter on each region for the number of documents she thought could be traced to that area. Europe, the Middle East, Asia, the Americas — there seemed to be no obvious geographical center to the distribution.

"If this is how Midori thought she'd find the tree ... I don't know. She'd have to look *everywhere*. Maybe the chronology helps a little bit, knocks the Americas out of the running ... but I'm not even sure of that."

She closed the map and swept away the sea of hovering documents. Interlacing her fingers behind her head, she stared up at the ceiling. A few minutes later, she re-opened the tablet and flicked through the documents again.

"Words, words, words," she said, "I wish someone could have just drawn a map, or written down some lat-long coordinates or something. How did people get around back in the day before GPS, anyway?"

She ran a few keyword searches and finally found the

word she was looking for: geodesy, the measurement and representation of Earth. Several books on the subject came up, and while she found the math a bit interesting, at last she closed those books as well.

"If there are any trigonometric equations or latitude-longitude calculations hidden in those texts, there's no way I'd be able to figure that out anyway, without being able to read the language."

She sighed and turned to Dom.

"Sorry. I need a break," she said, climbing to her feet and swaying a little, "Whoa. And suddenly I'm starving."

"Eat," said Dom, "Rest."

"What about you? Do you eat? Rest?"

"My need is not as great as yours. I will stay alert as long as there is a risk of Amos appearing."

Emmie felt her stomach twist a little at the reminder. She opened the door to go outside and jumped when she found Naoto standing there.

"How long have you been there?" she said, pressing her hand to her racing heart.

"Since Amaterasu left. I didn't want to disturb you, but she said you need a constant watch. As long as we're incommunicado with Falsens, I figured I'll take orders from her."

"Thanks," said Emmie, "Hey, is there some place to eat around here?"

∞

Emmie followed Naoto back to the main temple complex. The grounds were full of tourists now, and they made their way through a crowd gathered before the main temple gallery. A babble of Japanese filled the air as people young and old attempted to narrate home videos of their Enryaku-ji tour over the sound of a hundred others attempting to do the same.

Finally they reached a communal dining hall where monks and tourists mingled at long tables. Emmie joined a long line leading up to the serving station, staring hungrily at the trays of steaming rice and vegetables passing by in the hands of others.

"Any luck with that tablet?" Naoto asked quietly.

Emmie shook her head.

"I'd love to say it's all Greek to me. At least then I'd be able to call my grandparents about it. But unfortunately it looks like it's going to be way more complicated than that."

When at last they had their trays in hand, Naoto led Emmie away from the noise of the communal dining hall, outside and down a path to a little clearing with a view of the mountains.

"Do you mind sitting on the ground?" he said, "I thought it would be better to talk somewhere out of earshot."

"Honestly, I'd eat almost anywhere at this point," said Emmie, collapsing into the grass, "If that line had moved any slower, I seriously think I might have grabbed a fistful of rice off someone else's tray."

Naoto chuckled and looked away politely as Emmie inhaled her food with indecent relish. Emmie leaned back on her hands and looked out over the mountains.

"It's really beautiful here," she observed appreciatively, "It's funny. I kind of feel like I've been here before. I think Tomo must have borrowed some of this for *Kaisei*."

"I wonder if there's anything on the alternet that wasn't stolen from somewhere else."

Emmie laughed.

"My uncle once told me that stealing is just another word for inspiration. He was trying to make me feel better about stealing a photograph that my —"

Emmie's smile faded.

"Emmie?" said Naoto, "What is it?"

"I — I just remembered something. These photographs, in my mother's office. Photos that her sister took at some … some church somewhere. Turkey, I think, on this island in a big lake.

"I saw a photograph in a book I was reading, back there in the study. I just couldn't remember where I had seen it before. But that's it. There was a photograph of a big headstone with an Armenian cross carved into it, in my mother's office, right next to another photograph of a tree that I drew for my uncle's tattoo."

"I don't understand," said Naoto.

"Well, there are all these images worked into Midori's documents. Trees and crosses, sometimes whole landscape paintings filled with symbols. But what if they're not just symbols? The people who made these texts, what if they were drawing pictures of things from the place we're looking for? That would be sort of like a map."

"Those are really generic symbols, though, Emmie. And there must be — what? — millions, at least, of crosses — in churches and artwork and sculpture, all over the world. There might be thousands of Armenian crosses alone. The cross that your mother's sister saw could have nothing to do with the documents on the tablet."

Emmie sighed.

"I know it's a long shot. But at least it's a starting point."

∞

Back in the quiet room in the midst of the cedar forest, Emmie pulled open the image of the Armenian cross once more. Dom sat beside her looking at it.

"It really is a long shot," said Emmie.

"But perhaps it is no accident that you remembered this photograph now," said Dom.

"I wish I could remember the name of that lake, though," said Emmie.

"Van," Dom said promptly, "The island was called Akdamar."

Emmie looked at him wonderingly.

"You were there, too, weren't you? In Yosemite, the day my mother told me the story about how Nazanin died."

Dom nodded. Emmie looked away, remembering that day and the night that had followed, the expanse of stars that had taken her breath away, and Owen there beside her. But her voice quavered only the tiniest bit as she said,

"All right. Akdamar. Let's have a look."

She opened a map of the world and zoomed in until she found the tiny island in the midst of a great lake in the Anatolian mountains of eastern Turkey.

She downloaded the public domain geo-rendering of Earth, which was for many alternet designers the default terrain template for new domain designs. She spun the globe until she arrived at Akdamar, then zoomed down to ground level.

The rendering of the island was rough, unlike the more high-fidelity renderings that were available for the major cities and notable scenic preserves of the world. She assumed a point of view atop a small hill that looked down on a blocky approximation of a pink building. A floating marker above the building identified it as the historic Armenian Cathedral Church of the Holy Cross.

She navigated smoothly in a circle around the building, but it was too low-fidelity for her to make out any detail. She panned out her point of view to look across the simulated waters of Lake Van, out toward the snow-capped mountains beyond.

"Dom!" she gasped, "Dom, look at that!"

Dom, standing at her side in the small room, followed her gaze.

"Ah," he breathed, his eyes locked on the profile of the mountain range.

They turned toward each other, their faces mirroring each other's surprise.

"It's *Eden*," Emmie exclaimed, "Those mountains, I'm sure of it. I've spent a gazillion hours in this landscape."

She quickly switched views of the landscape, eliminating the surface of the lake to reveal the shape of the submerged terrain. Now they stood on great rock protruding from the floor of a deep valley. She turned to Dom, her excitement changing to bemusement.

"But I didn't take terrain from the public domain," she said, "These were just the mountains that I saw when I imagined this place."

Dom nodded.

"Yes. These are the mountains I showed you, mountains we saw together, once. These are the mountains surrounding the valley in Dulai where we spent so many centuries together. And this island — but it was no island, then — this was the place where you crossed from Dulai into Death."

"But it's the same place, then? The same place in both

worlds?"

"I never understood before," said Dom, "I saw the place you were going, that day we stood together beneath the tree. The place mirrored in the surface of the pool."

∞

Emmie could barely contain her excitement as she pulled up Falsens' security concierge and said in a rush,

"I have a consultation request."

"Please hold," the security concierge replied.

A projection of Falsens' avatar appeared a moment later.

"Miss Bridges," he said, nodding, "I'm glad to see that you are well since Naoto last checked in. He's been remiss in providing me with status updates."

"Yeah, I think he was busy before, patrolling or something, Amaterasu said."

"I was unaware that Naoto continues to be engaged by Amaterasu. I will have to have a word —"

"Maybe you could sort that out with him later?" Emmie said hurriedly, "I have an urgent request."

"I apologize. Please proceed."

"I need you to get me to a place called Akdamar Island, in eastern Turkey."

"May I ask the reason why?"

"You wouldn't believe me if I told you."

"I of course respect my clients' wishes to maintain privacy, even from me," Falsens said curtly, his voice sounding strangely like Emmie's mother's for a moment, "Please be aware, however, that any information you choose to withhold from me may impair my ability to provide the highest quality of service."

"Don't worry, Falsens. I'm not going to ding you in my review."

Falsens cleared his throat.

"Very well. Before I make arrangements, I would recommend performing a preliminary investigation of the area to determine whether there are any indications of local activity by Amos Eckerd or his associates."

"Oh. I guess that's a good idea."

"I will need your approval on —"

Emmie swiped the prompt and said,

"Sure. What else?"

"I need to make you aware of several issues that could influence the comfort and safety of your travel."

"Okay ..."

"There are currently travel warnings in effect for Americans in Turkey due to widespread anti-American sentiment in the country. In addition, due to the low penetration of alternet technology outside the major metropolitan areas, I anticipate that we will be unable to —"

"Okay, okay," said Emmie, Falsens' words already starting to run together in her mind, "I'll read the terms later."

"Very well," Falsens said coolly, "I anticipate that I can make the necessary arrangements within the next twenty-four hours."

A liability waiver prompt appeared before her. Emmie glanced at Dom, swallowed, and gave her approval.

∞

Emmie spent the rest of the afternoon sprawled out on the bed, poring over the library material she had found about the island of Akdamar. She read aloud the legend of the unlucky peasant boy who drowned attempting to swim to the island at night to meet his lover, a princess whose father extinguished the light his daughter had set out to guide the boy. She watched with interest a short documentary on the origin and historical significance of the bas-relief carvings that adorned the outer walls of the island's centuries-old Armenian church. She flipped through hundreds of photographs of the island that she extracted from books and magazines. She scanned abstracts of scientific journal articles about the geology of Lake Van, which had formed after lava flows from a great volcanic eruption had blocked the outlet of the valley.

She gradually drifted off to sleep, her immerger headset still on. Fourteen hours later, an insistent pinging roused her from a dreamless sleep.

"What?" she groaned.

"You have a status update," said the imperturbable security concierge.

"Ugh, Falsens," she muttered, sitting up, yawning, and stretching, "What is it?"

"Good morning, Miss Bridges," said Falsens, "I have come to report the results of my ground sweep of the southern shore of Lake Van and the island of Akdamar."

"What did you find out?"

"For the past year, all indications show that the only full-time residents of the island have been the two men responsible for the upkeep of the church museum. I performed extensive background checks on these men, as well as the government employees who operate the museum during the day. My scouts obtained biometric samples to confirm DNA matches between the caretakers and museum employees and the corresponding Turkish live births and school records databases. I have determined that it is unlikely that any of these men has connections to Amos Eckerd or the Stewards."

"How unlikely?" asked Emmie, unsure whether this was good news or bad. It was going to be a dangerous exercise crossing national borders illegally. But at least if the Stewards were guarding Akdamar there was a high likelihood that she was looking in the right place. Otherwise, the whole journey could prove to be pointless. She heard her mother's voice screaming an alarm in her head but tried to ignore it.

"I calculate the likelihood of Steward association with any of the Turkish nationals who frequent Akdamar to be less than five percent."

"Did you find out anything else?"

"The employees of the museum and the tourists who visit it come to the island by boat from numerous points of departure around Lake Van. Traffic to the island is highly variable with the seasons, with peaks in spring and summer. Over the last three years, there has been a relatively low volume of visitors to the lake, and even fewer to the island, due to the ongoing violence in the area."

"Sounds great. When can we leave?"

CHAPTER 16
Akdamar

Amaterasu accompanied Emmie and Naoto to the parking lot that evening as they prepared to depart the Enryaku-ji temple for Akdamar Island. Naoto climbed into the driver's seat and listened to Falsens' final briefing before the journey began. Emmie paused before joining him, turning to Amaterasu.

"I keep thinking about what my mother would say, if she knew where I was going. She'd be freaking out."

Amaterasu appeared to be above such concerns. She gave Emmie neither cause for fear nor reason to feel bold when she asked,

"And are you?"

Emmie considered the strange mix of emotions buzzing about inside of her.

"I don't know," she said at last, "A little, maybe. But I really do want to help Dom. Somehow, I feel like I owe it to him. Even though I don't understand how I can be responsible for things I can't remember, things I maybe did or maybe didn't do when I maybe was or maybe wasn't living some other life."

Amaterasu nodded, her eyes half-closed as she said,

"It is impossible to unravel cause from effect. Do what you believe is right, and do not be afraid of what may or may not result."

Naoto leaned out of the car window.

"Are you ready?"

Emmie took a deep breath, smiled at Amaterasu, and said,

"I guess this is goodbye."

"For now," said Amaterasu, bowing.

"For now," said Emmie, bowing back, a bit more smoothly now.

∞

Despite Falsens' warnings about the dangers and discomforts Emmie might encounter en route to Lake Van, the most discomfiting thing about the first twenty-four hours of the journey had been the seemingly endless stream of alarming liability waiver addenda Falsens found necessary to issue as Naoto guided Emmie through a complex series of covert transfers between planes, trains, and automobiles.

Emmie had been drifting in and out of sleep for hours, lying atop a pile of rugs in the dark hatch of an old truck, when Naoto's voice said over their shared channel,

"Are you awake?"

"Uh, yeah," Emmie said groggily. In the darkness, she could barely see Dom's shadow lying next to her atop the rugs. "What's up?"

"We're close to the border between Armenia and Turkey. There are a few hours left until sunrise. Falsens has an operative in the Armenian Border Guard who's going to help us through the gate. Just sit tight back there, okay?"

Emmie sat up apprehensively as she felt the truck slowing.

"Quiet, now," Naoto murmured.

"Calm down," Emmie heard Dom say in the darkness beside her, "Do not be afraid."

The truck came to a stop, and Emmie heard Naoto say something in a language she did not understand. She heard the voices of two or three other men. Her heart pounded in her throat, then seemed to stop beating at the sound of someone unfastening the hatch.

The hatch rolled up suddenly, and Emmie froze. It was only slightly less dark outside than it was in the truck, and it took Emmie a moment to make out a clean-shaven young man in uniform wielding an enormous Kalashnikov rifle and peering in at her. Emmie bit her lip to stifle a scream. The man raised his free hand in a non-threatening gesture, whispering in thickly-accented English,

"It's okay, it's okay. Falsens sends me."

Emmie slumped back on the pile of rugs, but the man extended his hand and said,

"Come, come. We go now."

Emmie looked at him uncertainly, then climbed down from the pile of rugs as quietly as she could manage. The young man gripped her arm, helping her down. He rolled down the hatch and shouted something toward the front of the truck. There was an answering shout, and the truck pulled away through a brightly-illuminated double gate of chain-link fence topped with razor wire. As the truck disappeared into the night, the reality of Emmie's situation came suddenly into sharp focus.

"Naoto?" she whispered under her breath. There was no

answer on the shared channel. Emmie felt her hands turn to ice and hugged her arms to her chest.

The young man with the rifle rushed her into a small building that stood on the near side of the fence. He pointed her to a padded chair in front of a desk and picked up an old-fashioned hard-line telephone. Emmie glanced up at Dom, who stood silent beside her, looking grim. Emmie could hear muted ringing in the phone's earpiece, followed by the garbled sound of a voice on the other end of the line. The young man said something, waited, said "okay, okay," and hung up the phone.

"Come with me," he said.

Emmie shook her head.

"Where is Naoto?"

"We meet him at the lake. Van, yes? The island?"

Emmie took a ragged breath and relaxed ever so slightly.

"Yes. The lake. Okay."

The man rummaged around in the desk drawer and pulled out a bag, which he pushed into her arms.

"Clothes," he said, "Wear them now."

Emmie peered into the bag, which contained a long loose-fitting garment and some sort of head scarf. She pulled the garment over her head and attempted to arrange the head scarf. The young man tried to help her, but he seemed as confused by the clothes as she was. At last he shook his head and said,

"Good, okay. We hurry now."

The young man turned off the light and opened the door, peering out toward the gate, which was illuminated by bright floodlights. He waved at her to follow him. They slipped out of the building and walked quickly away from the gate, into the darkness.

"Where are we going?" Emmie hissed.

"River boat," the man answered, "Two, three kilometers from here."

Emmie remained silent after that, though the man's boots crunched so loudly on the gravelly earth that she supposed it would not have mattered if she had kept up a steady stream of conversation.

The march to the riverbank provided ample time for Emmie to assess the gravity of her situation. She had no way to contact Falsens or Naoto. There was no telling what anyone else might do if they found her in one country illegally and about to cross illegally into another. She decided that all she could do was be patient and keep following this man.

At least Dom was still there, striding silently alongside her. Even if she could not have seen the worry on his face, though, she would have felt it through the strange connection they shared.

The rocky ground gave way to a strip of thick grass and a few scrub trees. Emmie smelled the water before she heard it, and soon they came to the riverbank. As she stood by the water's edge, the young man rustled around beneath a cluster of trees and uncovered a small rowboat turned upside down. He flipped it right side up and dragged it to the water's edge.

"Get in," he said, holding the boat steady. Emmie stepped in carefully, followed by Dom, and the man pushed off the shore and hopped into the stern. The boat turned slowly in the current while the young man set the oars in the oarlocks, and he began to row for the opposite shore.

∞

A burly, olive-skinned man with a dark cap and a thick mustache emerged from the shadows of a tree as the rowboat crunched to a stop on the pebbles of the Turkish shore. He reached into the boat and, before Emmie could protest, lifted her out bodily and set her on her feet. He exchanged a few tense words with the young man in the boat, who then pushed off the shore with an oar and rowed back toward Armenia. Emmie exchanged a fearful look with Dom and said, with as much courage as she could muster,

"Who are you?"

"Goran," said the man, with a deep voice that matched his barrel chest.

"Where is Naoto?"

"He meets us at Van Golu," said Goran, sounding almost jolly, as if they were going on a holiday, "The lake, yes?"

Emmie nodded nervously, and the man gestured her to follow him toward an old pickup truck parked on the bare earth beyond the green riverbank. Goran hopped into the driver's seat, and Emmie climbed in beside him.

They drove south for a long time on an unpaved road through a flat, barren landscape that appeared, in the bouncing headlights of the truck, to be uninhabited. As dawn brightened on the horizon, however, Emmie saw across the arid plain occasional ramshackle clusters of small, flat-roofed buildings, and farther off in the distance the incongruously modern sight of power lines. To the east, blurred by a haze of dust, loomed the awesome form of Mount Ararat, its snow-capped summit gleaming pink and gold. She had seen it for the first time only yesterday, flipping through photographs of the region after reading the story of Akdamar Island.

They came upon a broader paved road after a while, and

they continued south through a rural landscape that grew brighter, greener, and hillier as the sun rose. A few hours later, they were driving along a winding river when Emmie caught her first glimpse of the great lake off in the distance. Goran pointed ahead.

"Van Golu. The lake."

Emmie nodded. On the seat between her and Goran, she saw Dom staring out at the lake, his agitated expression reflecting the churn of fear and hope that she felt.

In the bright light of morning, as Emmie took in the beautiful mountain scenery and spied signs of more modern civilization rushing by — homes with new cars parked out front, low office buildings, cell phone towers, sailboats out on the lake — her nighttime fears faded somewhat.

Goran pulled off the road onto a dirt path that wound through a screen of trees. They came out on a wide, rocky beach. Before them, a small speedboat was moored at a short dock. Emmie felt every muscle in her body relax when she caught sight of Naoto standing at the helm.

Before the truck had quite come to a stop, Emmie pushed open the door and ran out across the beach, waving happily. Goran hopped out and followed close behind her.

"Naoto!" she shouted, "Naoto!"

When Naoto did not wave back, Emmie lowered her hand and came to a stop. So did Dom.

"Go on," said Goran, the jolly tone gone from his voice.

Dread filled Emmie, and she wheeled around to face Goran. He took her by the arm and led her forcefully onward. Dom trailed silently behind.

∞

Only when she stood beside the boat could she see the man seated behind Naoto. It was Amos Eckerd.

Goran steered her into the boat, and Emmie sank down on a bench seat in the back. Dom sat beside her, and his presence was a small comfort.

"What are you going to do to us?" she said to Amos, her eyes locked on the innocuous-looking silver object he was pressing to Naoto's back.

"Excuse me just one moment," Amos said in a gracious Southern accent. He said something to Goran, who responded by unmooring the boat.

"Well, now," said Amos, meeting Emmie's eyes again, "I'm so glad to meet you at last, Miss Bridges. I apologize that it had to happen under such unpleasant circumstances. Your ... security team has made it quite difficult to arrange a private meeting."

Goran jumped into the boat and took the helm. With the help of his unidentifiable silver weapon, Amos walked Naoto to the back of the boat, where they sat down side by side, facing Emmie. With his weapon now pressed firmly to Naoto's thigh, Amos brushed the pleats of his pants and straightened his collar with his free hand. He caught Emmie eying the heavy gold ring on his finger and flashed her a politician's smile, then continued talking as if the three of them were seated companionably around a dinner table.

"Now, I understand perfectly well how this might look, but I want you to know that no one has the least intention of harming you. In fact, I imagine that we may be able to help each other."

Emmie's eyes flicked to Naoto, who gazed back at her expressionlessly, and said,

"Whatever it is you want, Amos, just tell me. You can

have it. You don't need to hurt Naoto."

"Of course. I was hoping to speak with you about the storage tablet that Tomo Yoshimoto left to you in his will. Do you happen to have that tablet with you?"

Emmie nodded.

"Would you be so kind?" he said, extending his free hand. Emmie fumbled with the compartment on her immerger belt and withdrew the emerald tablet with trembling fingers. She dropped it into Amos' hand, where it plinked against his gold ring. Amos tucked the tablet into the breast pocket of his jacket.

"Thank you, my dear," he said, flashing his megawatt smile again. The motor churned, and Goran began to back the boat away from the dock.

"Wait," cried Emmie, "Please — Can't you let Naoto go? He knows nothing about what's on the tablet. Nothing."

Amos shook his head.

"I'm sorry. I cannot take the risk of further interruptions. You and I have a great deal of business to discuss."

The motor roared, and the boat set off across a light chop, splashing in the waves. The salty spray stung Emmie's eyes, and she blinked away the tears.

∞

Dom sat beside Emmie looking out across the waters of Lake Van toward Akdamar. Geologic time had rounded the profile of the little island, but Dom still recognized it as the peak of the hill he had climbed with Ava so many ages ago. To the west he saw the remnants of the volcano that had lit up the sky on his last day in the valley. To the east were the summits of the gentler, snow-capped mountains over which he and Ava had watched a thousand sunrises. And deep beneath the salty waves lay the memory of gardens, orchards, and vineyards they had cultivated together.

Amos spent the twenty-minute passage to Akdamar examining Emmie closely, while she looked away toward the distant mountains, her face drawn. Naoto remained unreadable and motionless while Amos' weapon bounced lightly against his thigh each time the boat crested a wave.

If there had been any hope of a savior on the island, that hope was dashed as soon as they drew in to the dock on Akdamar. On a chain slung across the two end posts of the dock, a neat sign read in multiple languages:

Notice:
Church Museum closed for seismic retrofit
Visitors prohibited

Goran tied up the boat, then took over Amos' job restraining Naoto. Amos jumped out onto the dock and offered Emmie a hand, which she ignored. Dom, Goran, and Naoto followed close behind as Amos led the way toward the church on the east end of the island.

Akdamar, alive with spring, seemed an incongruous backdrop to the solemn procession. New grass carpeted the rock-strewn ground and spilled from crevices in the well-kept stone walls and pathways. Birds warbled boisterously from the white and pink and red blossoms of olive, almond, and pomegranate trees. Rabbits sprang from one flower patch to the next, nibbling on the greenery. The heavy morning cloud cover had broken over the lake, giving way to foamy clouds scudding across a clear blue sky.

They came to the stone plaza before the old Armenian

church, and Dom looked up at the conical dome flanked by walls formed of the pale red volcanic stone that his stonemason hands knew well. He saw, in the floral and animal motifs worked into the church's exterior, rough echoes of his final carvings for Ava, though the work on these walls incorporated newer symbols, as well: faces of saints, mythical creatures, depictions of stories out of legend.

From the warm, sunlit meadow outside, they stepped across the cathedral threshold into a cold, dimly-lit sanctuary. High above, the crumbling plaster of the central dome revealed patches of the underlying stone. Before them stood a grim wooden altar to the Virgin Mary. Around them loomed three apses coated with the faded remains of medieval friezes. The decaying interior so repelled Dom that, for the first time in recent memory, he longed to stand within the soaring walls of Musaion.

∞

Behind them, Amos swung the front door of the cathedral shut and barred it, entombing them in the echoing stone chamber.

"This way," he said, ushering Emmie toward the altar. She stopped at the rope barrier, but Amos pulled it back and led them through, up several steps toward the wooden altar. Amos stepped behind the altar and knelt to fumble with something near the floor. He rolled the entire wooden altar forward, revealing a trapdoor that had been concealed beneath it. Emmie shook her head, wondering if all temples were home to such secrets.

"Come now," said Amos, gesturing to Emmie. She stepped forward cautiously and watched as Amos pulled open the heavy wooden trapdoor to reveal a narrow stone staircase carved through the bedrock, descending into pitch darkness. A cold rush of air emanated from the depths, and Emmie shivered.

"Ladies first," Amos said cheerfully, "Twelve flights of twelve stairs to the bottom. Watch out for the last one. It's a doozy, as they say."

Emmie looked at him fearfully.

"What about Naoto?"

"Goran will take care of him," said Amos, "Don't worry."

Amos pulled a minuscule LED from a pocket and flicked it on. Emmie flinched when Amos put his hand on her shoulder, exerting a light but irresistible pressure that compelled her to step forward and start the descent.

Amos' tiny light cast strange shadows on the unfinished walls, here and there turning small protrusions in the rock into nightmarish profiles and reaching arms. Ahead of her, Dom cast no shadow at all. Emmie tried to block out her awareness of everything except her feet, focusing on each rough-hewn step as it emerged from the darkness below into the pool of Amos' white light.

The staircase spiraled steeply down through solid rock. As they descended, the chill air seemed to grow heavier and harder to breathe. Emmie counted twelve times twelve, and the pressure seemed to ease at last as they neared the bottom and the stairs widened. She came to the last step, which, as promised, dropped over two feet to the ground below.

She hopped down after Dom onto the uneven floor, eager to detach herself from Amos' grip but unable to go far, as the pool of light cast by his LED extended only a few steps ahead. She turned to face Amos. His mane of white-blonde hair seemed to glow in the darkness, and his blue eyes reflected two piercing points of light. She thought she should be afraid of him, but her mind had grown strangely calm. She felt that her answer, that Dom's answer, was close at hand.

Amos lifted the light above his head and clicked twice. The pool of light tripled in size, and Emmie looked around.

They had arrived at a vault, whose ceiling was formed by three rows of three domes supported by sixteen round stone columns. The domes glittered with patterned mosaics formed by small tiles of green, blue, violet, and black. The colorful upper half of the vault contrasted with the rough-hewn bedrock beneath her feet, which was covered in a glittering, greyish-white powder.

A pointed archway opposite the staircase led out of the vault into a dark space beyond. As Amos ushered her forward through the archway, Emmie realized that she must be standing directly beneath the entryway of the church above.

She stepped through the archway into a cavernous chamber whose scale, in the darkness, could be guessed only because of a square outline in the ceiling above. This was formed by a few narrow panels of translucent stone, which glowed with a faint suggestion of daylight. This was the only source of light in the chamber other than Amos' LED, and the sum of the two was insufficient to fully illuminate the space.

Emmie could make out a large central dome circumscribed by the glowing square of translucent stone, as well as the tops of four pillars supporting the dome. Below the dome, the ceiling sloped downward and outward until it disappeared into the darkness at the edges of the chamber. Emmie had the impression that she was standing inside a hollowed-out hill, or perhaps a great tomb.

A trickling sound echoed through the space from some

unseen place ahead, and the smell of water hung heavy in the air. She looked at Dom, whose face she could barely make out in the dim light. He was gazing toward the source of that sound.

"Is this it?" she asked Dom in a whisper.

He peered ahead into the darkness.

"I do not know."

"Indeed it is," said Amos, hearing only her question, "It's taken a great deal of trouble for us both, but now here we are."

Emmie swallowed and turned to Amos.

"I didn't think what I was looking for was going to be in some underground cave."

Amos held up his light and ushered her forward, saying,

"Why don't we go and have a look."

Emmie followed her long shadow toward the center of the chamber, until Amos' light flashed suddenly on something monstrous, tall, and white up ahead.

"Stop," Amos said loudly, but Emmie had already frozen in her tracks. Amos caught up to her and shone his light ahead of them.

They stood before a massive, gnarled pomegranate tree, its swirling bark as white as snow, its twisted branches bare of leaves. She and Dom stared up at it together. Even in this ghostly state, Emmie recognized it at once.

"Yes," she said softly, "That's it."

At the base of the tree stood a shoulder-high slab of pale red stone bearing an inscription in letters that might have been the common ancestor of all the texts Midori had ever gathered. Emmie took a small step toward the stone to have a closer look, but Amos reached out and grabbed her arm, holding her back with a firm grip.

"I'm afraid that only those initiated into the mysteries are allowed to stand before the spring," said Amos, repositioning his light to reveal, just beside the tree, a round pool ringed with smooth tiles. Water bubbled up darkly from the center and flowed outward, emptying somewhere beneath the tiles.

"It seems a little late for that, doesn't it?" said Emmie, twisting her arm in a futile attempt to escape his grip, "I'm standing here already."

"In this particular case, we have considered the possibility of a rather unconventional initiation."

Emmie took a deep breath, trying to keep her voice level as she said,

"Who's we?"

Amos looked at her thoughtfully, then let go of her arm, taking a step back to stand between her and the spring.

"We have been called by many names. I think you have heard at least one?"

"Stewards."

"Yes. Stewards. And do you have any idea who we are?"

Emmie eyed him coldly and, with more bravado than she felt, said,

"I guess you're a bunch of murderers."

"Well, now, it's not as clear-cut as that," said Amos, sounding slightly perturbed, "I'll be the first to admit that there have been unfortunate casualties in our work. But over the course of time, one does come to accept the reality that sometimes a few must be sacrificed for the sake of the many."

"Or maybe over the course of time, one gets to be pretty good at rationalization."

"Now, Miss Bridges," Amos sighed theatrically, "I know you've suffered a great personal tragedy. For my role in that, I apologize. But before you start casting aspersions, consider the part you yourself have played in all this. Through your obsessive quest to put dangerous information in the public domain, you have imperiled yourself, as well as your collaborators."

Emmie felt sick at the thought of them all: Tomo, Owen, Naoto, Amaterasu, and perhaps the entire anonymous collective, as well. And, she realized suddenly, if Dom was telling the truth, the list might span generations. Midori might not have been the first to cross the Stewards.

Amos nodded as if he knew what she was thinking.

"Yes, well, you weren't the first, and you won't be the last, I'm sure. The prospect of eternal life has driven many men to take far greater risks.

"So perhaps you can forgive my ... rationalizations? Imagine a world in which every man knew that eternal life was within reach. What man would not desire such a thing? What man would not risk everything to obtain it? Imagine the chaos as men fought to control the source of eternal life."

Amos looked at her expectantly, as if waiting for her to agree with him.

"Look, Amos," said Emmie, frustrated, "I didn't come here for that spring. I don't care about eternal life. All I want is to have a look at that tree. That's it."

Amos chuckled.

"I find that hard to believe, given all the trouble you've taken to find this place.

"But be that as it may, your reason makes no difference to us. We Stewards have a sacred duty, to preserve what is beautiful and good in the world, to protect mankind from its own destructive impulses. We control information that would be dangerous in the wrong hands.

"Assassination is a regrettable expedient. It's also unsustainable in our ever-more-closely surveilled world. We risked a great deal of exposure trying to prevent Midori Shimahashi's research from spreading, and still you managed to piece together our secret. Our old methods are not up to the task of addressing emerging threats to information control. We're not blind to the fact. We've fallen more than a few steps behind the times.

"But you, you've managed to keep more than a step ahead. You probably could have evaded us for much longer, had we not had a rare stroke of luck coordinating a raid on Falsens' headquarters while you were in transit.

"We could put your talents to good use. With more practice, more resources, more time, you could be a tremendous force for good in the world."

Emmie stared at Amos in disbelief, then started to laugh involuntarily, a laugh that sounded slightly hysterical as it echoed against the walls of the chamber. When at last she managed to stifle herself, she sniffed and said,

"You're telling me you're a headhunter? You're making me an offer?"

"Help us preserve the peace and security of the world. Help us keep dangerous knowledge from those who would use it for evil. We will give you the tools you need, resources beyond your imagining, as well as the unlimited time that comes from the greatest secret we keep," he said, turning and extending an open hand toward the spring.

"It's a nice idea, Amos. But — It's just ridiculous. Don't you get it? This will all get out, eventually, one way or another. Information wants to be free."

Amos sighed, closing his hand and letting it fall to his side.

"A sentiment popular among your glib generation. But, no, Miss Bridges, you underestimate the depth of our resolve, the extent of our resources, and the importance of our mission. We keep the darkness of this world at bay."

Out of the corner of her eye, Emmie watched Dom walking slowly to the edge of Amos' light, toward the dark pool.

"Think, Miss Bridges. I am giving you the opportunity to stop the spread of evil in the world, to stop the spread of unnecessary suffering. You could help create a better world, a world of truth and beauty that endures."

Dom stopped and turned around, looking curiously at Amos. Emmie felt a quiver along her connection to Dom, some realization, but she was not sure what it was. Amos continued,

"You can save innocent lives. Lives that have already been put at risk by the tremendous information leak for which you are entirely responsible."

Emmie blinked rapidly, distracted from Dom by Amos' words.

"What? Whose lives are you talking about?"

"Well, it's difficult to predict. But it's inevitable, given all the material that slipped through our fingers into offshore locations beyond our reach.

"I would imagine … First, some clever scholars making astute connections as they translate the source documents. Then a thousand conspiracy theorists spinning out a thousand conspiracy theories, until there's a close enough encounter with the truth to inspire a curious visitor or two, perhaps even a team of treasure hunters with a swarm of reality television cameras, to come knocking on these doors. All of them will need to be dealt with. Every single one."

"Really?" Emmie huffed, "All that crap about 'regrettable expedients,' and you're telling me your information control plan is just to slaughter anyone who stumbles along into this?"

"You can help us do a better job, Miss Bridges. We need fresh perspectives, new ways of doing things. It can be difficult to adapt to new things, with so much memory of the old to contend with."

"Now there's the real downside to immortality."

"I'm sure you'd find that the advantages more than outweigh little drawbacks like that," said Amos, unconsciously smoothing back his hair and moistening his lips.

Emmie shook her head.

"I don't think so. I don't want to work with you. I don't want to work for you. All I want is to take a look at that tree, and afterwards I don't want to come here ever again. And I sure as hell don't want to tell anyone else to come here, knowing what you so-called Stewards are all about."

Amos nodded slowly.

"I understand. This must have been an unexpected proposition, certainly. But I have made an effort in good faith to show you what we can offer. I believe you could do more good with us than without. But unfortunately I cannot allow you to leave here under any terms other than your full agreement."

Amos withdrew the silver weapon from his jacket pocket. Emmie's mouth went dry, and she backed away a step. She exchanged a look with Dom, whose eyes had locked on hers.

"Could I have a minute, just to think things over?"

Amos nodded,

"Of course, my dear. I have all the time in the world."

∞

Emmie raked her fingers through her hair, staring up into the dim grey light drifting down from the chamber ceiling. She wracked her brain for a reasonable course of action, but her mind seemed determined instead to project a series of whimsical solutions onto the gloomy emptiness surrounding her. Her Amaranthian guild members from *Eleusis*, led by Otaku, stormed out from the shadows to pummel Amos into submission. A forest of writhing fractals sprang up from the ground, providing cover for her to run to the archway. The spectral tree in the center of the room morphed into the living, blooming tree out of hers and Dom's memory, growing taller and taller until she could climb up to the very top of the chamber and burst through the ceiling onto the sunlit hilltop above.

Emmie's gaze drifted downward, and she looked past Amos to the old tree bent over the dark fountainhead, its brittle, shrunken branches offering no hope of escape. As she watched, a glittering droplet on the tip of the branch stretching farthest out over the water fell into the dark pool with a plunk. The tiny ripples spread from the center to the edges, distorting the reflection of the pale branches. The ripples disappeared beneath the circular lip of smooth tiles, and for a moment the waters lay still.

A flash of reflected sunlight suddenly dazzled her. She blinked in surprise and saw in the pool a strip of clear blue sky framing the dark cliff across which spread the white tiers of the Temple City, gleaming in the morning sun.

"Dom!" Emmie gasped.

"What?" said Dom and Amos at once.

"There, don't you see —" she said, taking an involuntary

step toward the pool.

"Don't move!" Amos shouted, rushing toward her with the silver weapon in his hand extended, just as Dom shouted, "Emmie, stop!"

Emmie froze as she felt the tip of Amos' weapon brush the skin of her neck. She stared up at Amos wide-eyed, terrified. He shook his head in displeasure, nostrils flaring, and traced the icy metal point slowly across her throat as he stepped behind her. He reached around her with his free arm and pulled her into a headlock.

Emmie's eyes began to tear up from the pressure of Amos' forearm on her neck, and her eyelids fluttered. She felt the warmth of Amos' body pressed against hers and the scratch of his wool jacket sleeve beneath her chin. He smelled faintly of expensive cologne and cigars.

The ghostly form of the great tree swam before her eyes momentarily before snapping back into focus once more. She saw Dom's face drawing close to hers, his eyes filled with tears. His trembling fingers reached out to meet her cheek, but his touch was as insubstantial as the air.

"Emmie," he whispered, "I am sorry. I am sorry."

"Look —" she choked, pointing toward the surface of the pool, gritting her teeth against the pain of Amos' crushing grip, "There —"

On the surface of the water, she saw as clear as day a passageway. This tree was the axis around which the worlds turned, and at its root was the point from which each world unfurled. Dom must see it.

Emmie struggled to break free from Amos, to regain her breath to speak to Dom, but Amos lifted her off the ground so that her feet kicked uselessly. She felt the pressure of the metal point against her neck increasing.

With a tremendous effort, Emmie reached backwards over her head and grabbed two great handfuls of Amos' hair. He roared with pain and dropped Emmie to the ground, but she did not let go, instead pulling him with all her might toward the edge of the dark pool.

"Stop!" Amos cried, "You don't know what you're doing!"

"Dom," Emmie shouted fiercely, "Follow me!"

She leapt into the dark water, hauling Amos in after her by his hair.

She felt the water closing over her head, Amos thrashing in her grasp, and a strong current pulling them down, down, down. She felt the tip of his silver weapon strike her in the chest, and everything went dark.

∞

A thousand lives of Ava flashed before Dom's eyes as he watched Emmie tumbling into the pool, hauling Amos in after her by his mane of white-blonde hair. The light of Amos' sinking LED illuminated the two of them locked in swirling combat beneath the water, until the great undertow of the underground river grabbed hold of them, sucking them down into darkness. For an instant, Dom stood alone beside the great tree, staring down at the surface of the pool in horror. When the chamber around him began to blur, he knew that the sting of death in Amos' hand had struck home.

Dom's tether to Emmie snapped as her awareness drifted out of the world, and Dom felt his own awareness come crashing back to his body in an explosion of white light. He opened his eyes and was momentarily blinded by the morning sun streaming in through the open eastern entryway of his sculpting pavilion.

He climbed unsteadily to his feet. Before him stood the unfinished sculpture of Ava. He looked up into the unseeing eyes of stone, the face frozen in the moment of enlightenment. He squeezed his eyes shut, gripping his head between his hands as if to crush the memory of Emmie struggling helplessly in Amos' arms.

He roared with despair. Emmie had given him his chance to stand before the great tree once more, but whatever it was she had seen, Dom had once again been blind to it. All the suffering he had brought into her life, all the lifetimes she had sacrificed to return him to that place, all had been for nothing. She had once more been cheated of life, and still he was cheated of death.

"Dom Artifex."

Dom turned slowly and found himself face to face with Serapen. Her eyes flickered to the statue before returning to him. She made a gesture of blessing, and Dom lowered his head wearily, saying,

"Serapen Mohira."

"I come with word from the Oracle," she said gently.

Without raising his eyes from the ground, Dom said,

"I submit to the will of the Oracle. I submit. Only leave me in peace, and I will continue on the task I have been given, until the very last stone of Dulai crumbles into dust."

"But your task is at an end," said Serapen, "The time for your answer has come."

"No," Dom moaned, passing his hand over his eyes, "No. I must not follow Ava any longer."

"That may be. But still, your answer comes. Seek it, and you shall find it."

Serapen turned and walked away, her long white hair and

flowing robes whipping up around her as she stepped from the protection of the pavilion into a capricious ocean breeze. She disappeared, and Dom stared after her, his mind empty of all thought.

He stood motionless for a long time, until the wind changed course, rushing into the pavilion, swirling in the stone dust on the ground, flapping in the canvas walls. A gust ripped loose a section of canvas near the entryway, and out of habit, Dom reached for the needle on his tool bench to repair it.

As he raised his arm, a strange sensation of silky web sliding across his skin caused Dom to shudder. He frantically stripped off his tunic and looked down to see his arms and chest encased in the net of scarlet threads that had during his long sojourn with Emmie at last worked their way free.

He felt himself trembling, his breath coming in great gasps, and he tore the threads from his body, clutching them tightly in his fist.

He strode from the pavilion, out onto the bare rock ridge dividing churning ocean from still lagoon. He stared down at the long scarlet threads twisting in the breeze, helpless to escape his grasp. A great wind kicked up from the ocean, and he turned away from it to face the Temple City. The wind coursed over his body, and he raised his fist in the air. He opened his hand, letting go of the last remnants of Ava's mantle.

The fine net rose up in the wind and soared out across the lagoon, rising and falling until at last it disappeared from his sight somewhere out over the deep water.

Dom lowered his arm, and his eyes blurred with tears. The blue sky, dark cliffs, and white marble melted together, then re-emerged as he blinked the tears away. He gazed out at the unfinished Temple City, suddenly hungry for the work that had for so long seemed so bitter. His hand reached unconsciously for the hammer that should have been swinging from his belt.

And then he paused. An uncanny stillness had fallen over the waters of the lagoon, and the light had changed. He saw the reflection of the Temple City in the water, ghostly white branches spreading against a dark wall of stone, a mirror image of the great tree that had been Emmie's final gift to him.

In that moment of clarity, Dom saw the way out. There before him lay the doorway into the world that Ava had first glimpsed.

Let go, the Oracle had said.

He had seen Ava do it a thousand times before in a thousand different lifetimes, letting go of one world to enter another. Her awareness had longed to inhabit new places, to comprehend new things. For Ava, death had been nothing more than letting go of something old to embrace something new.

Dom looked up at the crown of the Temple City above the water, then down once more at its reflection. Heart thudding hard against his ribs, he took off at a run toward the precipice at the end of the ridge.

He leapt out over the water.

Down, down, down he fell, sky above and reflected sky below, until he crashed against the surface of the water. Breath and light and sense were knocked entirely out of him, and he drifted weightless, surrounded by dark water on all sides.

His last thought was of Emmie, her face pale in Amos' harsh artificial light. Dom had longed to touch her cheek, to say some last word of assurance: that this was not the end for her.

Dom felt a crushing pain in his lungs. A bright light rose before him, and he knew his time had come. He thought he glimpsed the green flash of Emmie's eyes before at last he closed his own.

The pain grew more intense, and he began to struggle, swallowing great lungfuls of water as he gasped for air. He felt a small, strong hand closing around his wrist, pulling at him. He thrashed away.

The hand let go, then returned, this time as a gentle touch upon his cheek. He opened his eyes beneath the water, terrified, and saw a watery light emanating from a point just in front of him. Warm fingers interlaced his own and pulled once more. This time, Dom followed.

∞

They emerged gasping and spluttering, kicking with all their strength against the undertow until they reached the slippery lip of tile ringing the dark pool. Emmie scrambled out first and reached back in to haul Dom out of the water by his sodden tunic. Dom coughed up a lungful of water and collapsed against the white tree.

They stared at each other in the dim light of the chamber.

"You saw it?" Emmie said softly.

Dom nodded, speechless.

"Wow," she said, shaking her head, "Just … wow."

The ground beneath them began to rumble. Emmie looked up, eyes wide. Dom struggled to his feet, then fell back down.

A bright light flashed from somewhere near the edge of

the chamber.

"Emmie!" a voice rang out. Emmie squinted as the bright light turned on her. It was Naoto, running toward them, flashlight in hand. Naoto stopped in his tracks when his light fell on Dom, and he held up a small silver weapon.

"No!" Emmie shouted, "Naoto, put it down!"

Naoto lowered the weapon but kept the beam of his flashlight focused on Dom's face. Dom raised a hand to shield his eyes.

"Who the hell is that?" said Naoto.

Emmie glanced at Dom, her mouth open, but before she could say anything, Naoto shook his head and waved them toward the archway.

"We need to get out of here."

Naoto led the way as they started to run. The ground began to shake harder, and above them came a resounding crack. Emmie covered her head with her arms. Naoto narrowly dodged a cascade of dust that began to pour down from the ceiling. A falling stone struck Dom hard on the shoulder.

They passed through the archway and into the vault, where a glittering, knee-high cloud of salt and soda had risen above the trembling floor. A terrible crash behind them caused Emmie to turn back, and through the archway, she saw that a huge stone had fallen, blocking the entrance to the chamber. A series of similar crashes followed as they pounded their way harder toward the winding staircase.

They resurfaced through the trapdoor behind the altar. The stone columns supporting the roof seemed to sway. At the base of one column lay Goran, bound hand and foot, apparently unconscious.

"Out! Out!" cried Naoto, turning back for Goran, "I'll be

right behind you!"

Emmie hesitated, but Dom seized her by the arm and rushed her toward the door. They emerged blinking into the bright sunlight, followed a moment later by Naoto, who was carrying Goran over his shoulders in a fireman's lift. A thumping noise overhead caused Emmie to duck fearfully. She looked up to see a helicopter circling.

"It's Falsens!" Naoto shouted behind her, "Head for the clearing!"

They staggered across the lurching ground, following Naoto toward a broad meadow uphill from the church. A flock of birds rushed over them, their piercing cries cutting through the rumbling of the earth and the droning of the helicopter. The flowering trees whipped and writhed as the ground shook them from the roots. The air swirled with white, pink, and red blossoms that had fallen loose from the branches.

They came to a stop at the edge of the clearing. Naoto heaved Goran to the ground and sank beside him, exhausted. Emmie and Dom looked back toward the church. Great cracks were spreading through the walls of carved stone, and the foundation seemed to be sinking into the ground.

The earth fell still, and, for a moment, the church did too. Then the ground beneath the building gave way. The walls crumbled inward, and the conical dome sank in slow motion as a great cloud of dust rose up around it. When the dust settled, nothing remained of the church or the chamber hidden below but a crater filled with a rubble of pink and grey stone. The only sound that remained was the steady beat of the helicopter blades far above.

Emmie looked up at Dom, who stood motionless as a statue, staring at the ruin. She reached out and touched his arm, wondering if he might not vanish before her eyes. Dom blinked, looked down at her in amazement, and touched the shoulder where the falling rock had struck him. He winced.

"There is no going back," he said softly, and Emmie knew it was true for both of them.

"This is what you wanted, isn't it?" she asked uncertainly.

The distant look in Dom's eyes faded, and he took Emmie's hands in his own. His fingers were substantial and warm, and his voice was fierce as he said,

"Yes. This is what I wanted."

END REALMS UNREEL EPISODE 1

The adventure continues in
Realms Unreel Episode 2: Bonds Endure

For more titles by Audrey Auden, visit
http://audreyauden.com/

Acknowledgements

No one, not even Emmie, succeeds in a creative endeavor without a little help from her friends. I had more than a little help.

Ben Andersen, Shelby Cass, Randall Farmer, Emma Gobillot, Lori Gobillot, Michael Guido, Mac Hampden, Natilee Harren, Theresa Kelly, Lyndsay Love, Smith Mitchell, Kirsten Schulz, Susan Schulz, Mahendra and Shobhana Shah, Neil and Jenni Shah, Samit Shah, Tristan Walker, John Wallach, and many others cheered me on throughout the writing of this book. Josh Braslow, Paula Gutierrez, Sandy Little, and Jesse Steinberg raised a glass with me the day I completed the first draft.

Sharon Flood read multiple drafts and gave the work an early vote of confidence that encouraged me to push on through months of revision. Robbie Auray devoured the manuscript with the wholehearted enthusiasm that every writer dreams her work will receive. Sandy Little engaged the opening chapters with the incredible thoughtfulness that sets her apart from every other person I've known. Madison Hampden convinced me to preserve the symbols and mythic themes that I loved so much but was unsure would interest readers. Diana Kimball provided an invaluable assessment of the strengths and weaknesses of my first draft using such kind language that even her criticisms could feel like praise. "Admiral" Chris Waugh held my work up to his high standard of artistic integrity, challenging me to produce a story that might live long and prosper in the imaginations of my readers.

Michael Pettit connected me with a wonderful network of freelance writers and editors when I sought professional help for my amateurish work. Maya Rock provided both the high-level substantive editorial feedback and the in-depth line editing that helped me see most and fix many of the weaknesses in my writing style and storytelling. This book is far from perfect, but not for want of her effort and skill.

Masterful teachers Dale and Carlene King at The Geneva School imparted their passion for classical literature to me, introducing me to the texts that inspired many of this story's themes. Professors Jamie Hutchinson, Anne O'Dwyer, and David LaBerge, along with my many other professors at Simon's Rock College, honed my critical thinking and writing skills so that, every now and again, I experience the pure joy of expressing what I mean with clarity and confidence.

So early in my childhood that I cannot fully remember or ever fully thank them for it, my parents Barbara and Ed Hampden gave me that most wonderful of gifts: a love of books and reading. They were my first readers and critics, driving me to pursue excellence in all my writing.

My husband Sumul Shah gave me the time and space to write this book. He read every draft, listened to every self-absorbed soliloquy, and celebrated every milestone. So many ups and downs pushed me off course along the way, but his was the steady hand that guided me through it all. Sumul pursues his dreams with a fearlessness that every day inspires me to pursue my own.

We're living in the future!

The San Francisco Bay Area is teeming with real-world magicians. Ben Andersen at DreamWorks Animation, Ian Steplowski at Pixar Animation Studios, and the team at Linden Labs who created Second Life are just a few of them. Their amazing work inspired a great deal of the near-future technology described in this book.

A lot of other cool technology went into the making of this book, too. The content creators, designers, and engineers behind Google Earth, Wikipedia, and YouTube made it possible for me to visualize and describe many locations that I have never visited in person. Literature and Latte, the makers of the outstanding writing application Scrivener, vastly reduced the effort required to organize my rambling thoughts and probably saved me several hundred hours of manuscript preparation tedium. I don't know how anyone wrote a book before Scrivener, and I'm glad I won't ever have to find out. The online writer communities at Protagonize and Authonomy were wonderful sources of peer feedback and support at the later stages of my writing process. The teams behind the Kindle and the iPad made it possible for me to have the gratifying experience of reading my early drafts as if they were already in print (and noting problems that made me glad they weren't).

CPSIA information can be obtained at www.ICGtesting.com
Printed in the USA
LVOW130252110912

298285LV00002B/24/P